TRIUM

Nicole de Leon

First edition December 2019

Cover art by Valerie de León

ISBN 978-1-7334844-0-4 (ebook)
ISBN 978-1-7334844-1-1 (paperback)

www.nicoledeleonauthor.com

For my mother
for when I was young asking where we were going
she said: "To the moon"

1

Coconut palms lined the avenue to the cathedral, dark under shadow. Gargoyles on the façade withdrew into themselves, hidden in corners, threatening all dared to peek. The flying buttresses housed familiars less intimidating and humanized, outcast by their species. Roots of stone launched to the beast, clawed down the cathedral; anchoring the heavens to the earth; its pinnacles vast like a forest of thorns. Architectural ribcage seemed incapable of bearing it, but mammoth walls, streaked with water stains, were hurricane-resistant rock withstanding centuries of tyrannical winds. The southern spire was taller of the twin bell towers, overpassing its sister by seven inches. Through the openings of the bell towers, processional rehearsals for Sunday mass imbued majesty, a just displacement. Far down below, the stained glass windows of the apsidal chapels waited to bridge light from the nearby ocean. Impressions upon its design were to brace the immense weight, but just, if not more importantly, receive light and reflect.

   The cathedral underwent a reconstruction in the late nineteenth century after a fire destroyed the sanctuary and the transept. The component most emphasized was the glory of light. Evanescent and fragile at day's dusk or intense and illuminating by dawn, light had to be the spectacle and the comfort. The patrons and architects spared nothing between finance and inspiration to affirm that the product of their collaboration would be nothing less than worthy. St. Luke's Cathedral would be the beacon of the West. Aside from the inviting beach, the magnificence of the cathedral would be the reason people journeyed to Shore.

It solicited the question then that when Jamie Diez thought of the cathedral, all she could envision was a specious haven, an accommodating welfare for a trap.

The western horizon was unkind when Jamie rode her bike up Foley Avenue. The sunset's rays dissipated as she rode east toward the purple of creeping nightfall. But she could feel the last remnants of warmth on her back. Autumns in Florida were predictable and yet somehow, this year, the cold had moved in early. Her fingers were numb despite constant flexing repetitions, her calves burning like wildfire. The closest room of warmth was at the end of this road and only that motivated her to push the pedals faster than the chain allowed.

Everyone in Shore had the cathedral imprinted into their minds. Everyone knew at least the important facts:

St. Luke's generated a lucrative economy into Shore.

St. Luke's was visited most by Pope St. John Paul II than any other religious or political leader.

St. Luke's would outlast every man-made landmark until nuclear war or the apocalypse left the world desolate.

"The end of us all," Jamie muttered, eyeing the cathedral.

The coastal breeze ushered Jamie silent and prodded her toward the beast's steps, dimly lit by the streetlamps. The moon was visible in the dark blue fields of evening sky, and hopefully would remain clear for her ride home. Most of Shore's streets were lit, but the moon was essential for a biker as headlights were for a car.

She found a place to stow her bike then picked up her mother's gift from the basket. Earlier that week Jamie's mother surprised her family with the news that her uncle Gabe was transferring to St. Luke's. Jamie hadn't seen him since before her brother was born, incapable of even remembering a blurry face. There were few pictures of her father's side in old family albums; the sole source from which she had to go off of.

Your father had a good relationship with him more than anyone else in his family. Her mother had told her after she protested being the courier. *Do it, for your father.*

It was a day before the third anniversary of her father's death and Jamie didn't understand why he was coming. He didn't come for Aiden's birth. Not for the funeral of his own brother. Only now, when it was just another year without him. He'd come when it wouldn't mean anything.

I don't know him, Jamie had said. *I don't care. Clearly he didn't. I'm only doing it because you asked.*

The fruit basket in hand, she approached the large façade and checked which of the cathedral's six doors she could pass through. The two in the center were almost twice as tall and twice as wide as the two smaller doors on each of its sides. Each tympanum engraved a city of figures from saints, palms faced outward and gestures guiding lost inside; to demons, hanging upside down with wolfish grins, stuck out tongues, and widened eyes intimidating and marveling any who noticed the focus of their gaze. Jamie chose one furthest to the right, under a figure with closed eyes, and pounded on the door. Her mother told her they were expecting her that night, and while bouncing on her toes, she began to wonder if the priests suffered from impaired hearing.

"Any day, any day." She looked around the portal. She knew little about architecture or churches but gave a chance to admire it from an aesthetic viewpoint. She had taken several photography classes in school and one assignment was to photograph historical sites.

Sunday mass had crowds in the hundreds on a good week, excluding Easter which was in the thousands at least, but the largest cathedral in the U.S. welcomed ten times more tourists a month than the average church and while admittance was free, donations were the heaviest traffic avenue for revenue.

Religion aside, the cathedral was an impressive sight from a distance; even more so when standing at its base. At its apex the height of the cathedral's spires were equivalent to an adolescent skyscraper, and even the front façade was four stories tall, with notable Christian figures carved in high relief. Both sides of her family were religious, but with just the three of them left, they had foregone Sunday service. Her father went on occasion when he was alive, since the habit from his youth never really wore off, but he did insist on the family going to church on Christmas. It never worked how he wanted, and so that was the only time Jamie went. Her mother never cared for it and her brother always opted out; he preferred his books and online trivia quizzes. So it was just her and her father. She liked it that way anyways. Just her and her father.

The reason he had lost touch with his side of the family was due to the fact they disapproved of his decision to marry her mother. Her father's side was devout and marrying someone who wasn't was a disgrace. They told him not to return home. Following the falling out, for years the only one he kept in touch with was Gabe, both brothers keeping it a secret. After all the years of silence, for Jamie, he was just like them.

The door clicked and Jamie expected to see a face, but no one stepped forward to answer. The worn wooden door slowly opened, well-oiled, uncomplaining. She entered by the wind's gentle persuasion. Extinguished flames left soft traces of smoke as she passed through the portal. The narthex was wide and for a small stretch, under a shallow roof. Candelabra linked to pillars dimly lit the way toward the stomach of the beast. Stepping to the edge of the nave she looked up the way a person looked over a precipice. The ceiling was almost as far up as the sanctuary's altar was ahead. The red tinted light from dusk streamed feebly through the rose window toward the far edges of the broad chamber. Between Jamie and the back row of pews was a vast open space, only interrupted by a large sculpture in the crossing. Its four columns were varnished and supported a flat platform, above it curved roots formed together like petals on a closed flower bud.

"It's a baldachin."

An expletive escaped her lips as she jumped, tightly gripping the fruit basket closer to her chest. The man approaching was Jamie's height, with short gray hair and a sparkle in his dark eyes. Jamie wasn't sure if he was overdressing for the Florida autumn with his dark gray robe or underdressing for it with his open-toed sandals. She brought her focus back up to his eyes, apologizing.

"On the contrary, excuse me. The others claim that I sneak"— he twiddled his fingers playfully—"nicknaming me the ninja of the priests."

She held back a laugh, regardless it was what he had wanted, and glanced behind him, wondering where he had come from. While searching the darker aisle behind him, he pointed up behind her.

"Our baldachin was designed after the Baldachin, the *Baldacchino*," he said with an Italian accent, "in the Vatican. It once umbrellad over the altar, before the reconstruction. Not as impressive to be sure, but one of the few gems we house here." He was standing by Jamie by then and crossed his hands in front of him before turning toward her as if just remembering she was there for a reason. "How may I help you young lady? We closed our doors for today several hours ago."

She nodded once and spared a glance down to the fruit basket. "I'm here for my uncle. He moved here from another church today—or yesterday. They wanted me to bring him—" she moved the basket in her arms and sighed, "—this. His name's Gabe Diez."

The name struck a chord. "Ah yes, Gabe. A shy soul, very quiet. He bears a very strong expression. I'm sure once he settles in he'll warm up to us. The little he's spoken of his sister-in-law and niece was in very high regard."

He hadn't met her brother yet, of course he wouldn't mention anything about him. Instead of saying what she wanted, she responded, "Really?"

"You must be Jamie. That's a very nice gesture of you."

"He knew I was coming. If he knew my mom he must have expected that she would send me with something."

An expression of awkwardness passed over his face, but it faded quickly and he smiled as he extended his hand back the way he came.

"Well, let me take you to him. And try to keep up." There was an amusement in his eyes Jamie recognized from her *abuelo*, someone willing to say anything to make her smile.

"Have you visited the church before?"

"Visit? I just admire from the trails." There were over a score of them snaking between the church and the beach less than half a mile to the east.

"Ah, yes, well you wouldn't be the first. Though—and I may be a little biased—but the splendor of the building really does lie within its walls." Jamie was afraid he was about to start proselytizing, but he pointed back toward the main chamber. "Not only the baldachin, but the altar is of pearl marble and bronze lining. Each morning, the rose windows shine on the altar like God's grace. I truly insist you return to appreciate the cathedral in the light. Florida may not have mountains to stand on but we have created our very own majesty to appreciate *His* majesty." The man pointed upward then chuckled to himself. "There is also the inner courtyard, the atrium, our lovely burial chapels, our outer stone garden with a fountain—I'm sure you've spotted it from the beach. As a relative of one of our own if we were still open I would have been happy to take you past some."

"Perhaps another day, Edgar," said a voice ahead of them.

Both Edgar and Jamie had reached the edge of the nave and the narthex where they looked to find a man in his late thirties step from the darkness. Similar to Edgar, he had a sparkle in his eyes despite the subdued lighting. What made Jamie hesitate a step was how closely he resembled her father. He had brown hair where her father's had black, but he shared his firm build. The jaw was sharper and a beard was growing, but the shape of his eyes and nose were exactly the same. His voice was unfamiliar, almost completely alien. They may be related, but other than the physical similarities, he was a stranger.

"Gabe," Edgar chirped. "I was just delivering your niece to you."

"Thank you, Edgar. My sister-in-law called several hours ago telling me to expect her." Gabe focused his attention on her. "It's been a while, Jamie."

A moment ago he was an alien, but how he said her name sounded so familial, and natural, she thought she heard her father's voice. It was strange that it only took her name, only a moment for this stranger to suddenly become her father. She hadn't realized how much she missed hearing his voice greet her, say her name, and bring up so many memories. Smells trigger memories. Sights trigger memories. But no one ever talked about how a sound, a person's voice, could register into the corners of a heart that ached for them. She hadn't cried for her father in three years and now here was the voice she didn't think she would need anymore.

A smile—one she hadn't expected to show to a relative she didn't know. "Yes, a long time."

Gabe smiled back, relieved that she was as open to him despite the many years apart.

"I believe I haven't seen you since your seventh birthday."

Her smile faltered.

Similar in everything but who he was.

The happiness slowly drained from her face. "It was my sixth."

"Forgive me," Gabe said, rubbing his jaw sheepishly. "You're right, it was the sixth."

Jamie's eyes which were alight now dimmed to a cold gaze. He didn't remember which birthday he last saw her. She could have told him it was her tenth and he would have agreed with her. Even though he was from the side of the family that was cut off, her father always praised his younger brother. Gabe was so special. Gabe was so considerate. Gabe risked so much. Gabe sacrificed so much.

The realization that her loathing had temporarily lapsed made her wish she had another body to berate her. After all this time, Gabe was no better than the rest of them. The Gabe he so highly praised didn't even come for his brother's funeral. He hadn't contacted her mother once and then all of a sudden, he does call, with the news he's moving to Shore and hopes he could become more involved in their lives. Her fickle feelings were easily swayed from one sentence to the next and now he was someone she resented. Hardly fifty words had been exchanged and she couldn't see how he could make up for it. Edgar stepped in the space between them.

"I'm sure you two have much you would like to catch up on. My dear"—he faced Jamie—"it was a pleasure to meet you." He turned to Gabe. "I'll see you in the morning. Please lock up after she leaves." He handed over the keys and patted his arm before walking away.

Jamie didn't want to be rude to Edgar since he was actually decent to her, but once he was far enough away that he couldn't hear, she pushed the fruit basket against Gabe's chest. His hands quickly caught it.

Gabe's lips twitched. "Your mother has always been very kind. You came all this way—I would hate to see you leave so soon. You're the first family I've seen in a long time."

By then it was probably too dark to ride in natural light. Jamie looked over his shoulder to the door.

"I rode my bike and it's at least a thirty minute ride."

"You didn't drive?" He looked at her surprised.

Her jaw tensed. "I don't."

He noticed how her eyes remained distant. They weren't narrowed, but somehow eyes wanting to remain distant seemed worse than eyes that were angry. Anger could be changed, negotiated with, and remedied. If someone didn't want to become closer with another, they only needed to keep away. And in a relationship where one most likely wouldn't come across the other, that distance would be easily kept. He nodded, adjusting the fruit basket on his chest.

"Have you brought a jacket? I hear it's getting chillier. It isn't as cold here as it is in Toronto, but I know you Floridians think low sixties is freezing. Come. Let's drop this off and I'll lend you something that will keep you warm." He extended his hand toward a hall hidden to the side.

She shook her head. "I've got thick skin."

"Who would I be if I let you back out into the cold without a coat?" he asked. "I can ask for the clergy's truck. I'm sure Ray won't mind. You can put your bike in the back."

A car ride was out of the question. She wouldn't be able to escape an at least fifteen minute drive, which would only be filled with unnatural pleasantries and lamentable conversation. She'd rather embrace biking home in the dark and cold. However, a jacket was another matter. Why reject a free layer of warmth when it was offered? It was more desirable than the first option and it would get her out of being in a car with him without having to gratuitously decline every offer he made. She decided.

They walked down a hallway and up a flight of stairs before Gabe found the courage to glance over his shoulder.

"How's Aiden? He's twelve now isn't he?" "

Gabe hadn't met him yet and since he couldn't get Jamie's birthday right a moment ago, she was surprised he even remembered he existed; let alone his age.

"He's like any other younger brother. A pain in my—" She darted her eyes up to him, who merely looked back to her after she paused. "Like any other younger brother I guess."

"I'll have to imagine," Gabe said, smiling. "It'll be nice to finally meet him. Perhaps it's a common trait for the younger Diez brother to take an interest in game shows. *Who Wants to Be a Millionaire* isn't the same since Regis left."

It was easy to resent Gabe since he never made an effort to reconnect with her family, however, he was doing what the others never did. At least now he was trying, for whatever reason. That prompted her to eye him suspiciously. He kept in contact with her father when he risked being disowned by his family. Jamie always wondered why he remained so close. Uncles, aunts, grandparents—they were supposed to spoil the kids. Not to say that on Rosario's side they didn't spoil Jamie and Aiden; they probably did more so because the other side was absent. It was just an unspoken mystery why the only person who reached for her father didn't try to reach out and get to know her. How was she supposed to just fill him in on their lives? How could she when he'd had the past ten years to try and hadn't?

Unlike with Edgar, she didn't hold back her tongue.

"Why didn't you try?"

They were climbing the steps in a narrow stairwell when he slowed his pace. "I suppose, a person like me can relay all the guilt onto himself, then make excuses to avoid ever trying to lessen that guilt."

Inside her, a monster she never realized was lurking, forced her to speak without thinking. "You were dad's favorite."

At this he paused on the steps. Jamie could only stare at his back since he refused to turn around.

"I made many mistakes with your father, many before you were born. The worst of them I've done was, however, after he passed. I never came to visit you, your mother, your brother at the funeral. I regret that."

"Even I'm not religious, but I would've thought you'd've at least given your respects."

He was silent for a moment and she noticed his jaw twitched. "Before coming here, I stopped by his grave." He exhaled after a moment, as if he remembered he wasn't alone, explaining himself to someone. "Losing my brother—it's not like losing a father. I can't imagine how your family handled his passing."

As if wanting to move on from the conversation, he continued forward again. Jamie nestled her tongue behind her lower teeth and followed. The second story opened above an atrium, presumably the inner courtyard Edgar mentioned judging by the stone sculptures of men and angels spread throughout the inanimate garden. At its center was a small terracotta fountain, unsetting and out of place amidst all the gray. Looking up, she noticed the moon shining brightly with not a cloud in sight. Her bike ride home wouldn't be obscured in darkness.

They reached his room and he set the fruit basket on a desk beside the door. He walked over to his closet and found what he had in mind. It would have been a good fit on him, but for Jamie it was large.

He stepped back in front of her, his eyes on the jacket he proffered. "Your father's." He placed it in her hands then moved back to the closet to close it.

It was a flight jacket, over-washed, old; but it had an intact dark brown leather collar, not severely torn or marked by stains. Jamie shrugged into it and moved her hair over the collar. The good thing about long hair was that it shielded against the wind, at least until she was on her bike.

"You're free to go, but I'd like to show you something before you do. I take it you don't come here often. I'd really like you to see something I promise you don't see every day." She was intrigued by such a high expectation and didn't respond. He smiled kindly. "Your mother mentioned you enjoyed photography."

"And?"

"It's sort of a church secret. They trust their new transfers very quickly it seems."

"I'm not part of the church."

"It doesn't have to be a secret. The church is almost entirely open to the public, or so they tell me, even this place is accessible to them."

The only interest Jamie had in this supposed secret was because of the spark in his eyes. There was a thrill that stirred curiosity, even from someone who didn't want to be near him.

Taking the silence as a yes, he led Jamie back down the hall except when they reached the staircase, they climbed up. They climbed two stories when Gabe gestured toward another stairwell. Jamie was convinced he was trying to lose her in the maze of the church. She could make it back on her own from there, however, any more secret stairwells and she *would* get lost. It seemed the church had other ways of trapping people.

The stairwell was open, the ascending stairwell on the far side of the tall chamber made Jamie take a double take.

"We're going to the roof?"

"Yes. We're in the southern bell tower right now."

Heights didn't intimidate her, however it still made her apprehensive when she evaluated at all that was left to climb.

Gabe sensed it. He half-turned his head over his shoulder. "Your mom mentioned you worked at a gym."

"Emphasis on the work." Jamie exhaled. "And yeah, it's a rock gym."

"You like to climb?"

The small talk wasn't warming Jamie up to him, so she turned her focus on the steps and controlling her breath.

Gabe seemed to think nothing of the climb and smirked, placing his hand on the handrail for the first time in several flights.

"It's a pity Florida doesn't have any cliffs to practice on." She didn't respond so he tried again. "Have you left the state? Georgia has some places. Not as impressive as some other states but it's the closest."

"No," Jamie sighed. "I don't go out of state often."

Based off of her tone, he decided to give up, and continued the climb in silence. Eight flights later, Jamie leaned against the railway.

"Are you some sort of a marathon runner? Or do you just have legs of steel?" The intonation was hard to miss. She rode her bike every day for school but climbing steps was a feat in itself. "This so-called surprise better be worth it."

Three flights later, Gabe opened the door to the roof. Jamie slowly walked past him toward the parapet.

The twilight of the night was beyond words. As high as they were, they were able to see just the last shadows of the sun. The skies burnt oranges were divided by a white barrier from the darker purples and blacks. The outline of downtown was several miles west. The city lights glittered like fireflies in a field.

"We don't fly often," she said. "Florida's so flat we never get to see the sunset. Not like a sunrise."

Her knees brushed against the edge and she crossed her arms over her chest. Gabe stepped beside her, holding his hands together in front of him. In that moment however, Jamie liked to believe she was looking alone over the world. She could see why anyone who climbed Machu Picchu or the Himalayas would praise deities for the view. For someone who lived in one place all of her life and who had flown only four times in her eighteen years, she could only appreciate it all silently.

"The view isn't taken advantage of by most visitors. I guess it has to do with the climb."

"I have no idea why anyone would think that."

Jamie looked over the verdant waves before her. The area they looked over didn't have a building more than two stories high. The only significant tower over the trees was her workplace: Shore's Rock Gym. But despite being flat, all of the culture in the roads, in the buildings, in the parks, and the lakes were hers. She was proud of it. Nothing amazing came out of this town though many came for the beach, others for the oldest cathedral in the country, so it was easy to dismiss her hometown for not being special. She'd lived in Shore all her life and today was the first time she'd seen how the day wished farewell to her home. Watching the traces of the sunset, as the stars shined behind her to the east, she started feeling thankful that at least now she had. There was something to be said of someone who arrived late, because at least they came.

"Come," Gabe said. "There's something I think you'll find more interesting."

He passed the door they entered through and walked under the spire, above cavernous and hollow reaching so high up it was as dark as Alice's Rabbit Hole. It was wide and nearly completely bridged the northern edge of the bell tower to the southern. However to the east and to the west, there was space outside of the spire's borders to allow its earthly visitors to sunbathe and sightsee over land or over sea.

Beyond the capitals of the columns the interior of the spire reached over two stories, shadows in its ominous corners housing spider webs and nesting coastal birds. On the ground surrounding the Diezes, boxes slouched depressingly. Some gathered in groups and others were scattered in solitary. Towering above the sea of boxes were statues, gargoyles, twice—even three times the size of the statues in the courtyard below.

They were massive, yet none looked as heavy as they appeared due to their stances. Most stood resolutely, one sat, one crouched. Seven total.

"Magnificent, aren't they?" Gabe said, looking from one to the other as he walked passed them.

"You could say," Jamie said, studying one whose tongue stuck out. Its face was menacing, his stance crouched and wings arched defensively. Even the gargoyles she thought of in traditional European Gothic cathedrals looked friendlier than this one.

"How did they get up here?" she asked, moving on. "They're so huge. I don't know how I've never noticed them before. You can see the canopy under the spires. I don't know how I missed them."

"Originally they were in the outer courtyard, but they moved them up here after the renovation. You know, they were the reason the cathedral was built in the first place."

Jamie passed another. It was squatting, its chin resting on its clenched fist, the other hand on its knee. It looked into the horizon; concentrated, pensive, and calm.

"Why?"

"They are the protectors of evil spirits. They were brought overseas from one of the countries of Europe. Age has no measure for them." He squinted as he looked from one gargoyle to another, giving respect to each one, respect to the sculptor.

"They were meant to be attached to the sides of the church," he said, "but for some reason, the church was unable to apply them. They were to be the centerpieces of their own portals all around the church, but funding of the construction only got them this far. Facing in to one another instead of outward. Perhaps they were only meant to make it this far. So here they wait."

The gargoyles were like the palm trees aligned along the avenue below, a final gargoyle at the end serving as the cathedral. Its face was not menacing, pensive, intimidating, or anything a gargoyle should be. It stood, its elbows bent by its side, its hands flexed, its legs bent slightly, one foot reaching forward. Its stance was frozen as if about to spring off the ground, to take off and fly. Horns like mutated thorns broke through the rocked earth, a single horn sprouting from his forehead like a third eye. But its face—she couldn't be drawn away. The face was dominant and focused, yet calm and controlled. She couldn't see how it could be the face of a gargoyle and not of an angel. Gargoyles were meant to be grotesque, repulsive, and vile, and while he had tusks protruding from his lower jaw, he didn't seem to want to repel the viewer.

Jamie stepped beside her uncle, not far from the statue, clasping his hands behind him. "Or maybe they were meant for you to get an A on your next photography project."

"You brought me all the way up here for my photo assignment? Did my mom tell you that, too?"

He shrugged. "It was worth the climb regardless."

The wings of the gargoyle reached higher than the others. The light was gone but the intricate details from the tips of its wings to the talons on its feet were stunning. If they were made of marble they could compare to a Michelangelo; if they were a painting they could compare to a Caravaggio.

Voices of the choir rose up the flights of stairs and through the granite walls to the roof. The sea breeze was soft that night and even at such heights, there was an ironic sense of warmth in the presence of monstrous statues.

"He's my favorite too."

"I don't know why, but he's captivating."

"He's called Trium."

"*Tree-um*?"

"It's more of an inside church joke," he said, walking around toward its back and pointing up at its wing. "A nickname of sorts. They only found *TRION*. Perhaps the sculptor didn't get a chance to finish. The records state the sculptor of the gargoyles was Italian. To triumph maybe? Triumphant? They just shortened it, roughly translating, settling with Trium." When he glanced over to Jamie, he felt he had long lost her attention.

Jamie's eyes followed the curves in its arms, its face, its outstretched wings. How much time had been spent creating him? Despite having the charm of any gargoyle, the sculptor secretly hoped for people to acknowledge his skill. Whoever the sculptor was must have wanted passersby to see his creation and *not* flee; willingly desire to admire this monstrosity. To admire the chaos is to admire truth. If one can admire what is tumultuous and what is monstrous, they cannot be frightened. It was a disservice to have him locked away—hidden, where no one could see him.

"Jamie," Gabe said uncertainly. "My being here is a struggle for you. I understand. I don't deserve to say this to you—I've been absent most of your life, but I would like to get to know you better. You and your brother. You two meant the most to Jacob and I would like to have what meant the most to him in my life as well. I'd like for you to think you can come to me if you ever need anything."

For the past few minutes, Jamie walked in a daze. Her mind was hazy, marveling at the gargoyles and seeing what few outside of the church have seen. It was like being entrusted with a state secret. There was responsibility and privilege to knowing these gargoyles were here.

That daze collapsed in itself as she registered his request.

Gabe watched her expression harden and he spoke as she opened her mouth.

"If you need something, I hope you won't be afraid to seek me out—about anything. If I'm not available, I encourage you to come here. The clergy will not mind. In fact, they might enjoy seeing a regular new face around. They mention that sometimes they come up here to think, to empty their minds. Standing so high up, it gives us a closer connection to God. I know you're not religious, but perhaps, it will refresh your spirit, or maybe heal it." Jamie looked back toward the gargoyle Trium as Gabe read how easily he wasn't growing on her. "And if not, they make for good subjects for a photo assignment in the least."

Jamie chuckled, unable to hold it back.

"Thanks, I'll keep that in mind Unc."

He said nothing more as she added it was time to leave.

The descent down the bell tower wasn't as onerous as the ascent; however, she immediately regretted agreeing to climb all those flights of stairs. The gargoyles and spectacular sunset were not worth the sore legs she'd have tomorrow. And she still had a thirty minute bike ride home tonight.

Avoiding his lingering glance as she rode down the avenue, she didn't turn back toward the cathedral until she was several blocks away. When she did, the door which silhouetted her uncle had closed, the entire front façade marked by branches of shadows.

Her eyes were drawn to the apex of the cathedral's southern bell tower. She couldn't believe she had climbed that entire building.

The gargoyles. They were visible now that she knew what she was looking at, especially the one called Trium. Had he been facing west the entire time? She swore he was facing south just minutes ago. He was—it seemed—looking her way.

Jamie shook her head. Of course not. The statue weighed several thousand pounds and it was entirely impossible for it to have turned west. It was facing south the entire time and the shadows were playing tricks on her. That and she had a long day at school. At such heights, the thin air affected her head. She thought she'd heard of people saying that some become light-headed easily at high altitudes. Florida only had hills; she hardly ever reached higher than thirty feet above sea level. It was just the climb and the reunion after a long week of work and school.

She turned down the avenue as clouds blocked the moonlight. The wind lifted her hair and slid down her neck to reach down her spine, causing an uncontrollable shiver to strike throughout her body. Closing her eyes for a moment and twitching out of impulse, she twisted the bike and the front wheel was knocked aside. She didn't fall off, but it caused her to land roughly on one leg. She hoped no one had seen that but to her dismay noticed a man with a newspaper under his arm further down the road, turning and walking away.

God I hope they're just being nice.

The front wheel had hit something though. A journal. It was dark and had the same texture underneath her fingertips as her flight jacket. Flipping it over to the back, she noticed it was frayed, worn off on the corners, and contained a penny-sized insignia at the bottom center she couldn't make out in the darkness.

There weren't any businesses nearby and no cars were parked on the side of the road. The cathedral was the closest establishment and it must have been dropped by someone on their way there. They might return to the cathedral and ask for it later.

Despite being so close, she wasn't willing to go back. She had had enough of her uncle and didn't want to chance being sermonized. Knowing her mother, she'd invite her uncle to dinner sometime soon anyways. She could give it to him then.

Tossing the book into the front basket, she leaned on the seat and rode down the street. Being less than a mile away from the beach, even behind the safety of a colossal cathedral like St. Luke's, didn't deter the icy sea winds from reaching her. She had to keep stretching her fingers so they wouldn't crust over the handlebars. Autumns in Florida were unpredictable, but this was the coldest one yet.

2

"About time you got home."

Sister cast brother an unfavorable glare three steps from the front door as he continued relaying the instructions.

"Mom called and said to heat up the oven ten minutes ago," Aiden said.

Said was too polite. He shouted it over his shoulder when he heard the front door open. He was slouched on the couch in front of the TV with Alex Trebek reading out one of the slots under the category: SCIENCES & STUDY.

"Speleology is the study of *this*. Rest assured, you won't need to spell it," Alex read.

"Caves!" Aiden said quickly.

"What are caves," said one contestant.

"Yes, pick again," Alex said. The contestant picked the last slot in the same category. "Hamartiology studies *this*, its origin arguably tracing back to the beginning of Christian teachings."

Aiden stood up and shook his hands as he paced back and forth. "Universe. Man—no that's paleoanthropology. Angels. Creation. What . . ."

"What are harmonies," said a contestant who regretted clicking with despondency.

Alex stared at the contestant as his lips spread into a grin. "Better to cover all grounds, huh? No, that's incorrect." Trebek waited for the other contestants to ring in.

When several seconds had passed, Aiden had an epiphany before lunging toward the TV. "Sin!"

The time limit beeper went off as Alex scanned the faces of the contestants. "The branch of Christian theology studies *sin*. Sin. Go again."

Aiden looked over his shoulder with a smug smile. Jamie leaned against the kitchen counter, knowing not to rest her legs just yet, and noticed her brother's expression.

"How the hell did you know that?"

He lifted a finger and waited for Double Jeopardy to finish before answering her.

"The beginning of Christian doctrines usually start with Creation, but 'Christian' is too liberal a word. So I had to assume he meant Western denominations of Christianity since the populace worships that. Now what do I know about that? Back to what I thought first—Creation. But why would Christians debate something that *had* to have happened? Because no—it isn't Creation. It's something more fickle. The first man and woman. Perhaps their race? Nah, the study of race has something to do with 'eth.' I don't remember exactly what it's called but I read about it once. What about the first man and woman do I remember from the times we went to church? The woman disobeyed—she screwed up the world for the rest of us. By the way great going." Jamie squinted at him as he continued. "So I thought knowledge—philosophy. But that's too easy and this is the hardest slot in the category. Honestly, it was just a matter of deduction by that point. What do *all* religious pipers talk about? You're going to hell! Repent! Tithe! Only then will you reach salvation." He pressed his palms together and shook them softly. "*Sin.* Sin is debated from theology to literature. You know I read an interesting article discussing Plato's *Allegory of the Cave*—"

Jamie was used to her brother flashing whatever he'd read recently but still there had to be a limit to how fast the thought process functioned in a human brain. "There's no way you thought all of that in two seconds."

Aiden shrugged. "Not for one with intellect." He flashed a smile at her and didn't turn away.

Her eyes scanned the embodiment of bravado and she jutted her jaw. "You look really creepy. Stop it."

Aiden returned his attention back to the TV. Jamie pressed the button to preheat the oven.

"Mom's going to be mad," Aiden crooned as he slumped back onto the couch.

Jamie let her head fall back. "Well then why didn't you set it? You were a big boy and came home all by yourself from Banafsha's house. Why couldn't you set it when she called?"

"Because I'm twelve."

"You knew I was running an errand to St. Luke's after work."

He ignored Jamie and she repeated herself. There was no response. When he was watching Jeopardy he was really zoned in. She yelled his name.

He waited for Alex to finish reading the clue before responding. "Would you really have wanted me to turn on the oven?"

She looked over to the oven. The time read 7:24.

A commercial appeared on TV.

7:25.

"How far away was mom when she called?" Jamie asked, her eye on the clock.

"She said she was coming from the grocery store."

"That's not a time, thank you."

Rolling her eyes, she left to shower and when she returned, Rosario was spreading the groceries on the counter. Aiden was beside her, reluctantly helping her put away the groceries she didn't need. Unrolling the towel around her hair, Jamie tossed the wet towel onto the back of a chair and pointed toward the TV.

"I'll help her. Go back to Vanna."

Without another word, he raced back to the couch.

"In a commercial break—" Rosario stopped, knowing it was a lost cause. She concentrated on peeling potatoes as she spoke to Jamie. "How did it go with Gabe?"

"As well as it would after seeing someone you haven't in over a decade," Jamie said. Only when Rosario glanced over at her did she capitulate. "He looked the same from the pictures."

"Really? It's nice someone can still look young after all these years. I want to take Aiden to meet him. Finally, I should say. He hasn't yet."

"Like he hasn't met anyone from dad's side," Jamie said sarcastically. Both continued in silence for a moment before Jamie continued. "Do you have an idea why he decided to move here of all places?"

"No. Believe me I was as surprised as you."

"You don't think he'll come tomorrow do you?"

Rosario began cutting the skin off of another potato. "It's the anniversary. If he wants to come, he can."

Jamie was silent a moment, then eyed her mother. "You didn't invite him did you? It's only a family thing—"

Rosario gave her an annoyed look and Jamie stopped. "That excuse will work with Victor but not with your uncle."

"I don't have a problem with Victor," Jamie said flatly.

Victor had been dating her mother for over a year now. The prior anniversary he didn't know them well enough to come. Aside from that, Jamie and Aiden got along with him well enough otherwise and with his young daughter, Riley. It was probably the fact that he was a single father too, which gained him points even if they wanted to have the reservation to dislike him. More Jamie than Aiden, but that goes without saying.

"And besides," Rosario rebutted. "When did you start seeing Daehyun Jang as part of the family? He's come with us for two years and you've never complained."

Jamie bit her tongue and cursed herself. She needed to stop speaking impulsively. "I'll be right back," she yielded, leaving to return her wet towel to the bathroom.

"Hurry back," Rosario said light-heartedly. Her tone shifted to a sharper one as she called into the living room. "*Mira, vago*! It's a commercial. Help me here until it comes back."

When the food was around the table, Aiden devoted his attention to the TV, leaning around Jamie. He chewed slowly so as not to have to look at the plate often. Rosario pretended not to notice.

"Speaking of Daehyun," Rosario said. "He called."

Jamie looked up from her plate of mashed potatoes. "Is he meeting us there tomorrow?"   "Actually he said he couldn't come this year."

Jamie nodded. "I guess this shouldn't come as a surprise. The fact that he's come with us these last two years should be recognition in itself. Not many would go to the funeral and continue coming to the anniversary after they've moved out of town. I knew it was only a matter of time before he wouldn't be able to anymore." Jamie sighed deeply but with satisfaction. "Now it can just be family."

Rosario was displeased at how Jamie spoke of Daehyun. Yes, he was the one who hit her husband's car, but he did the right thing. He immediately sought help that night and spent the rest of the year trying his best to make up for the accident. His senior year was spent doing community service and while it cost him his scholarship he applied for, because Rosario asked for clemency and she spoke with the university admittance personnel vouching for his character, he was able to attend the college he wanted. And even though he studied in California, these past two years he was present for the anniversary. This was the first time that Jamie had ever shown any emotion to his presence or absence.

She had always borne the day and let it be like any other. Rosario knew Jamie took her father's death the hardest—catatonic for almost a month—but one day she woke up early and made breakfast for the family. Every day after that was functional. Not like when her father was alive, but functional.

Jamie was silent for a moment before straying away from her food again, tilting her head toward her mother.

"So, you didn't invite him right?"

"I did," Rosario said, focusing on her food.

"Why?" Jamie asked, genuinely curious. "Why are you okay with him?"

Her mother studied her. "Why shouldn't I be? Why aren't you?"

"I just find it suspicious that after three years of nothing, he arbitrarily decides to move here. Shore isn't exactly a happening place."

"Well, St. Luke's is important to his denomination. And many other denominations and religious groups visit the church as well."

"Fine, I'll give him the church. *Pero* timing, *mami*. Why move here the day before the anniversary?"

Rosario looked to Aiden, who was now eating with blank eyes. "Hey, Mister Zombie man. Eat. You can't eat late and it's already past nine." He looked back at her with a smile he used to suck up to her. Jamie rolled her eyes as she fought for her mother's attention.

"You just think it's just"—Jamie waved her hands—"completely random?"

"Yes, I do." Rosario answered flatly. "And even if it's not, he was your father's brother. The one he was closest to. The only one who kept in contact with him after we married."

"What a pitiful excuse."

Rosario responded as if they had revisited this argument multiple times. "Jamie, did something happen when you went to visit? Did he say something?"

Jamie forfeited her focus elsewhere. "No."

Her mother looked content with not knowing any of the answers Jamie was asking, and that was the problem. The man who was so ideal in theory was probably just as much a mystery to her mother too. She probably knew just as much about her uncle as Jamie. It must have been out of her father's memory that she feigned respectability toward him. Gabe accepted her parents' marriage when the rest of the family didn't and got along well with her father, yet, he never visited. He kept away all of her life. Jamie couldn't accept him just because he happened to be in a handful of pictures from family albums that only collected dust.

"I'm not hungry," Jamie said, standing up and taking her plate to the sink.

Rosario pressed her lips together as she followed Jamie with her eyes. "How was school? And work?"

"Got a new photo assignment."

"That's interesting. W-what is it about?" Rosario turned slightly in her seat as Jamie walked past her to her room.

"Silhouettes," Jamie said. "Leave the dishes. I'll do them in the morning."

Despite the offer, Jamie knew that her mother hated dishes to be left in the sink overnight. They'd be gone when she woke up.

****

Aiden was by Rosario's side as the three walked down the lane to the grave. It was almost one in the afternoon, and the chill that was in the air yesterday was gone. A capricious "cold front. "

Jacob was buried in an afternoon like this a couple of days after the accident. Today Rosario wore a summer dress with pastel white, pink, orange, and leaf green while Aiden and Jamie wore shorts and a nice shirt. Rosario had her hands on their shoulders, leading the way they both knew.

The cemetery was a field of fallen meteorites. Once flying free in the vast expanse of space, with nothing to stop them on their path, now fallen, forgotten in its new home. Not many visited the cemetery unless they were burying the deceased that day. In the past three years that Jamie and her family visited, aside from the day of the funeral, they never saw more than three people at a time, if any.

Jacob's meteorite was twenty graves from the road, seventeen from a nearby oak tree. His neighbors were Stanley Morgan, who arrived several years before him, and Jeanna Swinten, who joined them a couple of months after. As they approached Jacob's grave, Jamie watched as a leaf was blown off the top of the headstone by a gentle breeze. Aiden looked down with a small frown, his chin tensed and his eyebrows slightly furrowed. Rosario brushed away the hair that went in front of her eyes. Jamie studied the grave, expecting it to have changed at least a little. She had visited his grave a couple of months back before her senior year started. No words then, and she wasn't planning on saying any now.

Jacob Manuel Diez
April 14, 1972
November 4, 2014

The words on his grave that read his name cried, as stains from the late morning showers still dried in the afternoon sun. The words and numbers that read his life line also grieved, lengthy streaks reaching the tops of the grass blades.

Rosario set the flowers down in Jamie's line of sight, and Jamie lowered her eyes to her hands.

"*Hola, mi amor*," Rosario said. "The Rays beat Pittsburgh last week. Though you probably already know that. I'm sure you didn't move from the couch the whole game." She smiled and lowered her face.

"I've grown three inches since you last saw me," Aiden said. "In a couple of years I'll be Jamie's height and then I'll pass her and mom. I'll be as tall as you before you know it."

"Not as handsome though," Jamie said flatly. "You'll be just as ugly as you are now. Maybe uglier."

Aiden turned with bitter words ready on his tongue, but Rosario was already scolding her. Jamie only half paid attention. Others were visiting graves on the opposite side of the road.

"Just the same as when you left," Rosario said to the grave.

"Not true," Jamie said, bringing her attention back to her. "Aiden wasn't a headache three years ago." She made a face to him when he turned toward her again.

"Well, you're—"

"Enough, both of you, please. *Cariño*, didn't you want to tell your dad what you've learned this year? Ms. Walters says that you're at the top of your class. All those hours taking online trivia quizzes and reading is proving to be worth it."

"It's all that Jeopardy and Wheel of Fortune. I'm going to be just as smart as all the contestants and all the winners. One day."

You'll be smarter, Jamie thought. It was going to get harder for him to remember their father as the years passed, but she admired that he still idealized him. He may not have been as close to their father as she was, but if he was still at the age to want to make him proud and not be told how their father would be proud of him, then Jamie wouldn't irritate him. At least for the rest of the day.

She looked over her shoulder back toward the other visitors, and it had been only a couple of minutes, but she saw a figure standing by the tree. He was facing toward them, and she focused her eyes to try and see his face. It was odd, he wasn't there before. Maybe her uncle had decided to come after all.

"What are you looking at?" Aiden asked.

"There's a guy over there," Jamie said.

Aiden leaned around Jamie and squinted. Rosario glanced back at him but didn't give it another thought.

"He's probably just visiting someone." Rosario reserved her attention back to the grave, Aiden following suit.

Jamie turned her back on the strangers. Her mother was right; they rarely came as a family to the grave. The purpose of coming together was so that they could give her father the proper respect. Silently rebuking herself, she forced herself to forget the figure and lowered her head toward the grave.

The time came for them to go and Jamie had long forgotten about the visitor. It was not until she was by the tree that she remembered. Looking up through its branches to the bright sunlight, she wondered why her uncle had kept his distance. Had her mother told him that Jamie didn't want him there? She couldn't decide how it made her feel, unexpectedly pleased or ambivalently disappointed.

3

Jamie's first class after lunch was photography and running down the hall, she was desperate to make it before the bell. She almost collided into a sophomore as she turned the corner to the classroom, bumping shoulders before issuing a quick apology over the shoulder. The bell rang. When Jamie caught Ms. Ava's attention, she merely pointed up.

"All right," Ms. Ava said, redirecting her attention to the class. "Your architecture assignment is due next week and so far I have two students' RAW drafts. Do any of the other fourteen of you want to tell me what you're up to when I leave you to work on your stuff?"

The class was small, yet the large room made her voice echo as their eyes watched her in amusement.

"We still have the weekend," one student said.

"Your outlines were due today," Ms. Ava said. "I've already extended it once. What will you be working on today if none of you have anything to work on?"

"We can work on layering," another student said. "The layering assignment counts for more than this one anyways."

"No," Ms. Ava corrected. "I spent more time talking about that technique but all assignments count the same."

"We can go around campus and take silhouettes. You have some digital cameras left over right? You didn't give them all away to Photo One and Two did you?" asked the first student, a smirk on his face.

Ms. Ava slowly walked over to his table and tilted her head to the side, smiling with the days troubles on her mind.

"It amazes me the ideas that you conjure up, Nelson. Why don't I just let slide how all of you 'forgot' to complete the assignment I've already extended, and just give you all As for showing up?"

The students laughed under their breaths as Jamie took out a notebook with the prints she took of her negatives, but negatives for the layering assignment. To be honest she was behind on that assignment and while the others might waste the hour, she was going to work on the pictures she took of some volunteers at the rock gym.

"So then what should I do about the students who actually did what I asked?" Ms. Ava said.

"Give 'em extra credit," suggested a third student.

"They're getting As anyways," said the first student.

Ms. Ava shook her head and went back to the front of the room. "I guess I'll have to fail you all. Really, these assignments aren't hard. These are your grades you're letting go down the drain."

Several students came to the classroom door which was almost always left open, pausing when they heard Ms. Ava berating the class. They weren't in Photo so they didn't receive a tardy stare like Jamie. She looked up and recognized few of the members of the Yearbook Staff. Their class was Ms. Ava's last period of the day, but Ms. Ava allowed them to come in their free periods to work as long as there were computers available.

Five came in, almost all from different classes, and sat at the table by the door waiting for her to finish. Ms. Ava sighed deeply as she waved her hand.

"Well, if the computers aren't going to be used, you might as well put this hour to use. I'll let you make up the chance to complete the assignment due today—though I want you to actually complete this outside of class. Seriously. There are two cameras in the closet, three to each camera. Each of you will have ten minutes to go out and really think about the assignment. Come back in time so that your fellow classmates will be given the chance. If you take your time on purpose, I'll give the As to the others and you will definitely fail. You know who you are." Ms. Ava stared down three students in particular who snickered in response. "The last ten minutes of class will be spent checking the pictures you've taken and you'll need to give me a short summary, proving to me you've actually learned something these past months."

The first two groups who were the most eager to get out of class rushed to the closet to get the best camera. Jamie made her way to Ms. Ava.

"I want to work in the computer lab to work on my layering assignment."

"I don't have your silhouette outline yet."

"I couldn't this weekend." Ms. Ava knew that it had been the anniversary and because Jamie was typically up-to-speed on her assignments, she nodded. Jamie slowly made a step in the direction of the computer lab. "But I have an idea of what I want to do. I'm pretty sure you're going to like it. You haven't seen it before I promise."

Ms. Ava arched an eyebrow. "But. There's a 'but' coming. What's the catch?"

Jamie sighed and snuck a glance at some of the students who were pulling up JPEG files on the computers at the back of the room.

"I can't take the pictures until this weekend. I work every day this week and it's too far for me to ride my bike late at night. Plus it's been getting colder." An over-exaggeration but used with the intent to stand in solidarity with the rest of the nation's dropping temperatures.

Ms. Ava studied Jamie and put her hands on her hips, slouching to one side. "What about the assignment for today? Have you got any partners?"

Jamie noticed everyone had chosen them already and thought for a moment before responding. "I have a couple of photos I can edit from last week."

"You can't use the same pictures from the layering assignment."

"They're at the rock gym also, but they're different pictures. I can use them."

There was no triumph in arguing against one of the few students who didn't actively miss her assignments. "I'm only agreeing because you usually turn in things on time."

"So I can go to the computer lab?" Jamie asked, pointing her thumb over her shoulder to the next room.

Ms. Ava nodded then turned to the Yearbook Staff. "My delinquent students decided not do their homework over the weekend. I'd like to keep them all here where I can watch what they're doing. Jamie, Cate, and Ian will be in there also but the rest of the computers are free for you to use."

Jamie picked up her binder and memory card and followed Cate and Ian into the computer lab. At least one seat in between separated the three as they heard the chatter in the next room escalate, only to decrease after a voice boomed for them to keep it quiet. The steps of the Yearbook Staff entering the computer lab broke the silence, followed by chairs screeching against the tile floor and computers humming as they warmed up.

The chair between Jamie and Ian pulled out and a student sat in it.

"Excuse me," she said to both of them, though concentrated on the computer screen.

Neither Ian nor Jamie responded, though both side-glanced her. The chair opposite Jamie remained vacant for a moment before another from the Yearbook Staff filled it. He was smiling to himself as he pulled the chair closer to the desk.

"You know Ms. Ava loves your work. She wishes you were on the Yearbook Staff to help with Michaela's lazy composition."

Jamie turned to him and shook her head. "Michaela's not bad."

The Yearbook Staff were Ms. Ava's children and were often seen at home in the classroom. It wasn't uncommon for students to come in and see work from them projected up on the white board. Jamie had seen all of the four photographers' works and they were quite good, expected of yearbook staff. Ms. Ava wouldn't let just anyone on her team.

"You're one of her favorites."

"Jay, you really want to tell her that with some of her other students in here?" said the girl beside Jamie. She looked toward Ian but he seemed unaware of their conversation.

"It's just one person's opinion," Jay said, smiling as he put the memory card into the slot on the side of his computer.

"To each one's own," said the girl, whose attention couldn't be bought.

"Just because I'm in here when I didn't complete the assignment makes you think I'm a favorite?" Jamie asked.

"Among other things."

"My photos are good and I usually turn them in on time."

"So?"

Jamie thought it was obvious. "*That's* why she let me come in here."

"No, no, no." He waved his hand. "She has favorites."

Jamie smirked. "Let me guess, you're one of them?"

He turned to her and scoffed. "Guess?"

Jamie pulled open a file of a picture of a five-year-old hanging onto the wall on an angle, smiling at the camera. He had short dark hair and gaps in his teeth with dark eyes that were warm. The lighting in the original photo was slightly dark, so she opened up layers to increase the brightness and exposure, though dimming the saturation to make it appear the photo had been washed and drained of some of its brightness. She stared at the picture, only bright for sake of the child's smile.

"Kind of sad, don't you think?" Jay asked.

She turned her face an inch toward him then undid the drastic change. In an effort to drive his attention away from her computer, she quickly said the first thing that came to mind.

"How's your brother? He couldn't come this year."

"Daehyun? Yeah, he's all right. I was expecting him to come this year, too, but he said he called your family about his plans."

Jamie noticed that while he smiled in his words, he was hiding his disappointment. Daehyun was his only sibling and they were very close; Daehyun had mentioned it several times when he visited her house. However, after moving out-of-state for college, their bond had stretched thin. The fact that Daehyun contacted Jamie's family before his own only confirmed that. She wasn't close with his younger brother so didn't see reason to fret over it.

"It was nice just having family. It never really bothered me that he came before, but, for the first time I could actually breathe."

She opened another file as she thought back on Saturday. Daehyun's presence was substituted with her uncle's, even though he didn't directly join the family in front of the grave. The fact that he just moved into town still scratched at the corner of her brain, and the fact she unintentionally was thinking about it again bothered her. At least so soon. She had work this week but she'd go to the cathedral again for those pictures. The gargoyles would definitely serve as interesting subjects. She'd even maybe learn why Gabe chose now to appear. There was definitely something there and even if her mother thought nothing of it, she knew her instincts were not wrong. She was a rock climber. Relying on one's instincts was paramount.

He had gone quiet and she smiled. "Anyways, the same old rock climbers can be tiring subjects, no matter how many cool angles and compositions I can think up. I've got a place in mind that can make up for being a week late."

"Are we talking about you being the favorite again?"

"Yes and no. By the way," Jamie said, adjusting the levels of the photo. "Your friends were missing you last week at the gym."

There was something she said that was entertaining as his expression unburdened again. "Oh really? The rock gym can't survive without me for a couple of days, huh?"

Jamie nodded. "Your club did seem quieter than usual."

"Are you saying that I'm loud?"

"I'm saying that you're the life of that little troop. It's inconvenient that there's only one rock gym in Shore."

"No, you don't mean that. No, no, no." He bit his lip as he refrained from speaking, but could not keep for very long. "So what place do you have in mind? Where in Shore could *possibly* be so great that work a week late suddenly becomes acceptable?"

"It's a surprise," Jamie said.

"Not for me."

"You could tell Ms. Ava." She shook her head. Obstinate. "I don't trust you."

"I'm not in the class. Come on I won't tell."

"You don't have to be in the class to speak to her."

"There's no negotiating with you." His chin tensed, remaining quiet for half a minute before trying again. "If I guess it then will you tell me?"

Jamie capitulated and he grinned proudly. He hummed before his first guess.

"Poppy's Old Theatre on Fifth?"

Jamie turned to him. "Wow."

"Really?"

Jamie held back a laugh as she looked back to the monitor. "No."

"Cruel, very cruel. It can't be Shore Beach or the Cliff." The nickname of the rock pier on the southern beach of Shore. He arched an eyebrow, still guessing but doubtful.

Jamie shook her head once with tense lips. He thought maybe she was lying but the beach was one of the two reasons tourists came to their town, it was too obvious. Maybe something less visited?

"The cemetery by the Bilem Site?"

Jamie's eyes widened a little at the thought. Why would she risk catching a ghost in the background? She shook her head.

"There's really little else in our pit stop of a town. There's no rivers, no lakes. What else? It can't be the cathedral. That's too obvious. Maybe somewhere near Embrujado Trail? By the way, isn't it a little fishy it translates to The Haunted Trail?"

"Well, *I* didn't name it that."

"So not the trails then, huh? Sneaky, very sneaky."

Ms. Ava's voice rose so that the people in both rooms could hear her. "All right, start wrapping it up. The first presentation will be in five minutes."

"Ah, well. I guess I'll just have to wait for next week," he said, standing up. "Vamoose!"

Jamie nodded her head once to the screen. "I just need to finish two pictures real quick."

Ms. Ava stopped at the portal of the photo lab and pointed toward the three in her photo class, though looked at Jay as she spoke. "Yearbook Staff will stay in here while the students present for the class. Don't make too much noise."

Jay hung his head to the side and raised his arms up. "Why'd you look at me when you said that?"

She smiled as she watched his expression feign well-earned culpability. "Minjae, we all know I meant *you* keep the noise down."

"You only say these things to me . . . More honest . . . More hurtful."

"It's because you're my favorite. Now stop being so dramatic. Cate, Jamie, Ian start wrapping it up." Ms. Ava returned back to the photo room.

Minjae turned over his shoulder to Jamie, who had been looking at him since Ms. Ava said the word, and chuckled as he mouthed:

Favorite.

****

Jamie had a long day at work and was tempted to ride her bike straight home but knew once she stepped into the house she wouldn't leave it again to pick up her brother. She stopped outside the blue house next door and left her bike in the driveway before knocking at the front door.

A woman with exhaustion in her eyes opened the door.

"About time."

Jamie smiled as she stepped inside, embracing the smells of nutmeg, garlic powder, and pancake batter. Silently, she followed her down the empty hallway, purposely kept dark, to the living room where Aiden sat on the couch. The room was spacious, with the TV set against one wall and the couch facing it across an open space. Behind the couch was room for the dining table and its chairs. There was just enough room to comfortably pull the chair out and not hit the kitchen counter behind it. Above the TV was a night seascape painting. Everything was open so Banafsha could watch TV from the kitchen, as she routinely did, while she cooked. The side of the living room opposite of the hallway was covered behind drapes, with a glass door leading to the backyard. Spread throughout the wall were many of Jamie's pictures, ranging in subject matter from pets on the beach to night shots of downtown Shore. There was a silhouetted picture of her mother and brother on one side and the Disney World castle on the other side. Jamie remembered being lucky enough to get a shot of them through the break in the crowd.

While Jamie had only known Banafsha for several years, she felt at home here. Coming to pick up Aiden regularly, she felt she was collecting her brother from more a relative than a neighbor. Banafsha was more family than Gabe would ever be. Blood didn't define family, as blood didn't prohibit her from having her father be her best friend. Being in Banafsha's house reminded her that no matter what, if it came to it, she would swear that Banafsha was her family. Not Gabe. Not any of his family.

The TV was turned on to a nightly singing game show he watched every week.

"About time," he said.

Jamie was exhausted from her long day but she managed to force a smile under closed eyelids.

"Banafsha is teaching you well I see. Come on. Your show will be waiting for you at home."

"Poisonous broadcasts," Banafsha said. "I don't know how your generation is so zombified by them."

Jamie looked at her and shook her head. "Who taught you that? That's not a real word you know." Her attention was turning toward Aiden when he quickly put his homework assignments into his backpack and tossed it over one shoulder, making his way to the front door.

"Aiden. Thank Banafsha."

"I see her every day."

"*Thank. Her.*"

He turned around. "Thank you!"

As he turned away again Banafsha raised her voice so he would stop. It was not with anger, but with the authority of someone who took care of another every day after school for years.

"You're the only one who can teach me words now? At least mine is a real word. Come on, it isn't hard. I taught it a long time ago."

Aiden relented. "*Shukriya*, Banafsha. See you tomorrow."

The front door closed behind Aiden as Banafsha turned back toward Jamie, resting her hands on her hips.

"It's amazing how your generation isn't satisfied with the language you have. Now you're making up words. No wonder no one understands you."

"At least you're old and have an excuse not to be up to date. If I ask what it means then *I'll* get a look and be laughed at. Be grateful you learn in the privacy and comfort of your own home."

"Old!" Banafsha waved the idea away as she went to the dining room table. She picked a seat and Jamie settled in one beside her. "You're not safe anywhere anymore. There was another shooting in Massachusetts. It started in a street downtown and the gunman ran to a neighborhood. Someone died! In the safety of the person's home!"

"Banafsha you know you can't watch the news. They're never going to tell you anything good, especially this past year. There's a shooting every other week and I'll never hear the end of it until the next one."

Jamie lectured her on this often, which is why Banafsha was eager to change the subject. "What have you got for me?"

"I don't have anything worth selling yet. But I'm planning a trip to the cathedral this weekend."

"Churches don't interest me," Banafsha said, picking up the glass she had in front of her.

"This is different." That failed to capture Banafsha's attention, so Jamie aimed to impress her with mystery. "But let's see what we see." Jamie closed her eyes for a moment.

"Getting a headache?"

Jamie shook her head slightly. "It'll calm down."

"I've been getting some in the afternoons."

"Not able to get your afternoon nap?"

"Not with all the noise our new neighbor is making."

"New neighbor?" Jamie opened her eyes.

"A couple doors down. Where the Garrods used to live. I miss that family already."

"You never spoke to them."

"That's why I miss them." Banafsha combed her hand through her hair and shook her head. "They never bothered me—"

"Aside from that one incident," Jamie interrupted, chuckling as she massaged her forehead.

"—*aside* from that one time," Banafsha corrected herself. "But they kept quiet. The kids were quiet when they played outside. The parents never had loud family gatherings. I very much enjoyed having them as neighbors. Now . . . now there's this new man. Young, maybe in college or thirties. I can't tell. You know how college kids are."

"You don't like him?" Jamie prodded.

"I don't trust him. He smiles too much."

Jamie laughed and leaned over the table. "Is there a problem with someone who smiles too much?"

"No one smiles all the time. But this man! He's like a clown. It's always fixed on his face even when he's not really meaning to smile in here." She tapped her chest twice and shook her head. "Listen to me, Jamie. Don't trust him. Never trust anyone like that." Quietly adding, "Like all those fake politicians."

Jamie considered her words for a moment then risked asking. "It doesn't have to do with something you've faced before does it?"

Banafsha made a noise like the question had been asked multiple times and she had refused to answer it multiple times. Which isn't far from the truth. Jamie had asked, always broad questions. The fact was that as much as Jamie cared for Banafsha, neither she nor her family knew anything about their reclusive neighbor; only that she came to America from Pakistan in the late 70s and any family she had is still there. She never returned and remained in America, neither keeping in contact with those with similar cultural backgrounds or establishing new relationships with locals. None that weren't Jamie's family.

"One of these days, you're going to tell me about your past. We've been neighbors for years now; since my dad died. We've become like family."

"There's nothing interesting enough to tell," Banafsha said, looking down at the glass in her hands.

Jamie lowered her eyes after a moment and nodded. "Tomorrow I won't work so late. I just wanted to make up some hours because of last week. Aiden won't be here past seven."

"Good."

Jamie stood up and pushed her chair in, taking a step toward the hall when Banafsha spoke up.

"It's late." Banafsha lifted her eyes to Jamie with an emotion in them, of sadness and memory. "But I'm sorry about your father."

There was nothing to be sorry about. It was years ago, so Jamie shook her head. "It was just the anniversary."

"I may not believe in many things, but your father was very important to you. Losing someone so close cannot be numbed just because enough time has passed. It still hurts every time you think of them."

"Death's just a part of life."

Banafsha studied her as Jamie studied her back. Neither responded and Jamie wished her a good night. On a regular visit, Banafsha would have told her to be careful closing the door on her way out or not to mess up her flowers by the front door, but tonight she remained in her seat and said nothing. She let the front door close and the emptiness swallow her and the silence shake her so that all left to hear was the buzz from the lightbulb. There was nothing to refute what Jamie had said. Death is a part of life. The rest was spent preparing for it.

4

The weekend would begin as soon as she got off from work and she oscillated between waking up early the next day to get morning shots of the gargoyles or waiting until the later afternoon. The shining background and the silhouette of the gargoyle against a sinking sun would coalesce for an evocative photo. Banafsha might even be convinced to buy it from her. Jamie tapped her fingers against the counter as she looked over the sign-in sheet.

"Era!" Jamie studied the list as she walked to the shoe closet.

"What's up?" Her coworker looked up from putting away a pair of shoes.

"I'm missing a waiver. I'm short one. Did someone change their mind after seeing the monster in the back?"

"I put all of them for today by the computer. I was logging them in but got called away."

"I checked. There's one missing."

"Jamie, they're there. Want to switch jobs while I check?"

Reluctantly, Jamie extended the list to Era who skipped to the front desk. Jamie didn't want to take the responsibility for losing important documents when it was someone else's segment. She remembered when a previous co-worker misplaced a waiver—temporarily—it was the first and only time she'd seen Noel in a temper. He didn't shout, but was clearly aggravated for the rest of that week.

Era returned to the bench by the closet and counted the waivers one by one as Jamie continued restocking.

"Thirty-one, thirty-two, thirty-three . . ." She loudly switched each waiver from one hand to the other. Jamie already heard the final one and slightly cringed, continuing her work. "Thirty-four! I told you I had them all there. You're lucky I didn't indulge in Noel's nasty gambling habit because then your pockets would be ten dollars lighter and I ten times more proud."

"Excuse me, what nasty habit?" Noel passed Era then Jamie, moving a box of harnesses and carabiners into the closet.

"A nasty *gambling* habit she said." Jamie smirked.

Noel raised his voice to be heard from inside the closet. "I'll remember that when you ask for another day off, Era."

"You're such a suck up," Era said, menace in her eyes, quickly and easily slacked. "What are your plans this weekend?"

"I have a photo project. Want to help?"

"Ha ha! Got a date. Hot date. Wants to take me dancing. Ever been dancing before?"

"Yup, with a hot date." Amused, Jamie looked up to a pouting face, but she shrugged and turned when a round of knocks banged at the front door.

The gym would be closing soon and the front doors were already locked. A customer stared through them as Era walked to the front, tapping her watch. The stranger mouthed wallet and Era nodded, letting him in.

The customer lifted his hands as he headed in one direction, apologizing profusely. He approached a bench by one of the side walls. "Two hungry kids with an annoyed cashier at a Wendy's and the wallet on the bench flashed across my eyes."

Era followed him as he peeked underneath one. It had been kicked beside a garbage bin. Resting his hand on his chest he exhaled. Era didn't have to lead him back since he did so voluntarily, but he waved farewell to Jamie and Noel across the room.

"Sorry about that. I won't get far without this. Have a good night! God bless!"

"God bless!" Era waved then locked the front door up. She was walking back toward them as Jamie studied her.

Jamie had worked at the rock gym for over two years and while she was amiable enough with all of her co-workers, it was no doubt that she was closest to Era, and from that, fairly knowledgeable about her friend. Era was two years older than Jamie, however would be graduating from college in the spring. Similar to Jamie, she had lived in Florida all her life, although in considerably more places than just Shore. Era had a healthy relationship with her family; closest with her eldest brother, a pilot, who gave her his benefits on flights and recommended foreign destinations. She was prey to cops whenever she succumbed to speeding, but always successfully utilized her charm to get off with a warning. Outdoor sports called to her, constantly active in anything physically challenging since elementary school when she was first introduced to gymnastics. Once bored she switched to karate; then bored again, switched to surfing. Her eldest brother took her and her other siblings to California when she was fourteen and stood before her first mountain, instantly in love. Every rock face was a new challenge. Previous climbs were like visiting her childhood home in the Keys. Even sky diving lost its thrill after several years. Her most recent venture was deep sea diving, however her joy lied forever with the mountain.

Sports and hobbies took up all of her free time and while excelling in school, she never thought of religion or politics or Hollywood. Sometimes even Noel was surprised at how out of touch Era was to mainstream trends or the latest celebrity scandals, and he was over a decade older than her. To Jamie, it wouldn't take anyone long to really know Era, as open and honest as she was with everyone. Aside from the menial tasks the staff rotated every other month, Era was content. She liked to give tips to beginners on how to top rope and the secrets of how to lessen your weight when climbing.

"Why'd you say that?" Jamie asked.

Era turned to her as she leaned over the counter. "Why not?"

"It isn't like you believe."

"Do I have to believe to say it back? It doesn't hurt me. It's just a courtesy."

"A courtesy our fair Jamie has to work extremely hard to pull off as genuine," Noel said, humored as he walked to the counter.

Era made a face at Noel as he walked past her to begin cleaning up the desk. Jamie was used to being picked on and ignored his comment, concentrating on Era.

"I just don't understand why you'd say it if you don't believe."

"I don't believe in a lot of things," Era said. "It doesn't mean they're not real."

"I'm not doubting the existence of hypotheticals."

"The question is why are you so sour about it?" Noel asked, looking up from the papers in his hands. Era watched her intently too, which beckoned Jamie to pause. She avoided their eyes.

"My uncle moved into town last week. He lives at St. Luke's."

"*Ooo*." Era held her lips in that shape for a moment. "Like *in* the church?"

"Did he try to convert you?" Noel asked behind a smirk, not entirely jocular.

"Unfortunately no. I could expect that and by expecting that make up some excuse. No, he tried empathy. Acting like he was sorry for being out of touch for so long."

"Maybe he's being honest," Era prodded.

"My mom doesn't suspect anything."

"For someone who says she doesn't believe in anything . . . you're very critical."

"Must nihilists be passive?" Jamie asked low enough to be under her breath, but loud enough for Noel to hear her.

"Not at all. Question anything and everything you see in the world."

Era nodded in agreement and they became quiet. Noel and Jamie refocused on their tasks when Era voiced a thought. "You know, I don't really believe that." Jamie looked back to her. Era shrugged after registering her expression. "I think you want to believe in something, you just don't know what. You're confused because there is so much out there. You say nothing because nothing is the easiest answer."

"So I don't want to put in the effort to understand differing opinions?"

"No, but maybe it's the most convenient."

Jamie walked over to the counter and crossed her arms, watching Era closely. "How convenient?"

"Neither of us ever met your dad but you were close with him. The fact that his side of the family was religious but none ever made an effort with your family, it turned you off to it."   "So,   I   don't believe in anything because people I don't remember convinced me. They believe in something therefore I must not believe in that god—deity."

"You're such a smartass," Noel remarked, still listening as he focused on the papers in his hands.

Jamie lifted her hands. "I'm really not trying to be."

And it was the truth. Era had never been so disputable about religion and Jamie's tone might have hinted toward sass, but she wanted to understand what she meant. A friend she thought she knew backwards and forwards now made her more uncertain than a child lost in a crowd.

"I think that your dad's side of the family did very little to make you believe that. I think it was your dad. You've said that he took your family to church every once in a while."

"He tried."

"So you agree he was a believer." Era gazed at Noel uncertainly and even though he nodded she shook her head, amusement on her lips. "That doesn't sound like a real word!" She laughed and looked back to Jamie. "His faith was important to him. And after he died his faith became the scapegoat. Interestingly more so than the person. You know I never understood how you forgave Daehyun."

The time had long passed since there was contempt for him.

"It was an accident," Jamie said. "At the end of the day, he was the one most scarred by it. Everyone loses someone, but not everyone accidentally causes the death of someone else."

"I think it's good that he didn't come this year. Your family needed at least one anniversary with only family present." Era noticed Jamie's expression and pointed it out.

"I think my uncle was there. I saw a figure by a tree—in its shade so I can't be sure. I put him to the back of my mind and when I looked again some time later he was gone."

"Spooky," Era said.

Near an hour after closing, the two of them finished cleaning and Noel finished transferring the documents to the computer. Jamie picked up her backpack and switched the ringer on her phone back on. "How did this conversation get so deep? We were talking about weekend plans a minute ago."

"It's odd. I never really debate these sorts of existential, philosophical topics." Era grinned. "It's fun."

"You mean you *don't* have these kinds of talks on first dates?" Noel said. "Back in *my* day—"

"Hush, Noel," Era said. "You call Jamie a smartass but look who's poking fun at me now."

"Well I can't help that you share your weekly escapades with Shore's shallowest"—he winked at them—"wannabe pro surfer tourists who always seem to be *so* shocked that we have a nice beach but lack acceptable waves. Go to California! Go to Hawaii!"

"They're sweet," Era remarked.

"Well who isn't with that charm of yours?" Noel said.

Jamie was putting her backpack on when she noticed a cockroach crawling by one of the rock holds.

"Jesus, it's November. Shouldn't bugs be sleeping right now?" Jamie shrugged off her backpack and shoved off a shoe as she made her way to its execution.

"Jamie, use the spray!" Era called out.

"By the time . . ." Jamie muttered under her breath as she climbed a few rows up before choosing the best time to squash it. After evaluating the remains on the outsole of the shoe and making a face, she hopped down and wiped it off of a paper towel Noel handed to her. As Jamie had gone to kill, he had gone to the maintenance closet to get cleaning materials. As she wiped the flattened bug into the paper towel, the sole began to bend away from the shoe.

"In time of some new shoes maybe?" Noel said, looking down at her. He wasn't a very tall man, not even six foot, just tall enough to look down under his dark eyes on her. He had suggested she get new shoes for weeks and in her pride, she refused to give these up. She bought them with her first pay check when she started working at the rock gym and had used them generously from school to work and home.

"I'm going to refuse on the basis of sentiment," Jamie said. She took the spray bottle and another sheet of paper towel before climbing again to clean what little remained of the critter on the wall.

"When have I ever been sentimental?" Noel looked back to Era who was placing a piece of gum in her mouth. "Is it possible for a sporadic gambler to be sentimental?"

"Sporadic my ass," Era laughed.

"Hey, you can go on your dates and Jamie can take her pictures but the hobby I choose happens to be gambling and for no reason, *I'm* the one looked down on. Why are we painted so monstrously?"

Era lifted her arms and pretended to play a violin to which Jamie laughed. When Noel saw enough he rolled his eyes and left to put the cleaning materials away.

"So where are you taking your pictures?" Era asked Jamie.

"St. Luke's."

"Really?"

"Hey, I never said anything about the architecture. A building and a mental institution are not the same thing . . ." She realized what she said and rephrased it. "A building and a religion are completely different things. You don't need to believe in something to admire it. And if it gives me interesting photos why not? Not a lot of people go there anyways," she said with a sarcastic swing. "I doubt anyone'll mind."

"Be sure to mind your p's and q's. You might not care one way or another but *they* might take offense. Ask before you take pictures."

"Better to ask forgiveness than permission. My uncle already gave it anyways."

"Oh!" Era nodded as she skipped to the front door. "Then just be careful. Don't let some priests corner you so we end up with a converted Jamie whose eyes have been opened forever."

A sly smile creeped onto Jamie's lips. "Would I let them fool me so easily?"

"No matter what you do, do us all a favor and get yourself some new shoes," Noel said, walking back into the room. "You don't want them to think you're there for shoes like that one guy from the Bible."

"Who are you talking about?" Era asked, adjusting her backpacks straps.

"The barefoot guy." Neither of the girls knew who he was talking about and he beckoned them with his hands as he struggled to remember. "C'mon, the really famous one. He walked around with no shoes."

"Barefoot generally means no shoes," Jamie said. Noel's expression flattened and she stared back innocently. "Drive home safely now."

5

It was later than she liked, but she'd spent most of the early afternoon doing the homework she'd ignored the night before, and was now coming upon the cathedral. The sun had a couple of hours until it set, so she slipped on the first shoes she found near the door and eagerly rode her bike to catch the light. The shoes didn't give her any problems until she got off the bike and the sole of one shoe flapped with every step she took. Rolling her eyes, she debated risking splinters and dirt on her feet. The climb was long up the bell tower. She wouldn't be able to take ten steps without grumbling about the broken shoe.

The blue in the western sky was still visible. She had at best two hours of sunlight left and trying to find the best angles for photos without a tripod would definitely eat up the precious minutes of natural light.

The church was open until dusk, so she forewent knocking. She spotted several tourists at the far end of the building, about half the size of her thumb's top phalanx, the baldachin the size of her hand. The rainbow of light streaming in wasn't as impressive as she'd been told, but it was more of a sight than when she came last week. A moment of appreciation later, she turned toward the direction of the stairs, bumping into an immovable figure.

Covering her nose and mouth, she looked up to a member of the clergy. His skin was dark, matching the bronze shade of the *baldacchino*, his wrinkles engraved, though one wouldn't have guessed from lack of gray in his closely cropped hair. He had a scar near his jawline that had been with him for most of his life. He pierced at her with brown irises, accompanied with a scowl that was hard to differentiate from being his natural expression or interim disgruntlement. Jamie stared wide-eyed then lowered her hand to apologize—how couldn't anyone after standing in front of someone as intimidating—but he spoke first, crossing his hands before him.

"The church is to close soon."

"I came last week when it was dark and no one said anything." Jamie furrowed her eyebrows slightly and turned over her shoulder. "And there are those people down there."

The man didn't look toward the people. He knew they were there.

"The last time you visited us was not the night before Mass. On Saturday evenings we close early. Perhaps you missed the listing of visiting hours after you helped yourself through the closed door."

Jamie looked over his shoulder hoping to find a paper with the hours of operation on the wall but found none. Ironically feeling unwelcome, she glanced toward the hall with the staircase she ascended the week before.

"My uncle moved here last week. His name is Gabe."

The man unlocked his hands to catch them again from behind. He released a breath and looked toward the staircase, contemplating something Jamie couldn't read in his eyes or in his expression. After a final thought, he turned to her, only then noticing the camera hanging by its strap over her shoulder.

She grabbed the camera and slightly turned away.

He didn't care to respond. "Family is always welcome. Of course." She knew it was reluctantly added. "You were coming to visit him?"

Jamie looked up quickly and pursed her lips. "I was going to go by his room."

He nodded and didn't seem to have noticed her extemporaneous half-lie. There was something about lying in a church that made even someone as irreligious as Jamie on guard. She *might* have gone by her uncle's room, since that was the only way up the bell tower that she was familiar with, and since the light was going, she didn't have much time to explore a new route. Feeling more relaxed now that the beacon of holy direction seemed to waver, she scrunched her chin and looked toward the hall. "Can I go?"

He nodded and lowered his gaze elsewhere. She didn't waste a breath leaving, only pausing when his voice rose up toward her, though not shown on his face.

"This is a holy place. Please do not extend your stay longer than you intended." He almost stopped, but continued after a thought ran through his mind. "Your uncle and others of the church should have plenty of rest before tomorrow morning." He released his hands and walked down the aisle toward the altar.

Jamie watched him for a moment then turned, muttering under her breath, "Who'd even feel welcome?"

Since mentioning her uncle she felt it necessary to at least try contacting him. It would be only a minute, nothing that would harm her day-long delay any further. Tapping on the door three times resulted in a subsequent ten second wait. When she was sure he would have heard it from inside his tiny room no matter how deep a sleeper he could be, she declared him absent and reset her new course for the bell tower.

The shoe flapped and in every step she grimaced. Discontent, she kicked off the shoe after moving from the small staircase to the second larger one. The ascension of the thousand steps had to be an analogy that Jamie spent much of the climb contemplating. Religion and analogies, she thought, always came hand-in-hand. Religion was only about teaching you a lesson because all man was the same. Selfish, inconsiderate, ignorant. That's why religions like Christianity always sought the heathens out—in the Americas, in Asia, in Africa. Even in the present day they came door-to-door or preached in college campuses, condemning the foul mind and dissolute heart.

Good thing I'm only here for the gargoyles. At least they're honest. Trapped as they are.

Once the door opened a crack, she immediately saw the progress of the setting sun. The bottom of the sphere was just starting to pass the treetops, and she clicked her tongue. There was no time to marvel at the sunset.

She slipped the camera off her shoulder and walked to the ledge, setting the camera to face the canopy that shielded the gargoyles. Sitting beside the camera, she took a picture, then took another vertically. Back to a landscape angle and setting it to a self-timer, she directed the camera toward her and created a good amount of space between herself and the camera, then sat on a bent leg as she looked out toward the city and the sunset. Usually, since she was using her digital camera more than her film, she would preview the pictures before moving on, but once she heard the opening and closing of the shutter she picked up the camera and moved on. It alarmed her when her battery warning began to flash, but she calmly and quickly moved on to the focus of her project.

She approached the corner of one of the columns and kneeled down, angling the camera up toward the interior of the spire. The priests had cleared the roof of the boxes and it made the set-up trickier. She'd planned on using a box as a makeshift tripod. For now, the floor and her camera strap would have to suffice. Next, she placed the camera on the ground at the entrance of the aisle, then set it for a time before running in the middle, keeping her back to the camera. Her photographing wires set to automatic, once hearing the shutter she ran back to take another, repeating the process enough times it beckoned her veins to pulse.

Now the time of the gargoyles.

She approached the first on her left, half standing, half crouching, its mouth closed unlike most of the other gargoyles, its forehead inclined forward. Its hands were militaristic, clenched into fists, though as one remained rested at its side, the other crossed over its chest and its nonexistent heart. Since the bent knee was low enough for her to reach, she took off the broken shoe and used it to climb to stand on its shoulders. There were markings on the wing she attributed to vandals before focusing back to the task at hand. Across the aisle from the most ghastly gargoyle, she had an eye level shot of its grisly presence. She turned toward the others, taking a picture of the gargoyles on her side and then a spanning shot of the other four.

Climbing down, she felt the need to explain herself. "It's for my photo project. I'm not breaking any church laws that jail people for climbing their guardians, right?" She chuckled as she jumped the rest of the way down and wiped her hands. She picked up her shoe and moved down the line.

Her assignment was architecture, but since she was already bending the rules by focusing more on the gargoyles than the actual building, she thought focusing on a theme of people and architecture might make for a better project study. It might even make the picture seem more warm and modern. She could look at the gargoyles, or maybe away. *Yes, away provided better contrast.*

The light from the sun had dissipated. The brightest light in the sky was from the waning crescent moon in the west. While she had taken many pictures that she was positive came out fine, she wished that she had started with this one. What was his name?

Trium.

With a mask of someone ancient and wise, she wondered who the sculptor modeled him after. He seemed to be too anthropomorphic to be meant as a gargoyle. Modeled after a human with a beast's face. What beast though, she wondered. A warthog mixed with a bat?

Since she had already climbed most of the other statues by that time, she figured one more wouldn't get her any less reprimanded if she were caught. It wasn't like she could break him; he was made of stone. A shot of her sitting on his shoulder might even look nice, like a child on their father's shoulder.

Resolved, she turned toward the eastern ledge of the bell tower as it was the tallest "tripod" that would support the camera and capture both her and the gargoyle's silhouettes clearly. She set the camera on the ledge and examined it for a moment before feeling uneasy. One rush of wind and there would go the most expensive possession she owned after her laptop. She used her broken shoe as a safety net between the camera and the ledge's precipice, then took off the other shoe and set it beside it. Before attempting the climb, she examined the quickest climbing route and meditated on it for a moment. Confident she could climb in the allotted fifteen seconds, she set it, then ran. The ground wasn't smooth to run on despite being rather undisturbed, but any pain her feet endured was masked by the need to beat the time. Running forward was easy, she only worried about the climb up.

She hadn't competed in an official speed climbing competition, but on slow work days she and Era would race. The fastest recorded speed was just under six seconds for about twice the gargoyles height, but she wasn't a professional and it wasn't a flat surface with wall holds. *And* she had a distance to cross before she actually started climbing.

"You don't mind keeping this between us do you," she asked the gargoyle. "I don't want to be the first person excommunicated from the church for climbing a consecrated treasure." She scoffed and then sighed. "Jesus Jamie, you really need to invest in a remote. You're talking to rocks."

She reached the top panting with few precious seconds remaining by the sluggish blinking to strategize about where she wanted to be. Since the gargoyle faced south, the camera was only going to capture its profile. She quickly sat on his shoulder and kicked her feet up as if she'd been moving them back and forth. She thought even if she didn't come out clearly, the silhouettes would; a girl on the shoulders of a giant statue. As she faced away from the camera, that meant she had to rely on the click of the shutter to notify her that the picture had been taken.

While waiting she peeked over its wings to look out into town, by this time lit up by its evening lights. The lights over Shore had already prepared for the winter holidays, resembling a Christmas tree. It was a sight to admire standing on her mountaintop. This would make an unforgettable cityscape she hadn't seen before. It was a distance, but she could discern which was her neighborhood and guess which of the houselights was hers. Her mom might be preparing dinner soon for when Victor and Riley came over.

Jamie looked back toward the wings and noticed markings similar to the first gargoyle. After forcing her eyes to adjust to the weak light, she distinguished the markings as letters. With as much care as sculpting the gargoyles, the letters were clear: AG.

A picture with the letters in the foreground and the city in the background? she thought. *No, it will be too dark. Maybe later.*

The camera must have taken the photo by then, though she hadn't been paying attention to listen for the shutter.

The next thing which happened, however, was ambiguous.

She had been turning to look for the dent in the gargoyle's neck to latch onto to help her up, but instead she mistook a shadow as part of the statue, and her foot slipped, and she suddenly became faced with nothing but twenty feet of open air. Without anything to grab onto, she fell. Reminiscent of a dream, she imagined the fall to be stretched, almost teasingly so. She hit the ground, or must have, as suddenly it became more and more dreamlike the more she thought about it. She could even see things, like figures and forms moving toward her— around her. It felt absolutely peculiar and the ambiguity of differentiating whether it was reality or a dream began to frustrate her. She didn't even feel any pain on her head or back or legs. It had to have been a dream. Or the first moments in a newfound comatose state.

But in dreaming the one thing people always take for granted than when awake is the element of time, and how a fall that lasted two seconds felt like twenty, or how being caught in the air by a moving shadow was masked by the adrenaline of falling off of a twenty foot statue. Time could be hours to seconds. Who knew how long she was in that silent pandemonium of a nightmare. Dreams proffered sounds and voices, not deafening silence. The moon had disappeared and she fell under the weight of shadow's night, eternal and universal. Nightmares used to always follow rules and end; this dark dream refused.

Lethargically opening her eyes, she was convinced she'd taken a short nap at the feet of the gargoyle and was still in her surreal, unescapable night prison. That was the first excuse why she saw what she did. Her mind automatically assumed it wasn't possible, which is why she made no reaction. Her heart didn't race and she made no movement but to close her eyes again. When she opened them for the second time, she slowly realized the nightmare's monsters had escaped and that this wasn't a dream. That moment was real. And what she saw would redefine her personal fears, her nightmarish terrors, and ethereal wonder.

Because what she was looking at were two beautiful, cosmic eyes, as expansive as the universe, with tiny suns of light at their centers. She wasn't alone.

And she screamed.

6

Monsters are terror; pure in nature as innocently a child is born. They were designed to remain in stories, nightmares, and cheap thrillers, but as Jamie watched the sun-filled eyes pulse as if it were alive, it became the monster. Crawling on all fours, Jamie turned over her shoulder and darted off, tripping over nothing and bumping into a column before reaching the roof stairwell.

The descent down the staircase, stretching so far down the world seemed a planet away, tantalized her. The descent required no effort. All the same, she felt she was running through water. The descent into hell never ended and the fear she never knew existed raced over her skin, compressed the veins, and exploded the muscles, nerves, and bones. High above her, far behind her, she heard steps. Trailing her. Pursuing her.

All she could do was breathe, allow enough oxygen so she could process instinctual commands like setting one foot forward before the other.

One foot forward.

Away.

The bottom of the bell tower and through the door, to the shorter descent of three stories, and then through the narthex.

A voice called her name from the darkness.

Fear kept her from keeping her back to the voice, impulsively facing Edgar, though retreating, stumbling backwards. Her lips trembled as she failed to warn him. She pointed up and then shook her head, insisting with her eyes.

"It's not safe."

He called after her, but she had already jumped onto her bike and rode down the steps to the road. She couldn't afford to spare a breath. She wouldn't be safe until she got home, switched the lock behind her. Looking back to Edgar wasn't an option. Looking to check both ways before crossing the road wasn't an option. Looking back up to the summit of the cathedral was *not* an option. What if they faced west again? What if they were descending on her now? They had wings. The shadows on the ground couldn't belong to trees. They were of flying creatures, unnatural, not unfriendly to the bewitching new moon. The monsters of her nightmares had power over the heavens. They hid the moon.

Damn the project.

There was no intersection to inconvenience her and no car horn to intimidate her. There was only home. The safest place in the world.

Rosario and Victor had been dating for over a year and due to both having families of their own and both occupying highly demanding careers, both in banking, their mutual dinner dates involved their children on a weekend night every other week.

Victor's daughter, Riley, was deeply invested in a crime show beside Aiden as the adults worked on dinner in the kitchen. She was four years younger than Aiden and while they had little in common otherwise, they enjoyed gluing their eyes to the television in search of the hidden mystery in crime shows, the answers to trivia game shows, and the comedic effect in sitcoms.

"You're not as smart as me," Aiden repeated again to the girl in pigtails. "That's why you can't keep up. It has nothing to do because you're a girl."

Riley had her arms crossed over her chest as she eyed the remote. It would be risky, but he had chosen what to watch for the past half hour. Not a moment to waste she launched toward the remote and snatched it, only for Aiden to exclaim, almost flipping the coffee table in front of them over. Puddles of CranApple juice spread over the wooden floor.

"Look!" Aiden said, reaching for the remote. "Now look what you did!" Riley had the remote locked between both of her hands as she stared back with wide eyes, ashamed she made a mess and worried how she'd be punished for it.

"*¿Qué pasó?*" Rosario took a step into the living room and spotted the dripping cups before Aiden could open his mouth. Her eyes narrowed on him and he heard it before she said it. "Clean it up. Now!"

"But she . . ." Aiden attempted, but his mother's back was already turned.

Victor stepped closer to the living room and examined the mess before turning to Riley.

"What happened?"

"It was an accident!" Riley said.

He pointed his arm after Aiden and, though not as loud as Rosario, was just as stern. "Help him."

She reluctantly dropped the remote back on the couch and followed Aiden to get paper towels. It was just an accident, but the more and more trouble she made here the less she found herself in her father's good graces. She learned that while he was not as strict at the Diez's house as he was at home, he did show his anger by being more reserved. The only plus at least was he was never as loud as Rosario when he scolded her.

Aiden was soaking the juice up with a mop and squeezing it into a bucket when Jamie burst through the front door. She barely noticed Riley and Aiden in the living room before rushing to her room.

"Jamie, you're back later than"—Rosario looked over her shoulder, noticing how her daughter wasn't listening—"Jamie?"

Though Jamie had shut the front door behind her, she couldn't chase off the feeling of eyes off of her back. Those eyes refused to disappear. They were in every blink, in the light of oncoming headlights, and in the shadows. Always the shadows. Always peeking from behind the darkness on the outskirts of the roads and sidewalks. That was when the whispers started calling after her.

She flicked on the lights and threw the door shut behind her, but it didn't move fast enough, so she pressed her palms against it until it shut against the door jamb.

It had never stopped once she saw the eyes, but now for the first time she noticed how much her hands had been trembling. She drew them to her chest, unable to feel safe until only walls surrounded her. As she scanned the room, she noticed the window blinds still open. It took less than six strides to cross the room, anxiously twist the window blind controls and blanket the curtains over it. She scanned the room to see what else she could cover. The air vent on her ceiling . . .

There was a knock on her door and she clutched her chest.

"Jamie, are you all right?" Her mother knocked again. "Can I come in?"

Jamie dithered, then opened the door. Her mother stepped back at the abruptness, but examined Jamie quickly.

"¿Mija, qué pasó?"

"I—I saw something," Jamie said, placing her hand on her chest as she tried to calm herself. "At St. Luke's. I saw something."

"For you to act this way?" Rosario asked, stepping forward and reaching for Jamie.

"Mom, listen! It was impossible!"

"Jamie, lower your voice. What is it that you saw? Does it concern your uncle?"

Jamie pulled away from her mother's hand. Why should she care about her uncle?

"The church. They have secrets. And no one in Shore knows!" Jamie laughed, her mother shifting away.

"Jamie . . . first your uncle has secrets, and now the church? I'm not sure what's stirring this on but I don't like it—"

"I was just taking some pictures . . ."

"You can tell me later. We have company for dinner—in case you didn't notice. You just walked by without saying hello."

Jamie stared into her mother's eyes and searched for the slightest concern into why she was behaving the way she was. It isn't like she made it a habit of acting hysterically. If anything Jamie didn't care about anything that happened. Life in Shore was drab and aching. Even with the terrorist and police shootings occurring week by week in every corner of the world; deteriorating coral reefs and the increase of endangered species due to pollution; heat spikes and rising oceans due to climate change; and despite the disastrous administration going up in smoke, her mother was supposed to assure her it would all be all right. To occupy all the feelings and emotions she couldn't. For the world. At least for her. But she was more worried about her uncle, keeping manners with people she saw often. More than about her daughter. Her.

Jamie felt her upper lip twitch as she reached for the door.

"I'm not hungry."

The door slammed in Rosario's face and this time she did react appropriately. She processed her daughter's actions for a moment before turning back down the hall toward the living room. Victor met her at the end of the hallway and she hinted at a smile before calling Riley and Aiden to finish cleaning up and to prepare for dinner.

Jamie shut the door and kept her hand pressed over it, glancing down to her desk beside her. On top of notebooks and assignments from English class was the journal she found by the cathedral. Engulfed in rage, she picked it up and tossed it across the room; followed by homework assignments, then books. Next were the clothes, shirts worn once and jeans hanging over her desk chair, laundry basket, and bed.

The lights. There weren't enough lights on. The ceiling fan bulb was on, but she turned on her desk light and then the floor lamp by her window. With no lights left, she reached for a flashlight she had in her closet and brought it with her to bed. She couldn't look into the light directly because the brightness would force her to see ring shapes. She stared at the window.

That's the direction they would come. It made the most sense that a creature of the night would crawl through her bedroom window. Her house was a single story. It would be only too easy for a creature to easily take out the window screen and fiddle with the window lock, lift the window she hadn't opened in years, hearing as it squeaked and deafened the cry of the creature before it stepped into her bedroom and . . .

Her eyes were pinned on the window, the flashlight already spotlighting it, her finger on the switch. Light would probably not kill it, but it might just blind it long enough for her to get away. A moment was all she had to spare and it wouldn't be something she would waste.

The moment stretched for hours.

Past the dinner. Past the departure of the boyfriend and his daughter. Past the clean-up of the dinner. Past the boy showering and then the mother. Past the goodnights. And past the house lights turning dark.

The boy went to sleep and then the mother. They didn't know Jamie would spend most of the night in brightness, staring at window curtains as if assigned border patrol. They weren't aware of how at 3:15 in the morning she dozed off, only to force her eyes open again. They didn't hear when the flashlight rolled from out of her hands onto the carpet floor at 4:50.

The shadows never came for her, but staring at window curtains and only window curtains could fool the mind from seeing movement when there was none, and noises when there was none, and shadows when there were none.

****

Jamie woke up to a slack jaw and a trail of dry drool. She wiped at it then sat up, remembering the window curtains. Strangely, she didn't dream of anything last night. It was better than having to suffer through a nightmare after the ordeal she went through last night, but having no dreams must have meant something grim. Her hand bounced around the blanket as she continued to focus on the window curtain. She relinquished her attention to search for the flashlight. After finally getting up, she looked over the edge of the bed and picked it up. The lights had been on all night, however she needed the flashlight just in case. Unsure of the time, she moved toward the window. It had to have been sometime in the day.

She rolled her tongue over the gunk on her teeth, rolled her lips together, then moved her hands through the curtain and the blinds to look outside. It was deep into the day, past noon, the sun as blinding as any Florida day. It didn't bring the designation of the Sunshine State to shame.

She shot her hand over her eyes, then turned back into the room. The abode of Chaos. She knew she had thrown things around, but she wasn't expecting such an aftermath. Not wishing to deal with the mess, she walked to the dresser and set the flashlight down. Once she spotted herself in the mirror, she noticed how bad she really looked.

There were unnatural dark circles under the eyes like she hadn't slept in days. Her hair was still tied up in a loosened ponytail, explaining the headache pulsing in her skull. She had eyeliner smeared toward her temple and nose bridge, in the eye socket, and below the eyes. She rubbed the eye crusts away and the dried drool from another earlier trail, rubbing the mouth gunk from her hands.

She needed a shower, and grabbed the first thing at the top of her drawers before going to the bathroom. Aiden heard her from the living room but said nothing. Even if he wanted to speak or had, she shut the bathroom door behind her.

When she returned to her room, she opened the window blinds and began to clean up. It was after picking up a shirt from the floor she noticed the journal from the cathedral. Curious, she tossed the shirt aside and picked it up.

The material under her fingertips felt different than when she first found it. It was softer and felt lighter in her hands, almost as if the words had spilled out and whatever vehement confessions within were expelled. Curious to what the insignia was in the back, she stepped closer to the window and flipped the book over. The picture was a profile image of a face hidden beneath a hood, only their nose and lips visible. The folds were incredibly detailed, and difficult to notice there was a tiny wing drawn near the bottom of the hood, hidden in the corner of a deep fold. There was a word, most likely a family name written underneath the insignia, but it was too small and worn away to read clearly.

Flipping the book to the front, she opened the front cover and looked for a name. Nothing identifiable as a name, but the unfinished word: pars.

Turning to the front page, she read the page quietly. The ink was faded. The writing was jagged, and not a straight column like a letter or in paragraphs like an essay; it was written as if the writer was unsure when to start or stop on the line.

Shadow upon shadow. Gleaming and clear the robe cannot contain the light within. A dance on the walls. Fire's shadow. Steps echo and dance flutters faster. The hall rises and falls and shadow upon shadow does not stop. Hours upon hours. No forward to anticipate. No behind to retreat. A turn to the wall, a sense of something upon the shadow. Not the shadow upon a shadow. A whisper. None should be heard in the hall of caved cries and fire's sway. First robe stops. Listens. Stench in the air fills the hall and the fire ahead brightens. Another. Approaches and speaks. First listens. Looks back to the second. The first of the whispers.

    Jamie arched an eyebrow and turned the page.

Words whispered. At first one. All know now. Shadow upon shadow only follows. First comes to a room. Scratches line the walls. Smoke and blood and dust fill the second. Does not stop. The room ends and opens to an open space. Far and impossible to end. No light to shine but fire's shadows. Plains and crevices. All the abominables waken, crawl out, see, cry in glee. Freedom. First lifts arms. Robe praises. Abominations below fill with hope, praise back. The whispers are true. First promises the whispers are true. Cracked bones, splinters, scorched bark appears beside first. First speaks to Destruction beside, first still looks forward. "Of a different kind say whispers. Of the East and of West." First looks to Destruction. "Find him." First looks to the abominations. First smiles. Shadow upon shadow knows.

    Unsure what kind of story this was, she turned another page. Whether this person was on something when they wrote it or not, she'd never read anything like it before.

Trapped. Chained. No escape. Human souls are food. Chewed, savored, swallowed, spit out. Eaten again. Stones thrown off of backs and land on explosions of dust and dirt to be picked up by the human souls again. Thrown and tossed. Eaten and spit out. Meaningless. All is meaningless. No brother to love and no master to devote. Spirals and water drops of uselessness and effects. Spur meaning. What meaning? Second asks first shadow. First does not listen. Whispers are forgotten. Time has leapt millennials. Human souls arrive at the gate from their dust and ruin in tears and scars. Only memories. New tears to be wept. New scars to fashion on skin. Ripped, sawed, torn, and beaten. Sewn together—

    There was a knock on her door and Jamie jumped, narrowing her eyes toward the direction of the noise.

    "What!"

    Aiden pushed the door open, swirling a spoon in a cup as he leaned against the doorframe.

    "Mom left to get some stuff for the house. She said to check on you once you woke up."

Jamie scoffed, setting the journal on the bed as she resumed straightening up her room.

"I bet she did."

"Well she did."

"Whatever, Aiden. If that's all." Jamie waved her hand for him to leave.

"She also wanted me to tell you that we're having dinner with Victor and Riley again tonight so you can apologize."

The wonders of having such a mother. Jamie never understood why she forced her to apologize. It was pointless if someone else was forcing you.

"I have stuff to do today and can't waste time playing remorseful daughter to mom's boyfriend and kid. I'll say sorry next time I see them."

Aiden smirked but shook his head.

"Mom isn't going to want to hear that."

"Of course not. That's why she likes you more. Because you make mistakes while I purposely make accidents. Now, if you'll be so kind." Jamie came to the door and pushed him out.

"You left yesterday to take pictures but last night I didn't see your camera. So it isn't like you're going to work on something tonight."

Jamie knew she'd forgotten her camera at the cathedral and was at pains knowing she had to go to that horrible place to get it back. Maybe if she asked Era, she might do it. She was working today, but— Jamie glanced at the time. Almost 1:00. She didn't go to work that day but Jamie could meet her and pick it up.

"I left it with a friend," Jamie said, reaching for her phone.

Aiden spoke quickly before she could shut the door in his face.

"I know that's not true because we got a call this morning from St. Luke's. They said you left it behind last night."

Her thumb was hovering over the call button, a hint of pressure from dialing. Jamie shut her eyes. Of course they reached out. They knew her number and probably informed her mom how insanely she behaved as she ran away from them. All that, and her mom still must not have cared because she was still forcing dinner with Victor and Riley. Even mentioned by someone else she didn't care what might have spooked Jamie out last night.

"What else did they say?" Jamie asked, slightly more polite.

"Nothing. They just said you left in a rush and they'll hold onto your camera until you come to pick it up."

"Damn it. My pictures are on there." Jamie noticed Aiden focus on her instead of his ice cream and she amused his curiosity. "They're due tomorrow."

"So . . . go to the cathedral?" Aiden said, a pause after each word.

"I'm not really in the mood."

Aiden opened his mouth to respond when they heard the garage open. Their mother was back. Jamie lifted her hand. "I need to change. Go away."

She closed the door and returned back to the journal. Whoever left it must want it back. Perhaps going to drop off the journal was the best idea. She wasn't enjoying reading it. If anything, it creeped her out more since last night.

There was another knock but instead of waiting to be let in, the door opened.

"What?" Jamie asked, turning back to them.

"Good morning," her mother said. She was leaning against the door with her arms behind her. There was a request in her eyes that asked for an explanation for the night before.

"Aiden told me," Jamie said. "But I need to go to the cathedral to pick up my camera. I'll try and make it back in time for dinner."

Her mom brought a hand forward, lifting the camera up by the strap. Jamie could only look at it as if her eyes were fooling her.

"No need. I was going out when a friend from work called and I stopped by her house. She lives near the cathedral and since I was in the area, picked it up for you. A priest named Edgar asked me if you were all right. He's a very kind man. He also said he found these."

She lifted Jamie's shoes. Jamie hadn't realized she had biked home barefoot.

"When was the last time you bought new shoes?"

"You didn't see Gabe?" Jamie asked.

Rosario shook her head and crossed her arms, walking to her bed and looking around the room.

"He wasn't available. But I left a message for him to call me when he could."

Jamie had half a mind to share that her uncle wasn't there when she stopped by his room, but knowing her mother, said nothing.

"Well, since I have my camera back, I guess I won't have any excuse to get out of dinner tonight." She moved to her laptop, already having slipped the SD card from the camera out. She inserted it into the slot when she spoke over her shoulder. "This will take a couple of hours but call me when you're starting dinner."

"I will."

Her mother left with a lingering glance that Jamie felt as intensely as if pressing the palm of one's hand onto a stove burner. Editing wouldn't take long, but her mother didn't know that. On one hand, working on the photos would only prompt those memories of angst, panic, and trepidation from the night before and if under her control, she wanted to avoid suffering two all nighters. On the other hand, she worked after school the next day. Afraid of discovering the pictures to be unsatisfactory while showing them to Ms. Ava, she pulled up the folder and browsed through the pictures.

They weren't bad at all. Of course some were blurry and some needed a brighter exposure, but all unedited photos have screens that make them flat and gray. Skipping through them quickly, she finally reached the last picture. It responded to her more than she responded to it, and after her eyes dried in an unyielding staring contest with the screen, she finally processed what she saw.

It was the image of her climbing Trium. There were two silhouettes. The gargoyle was facing left toward the aisle of the gargoyles. His upper body was bent like his legs hadn't caught up with the thoughts of his mind. The wings were stretched and spread out as if he were about to take off. The large silhouette's arms reached out under the second silhouette. While the second fell at a normal rate, the speed at which the larger silhouette moved had to have been faster. Yet, it was the larger silhouette that was clearer while the figure falling was ill-defined.

"Shadow upon shadow," she whispered.

An error popped up at the corner of the screen reading the battery was low and required a charger to be plugged in for further use or replaced with a new battery pack.

The image was impossible. There were no legends of gargoyles, yet she couldn't believe she had been the first person in history to have seen them move. The gargoyles weren't alive. They couldn't move. All of it was a conniving trick of the mind. She didn't want to admit it to herself, how even with the impossible, it still frightened her.

No, it was just a trick. All of the other photos had been normal. It was just this last one.

She moved the cursor over the image to delete it, but then hesitated. If she deleted it now then it would haunt her. Every day into the foreseeable future.

Tomorrow then, after she had a good night's rest. She'd look and see that somehow what she saw was manipulated, like a mirage in the desert.

Just like a mirage, she thought.

The computer shut down, unable for to wait for Jamie to stand up and plug it into the charger three steps away.

7

Trains of light disappeared into the popcorn ceiling. The nightmare felt like a trance-like descent. Primarily following one shadow, it was robed entirely with no hands, feet, or face visible. All around was darkness, though somehow shadows could still be discerned dancing on the walls. Hours upon hours she followed the shadow, having no control over any part of her body but her eyes, with only the power to look around and wish she could hide. Incapable of fleeing, she followed, linked by an unseen chain. Her heart begged to be free. Hours—it felt like days, simply walking, expecting to come across someone or reach the end of the hall. Perhaps she had been trapped in an infinite loop as the tenebrous murals continued to sway to unruly noise. When her eyes found the morning welcoming her, she'd never felt so thankful to be unchained from a dream.

Jamie expected to present the pictures she took when returning to class, but Ms. Ava had Yearbook to worry about. She didn't remember to ask for the students pictures until a couple of days later. Jamie quickly sifted through them, only really getting to the fifth one before Ms. Ava patted her on the back and moved onto the next student. However, during the next few days, Jamie kept seeing the image of the two silhouettes just when she managed to forget.

The days following she never pulled the last image up again, a streak of luck that would end as soon as her shift ended Friday afternoon. If it hadn't been for work, she would have almost always had the picture on her mind, the obsession itching to ask why she saw what was impossible. She was returning from the storage closet in Shore's rock gym when a voice called out in her direction.

"Moses!" Noel said. Clutching the box of harnesses, Jamie stopped suddenly at his exclamation.

"Lazarus!" Jamie said.

"Ezekiel!" Era said. Not many people were in the gym, but the few were preoccupied climbing and didn't notice the sporadic outbursts.

"Wise men," Jamie added.

Noel's expression fell, his eyebrows drawing together as he looked from one to the other. "What are you doing?"

"Isn't this some sort of name a Biblical character game? Adam—and Eve! *Ooo*, beat that!" Era said, jabbing a finger over to Jamie.

Jamie walked to the bench by the front counter and set the box down. "I just stepped in I don't even know."

Noel shook his head and set the waiver clipboard on the counter. "No—Moses. That was the name of the barefoot man. He didn't wear shoes because God told him not to."

"Ah." Era nodded. "You waited all week to tell us?"

"What are you talking about?" Noel said. "It took me all week to remember."

The girls chuckled. He was one to fret over trivial matters, letting it navigate his focus when there were more important things to worry about. He may not have Jamie's infrequent forgetfulness, but fretting over things that served no purpose seemed worse than forgetting something important. There was one time several months back he laboriously struggled to remember the names of the Easter Island Heads, giving Era and Jamie clues that the stones were certainly on the Hawaiian islands and they attracted hundreds of thousands of tourists a year. Being on work time with an unusual amount of customer traffic that day, they didn't have any time to search online and clarify that he was talking about the Moai. The southern Pacific island wasn't the only geographic pitfall Noel grappled with, he was positive that Napoleon died in banishment on an island in the Mediterranean and not in an island in the south Atlantic. There were heated words between himself and Era about the existence of an island name Saint Helena until Jamie diluted the argument when she pulled out a map. Quicker than he would've liked, it was well known within the gym's walls that his geographic awareness wasn't as serviceable as his knowledge on rock climbing or music.

"I think it beats your record for trying to remember the name for the Tierra del Fuego," Era said, a smile behind her eyes as she read the ceiling, a pen cap against her lip. "I believe it took you over three hours. And that was only thanks to Jamie coming and saying it—

what—within ten seconds of walking through the door?" Noel had his hand raised to refute that memory when Era pointed over her shoulder with her pen. "By the way, Jamie, your friends are here."

Over the way Jamie spotted members of the high school's rock climbing club: the Capes. Minjae was the belay for Bryden, a senior that was one of the first to establish the club. Though not exclusive to those with experience, their club was small compared to more prominent ones like the Thespian Society, National Honor Society, and National Beta Club. The five to ten who frequented the gym on weekends were rambunctious, even over the radio speakers which played mellow background music.

"My friends?" Jamie asked.

"Aren't they?" Era's eyebrow lifted. "Thought they were. My mistake."

"I know *of* them."

"Well you always take care of them when they come."

"Because you leave them for me."

"Because I thought they were your friends!"

Jamie's mouth opened when a man's voice called over from the beginner's belay wall. A father was belaying his daughter and she seemed to have gotten her rope stuck around one of the foot holds. Jamie complimented the father for not letting go of the rope in an attempt to loosen her himself. After making sure she wouldn't get stuck again she left the father and daughter, passing by the Capes.

One of the members, Vienna, flung her arm out to Jamie and beckoned her. "Hey, Jamie. Give us your opinion. Tell him he's wrong."

Another senior, Jax, who was the third point of the triangular conversation, stared down Vienna as he hung by the belay ten feet above them. "With you telling her what to think, how can she give us her honest opinion?"

"What?" Jamie asked.

"You've been climbing for a bit right?" Jax asked. Jamie gave a noncommittal nod. "Climbing in winter's frowned upon by parents and senior instructors alike, but another our age can agree. There's absolutely no more risk climbing in the winter than any other time anywhere else in the world."

"No," Jamie said, not fully committing to it before she turned to Vienna. "I mean there are risks either way. Only that in the snow there's more risks of avalanches. Or you might be at a high altitude—so acclimating. You could be snowed in, stormed in. Collapse through a snow bridge. Rescue efforts, if something were to happen, would be impeded by the weather. There's a bunch, you can get the full list from Noel."

"Exactly, you hear it all the time," Jax said. "Otherwise no would have risked the Alps or climbed Everest."

Vienna rolled her eyes. "I swear Everest's always your default rock."

"Is that your question?" Jamie asked.

"We've been planning an overnight climbing trip during winter break but some parents are stubborn to no end that climbing in the winter is absolutely and without a doubt idiotic."

"That . . ." Jamie tried to find the words and spoke slowly. "Doesn't surprise me."

"It surprises no one. I don't know why he asked you," Vienna said.

"Hey Italy, I wanted another POV. Okay?"

"Austria—you're thinking of Venice. Vienna's in Austria. I swear to God call me Italy one more time and I'll let you manage the rest of the climb on your own."

"What kind of climber deserts a fellow climber so heartlessly? Oh c'mon you like it." Jax smirked as he returned his focus on the rock holds and began his ascent.

Jamie stood in place as she crossed her arms and spoke to Vienna. "So, you're planning a trip?"

Vienna adjusted the rope. "All the Capes want to go. Our parents are half and half pretty much. But they all know we really enjoy climbing so this shouldn't have come as a surprise. I mean, it's our senior year. We should enjoy it." Vienna flashed Jamie a glance. "You know what I mean. You work here. You must want to climb actual rock faces and not pieces of plastic."

"Of course she does," said a voice behind them. "But there isn't exactly a 'mighty face' just around the corner is there?"

Jamie and Vienna turned to Minjae and several other Capes approaching from another wall they were climbing.

"Don't be snarky with me Jay," Vienna said.

"So you're telling everyone our plans now?" Bryden said, sizing up Jamie before tossing his harness to the nearby bench.

Vienna made a face but turned her attention to Jax, by this point not far from the top. "It isn't a secret."

"If you asked your mom what do you think she'd say?" Minjae asked.

Jamie unfolded her arms and shook her head. "Let me go climbing for real? I don't think she'd be up for it."

"Scared?" asked Caprice, a junior Cape.

"I'm sure she'd agree with most of your parents. Sending your kid across the country to potentially risk their life on a whim of an adventure . . ." Jamie shrugged.

"Whim?" Bryden scoffed. "We've been planning this trip for months."

"So where would you go?"

"Well I've had my sights on the Sierra Nevada Mountains for a year now," Bryden said, "but my parents prefer a range on the east coast. Can you believe it? Even if it's more dangerous!"

"I've heard Mount Harvard is great to climb in the winter, alongside Mount Columbia," Caprice added. "Or Blanca Peak. But they're in Colorado, not much better than California—"

"Still closer," Bryden interjected, winking at Caprice.

Caprice blushed and responded, "None of us want to try Mount Katahdin or Stony Man Mountain since they're more hike than climb. Yeah, but all our parents seem adamant keeping us in the East."

"To which we reluctantly inform them all the great places to climb are—of course—in the western half of the country," Minjae said.

"But your parents said no," Jamie said.

"Mine said maybe," Caprice said.

"Mine said no," Bryden said, then muttered. "Something about irresponsible."

"Mine said maybe," Minjae said.

"No," Vienna sighed.

"Maybe," Jax said, landing on his feet.

"It's an expensive trip anyways. How would you get there? Flying?" Jamie said.

"Well—" Vienna began, but was then interrupted by Bryden.

"Money's no issue. We just need to convince our parents. So far we only have club members. Maybe that's what's not working. How about it Jamie, would you be interested on an adventure? Maybe if we have someone outside the club they would see it isn't that serious."

"If I were a parent I'd think the opposite," Vienna said.

"She works at the gym. She's fully capable!" Bryden turned to Jamie. "What do you say?"

"A minute ago you didn't want her to know now you want her to come?" Vienna said.

Bryden rolled his eyes, and Jamie looked toward the front desk where Era was helping a customer with their equipment. She looked back at the members. "I don't know."

"C'mon," Minjae said with a small smile. "It can be an early graduation gift. At least that's what we're asking our parents it'll take the place of. It'll be fun."

"We might feel safer if we have an expert on site," Jax said, elbowing her arm playfully.

"I'm far from an expert. Talk to Era or Noel about that."

"Well, one our age," Jax said. "Just ask your mom. You must want to get out Florida. Experience something new."

"Don't let these Neanderthals tempt you," Vienna said. "We just wanted to hear your thoughts."

Several things occurred to Jamie. Her home. Her family. The strange dreams she'd started to have. What if she still had these dreams by the time that she went on this trip? But then there was being away from home. That was going to come eventually, though turns out not that big of an obstacle for herself. And money? She'd been saving for years. The most expensive thing might be the plane trip, because no matter how close it was, she'd do anything to avoid a road trip, regardless how cheap it would be in contrast. The biggest obstacle would be her mother as their parents were for them. What would she say? She *should* have no qualms. Aiden could manage, or maybe go over to a friend's house while their mom worked. There was obviously Banafsha next door, but Aiden might spurn that idea right off that bat. He already went there after school every day. They could call her *abuela*. Her mother's mother loved visiting them. A week in winter break wasn't too much time to ask. Maybe a little longer? Jamie never asked for anything, aside from begging to get out of her cousin's wedding. It isn't like she was that much closer with her mother's side of the family than her father's. Sure there were family gatherings and weddings and funerals in Puerto Rico, but that was a plane trip once every few years.

Jamie thought they were waiting for her to say she'd consider it, but then she noticed they were silently judging Vienna beside her. The condemned scanned the eyes on her from around the group and sighed. "But if you want to come, we'd really like it. Our club doesn't exactly have prerequisites to join."

"I'll see what my mom says." Jamie forced a smile and found Era fortuitously glancing at her. She left them with the professional courtesy to call her if they needed anything.

Back at the front counter, she waited for Era to finish reviewing the safety procedures with the customers. Not needing to accompany them to the wall, Era smiled over to Jamie and rested her hands on the counter.

"Fun talk with your friends?"

"I guess they've become that all of a sudden haven't they?"

Era chuckled and grabbed the sign-in clipboard. "Whatever you say."

Banafsha led Jamie to the living room where her brother was at the TV again. When Jamie made her presence known, it didn't even elicit the decent action of having her brother turn around. "Okay, another minute," he uttered. "The show's almost done."

"You've imposed yourself enough today. Let Banafsha have her TV back."

"Let him be. I'm not missing anything." Banafsha motioned for Jamie to follow her to the dining table. "Come."

Jamie sighed heavily as she sank into the chair. Banafsha was grabbing a juice from the refrigerator and brought a glass for Jamie. After Jamie drank half of it, she kept it in her hand. "I appreciate it. I haven't been sleeping well lately."

"You have a lot on your mind. Much more than what I used to when I was your age."

"That's not true."

Banafsha didn't show anything in her eyes. "You have tests and jobs and your future and college. And if you had one, a boyfriend."

"You sound like my *abuela* every time I see her. *Do you have a boyfriend yet?*" Jamie brought the glass back to her lips.

There was silence between them for a moment. "The new guy finally finished moving."

Jamie's eyebrows lifted. "It took the neighbor two weeks to move in? How much stuff did he have?"

"Well the moving truck was only there for a day, but he's been moving stuff in and out for days. Like he decided *now* after moving what he wanted to keep and sell and bring in."

"You're such a snoop."

Banafsha narrowed her eyes on Jamie. "Excuse me?"

"Of course I mean that in the most respectful way."

"Like being old? I am entitled to look out my window any time I want."

"Yes, forgive me." Jamie kept back a smile. "So, does he still smile incessantly?"

"More or less." Banafsha rolled her shoulders. "I guess I am a snoop. But you see more people than I do. Is that really so normal?"

"No, I'll have to agree with you."

Banafsha lifted a hand resting on the table. "And he looks paler than when I last saw him. He must see more sun than me and I think I'm darker!"

"That's because you have me to shine and keep you your beautiful shade of brown." Jamie stretched her arms and smiled widely.

"That's corny, Jamie," Aiden said, stepping beside her and rolling his eyes. "Good night, Banafsha. *Shukriya.*" Banafsha wished him farewell. "I'll see you at home Corny Connie." Aiden smirked and left.

"Even with all the TV he watches, he still reads so much. Learning so much. Your brother is very bright."

"I'd agree with you if he didn't just insult me two seconds ago."

"That's sibling spat," Banafsha dismissed. "He's very ambitious. He said he wanted to be an astronaut."

"All boys want to be astronauts at some point. He also wanted to be a pilot, a construction contractor, a CEO, and president. He'll change it at least ten times before he applies for college."

"From what I've seen he can do whatever he wants."

"Well as long he doesn't go with the church I don't care." Jamie slouched further into the seat.

"It would be a waste wouldn't it? But even the Pope is an influential man. And the Dalai Lama."

"Whatever. I'll support him with whatever he wants."

"You act like you don't care about him, but I know you like him."

"It's hard to like people who only try to sabotage the little free time you have, but I guess I'm compelled."

"It's why I love your family." Jamie looked up to Banafsha, smiling coyly. "Partially. You all have walls and you complain, but at the end of the day, you still like each other."

"I'm glad you just said like and not that other word."

"Sometimes you *have* to love people, but in this world, it's better if you simply like someone. Love is too much passion, too much expectation. Your love can grow to consume you, possess you, completely alter who you are, but liking someone or something is only a part of you. You will have room to like other things and other people and even if you begin to dislike something, at least you can grow to like something else easily."

"Have you ever loved someone, Banafsha?"

She had her hands crossed and was looking down at them. Questions delving into her past, Banafsha usually transitioned into another topic, however, on the topic of liking and loving, she seemed more open.

"I think it's quite hard to not love at least once by my age."

Jamie wasn't expecting her to reply. She only watched. Marveled. Entranced.

"When I was young I lived near a wealthy family with the most beautiful garden. They lived in an extravagant home with high walls and a gate at the front with orange tracery. I could see the green of the garden complimenting the gate through the openings and thought it was a small portion of heaven. One day the lady of the house saw me on her way home. I stared from the street as she got out of her car. I was maybe eight. Her house servant came out and spoke with her, but I just stared at the lady. She wore a beautiful Shayla, a very dark purple headscarf over neat, clean clothing. I thought she had maybe never gone outside in her life. It was a foolish thought, but you think those things when you're young and you don't know any better.

"She walked over to me and I was frozen with both fear of being scolded and fear of being belittled, but I had grown up being cast aside, my heart and my conscious kept me in place. She could no more hurt me than any other person in the world. But as she came to the gate, a folder in her hands in front of her, she bent down and asked me if I liked mango. What a silly question, I'd never had one before, but I said I did and she smiled so kindly. I thought she was an angel how beautifully she smiled. She extended a hand then led me inside. The house servant fetched me a mango and I wasn't shy. Not during those times. Not when you were so poor. I sunk my mouth through the skin and felt such a sweet juice bubble to my cheeks. I ate it all so quickly and all I could think was wanting another one. The lady must have read my eyes. She read my thoughts. And then she showed me where I could pick my very own. The largest mango I saw I could have. We went back outside and walked to the side of the house where the garden was. And . . ." Banafsha closed her eyes for a moment.

"I thought that heaven was real. So much green and so many colors complimenting the greens. All I ever saw in my life were the drab colors of gray and black and white. But red and orange and green and purple. Not just from a forsaken distance but a color I could touch with my own hands. I stared at such beauty with my mouth yellowed from the mango juice and my hands sticky from the fruit still in them. I was a child of poverty and yet I felt the richest girl alive. The kind woman let me pick one mango. Any mango I wanted. It was unfathomable to want something when you were poor, and even more so to have a choice. I found the biggest yellow mango I could find and actually took the time to enjoy what I was eating."

Banafsha was in deep thought, remembering each moment as if it were the most precious memory she'd ever had, one she'd thought of so many times before. Jamie carefully heeded how delicately Banafsha spoke. Any and every detail was important and deserved to be retold. It was a memory that Jamie would never have thought so precious, but it belonged to another person from another time who grew up in another culture. Pakistan during her youth was barely a country and was still in turmoil. Banafsha drew her eyes back to Jamie and held up a finger.

"*Just one. I'll let you come back and have one fruit of your choice once a week for every week*, she told me. Her servant would let me in to the garden where I could make my choice. *Just one*, she repeated. She wished me a good night and led me back to the gate. I licked my fingers the entire walk back home. When I got home I was slapped for not bringing anything for the rest of the family, but they never would have believed me if I said I only had enough for one person. So I apologized and said I would next time. I returned to the gate every week for years and would choose my one fruit. I would eat it in secret and never share it with my family. I always made sure to clean my face. I rarely saw the woman, but I became very close to the house servant. She was just as kind as the lady of the house. Sometimes she would share the extra servings she had from the house with me."

Banafsha stood up to put the juice carton back in the refrigerator. "I liked the lady of the house for what she did, but the first person I ever loved was the house servant. Even more than my own family I loved her. I just didn't know it was love until many years later, after the family moved and the servant left with them. They were Hindi and left to India. Many Hindis left during the Partition but some tried to stick it out against Muslims." Banafsha looked to Jamie. "You forget their face. Their name. But you don't forget how you evolved. One day you realize you are not the person you were before you met them, but a person you were meant to be. Because you loved them, because you liked them, because you met them. If only we could meet every person in this world, who would we be? What number is the boundary that defines who we are from that point on to the future people we will meet and shape? *Those* are the questions I want answers to, not what will happen after we die. We're dead. It no longer matters."

"I've often wondered who my ancestors were. What historical events were they a part of. What famous people did they meet."

Jamie felt brave and thought that since Banafsha was being open, she might squeeze something else out of her neighbor.

"So you were Muslim?"

Banafsha shook her head and took Jamie's glass, placing it in the sink and picking up the rag.

"If you want to label me. I was once, yes."

Valiantly, Jamie crossed her hands on the table.

"Banafsha, do you believe in a higher power? In another life after this one? In angels and demons and the like?"

The sink had few other dishes left behind by Aiden and Banafsha cleaned them quietly for several moments. Jamie must have hit her limit on how much she was going to get out of her and settled for not hearing another word, but then Banafsha must have been muddling over what she should or could share as she sighed before turning off the faucet.

"I don't believe in the God that Muslims believe in, or the Christians or the Jews. There must be something more after we die, but what? How can I believe that in all the world, the religion I have known growing up was the one and only truth. It is the one true answer to all the mysteries beyond life. True? Before even the earliest humans remember? It's difficult for me to believe. To truly believe. Angels and demons, they can be the messengers of God or the devil, but in all my life, I've only ever seen angels and demons in people. I believe that God was a great man and the devil his greatest enemy. Angels and demons are the people that obey and serve them. They are good and they are bad. But then again, people can never be just one thing. Of the people I've grown to know I never met a truly good person and a truly evil one, though I've seen many evil people; as much as I'd like to believe there is no more to their heartlessness and emptiness."

"That's an interesting way of seeing it," Jamie said quietly.

"I just believe in what I see." Banafsha wiped her hands dry and returned to Jamie at the table, sitting down slowly. "One day I'll learn the truth—we all will."

Jamie arched an eyebrow. "What of ghosts?"

Banafsha tsked and waved her hand. "What do you think? Why do you keep asking me all these questions?"

"I—I just . . ." Jamie fumbled over the words and shook her head, embarrassed.

"No, no, you got me blabbing my mouth all night. What do you think?"

"I don't know! Once I used to think it was true. Angels and God and all of it. Why not when my dad did? But then he died and it felt like a joke. Religion is just an institution, like school and government. You're taught it. I thought knowing of something greater than all of us should be self-taught, something we all experience spiritually since that's all we are. If we're really just souls walking with flesh suits." Banafsha made a face and Jamie clarified. "Meat suits? You've never heard that? Spiritually or not, I just never gave religion another thought. It was favored by those it did good for and rebuked by those it faulted. I was of the latter so it's expected I would argue against all forms and varieties. I feel it's just superstitious fluff that's widely accepted. But the dark stuff—for some reason I can accept that much more easily."

"Dark stuff? What do you mean?"

"Little devils lurking in dark corners, demons in the shadows . . ." Jamie hadn't realized how much she was sharing and instantly looked up to Banafsha's curious eyes, shutting her mouth. "I mean, like in nightmares. I see them much more vividly in dreams than angels."

"As long as they stay in dreams. You're feeling all right during the day aren't you?"

No, Jamie wanted to reply. It wasn't as bad as it could be, but it was new and felt very unpredictable. What if the dreams somehow came to life and jolting shadows on her peripheral began to reoccur in broad daylight? Would she then have to confront the problem?

Jamie cleared her throat and sat up.

"I thought we were just speaking in hypotheticals."

"Yes," Banafsha said, wiping her arms. "Well as long as demons in your dreams don't smile all the time like our new neighbor I think you'll be safe."

Jamie held back a smile and shook her head. "You really have a problem with this new guy. I need to meet him. See what his deal is. Is he crazy or on something? He *has* to be taking something. I need to reassure you."

"On my midnight walk I'll keep an eye open."

"Now that's not safe, Banafsha."

"What? I've been doing it for years. I like to walk. It's quieter at night."

"Very well. Since there's little more to convince you." Jamie stood up, stepping toward the front door.

"Oh, Jamie. Have you gotten anything for me yet?"

A blank expression fell over Jamie's face.

"Have you gotten your church pictures yet? Anything good?"

Jamie hung her mouth open for a moment as she thought back to the pictures on her flash drive.

"I'll let you know."

Jamie was at Banafsha's house for a time after Aiden left, so when she came inside her mom was cooking dinner. After a terse greeting and subsequent journey to her room, Jamie took out the SD card from the camera and pulled it open on her computer. She scrolled down the folder, past row after row of pictures, until she came to the final one.

A mirage, she thought.

The blurry image of her falling off of the only slightly clearer gargoyle made a shiver spike up her spine. The frozen image was enough of a mystery, but the daunting thought suddenly came to mind.

How did the priests know where to find her camera? Her shoes? They didn't know she was on the roof. It had only been a night between leaving the cathedral and getting her possessions back. The climb was a task in itself, meaning a journey rarely taken. How could they have found it? Had someone followed her? Did someone know of the gargoyles, of what they were, that they could move?

The fear of monsters; she had to overcome them. She needed answers. People in Shore had lived long enough in the dark.

MONSTERS IN SHORE.

That would make a great headline for the evening news at eight.

8

When Jamie told her mother that she'd be going to the cathedral to visit her uncle, it was only partially a lie. Like she told the priest before, she would pass by his room. She'd knock and if he answered then she could find some excuse to tell him why she was there. But she was there for what lay atop the bell tower.

It was the beginning of the weekend, *not a Sunday*; so as to avoid crossing the priest in a foul mood again. Several priests were huddled in a group at the edge of the narthex and nave after she entered the cathedral. When the priests directed their attention to her, she moved as if someone was expecting her. If someone offered to personally guide her to her uncle's room, or to him directly, then she'd have to deal with him before slipping away up the bell tower. But scanning over their faces, it looked safe enough when she didn't recognize any of them.

"Jamie." Edgar stepped from one of the side hallways, another priest following behind him.

Crap. Jamie quickly smiled and greeted him.

"Are you feeling better?"

She rubbed her neck. "About that. I wanted to apologize. I thought I saw something. You know a cloud in front of the sun, creating shapes like shadows that aren't there."

"Shapes?"

"Yeah," Jamie fibbed. "Like giant bees or bears."

"Bee shadows?" Edgar became further flummoxed as Jamie attempted to salvage her sanity.

"You know after further thought, I'm sure it was just a priest or deacon."

"Perhaps Cadogan. He has the build of a bear. That and he's very large-boned. And he does seem to be intimidating from a distance, especially in the dark."

Jamie waved her hands. "No, I'm sure he's a very kind man. I'm just—I had a long day and was just seeing things. I'm sorry if I alarmed you."

Edgar smiled. "As long as you're feeling better. Are you here for your uncle?"

"My uncle . . ." Jamie slipped the lie as rehearsed.

"If I recall correctly he was heading over to pray in one of our private chapels. Let me take you." He extended his hand in that direction at the same time Jamie brought her hands up.

"I couldn't keep you from your duties."

"Not at all."

"Um, actually, before we go," Jamie said quickly. "You can maybe answer me something." Edgar nodded. "My mom came to the cathedral last week and got my camera and shoes from you. I wanted to say thank you."

"You left it behind. I can't imagine the bike ride home was rather enjoyable lacking in proper footwear, and the weather has been dropping at night your feet must've been frozen by the time you reached home."

"I couldn't feel them." Her toes were the farthest thing from her mind that night.

"But, that's not a question," Edgar said.

"How you did find them? They weren't in an *easy* place to find."

Edgar lifted his eyebrows, releasing the hands crossed in front of his belly. "Why, I found them at the foot of the stairs."

Jamie kept her composure as her thoughts raced. How could he claim that? Was he lying like she was? Did he know she knew about the gargoyles? Her belongings were far from the bottom of the stairs, unless, he *did* find them there. Perhaps someone found them and left them there; but then why leave them there? Jamie couldn't believe him and only stared.

He misunderstood her expression. "I'm sure the camera wasn't broken though. It was left on the floor by the wall, so no one could step on it, your shoes neatly beside them. Is your camera not working properly?"

"I—I don't understand." Jamie couldn't call him out on lying in case he didn't know who found them. Perhaps he wasn't the right person to ask after all. Perhaps it was a coincidence finding them. "How did you know they were mine?"

"Elias told me. He remembered you carrying one that night. We assumed the shoes were yours as well."

So that's the rude guy's name, Jamie thought. She wondered if the priests had a complaint box.

"I appreciate you calling my mother."

Edgar nodded once and smiled kindly before looking over his shoulder to the group of priests nearby.

"You know," Jamie said quickly, looking over to the priests. "I think when I was with Gabe the first night he led me past a private chapel. I think I remember the way. You can carry on with your duties. I feel guilty."

"Not at all."

"I—um—" Jamie tried to think of another way to get rid of him as the priest beside Edgar touched his arm.

"You can meet us downstairs after," he said.

Edgar appeared burdened by responsibility, obligated to guide Jamie and yet expected elsewhere. He was turning back to Jamie when she rested her hand on his arm.

"I promise I'll make my way easily. Go. Please."

Edgar nodded, and the other priest thanked Jamie with a subtle one before turning toward the other priests.

"There's always someone around if you get lost. They'll be happy to guide you in the direction you need to go."

Jamie thanked him and watched him go as she made her way to the bell tower.

On the safe side of the roof door, her hands softened with sweat and she repeatedly rubbed them flat against her pants. This decision, coming up there alone with no one aware of her whereabouts, couldn't have been worse planning on her part. Her throat tightened. She felt the need to clear her throat lest it go scratchy, as if she were coming onto a cold. Fear was easy to face in theory, but facing the monsters was another mode of fear; too much of a step for bravery.

Who was this Jamie? Who ran from monsters and then felt she needed to be brave and face them again?

Her hand rested on the handrail, rampant with potential splinters. A moment was taken to allow her heart to tease. Far below her was the life she knew and the life she was safe in. Before her was the life that was true. Whether there really were monsters up there or not. Stepping onto the roof of the bell tower was the biggest gamble she would ever take. One step closer to learning if she'd been hallucinating, or one step to learning that there really was more to this life. If there were monsters, if they really existed, could they be spoken with? Reasoned with? Or was her discovery of their animation an accident?

It struck her.

That's all this was. All the nights fussing over shadows and mistakes and mirages: just an accident. One she'd get over. She'd step through the door, see nothing there, then move on. She'd go home, talk to her mother about a trip with the Capes. If not, she's saved money; she'd go abroad with Era after graduation and climb mountains and see as much of the world she can afford.

Her foot went forward for her. Her body couldn't wait another moment for her mind to let go of what could only remain in the mind. Plans. Thoughts. Ifs. Maybes.

The truth. It was what her body sought, and what it deserved to know.

The door to the roof was almost hidden in darkness, tiny streams of light sneaking through its cracks. The golden light wanted to lead her into another land of wonder and truth.

However, the world through that door was nothing but what she would expect. Reality. Nothing to fear.

Quickly turning the door handle, the door creaked open and the sun pierced her eyes. Rays peeking around vast clouds beckoned her to take cover and move toward the spire canopy. Only once behind the column did she lower her hand, stepping slowly toward the gargoyle statues. It was different seeing them in the daytime. Seeing them through natural light made them seem far less intimidating. The shadows cast from billowing clouds covered half the form of one, the entire form of another. But the clouds would move and dance and form shadows over the faces of the gargoyles, constantly altering their expressions. The same effect could be achieved when moving a single light source around the face of a person in the dark.

It was a lighting technique Jamie had learned in photography. A light source above the face of a person with a smile would give a light-hearted expression, but move the light source below and to the side without them altering the expression of the person, and their face may appear sinister and menacing. The shadows over the gargoyles' faces as she walked past them changed from threatening, to tormented, to mild. A scar became a cry of agony, and a tremor of self-condemnation overcame her heart and mind.

These gargoyles couldn't be monsters. She fell and what she saw was nothing more than a nightmare. That was all.

In front of the last one, she crossed her arms and meditated on its face far longer than the others. What was it about this gargoyle, to receive such attention? Was it a statue with purpose? Look at how preposterous she was being, treating it with the same respect the others did as if a symbol for revolution. It was no item of history or culture, merely a portion of the cathedral unfinished.

Stifling a chuckle, she shook her head. "You almost made me lose sleep. I swear I saw eyes."

Eyes of suns, with gravity; pulled by them. "Yeah, well, I came back. Officially nothing, so . . ." She pursed her lips, leaning on the heels of her feet before nodding. It was done now. "I can go home and delete that picture now." She backed up, still facing the gargoyle, Trium, explaining herself as if he deserved it. "You see I only made it worse reading a book about shadows and nonsense. I read it after I saw—*nothing*. But it was nonsense and what I saw was nonsense and listen to me—I'm talking to a rock. *Again.*"

She knew the truth now. It was a bump of the head. A visit to the doctor could have had her sleeping normally a week ago. She'd know for next time.

"Shadow upon shadow," she mumbled, then furrowed her eyebrows. "Damn it I should have brought that stupid book with me . . ."

She'd turned back toward the door when she heard something fall behind her. It was a small rock, not from too high up, but which fell from who knew what. It wasn't like she was standing underneath a construction site. Impulsively, she turned around.

The deep shadows of the gargoyles breathed, as if the wind was releasing them. They straightened rigidly before relaxing, as if they'd been stuck in a position for too long and needed to stretch. Their wings strained to unfold and suddenly yanked out, stretching themselves, acting separate from the rest of the body. The one closest to her that had "breathed" first curiously tilted its head down to look at her. Even though they came to a towering twenty feet in their stances, when they stood they rose even higher. She noticed it eyeing her and immediately looked away down toward the last gargoyle. Her peripheral missed how the other gargoyles stretched their heads up before looking down to the last one.

And that last one breathed like the others had, slowly straightening its back. Its wings, initially flexed out, straightened and returned to its fundamental position. It was made of stone, but it undulated as if lungs were inside them and had been kept pressed together for an inordinate amount of time. It blinked, and when it opened its eyes, she saw something that drew her to them. They were circular and white, glowing from within.

Suns.

It found her amazed eyes and held them. These were the same eyes she saw the week before. Shocked, she scarcely released a tightened cry. It was the type often in dreams, where the noise was pitifully spat out before being undeservedly drawn out.

Its head tilted slowly, a lion cautioning itself to make no movements that would frighten its prey. Living in a civilized society granted her the luxury of never having to fear for predators. But this, this is what true terror must feel like. Being frightened of monsters in the closet when she was young was miniscule compared to how she felt now.

And she had no one to thank as she felt her muscles pull free from the fear that kept her in place. Her feet began backing away and she turned and ran, her chest turning away from the unnatural beings before her head could follow.

"Wait!"

She didn't look back.

Through the door, she jumped over the steps down the staircase. It was at the bottom of the second landing that she stopped. Her fingers gripped the decrepit railing as she forced herself to reevaluate what she saw. Just her imagination. She didn't think about what else could've happened because she thought it too impossible. It should've been. It's like she was the naive 20-year-old in every horror film that does exactly what the audience expects of them.

No one would find fault with her if she broke her promise with herself about checking out the roof. No one would know.

They hadn't harmed her, though it looked like they could have. When they "breathed," they made such fast sudden movements they looked more elegant like a dancer—in complete control of their movements—than as frightening as a lion. One of them called out for her to wait. They had something to say.

Biting her bottom lip, she forced her feet up the steps. After an oscillating game with the door handle, she opened the door slowly, expecting to see the gargoyle statues waiting for her. However, only the sun welcomed her back, fall winds shifting the clouds south. She returned to the canopy with small steps, eventually coming to face the seven gargoyles.

The statues studied her curiously. It was only after a deep breath she challenged them back, staring with equal measure. She noticed new crevices in their faces, arms, and bodies as she walked past them.

One was hiding a graze at its ear, she only noticed after it looked from her to the gargoyle at the end. Another had a laceration stretching from the top to the bottom of the rib cage, a mark unseen because it had been mostly hidden behind the arm. The last she noticed was that one of the gargoyles' wings seemed to have been unfinished. It was a full wing, however the detail and layer of intricacy that was given to the others was withheld for this gargoyle. As the wing had been extended up behind him and since Jamie didn't inspect most of them, she never noticed. Despite the dissimilarities, they all had eyes of suns and fierce auras, overwhelming and breathtaking.

They surrounded her as she approached the final gargoyle, her body unable to keep from shaking.

It wasn't likely to happen a minute ago when she was running, but she managed to flatten her voice to a reasonably, normal-speaking tone. There was however, nothing to do about controlling the trepidation.

"W-who called out to me?"

All adjusted their gazes from the frightened human below to the one at the end. They morphed from stagnant rocks to breathing beings, they possessed some form of magic she had never imagined. None broke the silence for a long time and she wondered what else could exist out there. Was there a Father Time living in the clouds?

"I did." It was the gargoyle at the end. His voice was unlike any voice she'd heard before. It wasn't of an accent she could recognize, as foreign as it was in nature. The only word that came to mind when she heard it say those two words was ancient. If possible, more than that. Fragile. The statue could only be several centuries old at most, durable as it may be, and yet its voice seemed to have cracks in his words, though that could be attributed to the fact it was made of stone. And as if seeing them "breathe" wasn't enough, hearing them speak required a new sense of appreciation.

"H-how can you talk?"

"We are beings just like you. You have your science. We have ours."

"That's not possible." She shook her head, though the word "remarkable" kept echoing in her mind.

"Why?" he asked kindly. He tilted his head, though it was more of a friendly level of curiosity than his companions earlier.

"Because . . ." She found it entirely obvious. "You're not supposed to move. You aren't supposed to be able to breathe right now."

"Why do you? Did you not rise from the dust?"

Jamie was confused. What was this mentioning of dust? She didn't remember much from the Sunday School lessons, assuming dust had anything to do with the Christian myth. And dust had nothing to do with conception and birth.

"Your name's Trium?"

With heavy meaning, he nodded once. "I am."

"And why are you here? I mean I know you're supposed to be part of the cathedral, but my uncle said it never happened. Do you know why the project got cut short? Did you have any part of it?" Jamie examined the others faces as she spoke.

"We did."

"My uncle says you were brought from overseas." Jamie brought her attention back to Trium.

The gargoyle's form of amusement, a sort of chuckle, escaped his being. It sounded very unnatural and odd, but she could only stare as he continued chuckling at whatever he found amusing.

"We did. We came from overseas, and beyond the skies, and through All-time."

"Okay, but why? Why are you here?"

That question was either not meant to be asked, or not meant to be asked by her, because they all became statues again, holding still before twitching, and returning their gaze on Trium.

"There is much to share. Know that we are here for a purpose. One that we have been awakened for, through many rises of the suns and wanings of the moon."

"A purpose? What the end of the world?" Jamie said semi-jocular, though the humor was short-lived.

"No," Trium said tenderly. "Something far worse. There are things unseen that are much worse."

The humor remained as a shadow of a smile lingering on her lips, but at the dismal proclamation, it faded away. How could she be sure how serious it was when minutes ago gargoyles couldn't move or breathe in the first place?

"What are all of you?"

"Messengers. Protectors of the Father. We are here to guard, guide, and protect those that serve Him. From the dark lights to the spirits of the Fire."

It took her some deducing but God was sometimes described as being a Father figure. And she didn't know too much about the Christian myth, but usually beside God were . . .

She stared blankly at them. "You don't look like angels . . ."

"What do they look like?" There was genuine interest in his words. Of course, Jamie couldn't expect him to be an expert in art. They all have been on the roof or in a sculptor's workshop during the most recent periods of art.

Jamie shrugged her shoulders. "The church usually depicts them with a lightness about them. With long white robes and halos around their heads." She eyed around the group for a moment. "But saying it aloud does make it sound kinda foolish. It isn't like I'm an angel expert."

"Our true forms cannot be seen. It is a law that has been followed since the beginning of your world. On Earth, we take the shape of a man, whether that be organic or terrestrial."

Her phone vibrated in her pocket and she knew it was her mom. Quickly checking the time, she calculated by the time she got home it would be three hours since she left to the church. Internally, she groaned. Why did her mom have to need her at home *now*? There was a slim chance it was Aiden just trying to get on her bad side, though highly unlikely, and she silently cursed that no matter what, home was waiting for her.

Silencing the phone, she looked back up to Trium. "I have to go."

Trium tilted his head as Jamie began to walk backwards, the gargoyles moving out of her way as she neared them. Several steps away, as the gargoyles were beginning to move back to their spots, she stopped and looked around to all of their faces, the final statue to grab her attention.

"I'd like to hear more. Can I come back?"

"As long as you seek to return you shall be able to. The church is a place all are welcome." Trium's voice faded into the wind as he took the final steps back to the end of the aisle.

Not by sight, but it was heard as they took their final "breaths," solidifying into the lifeless statues they were.

Returning home she pulled up the final image on her computer.

"Shadow upon shadow." She brought her thumb nail up to her lips and pressed it against them.

It was real. *They* were. The photo wasn't a manipulation of light.

A soft knock on the door and Jamie looked up from her computer screen to Aiden.

"Huh?" Jamie asked, looking back to the screen.

"Mom wants you to come for dinner."

"I'll be there in a second."

Aiden stood in place, watching her. Her lip curled up in irritation as she waved him away.

"I said I'll be there."

Aiden clenched his jaw as he slammed the door behind him. Jamie stared mesmerized at the photo for several seconds longer before closing her laptop and heading to the door. She noticed the sick man's journal and put it on her desk so she could remember to take it the next time she went to St. Luke's. Certain that it wouldn't be thrown onto her floor and be forgotten again, she opened the door to follow her brother's footsteps to dinner.

9

Shadows danced on the walls. The shadows formed figures gyrating with other shapes of dimmed light. They swayed to the music of the screams; to the cries of damned souls. They snickered like firecrackers at the sounds, as it made them enjoy their dance.

Torment. Trials. Accusations. Revenge. Disgust. Hatred.

The creature walked down the hall where the shadows danced. It wore a dark robe covering its mass, exposing only face and hands. It was shaped like a human, walked like one, but was no human. Its scalp lacked hair and so did its face, its skin wrinkled and taut, its eyes black with small white pupils. It had a short angular nose and its mouth was natural in a tight grimace. It walked with no urgency and did not stop until it reached an open balcony.

The balcony extended over a cliff to a below deep and dark; a heart-quickening chasm, an abyss with no end. Over the pit lay plains of dust and dirt and blood. A tormented soul, a man, almost entirely naked and covered in dirt laboriously carried its load. Every step he took, the load fell from his back. A demonic shadow just as corporeal as the man whipped him each time the load fell. The fiend towered over him, rope and chains crossing over its shoulders and across its chest. A whip rested in its hand with another instrument of torture on its belt. It screeched every time the man dropped his load, as painful to hear as the whip was as painful to feel. But this abused man was not alone. Surrounding him were men and women being tortured by their own personal tormentors.

Swirls of dirt coalesced, forming a tornado. However the winds didn't make the dry atmosphere around them tolerable. It didn't make breathing easier. When the tormented would inhale, they would breathe in dust, dirt, and blood and their lungs would fill with it. The dust would swirl in their lungs and scratch at every sere and scraped corner.

"Drink your sorrows away they said!" a Sapling taunted his soul.

"You will feel no pain they said!" another Sapling cackled.

"This is what we all do they said!" The third Sapling cracked his whip and slashed it against his human's hunched back.

"Do you feel as one with them now?" A fourth Sapling laughed as he kicked his human, who had reached to pick up his sack, to the ground. "Get up!"

"Did they say the pain would go away? They call us liars. Filthy mortal scum." One Sapling shook his head with haughty disdain.

The humans dared not speak back. What good would it bring? Their superior was no better; in fact the higher the rank, the more unforgiving. The souls looked back through pleading eyes, knowing their pleas would never be answered. Even the gateway at the top of the hill served as ill-hope; not an escape; an omen of doom. All of their wrongdoings that they would forever carry on their backs, would and could never be requited.

The humans would pick up their loads and fall after a step and the torture would begin again. The seconds would feel like days. The days like years. The years were forever. And the thought that made them cringe: the souls had no destination. They would continue on forever dropping and picking up; being weak and becoming weaker. They would die to die again.

Stationary, the robed creature watched from atop the fortress balcony. The plains with millions to billions of souls stretched farther than the luminescence the flames in the horizon cast. Although he could catch a glimpse of his prize . . . There. Beyond.

His Darkness.

His fortress was on the edge of the plains; even if there was no chasm, it was a citadel never to be breached by the segregated souls. Religion, gender, sexual orientation, heritage, morals—it was too easy to cast them from one another. They couldn't even form together as one on the planet; they would never unite here.

Here, where no one could save them.

A shape stepped from out of the shadows and appeared several steps behind the robed creature. The shape took a form similar to the demons in the plains, of currant red skin and muscle of neglected darkness, engraved with crevices from two slashes to six. Identical in outer appearance in all ways but one: it was robed like the creature before him.

The robed creature did not care for those below anymore. It turned around and passed the shape. The robed demon did not speak, only hold a bow until the creature muttered below the screams.

"*Acario.*"

"*Erus,*" said the shape, quickly falling in step behind its master.

"*The incompetent down there only know of the human tongue. They do not know the freed language. Speak to me in this mortal jargon.*"

"My Lord General."

"The souls of men fall prey to pleasures and desires. Fortunate for us it is easy to deceive them." It would seem he was indifferent given the blank expression possessing his face. "More than before."

"The Darkness grows. Approaches closer."

"Gloriously, Acario. Look how it stretches from horizon end to horizon end. It is almost completely upon us."

The pall had returned after only two centuries. Planet centuries, not All-time. A tempest of mist and the source from which the damned souls had been born. It hovered meekly beyond the flames in the horizon until all that was left of the west was promise of oncoming doom. The last time the Darkness had appeared, it carried destruction, chaos, and heartache.

And rebirth, Erus thought. *Salvation.*

Acario waited for Erus to instruct him and after a fair amount of time asked, "Will I summon the Gatekeeper?"

The robed creature halted, slowly turning to face Acario. Erus' white pupils diminished into the dark of his eyes. He raised one hand and slapped Acario across the cheek. The servant flatly returned his head to his master's gaze as if he had done nothing.

"The Gatekeeper despises every beckon I make. If we have learned anything, it is not to be hasty. Neither he nor the Seven are to be summoned before the appropriate time. They are occupied. To disturb them is to prohibit future souls from temptation. What we would do if our family did not but grow?" The robed creature scowled at his subordinate. "Perhaps you have spent too much time watching the souls. You've grown restless." Erus narrowed his eyes. "Shall I assign you to another position?"

"No, my Lord General."

"Very well. Inform me when the Seven have returned."

"Yes, my lord." He bowed down and held his stance.

For the briefest of moments Erus concentrated on something of a shadow past Acario, then resumed walking down the hall, the demon not farther than a step behind. As they both fell silent, the screams of tortured souls consumed the halls.

Shadows danced on the walls.

10

Jamie sat up in bed. The journal lay shut beside her, her hand still marking the page she left off. She had picked it up last night, but struggled to remember what she read. Her nightmare clouded over the words minutes after falling asleep. Her dream remained vivid in her wake, she could still see the red darkened halls as if she were inside the tubes of a human organ, pulsating with flames to make the walls appear as if they were breathing.

Sluggishly, she set the journal on the desk where she meant to have left it last night. When she left her room, she found her mom tidying up the kitchen, returning cleaned dishes into a cabinet over the counter.

"I'd like to have one normal dinner at least some time with my daughter." Rosario didn't turn as she continued her menial task. "Maybe not every week but every other month or so would be nice."

Jamie picked up a glass cup and reached to put it away in the cabinet drawer adjacent to the cabinet her mother was putting plates. "I'm sorry."

"I'd like a little more than an apology."

"I went to the cathedral."

"You don't need to tell me where you went. I'd just like to spend some time with you when I'm home."

"You're right." Jamie said, stirring her mother to turn to her. "I'll be home tonight."

"*De verdad?*"

"Yes. You can even invite Victor and Riley. I'll apologize for last time."

"That would be nice. I'll make the call."

They finished putting away the dishes and Rosario went in the direction of the washing machine. "Wake up your brother. Oh, no . . . you haven't eaten breakfast yet. Never mind, I'll wake him." Jamie gestured that she would and left to his room.

His body was angled across the mattress, his right foot hanging over the edge, though hidden under a blanket that half-covered him and half-hung over the bed. He organized his room much like Jamie's, with clothes thrown about, though unlike her his books were neatly stacked by his computer desk. She stepped in the uncovered parts of the floor to the bed and shook his foot.

"It's Sunday," he grumbled, knowing it was Jamie and not their mother. Rosario would have already taken the blanket off him.

"And almost noon," Jamie said. "Mom wants you up."

"Ten more minutes."

"Fifteen max," Jamie said, already stepping back into the hall.

Jamie prepared eggs and ham, bacon, and sausage for the both of them as she gave him his fifteen minutes. He prepared their drinks when she started to bring the cooked foods to the dining table. They sat down together when Rosario had a bundle of Jamie's and Aiden's clothes in her arms.

"The sausage is good," Aiden said, placing a couple of pieces of bacon onto his plate.

"I tried a new sauce." Jamie yelled loud enough for her mother to hear from the laundry room. "Hey ma, have you called yet?"

When Rosario returned she said she did, then stood beside Aiden, reaching for a piece of bacon as she answered Jamie.

"He said they'd love to. You going to make dinner, too?"

"I have schoolwork."

"Fine. I was planning on ordering pizza."

Aiden became intrigued. "Can we have Orlando Supreme's?"

Aiden stared disappointed at the pizza box reading the name of nearest local pizza restaurant. He had just come from the living room where he and Riley had been playing her favorite racing video game. Not only had he lost because of a glitch in the game, or so he claims, but now the pizza was one he hated.

"What happened to Orlando?" he asked.

"I'm sorry, sweetie," Rosario said. "I forgot."

"I don't like this pizza."

"Want me to order Orlando for you now, Aiden?" Victor offered. "I can take the leftovers home. You'll only have to wait a bit for it to be delivered."

"Don't be absurd, we already have pizza here," Rosario said, turning from Victor to Aiden. "Really *cariño*, I completely forgot you mentioned it. We'll order it next time and I promise I won't forget."

"This is my favorite," Riley said, picking a couple pieces to put on her plate. Aiden side-eyed her and muttered inaudibly as Jamie chuckled.

If it's not me, at least I have a worthy substitute, Jamie thought. Everyone began eating when Jamie adjusted herself in her seat. After several cursory glances from her mother, she faced the guests. "Victor, Riley, I wanted to apologize for being so absent lately. These past few weeks have been unexpectedly . . . distracting. And I didn't mean to be."

Victor more than Riley showed his appreciation for her apology as the father spoke for them both. "That's all right. We understand. I'm sure you're starting to wrap up applying for colleges alongside your other coursework."

"I'm about done yes." Jamie nodded.

Rosario needed to put her two cents in. "Stressed about school or not, I won't accept her being rude and hiding away from just saying a simple hi just because she's comfortable with you. You're still our guests when you visit this house."

"*Yes, mom*," Jamie said.

"Rosario," Victor said quickly before Rosario responded—she already had her eyebrows raised and lips open. "Don't be so hard. Jamie's all grown up but she's still a teenager—"

"Don't I feel belittled?" Jamie muttered under her breath. Riley heard from the seat beside her and giggled.

"And all teenagers feel apprehensive about having dinner with their family. I know I did. Especially these days when families don't do this anymore."

"If Abuela were here she wouldn't behave so rudely," Rosario said.

"Your mother's family," Victor answered quickly, as if that reason was enough to eclipse all others. "Now, it's already forgotten. Roly Poly, you don't mind what Jamie did right?"

Riley shook her head with pursed lips, pizza sauce on the corner of them as they lifted in a smile.

"See? Already forgotten." He sat back, exhaling resolved. He'd settled tension between everyone in under a minute and felt very accomplished. Only once had the tension risen past salvaging, and it was concerning his daughter and himself. Thankfully on that occasion the matter was able to be resolved by the next day. The attitude that both Jamie and Rosario displayed was nothing compared to their daily bickerings of trash duties on Monday morning or why there were dishes left in the sink for three days. Now, mother and daughter resumed eating and with a satisfied nod, Victor picked up his slice and took a massive bite.

Rosario swallowed the pizza in her mouth. "Speaking of Abuela—"

"You brought her up in the first place." Aiden smiled.

"*Yes*, well . . ." Rosario ignored him. "She called and told me she already bought her plane ticket for Christmas. She wanted it to be a surprise since it's Jamie's last year and we don't know where she'll be a year from now."

"I'd still come home for break," Jamie said.

"You never know. You could be out-of-state and what if you can't afford to fly back? Or you make plans with some friends you make?"

"Actually—" Jamie moved her tongue around to get at the pizza bits stuck in between her teeth. "Speaking of Christmas and plans, I was wondering if maybe I might go with the school's climbing club on a trip to climb some real mountains."

"The school's climbing club," Rosario said ambiguously as neither statement nor question.

"Yeah, I see them at work every weekend."

"The school club that visits your gym. They want to climb real mountains? Where?"

"There's indecision as to where but if they get enough of their parents to say yes they'll officially plan it out and pick a place."

"Good, so parents have said no."

Victor, Riley, and Aiden switched from one Diez woman to the other with wide eyes, sensing the tension escalating again, albeit contained at the moment. Jamie wasn't perturbed, only tilting her head to acknowledge the fact.

"Several have. But most of the others have said maybe."

Rosario picked up her glass and laughed. "Of course, 'maybe' doesn't make you the bad guy immediately."

"So you're saying no?"

"I haven't said anything."

"Maybe once the details have been more thought out, the parents will feel more at ease," Victor said. "Like where you're going and have the stats for fatalities, injuries, how many people climb them, etc." Jamie glanced at him. Rosario focused her attention on him now.

"Exactly. I need all that info before I make a decision. So for now I'll say maybe." Jamie didn't hide her surprise and Rosario shrugged her shoulders. "Not 'no' because you're responsible and you've been climbing for a couple years now. And you're eighteen, I don't think I could stop you when you're *technically* legal."

A thought suddenly occurred to Rosario and she almost jumped in her seat. "Oh, that's right you mentioned Christmas. You'd want to go during Christmas break. Well then it's definitely no." She read *why* on Jamie's face. "Christmas means winter and winter means snow. Not in Florida—but there are no mountains here, which means you'll be going somewhere north. I don't want your first climbing experience on the real thing to be on top of hazards like ice and snow. So no. I say wait until Spring Break or next summer."

"This doesn't only concern me, mom," Jamie said, falling back in her chair. "Everyone's planning for winter break."

"When you have kids, you'll see my point."

"Would it just be you and the climbing team?" Victor asked. "Would there be no adults?"

"Not that I'm aware of no," Jamie said.

"I don't think I'd be a good parent if I let my daughter join a bunch of other underage teenagers go mountain-climbing during the winter," Rosario said.

"Your main beef is against it being in the winter than it being about our ages," Jamie said.

"Are no other parents going? Or an older sibling? It would at least make me warmer to the idea."

Jamie took a bite from her pizza, shaking her head.

"Call me what you want," Rosario said. "My answer is the same."

They were silent for a moment when Victor spoke up. He'd been watching the two of them try to reason with the other and considered a middle ground that neither considered. He had his hands clasping each other over the table as he focused on Jamie. "If you want, get more information on the days and I could maybe take some time off of work. I haven't climbed in a while but I still remember the key stuff. I can get my parents to watch Riley."

Jamie looked over to him. It was a generous offer, but how could she really have her mother's boyfriend tag along as the adult supervision for a trip that involved people she wasn't close with in the first place? Her expression slowly dropped and Victor caught onto it quickly, about to rescind the offer as her mother spoke up.

"It would reassure me a little more but even with an adult it makes me uncomfortable. For your first time . . ."

Jamie dropped the disappointment from her face and substituted it for a blank one. "You know what, it doesn't matter. The club members asked me what you'd say. I'll just relay you only have a problem with the time of year, not necessarily the trip." While she'd been fighting unforgivingly a moment ago, it hit her that she wanted more the opportunity to go and not had the real desire to.

"How would you get there anyways?" Aiden asked suddenly. "Plane tickets are expensive and you hate being in a car. Wherever you go it would take more than a day to drive there."

Jamie's fear of cars was well-known by her family and since her mother had been dating Victor for over a year, she would have told him by then why that was. However, Riley was still in the dark and voiced her curiosity.

Everyone around the table fell into a cavity of silence and while Victor and Aiden lowered their eyes, Rosario glanced at Jamie. Despite what Rosario and Aiden might've thought, Jamie didn't hold it against Riley. She was young and she hadn't had it explained to her yet, which is why Jamie managed to force a small smile. Victor teetered from Jamie to Riley.

"Sweetie, she's just uncomfortable in cars; just like you're uncomfortable at night if your closet is open after I turn off the lights."

Jamie wanted to tell Riley that it was just because her father was her best friend and he died after being T-boned, trapped inside his car. That ever since then she was tabooed by them. It was just an accident, but it was the reason she remained one of the handful of seniors at Shore High School without a license. It was why she always biked everywhere no matter the weather; not that Riley ever noticed. All the same, perhaps that was too heavy an explanation for an eight-year-old who still possessed a child's innocence.

Her hands began to sweat and saliva filled her mouth, causing her to swallow. She couldn't bring the words of assurance to Riley, so she sat there quietly. Any fire from her debate, which had already begun to simmer, had now completely vanished under the mention of her sole fear.

"Oh! I understand completely." Riley nodded, taking a bite from her pizza crust.

They all smiled softly at Riley, completely sincere in her assessment no matter how far from truly understanding she was. Even Jamie couldn't keep from being amused, though her eyes were still lowered. After a couple of breaths, she answered her brother.

"I thought of that. Once they picked a place, I *was* planning on buying a plane ticket and just arranging a car service from there. I'll have to take a car no matter what, but at least it won't be for over a day. Maybe a couple of hours at most."

"Honey, you've saved enough for that?" Rosario said.

"Since I don't have a car, I was planning on saving for college. It'll be hard to find deals since it's less than two months away, but who knows what luck I might find. What I might've found."

Rosario wiped her mouth with a napkin. "You've really seemed to have given this a lot of thought."

"Honestly I just found out two days ago."

Impressed, Rosario kept her lips together for a moment. "Well you know my answer. Get more details and we'll discuss it more."

"Fair enough," Jamie said, then added, "And I could still see Abuela. I won't be gone for weeks."

"She'll like that very much." Rosario smirked. "Smart to ask about this with guests over. Or is that why you wanted me to invite them in the first place? So I wouldn't be so unreasonable?"

"You call what we just talked about unreasonable?" Jamie said.

"Couldn't you tell?" Rosario said. "I'm sure I was much more reasonable than the other parents of the members. What's the club's name again?"

The disinclination to answer spread over Jamie's face. "The Capes."

Riley had been playing with her pizza and when Jamie mentioned the name, spoke up. "Why are they called the Capes?"

Jamie stood up to refill her drink. "Please don't ask."

11

Jamie pulled up the cathedral images on her computer. Minjae sat beside her in the photo lab, head slightly tilted to show he was listening as she finished relaying what her mother said the night before.

"I think the parents'd be more lenient if that's the real issue."

Jamie was willing to negotiate, if at the end, her mom complied. While there was nothing attractive climbing for the first time in the company of the Capes, it would be fulfilling to feel real dirt and rock under her palms—or gloves.

"They might say yes," he rephrased. "I think my parents would say yes."

"Say, wouldn't your girlfriend feel a little excluded if you skipped town over the holidays?"

"*Skipped town?*" Minjae pushed away from the computer and exaggerated an open mouth and raised eyebrows. "What are we in the '50s? Did they say that in the '50s?"

"I don't know. If I had a boyfriend and he took off during break I'd feel left behind."

"Would you?" Minjae turned back to his computer when Jamie didn't give him her attention. "Well, Emily's understanding. She already has to deal with Yearbook taking up most of my free time. What's one more little hobby going to take away?"

"I don't know her that well. I've never seen her at the gym. Does she not like outdoor sports?"

"A mountain to me is an ocean is to her."

Jamie had never heard that expression before and prompted him to explain. Not showing how amused he was that *that* had stirred her attention, he only partially grinned.

"I see a challenge. I see the rocks to climb, the different paths, the branches to grab onto last minute before you fall a hundred meters to your death. I see the sky above and the top of the peak, possessing beautiful views on both sides of its slopes for sunrise and sunset. Now she might see the ocean, a challenge *maybe*, but why try and challenge yourself when you can just admire the view? It might not be worth finding it once you cross it and you'll probably just face storms and be taken off course by foul winds along the way."

"And you're saying all women are like this?"

"No . . ." Minjae rolled his eyes. "Just some people are like that. Case study: Emily. She's great, but riding on the back of a motorcycle and cycling are two very different modes of transportation. Like jet-skiing and rowing. Flying and parachuting."

"I get it."

Silence fell and they both focused on their computers. Jamie was working on an exposure layer for one of the cathedral pictures. Minjae seemed to want to finish a sentence Jamie hadn't heard the beginning of.

"I'm not a misogynist. I was just trying to make an analogy."

"I got that," Jamie assured him. "Don't worry. You won't have to stay up tonight in fear I'll slash your tires or anything." She looked back to her computer screen as he studied her face, making sure she wasn't sparing him. Ms. Ava entered the room and instructed the photo students, ushering them back for a presentation.

Jamie followed the other students back into the class as Minjae remained where he was. He was the only one from the yearbook staff to show up that day, so left alone, he felt it necessary to begin humming.

When he glanced over to the photo room when the lights dimmed for the presentation, his eyes slipped over the folder Jamie had opened on her computer. It was scrolled all the way down to the bottom, and while he normally didn't snoop through other people's pictures, the last picture caught his attention.

He leaned over the desk and reached for the mouse, his eyes pinned on the last picture. He opened the image, scanning over the composition and memorizing every detail. The image was impossible. He had glanced at some of the pictures Jamie had edited before and he knew they were at St. Luke's, but he thought she'd been taking pictures of the statues located in the back courtyard. He hadn't realized his heart rate increasing and his breathing shallowing. The image—he wasn't expecting it. Not from Jamie of all people.

Double checking over his shoulder, he pulled out his flash drive, quickly plugging it into her computer and copying the image. The flash drive was safe in his pants pocket long before Jamie returned.

He remained ignorant of the pair of eyes that had witnessed the clandestine theft.

Jamie tightened her fingers around the bicycle handlebars as she walked down the road to Banafsha's house. The cicadas were dormant. Autumns in Florida were unworthy compared to northern states, even Georgia. They weren't so cold that there even "might" be snow, not even a blanket of frost over the grass lawns, but possibly mist in the air when one breathed or a shiver up one's spine if they failed to layer up.

While she'd told the gargoyles she'd return, it was unlikely the day before and a definite impossibility for the rest of the week. Work took up most of her free time and it would be dark by the time she clocked out. There was also the matter of operation hours she didn't want to review with Elias. She wouldn't try an excuse like seeing her uncle since by now he must've told the other members of the clergy that he hadn't seen Jamie either of the last two times she'd visited. The thought began to grow in her mind: *why hadn't he reached out to know why she continued claiming to visit and yet hadn't?* Or did no one ask about them? From the brief visits, she assumed the priests were close enough to share these things around the table at dinner. Their interests were the same; they must've shared family matters.

Jamie was several houses down when she noticed an unfamiliar face removing envelopes from his mailbox. Jamie spent a fraction of a minute studying the neighbor Banafsha felt an instant dislike for. From her cursory read, he was average height with light hair and light eyes. He seemed in shape based off the tight shirt. He had begun turning, smirking at one of the envelopes when she noticed he had a mischievous look to him. If this was him, Jamie understood why Banafsha would say never to trust him. Jamie was moving forward when his eyes lost interest in his mail and found her. He smiled politely and waved once.

"Can't believe how fast mail works down here." He held up the mail in his palm. "Back where I used to live it took at least two weeks before I started to see my name printed on the recipient line."

If she had any doubts before, he confirmed now who he was. This was him. Jamie glanced over his frame again. He had a good deal of dirty blonde hair, a goatee without the makings of a mustache, and light eyes turned dark by the setting sun. His face was handsome and the mischievous smile from before proffered—with his permission or not—a rather rugged look. Apparently smiling could be too much for her taste.

"You're our new neighbor."

"Oh, which house?"

Jamie pointed. "The brown one."

"Ah," he said, a smile still on his face as he extended his hand over. "I'm Ethan. Officially moved in as of four hours ago."

She introduced herself as she shook his hand. "Did you move in on your own? No friends or former roommates to help? I've seen the trucks outside for a while."

"I grew up with a bunch of brothers and have forsaken that life. This house is mine and mine just. It's honestly perfect for me. I've traveled for work for years and felt it was time to find a permanent place. Florida doesn't get cold in the winter and the house prices are affordable in this part of the state . . . considering."

Jamie leaned on a hip as she adjusted the bicycle against her. "If you don't mind my asking, but what'd you do that you had to travel?"

He opened his mouth, but then pulled her toward the curb as two cars passed each other not an arm's reach from where Jamie stood. They wouldn't have hit her, however being so close to a moving vehicle, let alone two, made her pulse quicken. She already felt her palms sweat over the handle bars and her ears rush. Cars rarely made her nauseated, only in cases like this when they were operating behind her back and going at a destructive speed, which for her was anything over five. Her fear had escalated to a point like the thrilling rush from a rollercoaster, quickly heightened and gradually sedated.

"You okay?" It was impossible for him not to be aware of the trauma she was struggling to conceal.

"I'm just a little nervous around cars. It's my fault. I shouldn't have been standing in the road." While sharing her fear was abnormal even for her, the realization that she had in fact shared her fear with a stranger made her terribly embarrassed. "Childish, I know."

"Don't be silly." He waved the hand that had taken her arm. "What was it that you asked again?" She drew a blank even though it was just moments ago, but he already recalled it. "I was a photographer—well, I guess am still. I haven't given it up. I used to work for travel magazines."

The minor scare she just survived from vanished from her mind. He laughed at her caprice. "I usually get reactions like that but not one so incredulous. Traveling the world, eating new foods and staying in rooms the size of closets, it's really too high in demand. The benefits of traveling don't outweigh the stress of the job. Airports and taxis and non-specific maps and people—especially sticks in the mud;

they can really be demanding. And difficult. And uninformative. And extortionists; you wouldn't believe how manipulative some people can be when they think you don't know any better."

"I used to want to be a photographer," Jamie shared. "For National Geographic."

"The pay's well worth it."

"Where did you used to work?" Jamie asked.

Ethan caught onto her question. "One I won't share. If I tell you, you'll just have a red X over the magazine and while I might not have found a home with them, many others have. But, to each their own, right?"

Jamie nodded and looked forward toward Banafsha's house. Her phone started to vibrate and she held it up.

"Duty calls."

He pointed with his thumb behind him. "There's a dog with his nose to the door as we speak. Separation issues. I walk him a lot so you'll meet him eventually. Have a good night." He smiled infectiously and nodded once before heading back.

Jamie watched him for a moment as he walked down the path to his front door. They only spoke for a short time, but the sunset was short tonight. The gold of the sky had already dissolved into a shade of pale blue, the clouds a wispy gray.

Jamie entered Banafsha's living room and noticed Aiden already packed, whisking past her and wishing a quick goodbye over his shoulder to Banafsha.

"Rude . . ." Jamie couldn't get anything else out before the front door shut behind him. "He must be tired. Victor and Riley came over last night and stayed until late. Banafsha, are you all right?"

Banafsha wore a haggard expression beneath her eyes, grouchiness over her eyebrows, and irritation sunken between her cheeks, nose, and lips. Jamie wondered if they had argued over something on TV again, since they both could become quite heated; both rather obstinate.

"It's a culmination of things," Banafsha sighed. "All things that are small and insignificant but all that involve people that are only small and insignificant themselves."

"Slow down, Banafsha. Is it something Aiden said?"

"Aiden is anything but small. He's talented and intuitive and kind. He'll be great one day. No, it involves other people I'm unfortunate enough to have to live in the same city with. The grocer gave me a difficult time again."

"What did she say?" Jamie asked, standing with her arms crossed by the kitchen counter. She watched Banafsha move around the kitchen, grabbing a bowl with vegetables, salad, and dressing before slamming the bowls down beside an empty plate.

"All the other lines were full so I go to the shortest one I could find. But of course when I'm next in line, the cashier switches out and it's the little leech who has it out for me. She does it on purpose. She doesn't look at me in the eyes as she scans and basically tosses it to the bagger. She says no more than three words to me, waving at the card machine. *Slide now, ma'am,* but the hate is all in her eyes." Banafsha dangled her fingers over her own as she dumped the salad onto her plate. "Prejudice. It doesn't matter where you go. There is always prejudice for my kind."

"I'm sure that's not it," Jamie said, trying to soothe her. "Maybe she was having a bad day. Sometimes I speak out of turn to customers and then regret it after I've cooled off. I've even gotten a couple complaints but we're only human. It happens to everyone. "

"It's always the same when she sees me. Either she pretends I'm not there or treats me with disrespect."

"If she says anything, you should speak to a manager."

"No!" Banafsha said, stopping to look coldly at Jamie. "Then I'll be like her. I'm not going to complain when she has done nothing. No."

"Why don't you go somewhere else then so you don't see her?"

"Must I, Jamie?" Banafsha lost all interest trying to act busy. "When I have come to this country and have lived here for years, much longer than even your parents? When a woman cannot even go to a grocery store without being ignored or spoken to like I do not deserve to be in the same continent? I am a citizen of this country. I respect every man for his choice of faith, political preference, sexual orientation, but because I am from the part of the world many Americans foolishly believe is part of the Middle East, I am not worthy of any form of courtesy? I used to be spit on back there, but how you Americans look at me, it is as if you have kicked the street dog." She turned away from Jamie, not wanting to defend herself anymore.

It took a minute for Jamie to feel the tension between them cool down. Banafsha let out steam all the time about many things that irritated her, but being at the other end of the rant for the first time hurt Jamie. It was as if she had been the cause of Banafsha's lividness.

Unable to say anything that would make up for her thoughtless words, she walked over to Banafsha and wrapped her arms around her shoulders.

"Aach!" Banafsha moved out from Jamie's arms and taking a step to the side, roughly slid the plate and salad bowl away.

Jamie rested a hand on the counter. "I'm sorry, Banafsha. I wasn't being considerate toward you."

Banafsha picked up a pear and knife, slicing it into pieces slowly before stopping mid-slice.

"It is not for you, my anger. I'm just an old woman."

Jamie smirked and walked over beside Banafsha, wrapping her arms around her shoulders again, leaning her chin on one.

"I don't mind you letting it out to me. It's kind of soothing hearing you speak so harshly."

Banafsha snickered, her shoulder bouncing lightly as she shook her head, continuing to cut the pear. However, the lightness of the moment ended when Jamie kissed her on the cheek out of good measure.

"Aach!" Banafsha shook Jamie's arms off of her and while she lifted the knife, she lowered it back down. She had her dark eyes on Jamie as she waved the knife around in a loose wrist. "Why would you do such a foolish thing when I have something that could slice you in my hand?"

"Because you don't get enough love," Jamie said, smiling mischievously as she walked to the end of the kitchen.

"I need an ear to hear me and then let those words fly out the other ear. I don't need your affection. I didn't just wake up after my heart stopped."

"It must be because I'm Latina," Jamie said with a forced frown, nodding as she looked to the ceiling. "We're all affectionate and have a diabolical need to comfort one another when we're upset."

"I'm not Latin."

Banafsha said the words with no inflection and while Jamie tried to hold back a chuckle, one escaped her lips. When Banafsha's eyes found hers, Jamie covered her mouth and forced a serious expression on her face.

"You're not affectionate either so stop cackling like a hyena."

Jamie's humor disappeared. "What else bothered you today?"

"That damned neighbor walks his dog around the time I take my midnight walks."

"You walk at midnight?"

Banafsha shot her a glare and Jamie shut her eyes and nodded, aware that she made a mistake.

"I crossed the street before we passed one another."

"Speaking of the devil, Banafsha, I just met him on my way here. He's cute." Banafsha rolled her eyes. "And I don't think he smiled too much. Just enough to pass as normal."

"What do you expect the face of a demon to be?"

"Banafsha, that's mean. Why is he a demon now?"

"You don't hear his demon of a dog at night? I'm two houses away and I hear it barking. I don't know why he still has it. How can he sleep?"

"I don't hear any dogs at night. Are you sure it's his? I think you're just making things up now. You never mentioned a dog when he was moving in."

Banafsha pressed her lips together and disregarded her thought. "Someone must have brought it after he moved in."

"Banafsha . . ."

"Isn't it time you go home now?"

"I want to hear more stories of your disappointment. If not me, who'll listen to you? You can't keep your anger in, it isn't good. As thanks for watching Aiden every day, I humbly volunteer my ears."

"That's all I feel like sharing. You can go."

Jamie made her way to the hall when Banafsha spoke up.

"Have you any pictures yet?"

One day, maybe over winter break, she'd print out the last picture and give it to her as a gift. Banafsha didn't celebrate Christmas, but it would be a gift to Jamie if Banafsha accepted it. Out of everyone she knew, Banafsha supported her photography undoubtedly. Always encouraging her specific photographic style and buying her photography books, and for her last birthday, a new lens. It used to be her father who always encouraged her.

But Banafsha filled in that void almost perfectly. She wasn't as loving and caring as her father was, but she did see something in Jamie that made even one of the most critical women be mindful to others.

"They'll be done soon," Jamie said. "Before Christmas I promise."

"Before the end of this term and everything is already due for grades? What a promise. Now go home. There's a crime show waiting for me to roll my eyes at for the next hour."

12

All week Jamie waited for the news. Her uncle exposed it all. Jamie had been lying. Going to the cathedral and not seeing her uncle . . . What was she doing? Where was she going and who was she seeing? But every day that came, no call. Every day Jamie wished she didn't have a job so she could go to the cathedral and ask them what had possessed her mind for the past week. Why they were there—why they were *really* there. They claimed to be angels and angels meant another form of life. A life in the afterlife. Were they once human? Was that fiction a derivative from some form of truth? Or had they always existed? Why exist in a gargoyle and not a human? Did they exist simultaneously in the gargoyle and back from wherever they came from? Or were they dormant in the gargoyle, alive somewhere else; and if so, how did she wake them up? *Did* she wake them? Or maybe the opposite, they're always waiting for someone to come, unaware of whatever's happening back where they came from.

They mentioned something worse than the end of the world. Maybe being cut off set them a little behind on recent developments. Maybe whatever End they spoke of was corrected and fixed and they've just been stuck unaware in the statue.

All week, question after question piled up in her brain, and to make sure she didn't forget one, she would make a note of it on her phone until she had nearly a hundred. She couldn't go to the cathedral because of the time of day, but she could research as much as she could about them. Her uncle told her a little, but there had to be more on their history. She'd spend a couple hours each night researching, but never found much other than a generic summary of the church's inception.

Since the searches on the gargoyles never bore much fruit, she would begin reading into Christian figures and tried to note the key ones in case the gargoyles mentioned them. It was confusing differentiating between the Old Testament and the New Testament characters, and especially confusing why there would be some books of the Bible with numbers after them. Were they all written by a different person of the same name, or were they like a book series that was divided into a trilogy or saga? At week's end, she'd had the sense to remember to bring the journal and remembering it was a stroke of luck. If it hadn't been for Aiden ratting her out about dishes, her mom wouldn't have forced her back to the house.

Jumping up the front steps, her backpack bouncing up and down, Jamie entered through the opened portal doors. There were many visitors in the cathedral, it being a Saturday, so no one noticed a tiny figure slip down a private hall at the end of the narthex.

So she thought.

A visitor did spot her, and feeling obligated, she walked toward them nearby the last row of seats. She conjectured which direction the atrium with the prophets Elijah and Jacob would be and wished the tourists luck. She'd never been inside at this time of day and since she had the rest of it free, she took the time to explore.

She walked toward the baldachin and tilted her head back to see the light of the rose window. Not as dazzling than during sunset, regardless, rather incredible. People used to stare into the permeable rose window, gazing into the sunlight's fauna, and believe that they were not alone. There was a deity in the skies who watched the whole earth and found a disheartened soul hidden beneath a chapel's roof; saw how lost they were in society, in their homes, in themselves, saw them and while they did not understand a human as they were not human themselves, cared. An omniscient deity empathized and would care for the human as long as they believed and prayed and held steadfast.

It was hard for Jamie not to want to believe that such an attitude could give her hope for a future. That simply closing one's eyes and bowing one's head and speaking louder with the heart than with the mind, that such faith could propel a lost soul out from the darkness and into the light. The light of the deity. Where someone so powerful could protect you and guide and love you. To not be in pain. To not be alone. All sorrows and worries cast away because of such comfort, of such love. But eventually truth and reality won over what she wanted. Believing in a deity was as much a hobby as believing there were aliens.

The smell of dust and old books suddenly filled her nostrils, as if it took standing in a centuries-old cathedral for five minutes for the aromas of old men and well-preserved relics to overtake the cathedral's visitors. The smell of all sorts of people. All manners of socio-economic backgrounds and interests and faiths—yes even non-believers came—walked down these aisles and left a little part of their lives behind. They traded only a handful of minutes to pray or an hour to tour the grounds, but at face-value a person's time was traded to be beneath the protection of the cathedral.

A line of faded ink from a dropped pen on a seat cushion caught Jamie's attention for a moment before she took another step forward, inward, toward the baldachin and the altar. On the ground at the edge of a pew, the corner of a tile was chipped and hadn't been replaced. The Bibles in the book holders were generously used, many with faded *Holy Bible* titles and bent corners. All around her, small moments of history that could have been made during last Sunday's church service or fifty years ago.

The metal vines and leaves of the baldachin were intricate gold, crafted to line naturally up the ascending column. Baldachins were canopies over altars or thrones she recalled, though this cathedral's baldachin lacked any form of honorary structure at its base. Walking beneath it and looking up with an expression no different than if she were seeing light from the bottom of a hole, her eyes marveled at the design of such a structure. Whorls of bronze intertwined with gold, expanding from a translucent crystal at the ceiling's apex. On the far edges were high reliefs of men and women and children staring up toward the center, some pointing, some lying down. They were dressed in a variety of fashions from simple robes to intricate gowns to military dress reminiscent of World War I.

"Our baldachin is our most expensive piece in the cathedral," said a male. Jamie spun toward the direction she'd just come, and felt foolish for not recognizing the harsh voice before. "Even more than our altar." Elias lifted his eyebrows.

"I can believe it. It has so much gold."

Elias stood in place with his arms held behind him, affording him a more authoritarian façade. His cool eyes almost impossibly matched such a hot tone. Jamie wondered if the resentment he'd had toward her was really toward *her*, or maybe he had something against her uncle and was lashing out at anyone with the same DNA.

Remembering her uncle formed a lump in her throat. She almost forgot. The con of a brother to her father. It'd been years since she heard a commendable compliment about him. Her mother wasn't close with him and so the last praises from her father disappeared into the recesses of her memory, fading as ghosts in a church graveyard. Perhaps the disdain Elias had against her uncle was well placed.

"Our Gabe is blessed to have such fond relatives, visiting on a weekly basis. If only all our relatives would be so generous with their time."

It would be stretching it to lie again and so she shrugged her shoulders, letting the lie from her lips go where it may.

"Actually, I'm not here to see Gabe." Elias wasn't expecting that and almost let that show on his face. He inhaled quickly to allow her to explain.

"Is that so?"

"In my last trip I discovered some rather marvelous sculptures and I don't know if it was the time of day, or just luck, but to my eyes . . . they seemed to *have come to life.*" She imitated a sincere smile as he studied her. She wondered if he knew how unembellished she was being. When her cocky grin didn't spur an appropriate reaction, she felt her confession to be too forward. Elias expressed feign amusement himself.

"As long as you credit the church, allow your artistic soul sail to the heavens on the Lord's river of light." Jamie scored a point for Elias and instantly his small grin fell, his glare hardening the longer he looked at her. "We'll be expecting you often from now on then?"

"My reasons for being here aren't entirely academic or artistic. Actually, a couple weeks back . . ." Jamie pulled her backpack around and searched around for the journal. "Leaving the cathedral I found . . ."

Elias seemed less interested than if she'd been preaching a sermon, and only looked at her face, not her backpack. "Whatever pieces of litter you've found near the church does not make it part of the church's responsibility." Jamie looked up. "Whatever you have found is none of our concern."

"But what if the person traveled away and didn't realize? It could be waiting for them if they call to see if they dropped it here."

Jamie thought him the worst Lost-and-Found administrator in the world and gave him a sour look, which caused him to exhale in submission.

"What is the item?"

She dug her hand in the backpack and felt the leather of the journal under her fingertips. All there was to do was lift it and hand it over, but there was a burden over her chest, as if something was telling her she shouldn't. The journal was someone else's, but there was a weight in her heart and oddly, a weight in the journal itself casting it down so it'd remain where it was. With her. A connection to a bizarre dream world with darkness and amber light, and one that piqued her interest and yet frightened her from ever being alone in the darkness again. She let out a breath and released the journal, instead moving her hand over a copy of *Pygmalion* and extending it over to him. He glanced down at the book and read the title.

"Someone left this behind?"

Jamie pretended to just realize what she was handing over and jumped in place, returning the pamphlet of a binding back into her backpack and shook her head as she explained the confusion. "Oh! This is for my class. I must have forgotten it again . . . darn."

Edgar walked down the aisle toward them as Elias opened his mouth. He had a pleasant humor about him as he switched from Jamie to Elias and back.

"Wonderful to see you again, Ms. Jamie. If we had known you'd be visiting so often, we'd have a welcoming party posted by the door."

Jamie adjusted her backpack as she shook her head. "That's really unnecessary. My visits aren't part of a new weekly routine."

"But it's so good for Gabe to be around family again. He told us how he hadn't seen much of his family since he was always away at church. It's refreshing to see family reaching out. Especially from someone so young." Edgar caught Elias' eye and smiled with deeper meaning hidden in his eyes. "Do Jamie's visits bother you, Elias?"

Elias held his eyes for several moments after Edgar emphasized his name and turned away.

"Cadogan sent for me, excuse me."

"I'm sure she will," Edgar said loud enough for him to hear, though his attention had returned to Jamie. Elias didn't respond, walking away, from what Jamie could tell, both of them. Was Edgar used to Elias and did all his encounters behave this truculently, or was it deeper?

"I'm afraid your uncle's not doing well today. I don't think he was expecting you. He never mentioned you were planning to visit."

"I wanted to return a book I found outside a couple weeks back but I had a little trouble finding it." She leaned to the side to show her backpack. "It must have walked out."

Edgar chuckled. "A book? What book?"

"It was thin and was leather or animal skin." Jamie acted like she hadn't already opened it. "I want to guess personal diary or journal."

"I'm afraid I haven't heard of anyone misplacing a diary but you're welcome to bring it here. We'll hold it in case someone stops by to collect it. You couldn't find a name . . . Address? Initials?"

She shook her head, biting the bottom of her lip as she noticed a deacon walking with urgency in their direction.

"Pardon me." He acknowledged Jamie briefly before turning to Edgar. "You're needed."

He took a step after him but then remembered Jamie. "I apologize—"

Waving her hand she stared back with wide eyes. The way the deacon spoke, she didn't think the attention was for someone accidentally slicing their finger with a kitchen knife. Without another thought she gestured for him to go.

"No, no need! I'm just going to look around on my own."

"Very well." He walked after the deacon who was by then reaching the final rows of pews and took several steps before half-turning back to her, his feet still moving. "Might I suggest the chapel of the apostles. Just to your right! Across the church library!"

A pressing force ushered him to hasten after his caller. Jamie waited a quarter of a minute after he was out of sight to walk back the way she came and slip down the hall to the staircase, then up to the roof.

Taking deep breaths, she headed in the direction of the gargoyles. A late autumn wind blew, cooling her back with a thin stream of sweat running down it. Late November it may be, but Florida didn't suffer harsh winters, hardly even cold ones. It would've been a perfect day to climb the bell tower if the weather was about ten degrees colder, even in the shadows.

She noted the shadows on the gargoyles, soft and adopted. It was strange for the winds to pass through them and not make them seem as menacing as they were meant to be. Unmake them from being soulless. There was something more.

It was a quiet moment she reserved to prepare herself. She used it calm her heart. The climb was not kind to friend or foe, and she didn't want their first glimpse of her to be of a heaving chest and hunched back. She mentally prepared for the impossible. It was a great secret—a privilege—to be the only one in the world who knew of them. But maybe there were others? The clergy had to have known. How couldn't they? They didn't seem to be frightened of them. And yet, they wouldn't broadcast of nefarious, belligerent monsters at the top of their skyscraper bell tower.

She marveled at them. Gargoyles weren't meant for such treatment. They were meant for much less. For the foolish to cower from and the brave to ignore as they walked through the broad cathedral doors. Large empty eyes, long piercing teeth hanging from cavernous mouths. Hands of age and torment and necks tough and thick, like rhinos whose skin withstands all but the deadliest piercing pressure. Sinewy fingers that curled and resembled wicked seaweed bending to a vicious wave. Arms of large bones, in the case of the ugliest gargoyle, but otherwise of taut muscle. Frames of damaged impairment, that mimicked the godlike marvel of Greek statues, then dipped in hot oil and scarred by flogging. Even weather wears at limestone, or whichever dark stone they were born from.

Enough time had passed and she exhaled. A week and a minute was long enough of a wait. She still stuttered over her words.

"I don't know the magic words. Abracadabra and open sesame." She twirled around, staring infinitely into their faces. "Um, Amen—no that's at the end. Hello. I came back."

They didn't respond and she tapped her foot for a moment before capitulating, taking off her backpack and sitting cross-legged. She looked at her nails then began picking one. Then another. Until she gave all of them her attention, before resting her elbow on one of her knees and resting her cheek on the palm. The wind receded and even in the shade, the heat began to settle again. She unfolded her legs in front of her and with one crossed over the other, she rested back on her hands.

"I've spent a lot of time researching." Her eyes studied the gargoyles then followed the ribs of the canopy where the vaulted ceiling came together. She pursed her lips. "Mainly Christian figures, but a little about you. If there had been other accounts of gargoyles coming to life in the world."

The fear that they might only come to life when it was near or past dark began to scratch at the edges of her mind. She came at midday to have more time with them, and at this rate, she would be talking to nobody but herself for the next five hours until it became dark.

"I didn't find anything. Nothing believable at least. Pseudo-science, you know. If we all believed what we're told or what we read on the internet, everyone would believe everything and then really nothing. I guess that's what separates us. Believing what we really think is true. Like, I couldn't believe what I saw when you first came to life . . . By the way, will that be happening anytime soon?" No movement in sight but by a bird in the distance.

"I guess I shouldn't be surprised. Maybe you're afraid of the light. I did come across some interesting stories. None really concerning gargoyles, but interesting. People who saw impressions and shadows of their loved ones; before their deaths, in a memorable place, by the church. I wonder if you can tell me if ghosts exist. I have to be open to ludicrous ideas now right?"

She began laughing and rolled her head back, wiping away a tear as she brought her head back forward.

"Somethings out there, that's for sure. All these religions, legends, myths, they stem from a small seed of truth. I believe that more than anything. But what makes one country's version more truthful than another if all are ideally stemmed from truth? Sure people wrote them and spread word and people are F-ing liars from here till doomsday, but what makes the Catholic church better than Hinduism? Why Buddhism better than Sikhism? Why something over nothing?"

There was a flapping noise behind her and she looked over her shoulder, spotting a pair of seagulls landing on the floor.

"I know there's the whole free will aspect, but you need to give us the benefit of a doubt. We can't just magically believe something is there just because of a couple of rumors and a couple of—no matter how fantastic and remarkable—miracles. We perform miracles every day in hospitals and through technology that would make people four hundred years ago call us gods. But we're just human. To err is to human—or something like that."

She thought she saw one of the gargoyles on her right, the one closest to Trium move, but after staring for a minute and nothing, she sighed.

"It's hard for me to share this with you believe it or not. Probably can't even hear me. But even a person without faith has their pride. It isn't that I don't believe in a god or I don't want to, it isn't even that I need proof to make me believe. It's just . . ." She struggled to find the words, grimacing. "I feel empty. Like it isn't possible for me to believe. I feel like an empty vase in a dark corner, not waiting to be filled with water or light or dirt. I'm just a dark vase in a corner who doesn't bother anyone like no one bothers me. That sounds so stupid *and* it makes no sense!" She stood up, walking past the gargoyles.

Rubbing the back of her neck, she tried to roll it around. "But, I do want to learn. Hearing stories about these people as if you actually knew them, even if they're vastly different from what people know from their Bibles. My dad's side of the family—they were hardcore religious people. Took the word of the Bible as if it were law. At least that's what I think of them. My dad and uncle might think something kinder but really, who chooses religion—that may be fallible might I add—over their family who are present and there? They didn't like my dad marrying my mom . . ." Not wishing to think too much on the thought but unable to think of anything else, she scoffed. "Bastards. I don't even care if you hear me now and I'm on the church. They're bastards and I'll call them bastards in front of any and all gods."

She hadn't realized but her voice had begun to carry, her hands beginning to shake at her sides. The slight tremors she could usually conceal and keep down were betraying her self-control. She wasn't like this, to lose it. Embarrassed for her body betraying her more than her words, she crossed her arms and continued her walk around the aisle, wanting to prove she could take over her self-control as it had done to her.

"I met them once. Barely remember most of the encounter but I was about seven. Aiden had just been born but he stayed with my Abuela. It was just my mom, dad, and me. We met them at a diner. They were all so serious, as if being happy wasn't allowed. They'd probably given it up for Lent. But I guess that isn't right since it was late summer." Jamie dismissed it. "It was my dad's parents and his two older sisters and one older brother. That side of the family's huge. I remember them all scowling at my father and any glances they made toward my mother were even more vicious. Out of everything that day, the one thing I can still see clearly in my mind was how my grandmother pointed her finger at me and my mom. The finger was pointed at us as if we were a broken plate by the dinner table and it had been our family's finest china. But it isn't like we were precious to her. She didn't care. None of them did. I'd never seen my father so angry beside that one time. Which doesn't seem right because all my life he told me they were still our family and were good people."

Jamie had returned to the backpack and sat back down, pressing her palm against her temple. She didn't know why she was sharing this and could barely remember how it came up in the first place. She had to have brought it up since she'd been the only one talking for the last ten minutes. She'd gotten lost in the memory.

Why was it so vivid? How could a memory remain so tangible? How could hate still be so hot and fresh? They never came up in her thoughts.

But the scowls and the pointed finger, it was pressed under her eyelids and she tried to force thoughts of school or work or her future, but that memory she never knew how much was suppressed surfaced. It was a mistake. She shouldn't have shared it with them. She shouldn't have remembered.

Leaning down to lay against her backpack, she shut her eyes and breathed steadily. Her hands folded over her stomach, she relaxed her mind to drift on its own to a more pleasant memory. Her father picking her up by one arm and towing her along like she were a football. They would go to the nearby park on weekends whenever her mom had to work—which was most days since her father only took on construction jobs he chose to spend more time taking care of Jamie and Aiden, and while she played near the other neighborhood kids her father would watch from the park bench. He'd be interested in everything she showed him and when it was getting darker and less kids were out and it was just the two of them, he'd play with her in the sandbox or inside the playground. And when it really got too dark and she protested to go home, he'd put her on his shoulders and walk them home. She'd feel like she were on the highest mountain. Happy even if the day of fun was over. Memories like this, with nothing but bliss. It was hard to imagine that such a warm man could come from a family like that.

Her mother's family was different. They were much warmer. The type of people that kept up-to-date with their neighbors lives because they were extensions of the family. Who'd invite you to family reunions and who'd dog-sit on less than a day's notice. Compared to her father, Rosario was somewhat colder, a somewhat firmer disciplinarian. However, while she was cold, her family was incredibly warm. Every family loves to spoil the kids and whenever Jamie would see them, they'd treat her special. It lessened when Aiden was born, but something within her accepted passing on the attention to him. Coming from a family of four to a large household of at least six, more often than not usually ten to fifteen, being thrust into such environments were off-putting.

And they loved her father. They accepted him into the family as easily as his family dismissed her mother. The clashing dichotomies peculiar since Rosario's family were just as resiliently religious in their faith. It was thanks to them Jamie found herself unable to completely close her heart to the gargoyles. As ugly as they may be, they represented some form of beauty every creature had whether organic, inanimate, or impossible.

"Jamie," said a distant voice. She muttered a response from her throat as the voice neared. "Jamie."

She peeked an eye open and saw a sky of stars, odd since there was still daylight. Focusing clearer, her vision straightened itself and narrowed on the two closest stars.

"Shit!" Jamie sat up quickly and backed up onto her backpack, resting a hand over her heart. The gargoyles watched her for who knew how long. If she knew better she would've suspected they waited for her to be off guard to scare her. She would've sworn she would've heard them had they begun breathing.

The gargoyle apologized. It was the one on Trium's left, the one she thought had moved before.

"No." She stood up. "I was dozing off." She brushed the remains of the ground off her pants.

"Not so close, Cato," said the gargoyle to her left. Oddly, the voice sounded higher-pitched than Jamie expected. Her eyes turned from the one called Cato to Jamie's. Could gargoyles have gender? "No one wants to be so close to a face like that."

"We woke her. The first thing she wants to hear will assuredly not be your babbling." The voice came from beside her, 9:00 in this gargoyle clock.

"It's quite entertaining to see others bear the end of protest," said the gargoyle to his other side, Jamie's 7:00.

Jamie chuckled as the gargoyle focused on her, a devilish grin on his lips. He was the one whose knee was used for her makeshift tripod.

"How do you know my name?"

Trium answered. "On your first night, the man shared it."

Her uncle. She distanced her thoughts from him.

"So you hear even when you're full-on statues?"

"Even pieces of rock, we all hear. The Earth hears us all."

Jamie kept back a smile. "I guess that answers the *does a tree make a sound in the forest* riddle."

"Do you not see the stars?" Cato asked. "Do not your astronomers believe the light from stars exist from extinguished sources?"

"Be careful what you start with him," said the 9:00 gargoyle, explaining Cato to Jamie. "He's tenacious to know all of man's philosophies and sciences."

"It's a theory." Jamie nodded. "My brother likes space so he would have more of an answer for you."

"A brother?" said the gargoyle at 3:00, who looked from Jamie up to Trium. Sharing only a momentary connection, he returned his attention to Jamie. "Younger?"

"He must've shared that with you." Jamie looked down the right side of the clock. "Do the priests know about you all?"

"They do," Trium said.

"That you come alive? Do you speak to anyone who comes up here?"

"Almost no one. Those who have come to us for a purpose, even for one they might not understand."

Cryptic, Jamie thought, studying Trium's mask. Behind such a façade, was it reticent or truly honest?

"So, I guess you'll tell me then, what's my purpose? Because I definitely have no idea."

Trium muddled over answering, they all did, because they just acted as if they were listening in the air for a siren that would call them away. Finally, 9:00 answered. "You mentioned studying figures from the Christian scripture. Are you familiar with Noah?"

Jamie nodded. "He built the ark before the world flooded."

"What of Moses?"

"He saved the Hebrews from further enslavement in Egypt and took them across the Red Sea." Remembering Noel, Jamie smiled. "And he had a thing about walking barefoot."

"And David?"

"David and Goliath? The one Michelangelo carved?"

"Do you know what they had in common?"

Jamie was reluctant to answer, shrugging her shoulder before she muttered the first things that came to mind. "They were lucky?"

"Faith. That He had what was best for them in heart. They had faith, by their free will, they would succeed in His Will. They all obeyed the Father. They all glorified the Father. To have in faith in one that one cannot see—it is remarkable. They and many took the blessings they were given, facing their fears and the pressures of secular influence to place their trust in Him. Times come when the world seems to fade, as if mankind could not become any more distant from the Father, and nothing can be seen of the world but corruption. People pray to Him and He answers them, in ill or in favor, always answering. He sends the people a prophet who the people dismiss like a plagued creature. There is a time still to come for change, one that has not been written. We were awakened to help defend the weak and protect the Father and His followers. When the time comes, the faithful will be asked to fight, and Victory shall be given for those who are true."

Jamie glanced to the female gargoyle, then back to the speaker, slowly understanding what he was implying. "So you're saying something is coming?"

"Not just something, Jamie." It was the 3:00 gargoyle. "A host. An army that will be fought by one just as fierce."

Jamie repudiated, casting an arm out. "Where are you going to get an army? There's only seven of you."

He ignored her comment and looked up to Trium, who obliged. "With faith, we will be victorious. A battle of faith is coming."

The voices surrounding her began to speak in another language, ancient, primordial, and somehow familiar. Inflections in their voices made the language melodic, if almost from a dream. Their wings jutted from their resting forms and began to flap faster as if prepared to launch skyward. The wind that accumulated caused her to go off balance. Surefooted, she stood her ground.

"What are you planning on fighting with? I doubt you have machine guns, nukes, or even bullwhips in your arsenals."

The gargoyles hadn't heard or they elected to ignore her. All of the gargoyles had spoken, she noticed, except the one on her 5:00. The definition of grotesque, a being of bone. He had paid close attention to the assembly of the gargoyles but from a safe distance. He leaned half behind one of the columns and concentrated on what the others were saying. If she didn't know better, she's say that he was just in the dark as she was. It couldn't be that though. It didn't make sense. She wanted to ask when slowly, as if gravity held a stronger tie on them than her questions, the wings of the gargoyles returned them to Earth and settled down.

She turned from him and tried a question a little easier to answer. "When's this battle supposed to happen?"

The gargoyle at 9:00 muttered something final before answering her again. "It is unclear. The last appearance of the army was—unexpected." He said it as if they were still preparing for it.

"When was it?"

"Before the renovation. In the first construction. Two hundred years ago."

"No more than that, Marius," said the one at her 7:00. It looked at Jamie with the same terrifying grin on his face. "This land was still green. Cities had not risen. There were forts and posts still lighting the beachside at night."

"Dominic you're perception of time is folding," Cato said. "It was ten years after we arrived, well into the nineteenth century."

"Well that cannot be correct," Dominic said, his conviction already faltering.

"So battles happen all the time," Jamie said, eyes round and lips pursed. "You guys'll win just like last—"

"No!" barked the female gargoyle. "No battle is like another. They are as distinctive as a human's fingerprints. No soul is like another, no matter its source of conception. Every soul lost because of the fatalities of such pride were taken by distinctive corruption. The battle to come will be more destructive than you can imagine."

"Settle, Sidra," Trium said firmly.

Jamie bravely spoke up. "I—I don't understand."

Trium softened his gaze. She was beginning to notice the miniscule twitches on the surface of the stone that signaled a change in expression. None of them had eyebrows or eyelids, their eyes seeming to be in a constant shape when open. It was slight, but in their cheekbones and only slightly more obvious in the adjustment of their white pupils, there was a shift in attitude, manner, and expression.

"We will not trouble you with grievances. Not at the present."

"Trium," said the gargoyle at her 3:00. "Perhaps for the girl to understand—for now, the beginning?"

Trium nodded while Jamie held her arm out and asked for him to wait. She walked back to her backpack and took out a notebook and pen, sitting down and looking back up. "All right, go ahead."

"It is unsettling for the body to run when it cannot walk, therefore I will not tell you of the Partner and the Weapon and who the battle is against until you know of our origin and our Father."

Fair enough, Jamie thought.

Trium sighed and sat down cross-legged, mirroring Jamie's position. It looked ridiculous, seeing a gargoyle in such a position she'd never imagined before, but it would be almost insulting to laugh. Even thinking about laughing seemed incredibly rude. Instead, she waited with wide eyes as he straightened his back, lifting his arms up.

"In the beginning of Earth-time," he began, "the Father separated the Heavens and the worlds. He knew that all around Him was darkness, so he formed that which would become light. And so, this was the first day."

Thunder could be heard from the east. All manner of gray surrounded Jamie from the gargoyles to the skies. Although behind the storm clouds, the sun had begun its descent toward the western horizon. Several hours had passed after closing her eyes.

Cato stepped forward as she was scrutinizing the sky. He pressed his fingertips together like he was contemplating what he heard, then rotated them in opposite directions, lifting one hand up and letting the other slowly fall away. In between his hands was a smoke-like darkness that emerged from nothing. With a gentle bounce of his hand, suddenly an orb of luminescence began to illuminate and float. Removing the top hand, he let the small glow float above the other palm. His fingers curled around an invisible sphere that surrounded the precious energy inside. He glanced at her, then looked back to the glow, which revolved around a center on its own. But what she observed, standing up, forgetting about writing and simply seeing, she noticed the glow was circling the center with a separate floating sphere of darkness.

Everyone observed the show and Jamie quickly forgot about pen and paper, approaching to marvel closer. It was interesting to see darkness as a separate agent. Not just what was filled with light, but an actual entity. Yes, on Earth it was observed as the absence of light, the remainder of space of that which was not filled with light, but to have it exist on its own . . . What was this science Trium spoke of?

Cato's hand bounced lightly and released the two spheres until they hovered down several feet away from Jamie.

The rain started to drizzle outside of the spire. The gargoyle beside Cato, Jamie's 3:00, walked to the edge and cupped his hands, collecting water. When he had what he needed, he walked over to Jamie and kneeled. He let the water run from his hands onto the floor, forming a puddle.

Trium watched the gargoyle then lifted one hand up while letting the other fall down. "The Father looked at the world and said to separate the water, one would be above and one below." Trium looked at the gargoyle and nodded, the recipient's eyes only waiting for the signal. The gargoyle raised his hand above the water as a magician would conjure his trick, and gravitated the water up. Half of the water rose and vaporized to form shapes similar to clouds while the water that remained below began to push and pull like ocean waves. "Immediately, the water separated. Above: float. Below: sink. 'The floating water would be called the skies,' the Father proclaimed. And so this was the second day."

The little glow of luminescence danced with the darkness, acting like the sun, shining the little days and when one was complete, hiding behind the sphere of darkness.

She noticed the most hideous of the gargoyles, the only one not to have spoken yet, step toward her. He approached carefully as if prepared to stop if she betrayed her fear. She met his eyes straight on and proved to him that she wasn't that spineless. Treacherous and sharp teeth rose out of his underbite, a rugged crease scarred in between his eyes. She wondered if he couldn't speak, and wanted to ask what she couldn't before, though curiosity wasn't potent enough to interrupt the performance. When he was near, he turned his attention toward the puddle, clouds, and dance between light and darkness.

"The Father looked upon the water below and declared that separate would be a dry ground called land. Amadrius." Trium motioned. The fearsome one allowed dirt to drop from his palm next to the puddle. "The water would be called seas." The little glow appeared from behind the darkness and illuminated the separation of water and land. The part which bordered them formed a beach, and the dirt near the water turned into sand.

Amadrius backed away into the shadows behind the nearest gargoyle, returning by one of the columns. Watching him retreat made Jamie pity him. Was it on account of her? So as not to frighten her?

"The Father looked over the land and proclaimed that plants of all forms and shapes and function would cover the land." Trium turned to Sidra, who stepped forward. A broken leaf fell from her hand onto the dirt and it sunk underneath like quicksand. Saplings grew to become minute trees and bushes, forming a wood with a blanket of grass replacing the dirt base.

"And so was the third day."

The glow began to hide behind the darkness.

"The Father looked out past the world and past the skies," Trium narrated. "He declared for lights to be cast out, to light the darkness and differentiate when the day was day and the night was night. To separate, He set the bright light of the sun to govern the day, and a lesser light of the moon to govern the night. He summoned for stars to be spread among the skies during the night."

Sidra passed her hand through the glow of luminescence. When she opened her palm another glow floated above it. As it danced alone, she clenched her fingers around it and trapped it there. As she unclenched, little sparkles fell into the other outstretched hand. The first little glow floated behind the dark sphere to display only darkness and then she threw the sparkles out toward it. They floated around the sphere like stars in the background and the glow came back out, smaller in size and dimmer in shine. The moon.

"And that was the fourth day," Trium said. "And so the Father looked at the Earth and wanted to fill it with not only life, but life with minds to think and behave according to their surroundings. He created animals to soar in the skies, and animals below to swim in the seas."

Marius stepped forward and grabbed part of the clouds. He then placed his hand over the other and blew into it, and when opening it, little birds flew out. He brushed his hands together like he was done. He then picked up a small pebble and tossed it into the puddle, and from the droplets of the splash, little fishes began to swim.

"And so that was the fifth day." Trium nodded once to Marius as he passed and looked over to Dominic. "Then the Father looked toward the land and created many animals that could crawl, trot, sneak, leap, and slither, and placed them in their own environments with others of its kinds."

Dominic picked up some of the dirt and sprinkled it over the land to form little mountain piles. From below, tiny land creatures emerged and shook off the dirt. Jamie watched as a lioness shook, as an iguana broke up from the surface of the dirt and sunbathed on a rock, as a monkey quickly dug itself out and climbed up the mini tree to swing from branch to branch, and as many others joined the animal kingdom.

"The Father then said for there to be mankind in His image, in which they will rule over the birds of the sky, the fish in the seas, and the animals of the land."

Dominic blew at the dirt and like a great wind, the dirt gyred into a contained hazy storm. When the dust fell, what remained was a tiny figure of a naked man.

"And when the Father was done, He said it was very good. And so that was the sixth day. When the Father gazed at all He created, He knew His work was complete. He declared for the seventh day to be blessed and rested, for those became the seven days of creation, the beginning of your world."

Jamie shook her head. "It's so much, in such a short amount of time."

"Of your world it was. And each day much love and care was spent to create the perfect home for you. Until you were ready to be with the Father." His voice was tender and devoting. "Why else do you think the Father took rest on the seventh day?"

Trium stood and walked over to the magical display and waved his hand over it. As soon as his hand passed, the clouds, water, stars, animals, and land vanished.

"What next then?" Jamie asked.

The rest of the afternoon she listened to the gargoyles share the stories of different biblical characters. Of the story of the first man and woman and their expulsion from the Garden all the way until the story of the flood. Marius was fond of the story of Abraham and his lineage, from Isaac to his sons Jacob and Esau, then to Jacob and his son Joseph. Jamie tried to ask more about the battle they vaguely hinted toward earlier, but they cleverly prevaricated and transitioned the conversation to another topic.

Though she couldn't really believe these people had done all the feats the gargoyles claimed, she felt them to be real. After several hours she finally understood it wasn't the stories, it was their interpretation. Trium spoke the most sincerely, masterfully reciting the stories as if he had countlessly many times before and it was only a pleasure to share them again. Sidra was rather fierce in her storytelling, imitating a sword in her hand when she delivered the stories with battles. Marius was the most soft-spoken, out of all the gargoyles voices, his represented a human's most clearly. Dominic was the talker, ironic since his statue was the one whose mouth was closed when they weren't breathing. He enjoyed referencing other characters Jamie had never heard of, leaving her to stare in ignorance. On Trium's other side, Cato was also a fantastic storyteller. He was the only one who would deviate from the story by referencing a person or event more modern and contemporary. Jamie wanted to ask where he learned all of this, but thought it a question for another time; they likely would equivocate the topic like they had concerning the battle. She was enjoying their stories too much to push it. The last gargoyle whose name she learned was Silas. He possessed the enthusiasm of the story without the loquacious flare as Dominic or dramatic re-enactment as Sidra. The purity of his storytelling came from an essence of peace and brightness for life that Jamie associated with optimists.

Each one spoke of the character's turmoils like they were the gargoyles', and rejoiced when they revealed their turmoils to be tests. The faithful were rewarded in the end. All the gargoyles took turns storytelling and all had their own style. All save Amadrius.

When Jamie heard her phone, she knew it was getting late. The sun had already set and she didn't want to end up getting locked inside. She said she would return soon and waited to take their final breaths.

On the bike ride home, she imagined all of the characters she learned about. While she browsed over the stories of the major characters, she wasn't aware how complex these stories could be. She now understood why the Bible was so thick. Betrayal and deception within the family was the most common theme from story to story, but no matter how different the times they lived in, it reflected people's ways in her own time. If in no account other than that, they had to have been real.

When she had gone to the cathedral in the past she had always feared the shadows around her. Tonight felt different. She was confident that it had only been in her head. Nothing had happened then and nothing would now.

That night she slept in peace.

The following day was spent much like the prior. They continued the Biblical stories and began mentioning names she was more familiar with, David and Goliath, but then diverted back to unfamiliar tales of men tasted by their faith like Daniel; Shadrach, Meshach, and Abednego; and Jonah in a large fish. And similar to twenty-four hours prior, she felt more confident on her bike ride home. No shadows were tempted to torment her.

See, she thought, *all in your head.*

13

Banafsha scrutinized Jamie while she watched Aiden pack his bag. Aware of eyes on her, Jamie drew her eyebrows together. "What?"

"You're spending a lot of time at the cathedral."

Jamie never mentioned it, and so she turned to Aiden.

"Oh, did the bug happen to mention it on his way in?"

Aiden made a face as he stepped up to them. "I mentioned it because she asked. It's called conversing."

"What a smartass—I swear you're lucky Banafsha even puts up with you."

Aiden rolled his eyes and walked past Jamie, then remembered something and turned to Banafsha. "We have a field trip to the Space Center this Friday. Mom told me to remind you. Before I forgot."

Banafsha nodded. "She told me."

Aiden turned back to the door, muttering to himself, "Why does she tell me to do things if she does things herself . . ." His grumbling continued after the door closed behind him.

Banafsha's eyes narrowed on Jamie again and while Jamie wasn't as perturbed as before, she finally let her head back.

"Why are you looking at me like that?"

"You're not converting are you?"

Jamie smiled sympathetically. "The stories are captivating—"

"They have to be!" Banafsha said as though rudimentary. "It's the cheese in the trap."

She made her way to the living room where Aiden left behind a mess of a puzzle. Jamie looked at the pieces spread out, her mouth agape. "I hope Aiden didn't make this mess. I know you don't have a dog, but you can lose pieces under the sofa or vacuum it by accident." Jamie bent down and started picking up pieces, placing it on the coffee table.

Banafsha guffawed. "He was actually organizing it for me. You should have seen it before. I had pieces everywhere!"

"Banafsha," Jamie exclaimed. "How dare you surprise me."

"What?"

"Being this way. Your house is the paradigm of order."

An eyebrow rose. "What gave you that ridiculous impression?"

"The fact that Aiden dropped one of your glasses a couple months back and you gave me grief about not having an even set anymore."

She dismissed Jamie and threw the puzzle pieces rather carelessly onto the coffee table. Jamie stared after her incredulously and stood quietly for a moment. "Did something happen?"

Banafsha made a sound in between a grunt and a scoff and ignored her.

"Go home. I want to be alone."

Tossing the pieces on the coffee table, Jamie didn't utter another word, in fear of provoking her further.

****

Bryden leaned against the climbing wall with his arms crossed. He and Jax were discussing a girl from their class.

"No," Bryden said, a curve on his lips. "She screams conservative. A crop of short black hair with bangs."

"With the same boring clothes she's worn since freshman year that don't compliment her figure?" From three steps away, Jax pulled the roll of rope out from its coil.

"Nice, Jax," Vienna said. "Knowing the only way you can describe a girl is by how generous she reveals skin."

Bryden jutted his chin out at Vienna. "Why do all girls get so touchy? It's true isn't it?"

"And you're a dick," Vienna said. "And that has nothing to do with what you're wearing but if you like we can start talking about that unholy side of humanity which is your fashion taste. What is that, shorts you've found in the dumpster?"

Bryden pulled the side of the shorts and shook it. "Clearance! Walmart!" Vienna rolled her eyes and Bryden straightened his back, leaning against the wall. "Got something against Walmart, Italy?"

Vienna pressed her lips together and refrained from protesting the nickname, though shut her eyes. "You've always been bitter against her. I'd like to wonder why." Vienna opened her eyes and looked directly into Bryden's. "I can guess why for two reasons." She arched an eyebrow. "Want to share if I'm right or not?"

Bryden scoffed. "Think what you want." Vienna didn't reply and he stared coldly as Jamie sensed the tension rising slowly.

"Who now?"

"Penelope Varano." Jax answered Jamie, though carefully looking at Vienna. His hands continued to snake the rope out of its wrapped loop. "We're not being indelicate, Vienna. I'm only describing her like any other person would."

Jamie sensed the tension skyrocketing now as Vienna redirected her glare from Bryden to Jax and stepped forward. "Have you guys considered asking your parents to push the trip back a couple months?"

Caprice nodded, opening her mouth to speak when Vienna spoke first. "My parents said it depends, but lately I've been thinking no." Her eyes dug into Jax's.

"Why?" Jax said.

"Mine still said no," Bryden droned. He'd been released from Vienna's line of sight and resumed his usual faulty character. "*Hell* no. It's like they don't trust me."

Vienna unclipped the bod climbing harness and tossed it to the bench, ignoring all eyes on her. Jax stopped unwinding the rope and watched as she reached for her backpack.

"Return that for me. I forgot I need to run an errand for my mom. I'll see you guys later."

"C'mon, Vienna . . ." His words reached deaf ears and she walked toward the entrance. As Vienna passed Era at the front desk, he tossed the rope aside and went after her. Jamie and the rest of the Capes watched as he called after her as soon as he was outside.

Caprice looked over to Jamie and shrugged. "They're always bickering."

"Are they together?" Jamie asked.

"*Say* they aren't—but everyone knows they are. Just because you haven't acknowledged it, does it mean you're not in a relationship?"

Bryden perked his eyebrows up and straightened up like a dog hearing his owner come home. "Oh really? If that were so then I've had many a girlfriend in my time."

Caprice rolled her eyes and picked up the rope Jax left behind, ignoring Bryden. "They've been fighting all week. Just a few words will knock them off balance."

"Are you sure it isn't more than that?" Jamie asked.

She looked up to Caprice, then spotted someone come inside behind her. Minjae pointed a thumb over his shoulder as he approached them. "What happened now?"

"Nothing to worry about," Caprice sighed.

"It's never nothing. Nothing happens all the time."

"Who cares?" Bryden asked. "We thought you weren't coming."

"Last week was the last football game of the year," Minjae rested his hands on his hips. "Yearbook takes priority you know. Ava's really starting to wear the staff down."

"I haven't seen you in photo," Jamie said.

Minjae nodded, keeping silent for a thought. "Ava's sort of banned me from coming for a little while."

"What?" Jamie mocked. "Her favorite student? No!" Minjae failed to suppress a grin as he sat on the bench, watching Bryden hook himself up. Jamie stood nearby. "Have you asked your parents?"

Without context he knew what she was talking about and shook his head. "I haven't had time. I will soon."

"Mine's close to bending," Caprice said, stepping on his other side, looking down at him. "If yours say yes, then mine definitely will. They trust you to be the most responsible out of the group."

"Thanks for the compliment. Don't rely too much on them."

"Or you, Jamie." Caprice focused her attention on Jamie. "If you just join the group and your mom says yes like that, they might not be so skeptical."

"Would that really work?" Jamie asked.

Caprice shrugged, smirking. "Probably not. They'd probably think I was lying. Wouldn't be the first time. Oh, I think you're being summoned," she said, pointing behind Jamie to Era. As Jamie turned, Bryden was calling for Caprice's attention.

"So," Era whistled as she bounced on her toes. "Do you plan on never asking me? Or do you just like me bottling things up when you know I can't for long?"

Jamie had sensed Era wanted to share something since her shift started, but was preoccupied with checking and chaperoning some kids on the bouldering rocks. Era did have a tendency to go on and on once she got excited and so Jamie had kept silent.

"What? Have a hot date tonight?"

Era showed all of her teeth and then covered them behind flat hands. "He's something, Jamie! He loves outdoor sports and he knows the difference between foundation and concealer."

Jamie's smile began to wane and she began studying her friend. "Era, are you sure . . ."

Era's expression fell and she almost sneered back. "Really. It wasn't just me. He walked over and flirted first."

Jamie let bouncing eyebrows say it all, but Era picked up a crumpled up piece of paper and tossed it to her. "When have you ever seen me approach a guy first?"

"Maybe it's a good time to start?"

Era waved the idea away. "Anyways, we have a date tonight. So, I was wondering if maybe, possibly . . ." She fluttered her eyelashes.

Jamie had planned to stop by the library after work to check out any records on the first cathedral or on the renovation. The city library was much closer than the cathedral and so she figured she might investigate more into the genesis of the church before seeing the gargoyles again. Era was supposed to close and Aiden had his field trip, and while she wanted to take advantage of a night without responsibilities, she knew if she told her friend no she couldn't go on a date because she wanted to go to the library that would make her more pathetic a friend than usual.

"I'll owe you big time?" Era prodded further, biting her bottom lip and tilting her head forward.

Jamie couldn't refuse her. The buildings would be there in the morning. She could stop by there first before heading to the cathedral. The answer was on her face and Era jumped in glee as Noel approached them with a box of harnesses in his arms, wondering what could make anyone be that happy when they would be working for seven more hours.

Jamie tried to be quiet as she closed the front door behind her. It didn't escape her notice one of the lamps was on, her mother still awake in the living room. She was seated on the sofa with several folders around her, her laptop on her lap and a pen in hand.

"Home," she said loud enough for her mother to hear, walking without any intentions continuing the conversation.

"I thought you'd be home hours ago."

Jamie mindlessly went to the loveseat and after sliding her backpack off her shoulder and dropping it beside her feet, sank in its cushiony depths. "Era wanted to switch shifts."

"Don't you work tomorrow?"

"No."

"Are you hungry? There's left-overs."

"What is it?"

"*Arroz y habichuelas. Arroz con* chick peas. *Amarillitos.*"

It didn't sound appetizing. "I'm not hungry."

"When was the last time you ate?"

Jamie was dozing off and the part of her still awake hoped that her mother would let her sleep, but her voice came back.

"*Mira, vete a dormir.*"

Jamie continued to doze off when suddenly her mother's hand took hers.

"*Cariño.*"

An eye opened, curious if Aiden was nearby. When she noticed he wasn't, she looked up to her mom, smiling kindly down to her. The endearment was reserved for Aiden, and hearing it used for her felt unsuitable, as if she were the baby of the family again.

Ever since Aiden was born, Jamie noticed how her mother seemed to tend to Aiden more than her, garnering all her focus and love on him to make sure he grew up strongly and safely. And she hadn't minded. Because she had her father, who she believed favored her over her brother. It wasn't ill-intended and Jamie knew that he loved Aiden undoubtedly. It was only her father catered to her as her mother catered to Aiden, each parent with their favorite child.

Jamie remembered one Christmas several years before her father died when her *abuela* mentioned it to her mother, rebuking her for her lack of attention to Jamie. They were in the kitchen and Jamie was around the corner, eavesdropping the way all ten-year-olds do, realizing for the first time her mother loved her in a different way. She had always assumed that she loved them both the same and more attention had to be given to Aiden because he was the baby. However, hearing the words from her mother's mother opened her eyes. Love could be split. As her mother loved her kids differently than she loved her husband, her mother loved her differently than she loved her brother. She listened as they went back and forth. One criticizing and the other lashing back. Harsh words shielded and deflected with harsher words. The jolly season became colder and darker than she dreamed it would be. Most of the words flew over her head, becoming less than words, more guttural and vicious as they went from English to Spanish and back and forth, but the sounds were still there, a faint heartbeat in a winter's chill. Her father found her and took her in his arms.

"*Mi angel,*" he said, kissing her cheek.

"Why are they fighting? Is it because of me? Did I do something wrong?" Jamie asked when they reached outside. It was a cold Christmas and her breath floated in the air.

"No, they're arguing because they love you." It didn't make sense to her and she told him. His chuckle, a sound warm and comforting, made her forget about the two women inside. He rubbed his thumb against her cheek. "When people fight over something or someone, it's because they care too much about it to let the matter go.

Your *abuela* loves you and your mom loves you, but sometimes she doesn't understand why your mom raises you the way she does. She doesn't expect her daughter to raise her children differently than how she did, but I promise you that both women are perfect mothers who care about their children more than anything. *¿Lo entiendes?"*

Jamie nodded though she didn't really. If people were arguing over her, how could it be because they loved her? Why was it not because one was actually unhappy with her? Perhaps the love she thought she understood as a mother's love was merely tolerance. Not all mothers loved their children, like her father's mother. If someone who should love you by right couldn't, how easy would it be for tolerance to become disapproval, disgust, in turn regretting the very life you brought into the world? Had she done something wrong? If she apologized enough times, would it earn her back the love that had been lost?

Jamie sat up, taking her hand from her mother's grasp. The drowsiness unexpectedly eluded her. "I'm going to shower. Is Aiden in the bathroom?"

Rosario shook her head, stepping back to lean against the arm of the sofa. "He went to bed. He's upset with me."

Jamie picked up her backpack and moved around her mother, not allowing that last bit of information to prompt her to ask why. It was small, and she had no real reason to be mad, but in that moment she understood how Vienna could suddenly flip and be mad at Jax after only exchanging a few words. For her, it had only been one. An endearment. It hadn't occurred to her before but she didn't want to be pampered or given attention.

The time had passed for that.

14

Jamie munched on a turkey sub as she listened to one gargoyle share stories of men from the New Testament. The stories were less about the family and more about the individual. And while the characters in the stories would meet one another, they seemed more independent. She drew a better relationship and empathy with them.

Marius' hands grasped the opposite arm. "Lazarus, risen again. The only man to have been dead longer than the Son."

Jamie swallowed the wheat grub. "But . . . he waited. He deliberately waited two days to see him. Don't you consider that shameful?"

Sidra narrowed her eyes down on Jamie, and Jamie avoided her gaze as best as she could, turning to Trium and Cato who in contrast seemed untroubled by the accusation.

"The wait was necessary," Trium said.

"But his sisters grieved," Jamie said derisively.

"And so did the Son. He wept. Tears not of the Father, but of a human. His heart was no less tormented by death."

"His own death would come," Cato added. "It was Lazarus' death that would reveal to him the woe that his mother and his apostles would feel in His inevitable death. He knew their pain would come again soon. And his heart *grieved*." Jamie shook her head, unable to accept.

"You do not understand," Dominic said, stepping in front of Marius. "To grieve as a human is not as a child of the Father would grieve, for you grieve for the present. The emotions of losing someone dear to you is a rush of the tide, powerful and unstoppable." Jamie's gaze hardened as he continued, though his voice remained composed. "A human may feel the loss and emptiness of another, as if they have been cheated or wronged. *The human should have stayed with them longer. It is not fair.* These are thoughts we have heard countless times. But to grieve, as a child of the Father, is to feel an emptiness that is . . . missing."

"No, that is the wrong word," Silas said. "It is the emptiness of oblivion, as if sucked into a vacuum and the universe had morphed into nothing. It is not an emptiness to feel. It is an emptiness of being."

"As I said, grief of misplacement," Dominic said. "The Fallen were lost from the Heavens but not truly gone. Though their souls were damned, their lights had merely gone astray. Their existence did not become obsolete. And our grief surpassed their greater vice of going astray."

"We are desolate," Silas said, "only where our thoughts reside. In our hearts, there is Light. He is there."

"On Earth, death is final," Trium said. "But death is not final with the Father. Death is only the test. One that man is prepared for or he is not. One that he will face in fear or face willingly."

"You don't understand," Jamie said. "To you, you know what happens after people die. You know who goes where. You aren't left behind wondering if they're all right—if they chose the right path after all. We're just left behind, unable to breathe in meaningless days. We're left in the dark, unsure why we needed to be separated when we did. But you wouldn't know that would you? Because as you've said, you've only ever been in the light. You know about this test and what comes after." She waited for a small spell of sadness to wither away before continuing. "Well take it from someone who's always lived in the dark. You're wrong. You don't know grief. You can watch the world's population dwindle to the last living person and never feel what I've felt. What a *human* has felt. You don't know what it is to grieve because you aren't human."

The gargoyles looked to Trium for guidance. They could not explain it in a way that she could understand as much as she couldn't make them understand. It was impossible to explain grief to a creature who hadn't endured it. And she may have only lost her father, only one person, compared to countless others in the world who had lost their entire families from war to disease to famine to tragedies, but her grief was more powerful than any other. Because it still lived in her. She could not wash it away. There was a point of acceptance that she had never been able to reach.

How many times had she heard segments of the Kübler-Ross model from movies or random trivia bits from Aiden, that grief could be overcome by acknowledging the emotional shifts in its post-stages. It always led to moving on, because every hurtful and jovial moment in life ends and another comes. Tragedy and pain is transient, evanescent, and never meant to be abiding. But if it were love, no scientist or idealist would contend that love, true love, is fugitive. Jamie knew if someone meant enough to you, theory couldn't replace anything that was written by nature. Because if science could analyze something as precarious as emotions, as easily and predictably as the physical world, then people would be no better than robots of science fiction.

The gargoyles could show her magic and have her bring down the reservations she'd held against religion, but if they could tell her how she felt, then it meant that their science could predict human nature and if they could predict, how much longer would it be until they could alter human will? Or had they already learned how, using flash techniques and marvel tactics like their science of Light under a familiar pretense like magic?

Trium's eyes remained on Jamie. He needed to elucidate color to a blind man.

"My brothers are wrong. It is not that we cannot or do not, but because we have no reason to. It is true that we cannot understand how a human may grieve or know what it is to feel the wind. You might think us cold and heartless. But there is a truth that we are aware of and because of our faith, we need no reason further. We need not grieve for separation as humans. The Light shows us the truth and for us it is enough. No child of the Father may understand the feelings of a human but the Son or the Partner, for they are the only ones to have lived among humans. Grown and lived alongside them and yet have seen the splendor of the heavens."

Jamie arched an eyebrow. "Partner? What Partner?"

All of the gargoyles focused on Trium, even Amadrius, hidden behind a column. His eyes looked hopeful for the first time, Jamie thought. And when he looked at Jamie, there was no trace of fear.

"The Earth had its first man and first woman. And at the end, there will be two of different kinds to walk the surface of the Earth, until the last souls return through the Gates of Heaven."

"What do you mean two of different kinds? Different kind of what?" Jamie asked, glimpsing at other gargoyles but always returning to Trium. "Like Adam and Eve, a male and female?"

"That one is a different sex is not what makes it significant," Trium said. "The Partner is destined to roam the lands of the Earth with one that is unlike the other. In almost every way are the two different."

"This Partner then, he's already aware of this battle you're so happy to prevaricate?"

"They are."

Jamie chewed on the corner of her lip, trying to gather together the tidbits of information she learned from them and word it in a way that would trick them into finally explaining why they were there.

"You said you were awakened."

Trium nodded once, his white pupils swallowing the black abyssal socket before diminishing to their normal size. His fists, which had been curled, loosened by his sides. The overall rigidity of his form seemed to feel the wind for the first time as the rugged and weathered surface of their gargoyle skin seemed to shift and slacken, as if the muscles under the rock face relaxed. The wings of the gargoyle seemed of an independent mind, alive and aware.

"We were."

"By who? Who woke you?"

"A high power," Silas answered.

"Because they know about this battle," Jamie said delicately. "That it's coming soon." None answered and she turned to look over their grotesque masks. "Were you wakened before the last battle? Did the sculptor who made you know what you'd become?"

"Our artist was tormented," Marius said. "He struggled to continue yet found it impossible to stop."

"What was his name?" Jamie asked breathlessly.

"Our artist?" Trium contemplated.

"Dario? Claudio?" Marius meditated.

"Antonio," Cato affirmed.

"Esattamente!" Marius nodded. "He had trouble saying his words clearly but he was a talented sculptor."

"Antonio," Jamie said. "Did he have a last name? Antonio what?"

"His last name? Antonio"—Marius fumbled over remembering for a long time—"We never learned his last name. It wasn't exactly a formal introduction. We wouldn't have even known his name if not for someone calling him."

"How did he know what you were though? You're beings of another universe, one that predates the world. It isn't like heavenly beings talk with people often."

"That is one way to see it. Angels are not to communicate with human, not for over a millennia. They are not of your world. And be that as they are separate, we still watch and protect when it is our mission to."

"You're talking about guardian angels."

"Guardian angels," Marius weighed the words on his lips. "There are those. But they do not hold the power to protect you from every source and every will. When the Father first made man, He gifted you with free will. From that gift, all may use or abuse it how they best see fit. By their own purpose."

"So then what do you protect us from if it isn't the world or evil?"

"Those are two very different questions. The world is not the same as evil. Evil is its own matter. It is evasive as Florida storms, sometimes a hindrance on the horizon only to never come, or only to come when there was no warning to caution you. While the world is full of evil it does not make the world evil. Guardian angels know the matter of men and the matter of evil, and with that knowledge they know they do not mix well. So when one is full of evil it will be as if he is not the matter of man." Marius held a spread hand over his chest. "It will be as if he has changed the very essence of himself."

"Every person is blessed with an angel," Cato said, "and they can help a human only so much as the human allows. It is the person and only they who make the choice. Freedom of will is a sneaky commerce. With some faith and some strength, one can be invincible with an angel by one's side. However, we are all not made alike."

"So then some of us are already pre-destined to be damned. Since as you say some are created and aren't saved because their angel isn't the strongest. That isn't fair."

"Humans made a choice a long time ago to dictate what is fair and what *is*," Silas added, stepping beside Cato.

"We can't help what someone did thousands of years ago. Why should we be punished for what they did?" Jamie began raising her voice, allowing emotions to betray her. Despite the unbalance, they never rose to the bait. Their masks and their voices remained steady.

"You are. But all make mistakes," Silas said. "Thousands of years ago and today. However our Father is forgiving and merciful. He gives humans the chance to pay for their transgressions. He loves His children like any father or mother would."

"Not every child's so blessed to have the love from the parent . . ." Jamie bit her tongue.

"While His children may have worldly parents He is Father of all," Marius said. "He loves and can forgive all. But if a person does not accept this or does not ask, how can they be forgiven? They will have to live with the consequences of that simple truth."

For two weeks she'd heard the gargoyles stories of all that God had done throughout time; how all of the things he had allowed to have happened was because it was meant to, from miracle to tragedy. However believing in someone who wasn't there was absurd. As much time as she'd spent with them, to her, that truth never deterred.

Even though she had a rough start with what to believe—all of her life up to that point—she had to think about what they were saying and how it applied to her life. Why come alive for her? Should she continue to return even if by the end she would leave with the same beliefs as when she entered? They said it was the person's choice. It was her choice to not believe.

While she may not believe in their God, she did believe in them. Why was it so wrong to believe in what you see and how you feel in a moment? She admired how much they believed, even if she couldn't understand it completely.

Jamie focused on Trium. "Why don't you say his name?"

"His name?"

"God."

"No, we do not say His name. We are beneath nothing compared to Him."

"If you feel so inferior to him how can you fight for him? If he makes you feel less than nothing."

"Because, He is our Father," Trium said. "How humans rank loyalty is too foreign a concept compared to how we are loyal. He does not treat us differently. He loves us all one in the same. Your history dictates that you must fight for a belief, a cause, a debt. But our history, our divine culture of a belief does not dictate. It simply is that we are what we are, our very existence does not exist to do anything but. We are loyal, we are true, we are all for Him. When humans believe they can be even remotely equal to Him, it is the darkest form of blasphemy that could ever exist in any existence. It is darker than them worshipping another over Him, darker than not believing in Him, darker than imagining any existence without Him. We will crumble to dust if we even attempt to say His name. You cannot say His name with your tongue—your language, but He understands you just as if you spoke His name. We are but particles in the universe, and He is the universe. Try to imagine seeing the most expansive form from beyond your world, beyond your universe, beyond your imaginative thought of what the universe could be and even then, He is much more. When the time comes for all to see His glorious Light—for He is much more than a form—the universe will shake with unification. We will all feel, see, be one. And after, after all that is predicted has passed, we will all be in *paradisus*. For forever, past forever, Earth-time and All-time will cease to exist and transform into measure that is more sensible. And He will love us all. He will love us forever. Because when you love something, with a love incapable of words, forever is undeserving."

Jamie hadn't realized that in his homily she had become drawn into his words. How could something as important as a human life feel worthless then precious when all that was said was to demonstrate how miniscule she was?

Her voice gave out on her as it cracked. "But did Antonio know of you? Did he believe, too?"

"Our arrival premeditated the battle, however, we were not wakened until the destruction had already begun to stain the air. Much too late," Dominic said, watching the other gargoyles as if to make sure he didn't say the wrong thing.

"What if I'm too late because you wouldn't tell me now?" Jamie scrutinized the others when he didn't reply. "That's it? That's all you're going to tell me?"

"There will be a time to tell you of the battle. The time for it is not now."

This was the first time Jamie looked at them and didn't believe them. They were deliberately withholding the answers. Why? What reasons could there be? She should know more, be prepared, so when it came she wouldn't be as clueless as the rest of the world.

Jamie surrendered her hands to her hips. "At least tell me who's the battle going to be against. Whose army?"

"A name . . ." Trium meditated.

Cato stepped beside Trium, resting his hand on his shoulder, watching his friend closely. "One that we will not utter here, my brother."

"Is it a name I might have heard somewhere?" Jamie asked.

"No," Silas said gently. "The army is by one you will not have heard of at all. One who is a legend without the myth."

"Why not?"

Sidra looked weary as she spoke, walking to one of the columns with her wings shrunk. "Despair. Destruction. Arrived—too late." She wrapped her hands around the column, lowering her head to it and speaking in another language, one Jamie had heard only once before.

"What—what is she saying?" Jamie asked, not aware she said it loud enough to be answered.

"The tongue of the Song," said Marius.

"The song?"

"Our language. Our jubilation amongst gloom. The children of the Father will sing, and be joyful, for none that are in the Heavens will ever have worry or sadness in them. She is Singing."

Jamie thought the language enchanting, nothing compared to what she would consider singing. There was a delicacy in the melody of her stresses and her cadence, and the inflections in the unearthly lilts of her consonants and vowels. It closely mirrored the voices of the church chants.

"She draws away from the Darkness," Cato said.

The light from the day had dimmed to overcast clouds, however the sun still shone in between the pockets of open air and even now it created stark shadows from the columns and parapets.

Jamie's focus returned to the gargoyles. "Why?"

"Though it is past, it still lingers. The memory exists as patently as you before us. Unlike a scar, there still lies traces of pain."

Amadrius had walked to the parapets on the eastern wall and was looking over them before suddenly flapping his wings, creating a sudden gust to make the pleasant weather cater to an unknown's capricious, icy whim. Jamie and the gargoyles turned to Amadrius, who looked over his shoulder at them with trepidation in his white eyes, before he pushed off of the parapet and returned to the gargoyle aisle.

"What happened?" Jamie asked, unreasonably since Amadrius never spoke.

Cato spoke in the tongue of the Song, halting Amadrius in his return to his locality. There was no response, sharing silent thoughts and expressive stares with one another that everyone but Jamie understood as one by one the gargoyles began to move. Amadrius found his home and he crouched, opening his mouth wide and sticking out his tongue like the first time she saw him. Her eyes were not drawn away until long after he had solidified.

"Did he see something?" Jamie asked, turning from Amadrius to the others.

"The day grows late," Silas said, solidifying into a sitting position beside Amadrius. One hand rested on his knee as the other hand came to his chin, his eyes fading gray as he looked up in contemplation.

"It's not even five. You can't go yet!" Jamie's words fell on deaf ears as those across the aisle: Dominic, Sidra, then Marius solidified. Dominic crossed his arm, his mouth closing as he knelt to one knee. Marius glanced heavenward one final time, his fingers skimming its mirror opposite before they fell to his side, palms upward, his wings fanning around him like a frame as he dropped his gaze across the aisle to Silas. Sidra bent her knees, one hand settling across the opposite knee, her wings shielding her body, her head bent in submission.

Jamie's eyes desperately turned to Cato, who only glanced a final time to Trium before extending both finished and unfinished wings up, his breath from animation lost into air.

"Trium."

His mask was soft. The gargoyles had fled because of Amadrius' episode and Trium seemed to be the only one who was not perturbed. The kindness remained. There was no fear in Jamie because if he was not afraid, she didn't need to be either.

"Please. Don't leave me yet. Don't leave me in the dark."

"It is not darkness that I leave you." Jamie hadn't shared all that was on her mind and brought her lips together. Trium regarded her restraint with gentleness in his eyes. "If a gargoyle can come to life and ask a question, would you listen to what was asked of you?"

Once when Aiden was only a toddler, Jamie sought reassurance that her parents hadn't completely forgotten about her. Without saying a word, her father took one look at her expression of abandonment, picked her up, kissed her cheek. He led her away from her brother and her overbearing mother to the backyard swing, where he pushed her until it grew too dark to see. They laughed and were silent, Jamie at peace either way so long as they were together. He asked her if he could ask a question. Rising and falling. She said yes. Rising and falling. He asked if she thought her mother didn't love her. Rising and falling. Rising and falling. Rising and falling. She said she didn't know. Rising and falling. He said it was *demasiado imposible* for her mother not to love her. *She loves as much as me. More. Do you doubt me?* It was one of her earliest memories. It was the first time she felt like a child for not having enough trust in her mother to love her as much as her father. It was the question, the most important question, when Jamie the child became Jamie the sister, a growth of a lifetime in a single evening on a swing set. It wasn't that love was deterred or was waned by the affection for another. It wasn't that she wasn't important enough. She felt foolish for having to be reminded that they loved her.

"Yes."

"Will you return? After you have taken the steps? Do you have the faith and strength of that which is required, to return?"

The skin between her eyes folded in as her eyebrows came together, the softness of the afternoon air settling over her skin like the sun on a cloudless day at the beach.

While she was disappointed this was the end of her lesson, she smirked as if she were in on a secret no one else around her knew. "There's too much more to learn."

Trium shared a final glance with her before his shoulders slunk forward slightly, lifting just an inch as his knees bent, one foot stepping forward slightly. The tusks from his underbite separated from the upper lip as he exhaled his final breath, his mouth the source of the solidification process. It traveled down his neck and slid down the spine, meeting at the hinges of the wings and traveling up them until they stiffened in an open, light expanse. The arms lost their air as the fingers twitched for the last time. The legs and feet rooted into the ground.

It seemed to Jamie that they were becoming more physical in their attempts of evasion. The next time she saw them she knew she needed to be firm. The answers to her questions couldn't be withheld any longer behind excuses of her not being ready. Nothing could be so bad she couldn't handle it. After losing the most precious person in the world to her, she had mastered the ability to handle any doom-laden prophecies.

Curious as to what directed Amadrius' attention, she leaned over the parapet to look down the bell tower, finding nothing below. Discontent, she returned beside Trium, looking up his frame and wondering how he came to be. Yes, he was made, but how and why did he come to possess *this* statue? Why did the architects choose to build a church here?

Walking down the aisle of the gargoyles she glanced up a final time to Dominic, not used to seeing him so still and with an expression of regression. She had taken a step toward the stairwell door when she spotted the markings. She had forgotten she had seen them just a month before. Confident that he wouldn't mind, she quickly made her way up his leg and leaned over to the wing, pressing her face close to the markings as if there was less light to show. Her fingers passed over the letters: AG.

The sculptor perhaps, she thought. *If they won't tell me, I'll find someone who will.*

Aiden was sitting against the couch on the floor in the living room, simultaneously watching a show on TV as he scrolled down the web browser on his laptop. Rosario was in the kitchen on the phone discussing an upcoming regional manager visit at the bank. Jamie sat on the couch near Aiden and noticed him have no interest on the TV. Game shows and late night documentaries were treats. Something was wrong. She remembered what her mother said.

"Are you and mom talking again?" Jamie leaned over and rested her elbows on her knees, folding her hands together. "Mom said you were mad last night. What'd she do?"

Aiden barely shifted his eyes in her direction as he looked over the top of the laptop to the TV.

"Whatever she did," Jamie said. "I'm sure she didn't mean it." Still no response and she nudged his shoulder with two fingers. "Don't be mad at her for too long."

"You stay mad at her for as long as you like," he rebutted bitterly, refusing to look at her.

"Don't follow in my footsteps. You're not petty like me."

"Oh so you admit it? I can be petty. And hold a grudge. As the younger child I'm allowed such shortcomings."

Jamie gazed down to her hands. The reason she told him was because she knew her mom hated disappointing him. She hated ever being the bad guy in his eyes and even when he needed to be punished, it was always their dad who did it.

"I'm sure you won't think it's so bad in a week."

"How about you just mind your own business?"

Jamie's eyes widened as she stood up, her hands raised in surrender. "It's none of my business."

Jamie retreated to her room, then returned to pick up the backpack she left near the couch. When her back was to him, Aiden looked over to Jamie, his expression more sympathetic as he pressed his lips together, words caught trapped behind them wishing to come out.

By dinner Jamie saw her brother and mother had slowly made the steps to making up, accomplished enticingly by their mother as she made Aiden's favorite dish: brown rice and chicken with *tostones* and *Budin* for dessert. Rosario mentioned that she invited their uncle to dinner the following night, to which Jamie pretended she didn't hear to shadow the weariness she felt. What if her uncle exposed her? She couldn't decline the offer since her mother already left a message for him and she couldn't back out because what if her mother mentioned Jamie's frequent visits to the cathedral? No, she needed to speak with him before it happened.

That night she had another dream of the figure in shadows. He didn't walk down halls like the first time she saw him, but stood on a balcony and faced countless numbers of other shadows. It spoke in a language she didn't understand, in a volume loud enough it reached the far ends of the lands; elevated over the roars of the crowds. All in unison. All in a shared cry. Jamie stood beside the figure, as if she were his right-hand man, second-in-command, successor.

Before the roars ceased, the figure turned to her. She couldn't see his body, however she knew lied hidden beneath his hood was a glare intended for her. As real as pain, she felt a shiver run down her spine as she listened and heard his words echo in her mind. She didn't know what was said, but it was wrong. The fact was undeniable. And also this: deep down, she knew whatever the shadow had said, he was pleased.

15

Despite having a rough night, Jamie woke to the news her uncle wouldn't be making it to dinner. Acting less than pleased, she departed on her bike in the direction of the town library. She'd hoped to strike some luck discovering more about the origins of the cathedral and the gargoyles.

Jamie wandered through public records, unsure how to properly search. It might be easier to start from the cathedral plans and go from there, so she ran her finger down the spines. Elementary, but it helped her to remember which titles she'd read.

The city archives offered everything from the founding of Shore to the present. It suddenly hit her it was about to be an incredibly tedious day. There was so much she had to look through that when she took her first break nearly an hour later, she wondered if perhaps she should start searching from the little that she knew.

The initials on Dominic's wing had the letters AG. A name. G must have been the surname. After an hour she found something with construction, but it was Gajos and he was the architect for the city hall. More time passed and she found an RG, but the person was affiliated with the cathedral and not the gargoyles themselves. If anything, it was a step in the right direction.

After three hours of going back and forth and revisiting documents she had briefly scanned over, she had begun to become discouraged. It was a long shot finding anything about the sculptor, but simply searching on the internet for gargoyles on a cathedral over two hundred years old was more improbable.

Her stomach began to growl and she compromised with it, promising to leave soon.

The voice on the speaker suddenly came on. "Because of an alert on the tropical storm Ophelia, the library will be closing in ten minutes." The person handling the mic dropped it loudly, causing Jamie to jump. She checked her phone. Almost four. It felt like a wasted journey.

A tall librarian in her thirties was restocking the shelves nearby and glanced over her glasses at Jamie. "Do you need help finding something before we close?"

Jamie sighed. "I was looking for a name, but all I have are the initials."

Bringing her lips together and bunching them to one side, the clerk stood up. "Um." She reached on her tiptoes to place a book on the top shelf. "Do you know what the initials are for?"

"It has to do with St. Luke's." Jamie began to gather up the papers and folders she had scattered on the table.

"Well, if it has to do with something specifically inside the church we won't have any records on it. But if it has to do with the construction or designs or plans—" She reached another book on the top shelf. "You might want to check the ledgers dating back to its development. Check late 1700s. I'm not sure of the designer or architects of the church but I'm sure it's documented somewhere in them. And when you find out a name you should go over to the cathedral and ask to see their records."

"Do you think they would? I thought that sort of thing would be closed to the public?"

"Is this for a school project?" After finding a number on the shelf, she looked over to Jamie.

"Um, not exactly. Just a sort of personal project I'm working on."

"Well it wouldn't hurt to ask. I'm sure if you say it's for something important they wouldn't mind."

Asking the church came with risks that she'd rather avoid. However the only way she would learn anything would be through any other means than the easiest. If only the gargoyles would just tell her what she wanted to know, she wouldn't need to go through all this hassle. Out of spite she felt maybe they were doing this as some sort of test, to see if she was worthy to be told. And even if she did know, what could she possibly do? Tell the world? No, too hysterical. Tell the local news stations? Would anyone believe her if she began spinning tall tales of the statues atop the cathedral bell tower?

Unsure if all of this would be worth it, she jumped on her bike and headed toward the cathedral in hope that she'd be able to research at least a little before it became too dark.

Of all the visits she'd made to the cathedral, this ranked first above all of her most clandestine drop-ins. Never before had anyone tried so hard to avoid detection by omniscient supreme beings under the very roof of their station. What kept her head from possible discovery was that this was meant to happen. She wasn't there for the gargoyles; she was inadvertently defying their intentions of her knowing the truth from when *they* deemed was the right time—whatever truth they were so willingly insisting on keeping from her. If she already knew of a battle, what worse was there to know?

Upon entering through the doors she came upon a member of the clergy and asked for Edgar. There were two reasons she didn't ask for her uncle. One, his brief occupancy at the church gave her doubt he'd have any authority accessing private records. Second, she still didn't want to see him.

When she spotted Edgar walking from one of the passageways, she noticed the same look of urgency he had the last time she saw him.

"Jamie, wonderful to see you dear. I'm sure your mother told you your uncle was unable to make it—"

"She told me." He raised an eyebrow and listened. "I'm actually here for another reason."

"Yes, what's that?"

Jamie rocked from one foot to another. "I was wondering if I'd be able to see the records of the church."

"Records?" He glanced to the side as if the answer lied elsewhere. "What for?"

"The records you'd have on the construction. You do have them don't you?"

"Yes we do but—"

Jamie nodded, capitulating. "I'm not allowed to see them." No one ever says "but" that leads to an answer you want to hear.

"No no. You may it's just we have a protocol, a matter of doing things when those outside of the church wish to review our documents. We're rather strict chaperones, wishing to keep things as preserved and organized as possible. Furthermore, you'll need a member of the clergy. Unfortunately the congregation and myself are needed at the present so there will be no member to supervise you."

Already feeling energized by the opportunity for free range on her search, she smiled and waved a hand modestly. "I'll keep everything in order so it won't look like anybody was there, I promise."

Edgar was still unconvinced and he eyed the direction he meant to go.

"If all of you are busy," Jamie said smoothly, "I know someone who'll be watching me and making sure I keep to my word." Edgar tried to think of who she was thinking of and after coming up blank looked over to her. She emphasized her eyes upward, holding them a moment before landing on him again. He studied her for a moment, then nodded accordingly.

"Very well. We are never truly alone. Come, I will show you quickly."

Edgar took her down many passageways until they came to the church's library. He showed her where all the fitting records were kept and departed after a hesitant lingering glance, followed swiftly by a distressed look of urgency. Not eager to land him in trouble or to lie if anyone asked, she shrugged off her jacket and began browsing immediately.

She began as she had in Shore's public library, looking for a section where they organized the documents by name. Everything was similarly organized like in the library, only the lighting was darker and the source of it were lanterns spread on top of desks, stools, and book stacks across the room. She found the shelf where the names with G were stacked and ran her finger over the binder spines.

"Antonio, Antonio. Where are you?" The pages flipped quickly as she scanned the names. Folder after folder she searched, setting everything in the place she found it before moving on to the next one. Going back and forth folder after folder was time-consuming, but it was to make sure she put everything in its proper place. People saw Edgar lead her there and she didn't want to risk getting him into trouble.

In one of the first folders she read over the name Ricardo Gallo and learned he was one of the prime attributors to the designs of the cathedral. Back in the library she saw the initials RG, but then there was another architect: Roberto Antonio González. He must have been one of the partners with Ricardo. Though the Antonio seemed coincidental, she wasn't going to spend any more time digging around for RG when she still needed to find AG.

It wasn't until she began to notice that while the area was for the surname G, it was organized not by last name but profession. She needed to pass the folders on the architects, the designers, the glassmakers, the laborers, the painters, the patrons, the plumbers, the roofers, the sanders, the smiths, the stonemasons. No—stonemasons were two professions too far. Picking up the folder on the sculptors she handled the fragile ledgers assiduously. They listed the names and the commissions they were assigned to. She scanned down the list searching for Antonio and all names with the initials AG. She stopped at several names but they were commissioned for other projects like a handful of the statues in the outer courtyard or the fountain in the back gardens.

She flipped the last page over and found it blank.

Defeated, she sat back in her chair. That couldn't be it. She wouldn't accept it.

She went over all the names again. Maybe before she'd been too anxious and accidentally read over it. There were nearly a hundred names for sculptors alone. But reaching the final name only made her relive that defeat once more.

Why would the sculptor responsible not be listed? Or maybe they were under another name and AG was just a pseudonym so they wouldn't get in trouble for marking the statues. Why put her on this hunt if she was going to end up at a dead end? Maybe the gargoyles lied about his name so if she did snoop on her own she wouldn't get anywhere.

But, why lie?

The papers returned to their respective folder and she walked back to the shelf. Just as she was about to put it back she noticed a small notebook in the back. Reaching past the books, she took out the booklet and opened to the first page. The writing was in cursive and barely legible, but it was in English. In almost every page there was a date with a small inscription. Each page consisted of one day and the entries began from 1652 to 1738. There was no name in the front or back cover, so whose it belonged to would remain a mystery for now.

Just as soon as she flipped to read the entry she heard footsteps approaching from down the hall. Without a moment to think, she quickly slipped it under her arm and returned to the table with her belongings. She put her jacket on and hid the notebook under some folders in her backpack. She grabbed the candle and right as she reached the doorway, so did Elias.

Of all people, she thought. *Are there no other people in this church? I see this guy more than my own uncle.*

"I saw a light," he said, eyeing the candle for a moment.

"I was borrowing it."

"In here? What for?"

"I—" She sighed, pointing with her thumb into the room behind her. "Was just checking the library out. I've been here so many times I wanted to see what there was." That was the most ridiculous excuse in the world and she did her best to conceal the lie from exposing her.

Elias had never taken kindly to her presence and didn't disappoint her now, however there was a glint in his eyes that second-guessed her.

"Those outside of the church are not allowed to browse the library's selections without a chaperone."

"Edgar trusts me enough."

The impassiveness in his face dissolved to a hardening intolerance. She also noticed that as she switched the candle from one hand to the other, that he bore a bruise around his eye, extending toward the temple. She held her breath and studied it, then quickly focused back on his eyes.

"Edgar was unwarranted." The eyes looked down to her bag and while already holding her breath, she stiffened. "I will need to check your bag."

"What for!" She scoffed. "I didn't take anything." She let the words come out of her mouth so easily she would've fooled herself.

"As you've come to an isolated section of the church in a room that is otherwise locked and restricted to outsiders, I find that my request is not unmerited nor gratuitous. The rules are placed and while Edgar may overlook them, I will not. Had he been with you there would be no issue. Or if you had waited for him to return, then you would not feel disinclined."

"Listen, I didn't sign some contract stepping through the threshold. This is my personal property and I don't give you permission to look through it."

"And you weren't given permission to look through the church library."

"I told you Edgar did."

"His permission does not supersede the rules."

"Well then take it up with him. I'm going home."

"If there is nothing to hide then you will be on your way shortly. Now show me what you have in your bag."

Jamie felt her lip curl slightly and pulled her backpack off her shoulder for show. Perhaps if he was convinced enough he might back off. She unzipped the bag, taking out the copy of *Pygmalion* she had since the week before and glared at him for a moment before placing it under her arm. She took out a school folder, then put it under her arm. She had three more folders and would try and buy time taking out each one at a time, but if he recognized the book, then there was no talking her way out. She'd probably be banned from returning to the church. And since this guy had it out for her, he might just call the police and charge her with attempted robbery.

The last folder was the only wall hiding the small notebook and her fingers were already reaching inside the backpack when footsteps echoed from down the hall.

"Elias, how thoughtful of you to keep Jamie company." Edgar approached as Jamie stuffed the book and folders under her arm back in the backpack. Elias turned over his shoulder to Edgar.

"I was not. In fact I was informing her of the rules."

Edgar waved his hand. "I'm afraid she made quite an argument."

"Convincing rebutter or no, we have rules and they specify no person that is not a member of the clergy may wander the library selections without an escort—"

"Dear man! Enough with the rules. For a man of faith you have very little in those outside of the church."

Elias leered at Edgar and faced him straight on. "*Someone* needs to follow them."

There was definitely something going on between them and Jamie didn't want to involve herself further. She feared getting caught in the crossfire of two aging disciples that would harbor her there for another hour. Tossing the backpack strap over her shoulder, she moved to the side.

"I hear you. Boy your message has been heard! From now on I'll come with a clergyman."

Edgar seemed as eager to get away from Elias as much as Jamie, directing his attention back to her. "Did you find what you were looking for?"

She nodded, handing the candle to Edgar as she took a step away.

"We're not done searching your backpack," Elias said after her.

Jamie stopped and turned back. "There was only a folder left."

"What is this? You were searching her backpack too? When did we become airport security, Elias?" He looked to Edgar and opened his mouth, however Edgar spoke first. "Go on, Jamie. I apologize on *the church's* behalf."

Not giving Elias a chance to refute she quickly ran down the hallway and exited the church.

It was hard for her to believe she took the notebook and got away without getting caught. She wasn't stealing, only temporarily borrowing until she read what was inside. She'd return it as soon as she had. Leaving it behind would've been risky. She couldn't have gone back to the library with Edgar or someone else watching. She'd just read it and see if it had anything related to AG and if not she'd return it back soon.

Stealing from a church. She slapped her forehead. That had to be a triple sin. She hoped she wouldn't go to hell for it.

Returning home she found her mother and brother preparing dinner in the kitchen. After a brief acknowledgment she retreated to her room. She closed the door and took out the notebook, studying the text under better lighting. Based off of the writing she guessed the writer to be a male. Not many women had any involvement in construction back then and if they did it would have to have been the rare exception. It wasn't the norm back then; it was hardly the norm now. She eventually came upon an entry that seemed to be getting her somewhere.

May 06, 1652

The Pope has commissioned nothing. Tasteless, uncultured swine. He is too busy with pleasure of secular influence. I must spend my day drinking to pass the time. My dream last night inspired me.

June 03, 1652

The stones have arrived. I begin my work. My first messenger has begun to take form. I will first shape his torso, his legs, his head, his wings.

July 26, 1652

I have finished the body and the wings but the face is unclear. I cannot see it. I fear he will see me when I am done.

December 27, 1652

These past months have been long. I could not sleep and when I did I have been tormented. Evil shrieks in the night slowly crawl into my room and taunt me. They have taunted me every night. I have not been able to write for months because they always come. It is today when I have finally finished his face. Such terror will protect me. He is my guardian angel. He triumphs over evil. That is what I will call him. Trionfante.

This had to have been the sculptor for the gargoyles, Antonio. And the statue, Trium. He spoke of the demons like the one she had dreamt of. What happened to him?

January 18, 1653

I have begun my second guardian. My dreams tell me there are six more to fight. Six to be like Trionfante. In my dreams, only dreams, I am safe.

March 05, 1653

I have begun on his face. He is marvelous. In my dreams I hear him. Cato. Trionfante and Cato wait for their brother warriors to be born.

May 25, 1653

Sleep evades me. I have begun the third warrior. But my guardians of the night are nowhere to be found. The forms of evil are the only ones who find me.

October 12, 1653

I am sorry my friend. I have only seen demons for months now and have cursed you. Cursed you like they have me. You will be Amadrius. You will be God's love. Your name will not curse you like I have. This is the only gift I can give you.

Poor Amadrius. Antonio only saw evil at night so he brought those nightmares with him into the light. He made a gargoyle, purposed as a guardian, cursed as a monster. The irony drew a cruel cough out of her. She read through the rest of the entries until the day he completed his last gargoyle. Marius and Silas were made next with pleasanter faces in the following year, followed last by Sidra and Dominic in 1655. There were a couple pages left but Jamie reflected on what she had read so far.

Antonio was paranoid. Almost every entry acknowledged their presence or lack of it. But most of all he was frightened without the gargoyles. It started from a dream. That answered why he made them. Now the question became why did they come to Earth in 1652? Why did they reveal themselves in his dreams?

Aiden called Jamie to dinner and while she sat at the table, her dinner was spent in silence. Aiden complained there were still three weeks left of school until winter break started. Rosario mentioned how year-end was going to overload her on work and as she finished she looked over to Jamie, expecting her to complain about school or work.

"You mentioned you were going to the library," Rosario said. "You haven't been there in years. What made you want to go all of a sudden?"

"Research," Jamie responded.

"I wouldn't have expected to see you go to the books. Doesn't everyone use the internet now for projects?"

Aiden rested his cheek on his fist. "My teacher wants us to use only books as sources for our next English paper."

"Mr. Penn? Really? Isn't he your favorite teacher?" Rosario said.

"He may be young but he has the soul of an eighty-year-old. Doesn't believe in technology. He considers it kind that he allows his students to type our reports."

Jamie listened as Aiden continued to complain then compliment his favorite teacher. Eventually she retreated to her room and opened the last pages of the notebook. The handwriting shifted, acknowledging it as someone else's. The dates also were much later, realistically unable to be by the same person. She read over the beginning entries, noticing some distinctions that made the author a different type of artist. She also surmised him to be the designer of the cathedral, in some way related to Antonio. Unsure of what the word *nonno* meant, she made a mental note to search it later.

March 13, 1725

Construction of the church has begun. Roberto and I designed the most glorious cathedral in the west. Nonno's legacies will be brought in the next months. Once they arrive and the church is complete, the eastern and western world will all know that nonno was not crazy.

So this person was related to the sculptor. He said "Roberto and I." This must be the other designer Ricardo.

October 3, 1725

The statues are here. They will be the guardians of the cathedral. They will face the west, south, and north. As I observed the workers unload them I felt an unnatural chill in the wind. The dark clouds gathered as if in meeting. The whispers of old men were silenced by the statues magnificence. This is what Nonno would have wanted. He wanted them to protect the weak, to guide them in the right way.

July 28, 1728

The days are longer. The sun is hotter. The men are weaker. The statues have been brought to the courtyard where they have yet to be placed on the cathedral. No men will touch them.

August 17, 1728

    We have run out of funds. The construction has stopped. The statues remain in the outer courtyard. They are waiting.

January 19, 1733

    Almost five years and six months since the construction of the church abruptly stopped. Plans to begin again soon.

Jamie read over the next entries, summaries over the next several years stating the progress of the construction. It wasn't until the last two entries did she begin to think that this person had anything more to do with the statues.

April 2, 1738

    The cathedral is finished. It towers over the trees. It can be seen from the ocean not a mile to the east. The final task is to set the gargoyles. But in my heart, I'm beginning to feel there is more to what Nonno told me about them. What the workers have whispered. I look at their faces. They are but masks. This not what they really are. They are more.

April 4, 1738

    I woke from my dream with a fear in my heart. A fear we all should fear. Nonno spoke of these gargoyles like they were his family. And last night they spoke to me. They said to prepare for a battle. A battle that would be worse than what I could ever imagine. They instructed to be left at the top of the bell tower until the messenger comes. When the partner would come, they told me not. Who knows when men will overcome their fears and cast them upon the cathedral's tower? In my heart I fear for my family. I fear for the townspeople who live here. But Nonno had faith in the gargoyles. I will have faith in them. I shall remain until I know that the partner comes and the guardians protect the people. Perhaps this was my purpose. May God be with all.

        -RG

A battle worse than he could imagine? Those were the same words the gargoyles told her. They said this centuries ago and the battle never happened. Why should she prepare for something that would probably never come?

Unlike RG, she wasn't going to wait the rest of her life.

16

The steps echoed in the dark hallway. There was one set of steps, two. The first set was firm. They belonged to one who commanded mighty forces, who could shake the ground with their voice. The second set of steps was light, belonging to one without power anywhere near as great as the first's.

However, the first steps, though ground-shaking, were quick. Whoever they belonged to—was late.

As they approached the end of the hall, even before they turned the corner to the high-beamed doors, shouts could be heard. They were tumultuous and obstreperous; a clear sign of an argument between acquaintances of long past a time. The topic at hand was not between two but disputed between many.

The massive doors of the turbulent room flew open as if a great wind rushed through them.

The footsteps of the dark hallway were of the robed creature. Though his hood was up, it was undeniably the creature as the second steps belonged to the robed demon. Acario would not submit so willingly to any other in this manner. They stood at the entrance of the large room, along the walls lesser demon Saplings stood at posts every few feet from each other like guards in a palace. At the center housed a long table. Surrounding it were seven large clouds of smoke and at the far end, one prodigious, repulsive, scarred demon. The dispute was solely between the smoke figures. The demon at the end of the table had its feet propped on it and was leaning back in its chair. Its face was amused as it watched the smoke figures argue, fiddling with something in its hand. Its expression reflected pleasure of watching someone else receive the blame for trouble they created.

"Apologies for my tardiness. I was"—the creature briefly glared at the demon beside him—"misinformed."

The closest smoke figure to the creature turned to him. Though there was no face, Erus knew where the front was. "Who gives a damn for your delay! Where is it?"

"Why should you be the one to know first?" proclaimed a smoke figure.

"Why must we always argue?" said a smoke figure calmly, the only placid one of the seven figures.

"My brothers, it is forthcoming," Erus said. "Patience is a gift. You would not wish for the storm to come early and all our waiting to have been in vain."

The first smoke figure to speak thrashed about and spat out gobs of ink and sludge before settling down to a state more comprehensible. "Damn your riddles. Tell us where it is!"

Another smoke figure approached Erus, raising him high above the ground. Erus lifted the eyebrows as if they were there and calmly asked, "Must we always default to violence?"

"It's never failed me before," threatened the smoke figure. Nevertheless, it set Erus down.

"We have waited and waited, doing what is demanded of us like we were meant to, and here you rule, as if by birthright. Relaxing, as if on vacation!" accused another smoke figure.

Erus was unfamiliar with the term, his nose twitching. "Clearly your vernacular has become one with the mortals, brother." Almost in cruel jest, Erus faced him tilting his head to one side. "What is vacation?"

The smoke enflamed to a boisterous hue of burnt orange. "Patronize me further and I'll send you there permanently you pretentious fool!"

The scarred demon at the end of the table chuckled.

"Shall we continue on this infinite loop of who bears the most vice or will be reach the point of this meeting?" sighed the smoke with the smallest mass at the palaver.

" My brother, I do not take joy displacing you from your tasks and wasting your time," Erus said. "Or any from the rest of you . . ." And had the smoke figures eyes, they would have rolled them. "But alas, we come to it. Follow me." The robed creature walked past the party surrounding the table to the balcony at the far end of the dusky chamber.

The smoke figures followed, cursing at each other and at their tardied host. Erus ignored them for more his sake than theirs and pointed out beyond the plains. The flames of the horizon were hazy, yet farther than what the common eye could see nestled a Darkness. It rumbled like a storm, but did not move, remaining a distant shadow.

"*There* it is my brothers."

"Marvelous," proclaimed one smoke figure.

The robed creature was content but held its grimace.

"What are you waiting for?" demanded a smoke figure, the one who had lifted Erus "Summon it."

"What? Do you take me for a fool?" A rhetorical question, he continued before any could answer. "I have not gotten everything in order. There are whispers of an imbalance which I must clean up, though they do not in any way disrupt nor hinder any of my plans. Curses of spite if I'm an angel! But I promise you my brothers, the time is nigh, your shackles will be demolished and all our freedoms restored."

"Have you truly considered all the components of your plan?" asked the smoke which seemed to struggle to keep altogether. There were no winds on the high balcony of the fortress but there were gusts of heat and currents, products of the flames on the far reaches of the lands. "What if something were to wrong? Or if something comes along you hadn't considered after the bodies are slain and the skies are putrid with triumph?"

Erus didn't consider it a possibility. "Nothing will."

"You have failed before. You did not heed caution then and look where it's landed you."

Reminders of his chaotic failure were infrequent at best, though Erus refused to squander any ill-will on one of his few allies. He needed all of them, even the unwilling Rephastion. Even if he did nothing, merely his presence would accumulate masses in support behind him. Erus grasped his hands behind him. "A slap on the hand. Tier made a ruckus but Paxiphen lacked notice anything had occurred . . ."

"And what of the Grand Master?"

Erus curled the side of his lip as if he wanted to smile, but couldn't. "Oh, the Grand Master merely sent me back to the hell hole I was in before. Hardly a punishment."

"There are other variables to consider," said one of the figures of smoke beside Erus. "Our ears hear more than yours, brother. Rumors of a Weapon, on Earth."

Erus faced the smoke, concentrating on the source of the voice. "I hope, brother, you are not humoring me in fools' tales."

"Rumors are rumors," rebutted the smoke easily.

"What rumors?" Erus contested, inhaling a breath to keep from exploding. "Who could've said it that you, my damning Avarice, would deem it reliable enough to believe, let alone communicate to me."

"Darling Erus, mistake not that because you sit on a throne in your fortress of dust and smoke and illusion of power that you are *above* us."

Erus risked enraging them. "It is you who comes and goes as couriers."

"If I recall," said the belligerent smoke figure more calmly, "it is my brothers and I who have created the portals and possess the power to use them. It is my brothers and I who have been leading the souls here to you."

"Come now," Erus said with a light heart, as the absentminded smoke figure neglected the fact Erus created a portal on his own before his last failure. It extracted every drop of power from him. He had to conceal his weakness for centuries using bombast and threats. "You mustn't take all the credit."

The smoke figure suddenly swallowed him whole as Erus stood still, allowing the smoke to freeze him then tear him apart. However, the smoke did not give way. While skin may have torn, bone collapse, his form returned to its natural state. When the smoke had enough, it reversed the track it took when swallowing him. It hovered above him and waited. Erus did not flick off the remains of smoke off of his face but simply blinked.

"Have you depleted your fun? Remember, nothing changes for you if you make an enemy of me."

"If anything goes wrong," said a smoke on the far side behind Erus, "there are worse enemies than us to worry for. There are things worse than hell on earth."

"I know," Erus gritted through his teeth. "It is precisely why I haven't given up, *failure*"—Erus flashed his eyes at the smoke who swallowed him—"or not. Why I'm giving you a chance to escape this hell I've endured for epochs. So disregard your rumors on Earth. Nothing is true there. All you should fear is here with me, and I assure you there is nothing to indulge in fantasy here."

"If you are sure. You have nothing to fear if what you say is true. But if it is not, I promise you, you will regret this. You will regret screwing us."

Erus sighed. "Always intent on revenge?"

"Always intent on being an ass?"

"An ass? My brother, I do believe you require recess from your duties. The mortal cabinet of insults still pools on your tongue."

"It is a vulgar term in the human tongue. Ah—never mind! If you are to become more acquainted with mortals you will have to learn of their tongue and of their minds."

"But I have no plan to," Erus said calmly. He turned away from them and walked next to the scarred demon. "In fact, I have someone else in mind."

The supercilious smile the silent demon haughtily flaunted the entirety of the evening suddenly became lost.

17

That was when it started. Nightmares slipping into her conscious state. Class after class she was driven to distraction, unable to focus on the teacher or the students with the hazy images lying behind lethargic eyelids. The only calm she could find was in the yanking of her hair. Pinching her skin. Biting her tongue.

Pain was the only neutralizer.

There was an image inside St. Luke's; a warm tint blanketed the silver columns soon hidden under shadow under the shoulder of the vault ceiling. The rose window shone in a festive kaleidoscope of blues and purples, overall mirroring the festive December season. It was toasty inside, sheltering those from the fierce winter chills outside. The yellow lights from the lanterns were frozen erupted starbursts, their rays extending farther and farther from their cores, an infinite white that blinded while capturing the eye. Such a light too bright for a lantern.

She had been staring at the screen when the seat beside her filled. It was slow, but her attention returned to the present.

"Your buddy's not here today."

What buddy? she thought, unable to recognize the voice. Alric smiled evasively as he logged onto the computer.

"Do you mean Minjae?" Jamie asked.

Alric nodded and sighed, crossing his arms over his chest. "He's sick. He won't be here all week."

Jamie looked back to the screen. "Why are you telling me?"

"Thought you'd like the company."

Alric rarely spoke to her. He was always fooling around and procrastinating with his friends. There was something off when someone from a different group of people suddenly wanted to converse with you. If she hadn't been having headaches all day she would've been less suspicious. Usually in class she ignored how incompetent and disruptive he was, but now it was nettlesome. As if the bug she'd ignored that had been flying around her ear suddenly began to land, crawl in, echoing its helicopter wings toward the eardrum until the vibrations became deafening white noise.

"You're usually on your own," he said, flicking his head toward her for a moment of attention, then returning his focus to the computer again. "You don't really hang out with anyone you don't know, do you?" This inquiry was becoming personal. What was this? "How well do you know Minjae?"

Jamie didn't know Minjae well. She only knew *of* him. Ironic since they were closer in age. She had a better relationship with his brother, if she could even call it a relationship. She'd regard her acquaintanceship with his older brother as tenuous. The younger was merely an acquaintance of an acquaintance. They've shared classes occasionally and obviously she saw him a lot at Shore's Rock Gym, but she didn't *know* him.

"I know his brother."

Alric waited for her to continue and when she didn't he spoke for her. "He's a good guy."

There was an odd sense of protectiveness over him that made the air within the room suddenly rigid.

"Is there something, Alric?"

"A good kid's a good kid, and not likely to change. But some time or other all the innocence we give to kids when they grow suddenly fades. We don't know if it's a birthday or an accident or some other event. It's almost metamorphic."

Jamie kept her mouth shut. He wasn't humoring her out of boredom.

"If someone was guilty of something, should the person they were guilty against have the right to know? I do."

"I think if someone's beating around the bush this long it's because they're trying to drive me into a state of aggravation. What do you want to share so badly?"

Almost as if he were an overprotective brother, he softened his expression. "You shouldn't trust him. Don't you think it's weird he's talking to you all of a sudden? He's known you for years. He's always had the opportunity. Even after your dad's accident he never did. So why now?"

It hadn't bothered her before because there hadn't been a reason to. People became friends after being acquaintances for years. There was no phenomenon in that. What was weird was being asked to go on a road trip with people she'd only spoken to professionally. It was weird talking to Alric as if they were gossiping about the biggest scandal on campus. It was weird that her uncle had moved to Shore and made attempts to reconnect with her family *now*.

Jamie studied Alric who by now was more invested in the conversation gone amiss. Had he been polite and spoken casually with her, even in an off day like today, she might've been content. But this fishing around, talking so brazenly when Minjae was sick was deceptive. He was revealing something she'd never realized before.

"You're good friends with Emily," she said. A flicker of surprise passed over his face and she nodded. "I don't know what beef you have with him but I don't know him well enough to gossip, especially when he's absent."

Suddenly, a moment of honesty satisfied him. "He's been distracted."

"What goes on between them isn't my business."

In an abject voice, he stared at her and said, "Why should he pay attention to you?"

Her teeth ground together as she stared back just as coldly. "What? Are you her guard dog?"

"That's weak."

"Oh like I care how belittling my insults are. Listen, let's just mind our own business shall we? Does Emily even know how gallant you're being? She seems nice. I'd like to think no."

The tension between them was now equal in acrimony. When she felt she'd said enough to appease him to leave, he smiled blankly. Such a shift in mood unsettled her and she gulped. He studied between her eyes, the smile unshackling itself from any chains of insult, preparing to cast them elsewhere.

"And here I thought you were talking 'cause you knew. Fine. If you won't acknowledge it I'll enlighten you. Minjae likes you."

No response was as appropriate than when she immediately scoffed in retort. "Is that your plan? Try to wedge an innocent third party in between them, dragging someone unaffiliated into a fight they have no interest in joining?"

"I'd hardly call you innocent. Honestly I think you've known all along."

Jamie turned to the computer with her jaw clenched, her palm pressed hard against the mouse as she unabatedly moved it across the pad. "Take your bullshit with you. I'm not listening anymore."

"Whether you believe it or not it's true. Everyone's been hush about it long enough. I just hope people move on from it now 'cause honestly it's been more annoying having to watch you act all ignorant. You can't use your dad's death as excuse anymore."

Her nostrils flared, but she refused to rise to the bait. He'd had enough of their conversation too, shoving his chair and leaving. The whole conversation had distracted her from the throbbing in her head, but it returned once she began to calm down again. Unable to ignore it, she pressed the palm of her hand into her temple, staring at the opened image. The sunbursts of light seemed brighter now. She clenched her teeth and shut her eyes, willing the class to finish soon.

Jamie searched from the kitchen medicine cabinet to the mirror cabinet in her mother's bathroom and couldn't find any aspirin or ibuprofen, which made her slam every door she passed through. Work wouldn't be skipped—what would sitting at home but nothing but her nightmares for company do her, so she was more or less sour to everyone who spoke to her. Noel and Era caught onto her bad mood but sensed since it happened so rarely, it was something outside of her control. They kept her to deal with as few people as possible for the rest of the day, which only made her more frustrated as that meant more time alone, and the more she was alone the more she would think back on her nightmare, and how childishly fearful she became just thinking about it. Dreams weren't meant to be real and they shouldn't be so vivid this far into the day. Most forgot their dreams minutes after waking up. But the hours she spent watching the clouds of smoke . . .

"I'm going to the store for medicine," she said aloud, stepping back into the kitchen.

"You still have your migraine?" Her mother shifted in her direction but kept an arm out toward the pot on the stove, continuing to mix the shrimp stew.

"I didn't go to the store because I thought we had some here," Jamie said bitterly.

"I can go get it for you. It'll be faster if I drive than if you bike. You just need to finish the soup."

"We all know I'm more competent at cooking," Aiden said, standing up from the table, eager for the dinner to be finished. Rosario tilted her head and he shrugged. "Well I am."

"Maybe fresh air will help. I've been inside a building all day." Jamie went to the table and picked up her sweater. The cool air of the evening would help, however, being alone wouldn't. Walking alone at night knowing nightmares aren't real seems easy when you're in the comfort of your own home. She needed something to distract her, even if it would hurt to think during the present. She glanced over to Aiden who had returned beside the table. "Do you mind keeping me company?"

Aiden studied her and wondered why, however he didn't share a skeptical glance like he usually would have. He reached for his sweater.

How he simply accepted the request made her hesitate. "Really? You don't mind missing Jeopardy?"

Now he rolled his eyes. "Do you want me to come or not?"

Jamie looked to their mother who only watched them warily before jutting her chin out the door. "Be quick. Victor and Riley will be here soon. I don't want to make them wait."

"You can start without us," Jamie said.

"I wouldn't if either one of you wasn't here," she said with conviction, daring Jamie to challenge the validity of it.

The closest pharmacy was a fifteen minute walk. This night could make it ten. The temperature was in the high sixties, perfect to watch the stars on a clear night like this one.

"Why'd you want me to come with you?"

Jamie admired a house been decorated with Christmas lights. The month had barely begun and people already had sleigh bells ringing from jovial automated Santa sleighs and blinking lights around reindeer figures. She didn't understand the hype of the season as she answered him. "Why'd you agree?"

He shrugged, not willing to audibly reply, inducing Jamie to see why. She'd seen that expression before when their mother had hidden the fact she was throwing him a surprise birthday party one year. He knew something was going on but couldn't predict what she was planning. He was grumpy all day until the party itself in the mid-afternoon.

"Are you still mad at mom from last Friday? What'd she do?"

He pressed his lips together and focused on his feet, keeping silent. Since she knew she wouldn't get an answer out of him if he didn't want to speak, she tried to get him talking about anything. The migraine contracted against her skull.

"How was your field trip? Did you learn a lot?"

"Nothing really surprised me." Jamie noted a smirk on his lips before he continued. "Did you know shoe insoles were first designed for astronauts?"

"Didn't you?" Jamie said, pressing her palm to her temple.

"What about memory foam?"

"Come on. Tell me something new."

"Solar energy?"

She knew now he was teasing her and she bumped him with her hip.

"I know you're smarter than me and all, but I'm not *that* dumb."

"The Soaper Soaker?"

"The kids toy from before the millennium? Aren't you too young to know what that is?"

"What are you talking about they just came out with a new model a couple of years ago. And if anything *you* shouldn't know what it is."

"I remember a childhood that involved going outside and playing with the neighbor's kids."

"Clearly ages ago. You have no friends."

Jamie bit her tongue and looked forward. They had reached the edge of the neighborhood and were waiting to cross the street. Aiden looked up at her and grimaced.

"I'm sorry. I didn't mean it."

"You're right. I have no friends. Boo hoo me." She caught his eye and then smirked as he studied her, bumping him again. "I don't care. I'm empty inside anyways. What do I have to offer besides sarcasm and a resting bitch face?"

"You're not empty."

"I feel faded. Like I'm just the lingering traces of dad. That for me, every moment, is just a matter of time."

"There's more to you."

"I'm not smart like you. Motivated. I'm rather a poor influence on you Aiden. Aren't you embarrassed to have a sister like me? Don't answer that." They were crossing the road when she noticed Aiden had his arm hovering around her, as if guiding her across the street, though didn't remark on it. "Anyways, I don't really see what I'll do in the future. I don't know what I want to major in. All I know is if there's a college for me, it's far away."

"Why far?"

Far so she wouldn't have to be reminded how Shore doesn't offer anything. Yes she had family and that should be enough, but it mostly just reminded her of a childhood that would only ever remain a colorful memory in a bleak reality. Ever since her father died she went through each day with dread instead of hope for something unexpected and wonderful to happen. Wonderful in an act of kindness or as simple as a stranger's smile. One day when she did receive a token of kindness from a stranger, it did little to alleviate the emptiness within her. Her life seemed to be mechanical. The mundane and monotonous cycle of a machine in a factory. All she was were cogs and oil and the conventional makings of an organic device. Would her inner workings stop working in ten years? In five? Within one?

"Is it because of mom?"

Her mother was part of it. She'd lie if she said no. Yes her mother wasn't awful and no she wasn't the best, but there was something about how her mother always seemed to value Aiden more. There was something about not feeling as loved to capacity that was ever enough for her. Everyone loved in their own way, but she could see it. In her mother's eyes, she could tell, that Jamie wasn't what she expected. She expected more. Of something Jamie would never know and would never ask.

"Is it me?" he asked subdued.

"No." Jamie wrapped her arm around his shoulder and brought him close to her side. "Don't be absurd. Don't get me wrong you're a pain in the ass but no, I would miss you."

"You're not empty," he repeated. They were close to the pharmacy and she lowered the tips of her fingers from her temple. "You have your photography. I've seen your photos and they're really good. Evocative and grounding. Even better than some of the things I've seen in magazines and TV. You could maybe go into that."

"And do what?"

"There's photojournalism. Since you don't like being home"— he looked away from her—"you can travel the world. Express yourself through what you see. You like to learn new things. It might suit you. Plus you're stubborn."

"And here I thought you were trying to make me feel better."

"I mean you can go after a story and not get scared off. You can champion for good causes. Fight the world. Save it. Be as great an ass as me."

"Why are you taking an insult as a compliment?" She pulled at his ear and shook it. "Obviously not as smart as I thought."

They stepped into the pharmacy and headed toward the medicine aisle.

"People call me names all the time. I guess I've become desensitized to insults."

Jamie paused. "People make fun of you? For what?"

"They say I have an accent."

"You don't."

"You're desensitized to me."

She clenched her teeth as the migraine continued to incessantly remind her of its presence. She turned to the rows of medicines and tried to find Advil.

"Have you tried Tylenol?" Aiden had the box in hand and she ignored it.

"That weak crap doesn't work on me." She found the Advil and gestured to the front. When they got in line he picked up a Kit Kat bar and smiled at her. She didn't say anything and paid for it quickly. Once back in the cool night air, she felt more relaxed. "You should have brought your bike so we could've gotten home quicker."

"You're the one who insisted we walk."

"Yeah, well you're the smart one you should have thought ahead."

He ripped the corner of the wrapper and ate a piece, offering another to her. As if just registering what was in his hands, she scrutinized him.

"Mom's not going to be happy you had dessert before dinner." She took the piece he offered and ate it quickly. "Just make sure you clean your face before going in."

They walked in silence as Aiden finished the candy, licking his fingers before folding the wrapper neatly so no chocolate residue from the wrapper stuck out, then stuffed it in his pocket. He pursed his lips as they walked down the block. "You don't hate mom do you?"

It didn't need saying but she knew a question like this, asked from a person like Aiden, was genuine. "No."

The feelings she felt by her mother oscillated often between disregard and relinquished, however she could never honestly claim her mother hated her nor the other way around. Once someone hated someone, truly felt a gap between someone they never wished to have crossed, then there was no going back. Deep down, she still wanted a moment where her mother would look at her and she'd know that all the years up to now had been misunderstood miscommunications. That while they argued, all moments of doubt had been mistakes. She'd do anything for her. A mother's love couldn't be defined although up to now it could. Her mother loved her brother more and she was beginning to love Victor and Riley too. It grew to include them. For once, she wanted to be the only thing her mother loved.

"As much as I argue with her I don't hate her. I don't hate anyone."

"I think so."

Jamie looked over to him, arching an eyebrow as he found her eyes, dim under the darkness between the street's lampposts. They were five posts away from home and in the darkness, she had begun to feel apprehensive again. She wanted to move forward into the safety of the light, but her brother held her there.

"What? No I don't. Who do you think I hate?"

Aiden stared long into her eyes, as if intentionally wanting her to cave and implore him to answer. However he sighed, then shrugged, and broke their connection and continued forward again.

"No one. Never mind."

"No tell me."

His head bounced up as his attention came upon something unexpected. "Victor's car's in the driveway. They must be waiting. Let's go."

She walked after him. "Aiden, tell me. Who do you think I hate?"

No response made her quicken her pace and snatch his arm, spinning him back around. It was a short moment but as she did, his eyes had an orange flame in them that dulled quickly to reflect the lamppost light in his irises.

She took a breath. "Tell me."

"Dad. I thought you hated dad." Jamie didn't refrain from showing how outlandish that was, but didn't need to respond as he exhaled a final time, never straying from her eyes. "After he died, you weren't yourself. But after a while, after life without him became normal, I think you turned to hate yourself."

"Why?"

"Because. You got left behind. You were alone."

"I don't hate myself for being alone. I can handle being alone. I handle it perfectly."

"No one should be alone."

"I don't need anyone else."

"Everyone needs someone else. A husband or wife or a friend or a child. No one's born destined to be alone."

"Some are."

Aiden slid his hands into his pockets as both Diezes remained in place, content with staring at one another until the other yielded. Brother and sister shared stubbornness well.

The medicine worked slowly but an hour after dinner ended her headache was gone. She contributed little to the night's discussions, but that strayed little from her recent dinner habitudes. No one said anything, only Aiden's wandering glances really pointing it out. Jamie didn't speak with Aiden for the rest of the night as neither was happy with the other.

Safely retreated in her bedroom she settled into her bed, regarding the journal she took from the church. Antonio's journal. Shared with his grandson. Why was it in English? It was highly unlikely that a 17th-century Italian man wrote in English.

The season's winds blew unabatedly against the window and she pulled the quilt over her head. Apparently the night tricks wouldn't be content until she was theirs. In a wicked twist, dreams seemed more comforting. All she had to do was face them. Nothing could happen to you if you were asleep.

Jamie yanked the rope out of the carabiner as she blinked hard, forcing her eyes open after closing them for too long. Era entered through the front doors and waved at Jamie as she set her purse under the desk.

"You look awful," Era laughed, leaning over the counter to get a better look at Jamie. "Have you not gotten any sleep in the past week?"

"No," Jamie said sourly. "Where have you been?"

Era beamed, immediately forgetting how Jamie was drowsing off. She jumped to sit on the counter and kicked her feet back and forth. "These past few days have been perfect."

"You mean you've spent the past four days with your date?" Jamie asked, waking up now. "Jesus who is this guy?"

"The most interesting man I'd ever met."

Jamie softened her expression. "More so than Ivan or Immanuel?"

Era leaned back on her hands and admired Jamie as if she were the subject of interest. "He listen and engages and we just click you know?"

"Careful, you're sounding dangerously close to those girls you hate."

"What girls?"

"The girl who falls instantly in love and the fantasy of this guy you shared a couple nice exchanges with. *Compliments and smiles—it's a trap, Jamie. You can't fall for that.* None of this ringing a bell?"

"Excuse me if I've just enjoyed little salsa and dirt biking."

Jamie stood up and laid the equipment in her hands down, exhaling deeply. "I haven't been getting sleep lately and I was expecting you earlier in the week. I'm sorry."

"Is work completely chaotic without me?"

Jamie pouted and kept her eyes closed. "Yes."

Era hopped off the counter and wrapped her arms around Jamie's shoulders, squeezing them before resting her chin on one. "I'm back. Never fear."

"Well, well, well look who's finally made it out of bed?" Noel said from behind them.

Era stepped to the side, a hand still on Jamie's arm. "Don't give me that attitude. *I told you* I wasn't coming in Monday and Tuesday."

Noel smiled and tapped the clipboard in his hand on Era's head, then moved to take the box of equipment Jamie set down. "If all of us just took off work because of a new boyfriend or girlfriend then nothing would ever get done."

"Oh come on, Noel. It's the honeymoon phase. Plus, I wouldn't say he's my boyfriend." Era pursed her lips, looking at her nails. "He's just someone I have fun with for the time being."

Noel made a face and tapped Jamie on her arm. "I better not hear this from you once you graduate." He turned back to Era. "Don't be putting any funny ideas into the heads of the rest of my staff. I'd like to keep them untainted for at least some of their youth."

"Untainted?" Jamie and Era asked at the same time.

Noel flicked his finger in between them. "God. It's already starting."

"I'd hardly call Era's casual raggle-taggle with the opposite gender tainting at all." Jamie linked eyes with Era then mouthed, *At all.*

Era sneered at her before shrugging and walking to the computer. "Tease all you want. I don't care."

"So when do we get to meet him?" Noel asked, looking down to the clipboard.

Era turned around. "Meet him?"

"Yes," Noel said. "It's customary for the family to meet the groom before the wedding, don't you?" He looked to Jamie and she withheld a smile. Era rolled her eyes and waved them away as Jamie and Noel laughed at her. Noel tapped Jamie on the head as she subsequently rubbed the sore spot with a frown. "Good. Now that you're awake. Go clean the front window will ya? Maybe some fresh air will keep you that way until the day's over."

Jamie frowned when suddenly Era leaned toward the cleaning basket and picked it up. "Even though you made fun of me I'll still do it for you. I'm the best aren't I?" She hopped beside Jamie and tilted her cheek out. "Kiss." Jamie shook her head then pecked one on her cheek, watching as Era walked away.

As Era passed through the front door Vienna entered. There was a burden wearing down on her face and she stepped up to Jamie, placing down her membership card and cash.

"Belaying."

"How many?" Jamie asked, not looking at the cash.

"Just one."

"Oh . . ." She rarely saw any of them here alone.

Vienna spoke with a tight jaw and an evasive gaze. "Not in the mood to be around them."

"All right," Jamie said, taking the cash and checking her into the computer. "Once Noel comes back I'll head over." Jamie handed her back her card and the equipment. Since it was a weekday there was a slow crowd. As soon as Noel returned, Jamie left the check-in to him.

Jamie double-checked the equipment before nodding for Vienna to go ahead. Vienna had watched silently, not realizing that Jamie was waiting for her to open up about what was wrong. Vienna was around ten feet up the wall when she paused.

"Jax pissed me off." Jamie figured as much but didn't say anything. Vienna only took that as cue to continue. "He's insensitive and a gossip. It just pissed me off how he mentioned Penelope the other day."

"Maybe she was just the first girl who popped to mind. I don't think he meant it personally."

Vienna scoffed. "Oh please. I know you don't mean that. Jax doesn't think what he says affects anyone. Like we'll just take it as a joke."

"He made an effort not to insult you." That meant nothing to Vienna. "Do you know her?"

"Known her for years. We're not as close like from elementary school, but who is? Jay hung out with us since we live near each other. She keeps to herself is all."

"Has he apologized?"

The corner of her lip twitched. "Jackass called a couple times."

"See? Listen I'm not saying this to take his side, but he does seem to take care of what he says in front of you."

"Doesn't try hard enough to me."

"He"—Jamie loosened the rope—"just does what he knows. He has two older brothers doesn't he?"

"Yeah. So?"

"He doesn't understand girls. And as the baby brother he only knows how to defend himself. I know. I tease my brother all the time. He always says anything to try and get under my skin." Vienna reached the top and hung her head back, meditating on a thought. She looked over her shoulder.

"It's Bryden," she said coldly. "I swear he only ever acts like a pompous jackass in front of Bryden. And unfortunately he chose the idiot for his best friend."

Jamie let Vienna down and when she reached the ground, Jamie watched her as she began to loosen the knot. "You like him?"

Vienna rested her hands on her hips and nodded, slowly looking back up to Jamie.

"Did you join the climbing club because he was in it?"

"What's up with this psychotherapy questionnaire?"

Jamie smiled as Vienna's expression softened. They moved through two other walls before Vienna reached her final wall for the day.

"Are you going on the trip? Enough of our parents have been changing their minds after renegotiations. It'll be during spring break."

"I haven't thought much of it. I don't know."

"Is it the long drive?" Vienna asked gingerly.

Everyone knew that Jamie biked everywhere but no one knew her fear of cars. No one outside of her family mentioned it. She thought maybe no one cared, but having someone ask her all of a sudden startled her. If Vienna noticed this what else did she and others notice about Jamie she thought she disguised so well? Clearly keeping to oneself wasn't enough to go unnoticed.

"Road trips aren't my thing."

"I wouldn't want to be in a car full of guys either. Especially not for road trips that are over a day long. I'd think you'd really enjoy it though." Vienna smiled blandly, making it hard for Jamie to flat out refuse the invitation.

"I want to climb a real mountain. Maybe another way."

"Flying? It'll be more expensive than just chipping in for gas, but I guess you won't be in a car for so long."

"I'll think about it." Jamie lied, though tried to flesh it out to make it more convincing. "My mom never said no anyways."

Vienna patted her arm and then walked to the wall. Jamie wasn't sure she was *that* eager to climb a mountain. Being in the car with her mom when she had no choice was one thing, but being in a car with the Capes was completely out of the question.

18

The cathedral was quiet as Jamie made her way through the vestibule then up the stairs. As she passed the level of her uncle's bedroom she paused, considering knocking and seeing if he was alive. Her mother hadn't mentioned him since cancelling last week and neither did the priests whenever she passed them. They had to have mentioned seeing her to him and yet he never questioned anyone why he never did. Yes she was harsh to him in their last meeting but did he really take her disdain of him to heart?

The moment of reflection passed.

She couldn't let pity give him excuse to be pardoned for all the years of nothing. No. Whatever moment she had just now was thanks to the gargoyles and her talks with Vienna. Over the past week Vienna had sought out Jamie's company as Caprice was more often than not in the company of Bryden. Vienna and Jamie's chats made her feel less empty; more useful and trusted. Grabbing onto a chunk of her sweater, she wrapped her arms tightly over her chest and moved back down the hall to the bell tower stairwell.

Once reaching the roof she noticed a disruption in the air. It had been blowing fiercely moments ago inside the bell tower as the winds became trapped within the cavernous walls, unable to find the current to escape; however, on the roof, the air lingered like heat sitting on a summer day, and never once had the gargoyles been awake and breathing before she had greeted them first and yet there they stood huddled together, focused in on an invisible entity at their center.

Jamie walked behind the closest gargoyle, Amadrius, and lifted her voice loud enough for him to hear. "How'd you know I was here?"

With terror in his eyes he flung around to her. In less than a second, in too short a time for him to calculate who it was behind him, he turned back to the other gargoyles and flapped his wings. The winds that the wings created were powerful enough to stir those around the cathedral and to make her colder than she was by the gales in the bell tower. Could storms be made from such wings? It didn't seem possible because as mammoth as the gargoyles were, they weren't large enough to conjure winds that devastating. The sounds from the wings echoed loudly and she covered her ears, bending away to make sure she wasn't smacked by a rogue wing. "What's wrong?" she yelled, before noticing a shadow behind him slip from one corner of her eye to the other. Was someone else there? She moved in that direction but stopped after gaining several steps. The gargoyles were turning to face her and had spaced themselves out under the canopy.

Amadrius blocked her lingering gaze and kneeled down, motioning her toward the others with an arm, keeping his head and eyes away.

"Were you expecting me?" Jamie said. She didn't fail to notice how Amadrius slipped away to the columns like he did every time she visited.

"We're always expecting you," Cato said.

"Was there someone else here?"

"Did you see someone?" Marius asked.

"No. I just thought I saw a shadow slip by." She swallowed, chancing a glance in the direction she saw it.

"Is this the first time you've seen a shadow?"

"No—" The migraines have become a daily inconvenience and she elected that thinking of the nightmares and dooming shadows had aided them. Bad thoughts only harbor for them to set up port and linger. She decided it was nothing. It couldn't be anything. Besides she never saw those sorts of shadows in the daylight and while the clouds were overcast, it was past midday. It was dark, but not enough for anything to be watching her from the darkness. Not yet. It was best to redirect her focus. "Why are you all breathing?"

"There is much to discuss," Trium said.

"Like what?"

"You."

"What about me?"

"Jamie, there are things you must know. The time you will be tested for the battle is forthcoming."

"Okay, but none of you have been too keen to disclose *anything* about this apocalypse. Your lessons haven't necessarily been top-notch stuff. You've just been telling me stories, as interesting as your presentations have been. We haven't even gotten to Revelations—which by my research tells me is the most relevant to your battle." Once she learned what Revelations entailed she had set high expectations for their renditions.

Trium's wings lifted up then settled down again. "You must trust that we are teaching you what you need to know for the right time."

"Well apparently I'm not the only one you've been teaching so I think I have a right to know exactly what needs to be known now."

"Not the only one?" Sidra said.

Jamie's jaw tightened and she nodded once. "I read that you've preached this battle before and *it'd be worse than they'd ever imagine.* Funny since that's exactly what you all told me."

"And?" Dominic said.

A rush of blood rang in her ears. Waves of anger built inside her and she used every ounce of willpower to keep them inside. "And . . ."—she managed through gritted teeth—"you told him this almost three hundred years ago. That's basically since the beginning of the country. How am I supposed to believe that this mythical battle of yours will even happen in my lifetime?"

"Jamie," Marius implored, "you must have faith in us and the stories we tell you; the warnings we give you. We are thinking what is best for all. Believe in us. You must now."

"It didn't matter before . . . Tell me the truth. Were you made for this battle?"

The leader of the gargoyles was the authority figure when discussing equivocal providence. "We were."

Jamie would've had greater luck getting an apology from her father's aloof family. "Against?"

Trium was quiet for a moment. "You are not meant to know at this time."

"Why not?"

"Because you are not ready." Trium spoke with an acceptance for a fate that still held the opportunity for change. Jamie could only stare back tongue-tied. She didn't understand how anything could be too much to bear. Her father was taken from her. She'd seen soulless statues come to life. No combinations of words could send her over the edge now.

"Please be patient," Silas said. "You will see the greatest rewards are to those who are patient."

"You sound just like those damn priests down there. Preaching, lecturing, sermonizing. I thought you all were more than that. Patience?" Jamie forced a smile on her lips. "I think I've become a master of patience since my dad died. Waiting to be embraced by someone I love the way he used to. To be missed and thought of by someone who mattered. But you're all just slaves to religion. This damn religion that allows you all the power and knowledge of science and history and time and yet you have to keep it from me—*why*? Because I'm human? I'm this great person because you come to life in front of only me and yet you can't even share what that reason is. I'm not ready? Well *I* wasn't ready. I wasn't ready to lose my dad and yet here I am. I'm more than capable to handle anything you incessantly wish to keep secret from me so *tell me*!"

The gargoyles said nothing. Eyes of suns measured her, perhaps feeling hurt, feeling betrayed, or simply waiting for her to continue as if they were being reprimanded for good reason.

Her mouth hung open as she breathed heavily, beginning to notice how mercurial her disposition had become. And her dad . . . She never spoke about her dad to anyone. Why did she suddenly bring him into this? She closed her eyes.

When breathing in, she realized why. He was a spiritual man. A man with a religion. While he wasn't a consistent practitioner of a certain denomination, he had been brought up by the church and his family was still utterly devout. Somehow yelling at them reminded her of how he used to believe in the same stories they did. He knew these stories just as well. He would go to Sunday school and hear these stories and believe in a God that loved just as faithfully as the love they held for their Father.

"My dad was religious." She wiped her mouth and stretched her neck, craning her head up to look at them. "I've never mentioned his death before." Her tone had weakened substantially. "Aren't you surprised?"

"We are not," Dominic said.

"I never told you."

"You never had to," Marius said. "We knew."

"How could you? No one told you." The only obvious choice immediately came to mind. Of course. She must've looked ridiculous to assume her uncle had never visited them on his own. He was the one who showed her the gargoyles in the first place. She'd foolishly thought that since she never saw anyone else no one ever came. But they had to. There's no way the gargoyles only ever came to life for her. There was nothing special about her. She didn't have the faith they did.

"We are messengers of the Father," Dominic said. "Though we are on Earth it does not mean we cannot communicate with our brothers and sisters."

"You mean you talk to other angels."

"Yes."

"And people who go to Heaven?"

Based off of their reactions they knew the question would be asked.

"To an extent," Silas said.

"So you've spoken to my father?"

Again they said nothing. Jamie let her arms fall to her sides.

"My dad never forced his faith on me but I know he believed. It was partly the reason why leaving his family was so hard. In a way, he loved my mom more. But he and his brother—my uncle, the one who showed you all to me—they didn't believe what the rest of them did." Suddenly thinking of her father made her more emotional and gentle in disposition than she expected, just like she became fiery whenever she thought of her uncle. "He believed. He's in Heaven."

Whether Jamie found commonality in religion, she never once thought that her father would go to hell or any purgatory where the irreligious go. Murderers deserved to go to hell. Thieves and rapists and psychopaths and liars and blasphemers and soulless people. Not men who love their family over everything else, still with the capacity to show compassion to others. If he was alive and it had been her mother who had died, she knew he'd forgive Daehyun just as easily as her mother had. She knew that he would make an effort to stay in touch with her estranged sibling in the cathedral if one day out of the blue they decided to move there. People who are kind don't go to any religion's hells.

"If you believe that he is, that is all that is important," Trium said.

"You're not even going to give me a straight answer?"

"Everyone will have their time to know who is in Heaven and who is not. Yours is not now."

Frustration, aggravation, impatience, hatred, and every burning feeling she could possibly feel ruptured all at once in that answer. She took her backpack off and set it roughly on the ground, then zipped it open quickly, fishing for the notebook and rashly flipping through the pages.

"Is there something you'd like to tell us?" Sidra asked.

Jamie stopped looking. She'd found it. The entry Antonio had mentioning seeing demons. It was for this entry that she had come. To ask them.

She held the journal open to them. "I found this notebook in the church library. The majority of the pages talk about you. The writer's Antonio, the one who made you all, and he says repeatedly that he saw shadows. He believed you all were his guardians. Genuinely. You can see it in his writing." The hand with the journal lowered. "But you abandoned him. You all stopped protecting him. Reading this I began to see that he and I had something in common. At first I thought they were nightmares but deep down I know they're not."

They remained silent, allowing her to continue. She closed the book and held it over her chest. "Antonio was starting to see unnatural forms when he was awake. Time passed and he became more and more scared, eventually simple shadows got to him. I've read this diary about five times and each time I began to feel what he was going through each day." Feel so much she almost wanted to share her fear with them. "When he finished Dominic, almost two years after the nightmares started, *that* was when he started to recover. If only in *his* mind, not in everyone else's. Did he never tell you this?"

"Though we come to life for you, it does not mean we come to life to all who come to us," Cato said.

Marius nodded in agreement. "He had spoken to us, but we were not meant to speak to him."

"Two years. You all don't have a perception of time, do you? He was terrified. You couldn't have made an exception and reassured him? Lest you forget he made you all."

"The terror would not last," Marius said to comfort her.

Translation: they would have done nothing different.

All week she had struggled to go to sleep because she still heard the eerie wind against her windows every night as if Banafsha had set up a large creeping fan outside and was taunting her. And every night she never checked to see it was nothing in fear she *would* see something. Eighteen years old and she was as fearful as a child. Afraid of the dark and afraid of monsters lurking outside her window. She talked big but the nightmares had broken the rules. They'd come to life. They stalked her in her wake. There was no peace except within the church walls and amongst the gargoyles, but after a month since first laying eyes on the gargoyles, she saw a shadow when they didn't. The roof of the bell tower was meant to be a buffer zone. Now there was no safety. None in having faith like Antonio and none in lacking it. Words, that's all it was to her. Believing in them. It wasn't enough to say them. She needed to believe it.

And she didn't.

Her throat had dried and the first words cracked as she tried to speak. "The reason I am telling you is because I had a dream last night.

It isn't the first time I've had a demon in one or seen a moving shadow, but it's the first time I heard them speak, in English anyways."

Whenever they spoke, she never failed to notice it was in a tongue that wasn't her own and yet it never disabled her from following what they said. Now hearing them speak in her language, as if taunting her so that she wouldn't be able to use foreign language as an excuse that her dreams weren't real, made her begin to doubt that the shadows were only imaginary. They could come to life. It was easy to believe in something once you saw it with your own eyes.

"What did they say?" Trium asked.

Jamie told them the dreams she'd had of the figure in the robes: the dream following him down the halls for hours, the first dream in which he spoke, and the most recent dream. She had trouble remembering specific details and she may have switched certain details from one dream with another, but everything she remembered she shared. They never interrupted her. Listening. Imagining all that she saw as if it had been through their eyes.

When she finished they looked at one another, keeping her out of their silent conversation even after she'd shared everything.

That was it. Even after being completely honest with them when they didn't deserve it, they still kept her in the dark.

"Do you know who they are?" Jamie prodded. "Erus and Acario?"

"Acario is a name," Cato said, as if this information was allowed to be shared. "As is Erus. Erus can also be used as a respectful term for a master of a house or for one who possesses high rank."

"So they're real? Those creatures and souls are real?"

Of course it could all be absurd, only dreams. But if they were . . . it'd mean something she couldn't imagine. She could see things at night today when months ago she was unaware of their existence at all. Had she become an oracle? Or were these scenes from the past?

Trium knelt down, eyes constantly on hers as all other eyes looked down on at her with the same distant and ethereal gaze.

"What I tell you is very important for you to understand." Trium spoke softly and gravely, as reverently as he had when he first spoke to her. Jamie nodded that she understood. As long as it was the truth she would hear him out. The suns in his eyes diminished in luminosity. "Dreams are not always born of reality. What you dream does not make it real. You must be wary for when a dream is simply that. Figment and only figment."

It wasn't the answer she wanted to hear. There was something in the execution that, perhaps spoken delicately so as not to set her off again, she wanted to question, but what more could be asked when someone didn't want to give up the answer? It was difficult for her to accept how others could be just as stubborn as she was but at least he clarified that the demons she kept seeing in her dreams were nothing more than imagination. The only harm they could do to her was by her fear of them, all within the dreamscape. They couldn't harm her any more than a boogeyman or chupacabra could. No demons or monsters could touch her.

Marius grasped his stone hands together. "The Father is always with you as long as you believe He is."

"The sculptor and I have nothing in common?" she said.

Trium nodded.

"Was there something else? Something you were going to tell me? Something I needed to know?"

The gargoyles looked to Trium who only kept his underbite closed. He was keeping something from her. He avoided her eyes. He needed to avoid being so obvious if he was going to continue this unreasonable quest of keeping her in the dark.

"You wish to know more of our science?" Trium asked. "Your science consists of many studies. Studies ranging from your world, to the causes of nature, to the reason of the universe. To understand our science is to understand and believe this simple fact. Our science is wholly made of the Light. The Light is in existence because of truth and love. All which the Light is is from the Father. The Light *is* the Father. He is science as He is history. He is past, He is present, He is future. He made and makes everything to exist. Through the Light everything is visible, everything is conquerable. Power comes from the Light as a way of means, as a tool to assist in spreading this truth, this faith, this selfless love."

"Light is also your God? That doesn't make sense."

"The science exists because the Light and the Father exist such as the Holy Trinity is three as well as one. The Light is the path to the Father, yet is the Father as well."

"How did Light come to be? One had to have come first."

"No one came first. They have always been."

"This Light—is it also good?"

"The Light is."

"So that means there is a bad? Like a darkness?"

"There is corruption, a Darkness that blossomed from man. Do you remember the story of the Fall? The fruit was of knowledge. Not that knowledge is evil—but the lust for something when it is not meant for someone to have. Many, beyond many do not understand this. With knowledge comes power and since the Fall, it is the nature for man to want power even in its most innocent forms."

"Why did God even give man a chance to be evil? Why not just create us like angels to only live in the Light?"

"The existence of all existence is a choice. Even our brothers and sisters who had only lived in the Light fell. Our Father knew this. He offers the choice to his children, born of All-time in the heavens or on Earth."

"The corruption could have blossomed from fallen angels. Corrupt*ing* comes before the corrupt*ed*."

"The mistakes our brothers and sisters committed were in act for another. Misled loyalty. Corruption of man is selfish, for themselves or for their posterity."

"You said before that you all exist because you were meant to serve him. That wasn't a choice."

Trium's eyes shone brightly. "We all have a choice. Did not some of His children become cast from the Heavens to the darkness? They made a choice. They chose to oppose their Father, their Creator. But for those faithful to the Father lies the truth in our nature—which only those full of Light—may possess. We are not like man to be born into our nature, but after we made the choice to be loyal to the Father does our nature state who we are. The Light is our science, like in your world there are laws that are ignored and broken. A choice. For those that understand and believe will be rewarded. For they who place their trust in the Father will not but have eternal life and love everlasting. They will not know fear."

"This darkness they were cast to," Jamie said, "isn't it the same corruption as the corruption of man?"

"There are many arms to darkness. Darkness of knowledge, darkness of history, darkness of the mind—the list goes on. But the body—the core—is the Darkness where those who practice evil draw their power. The Darkness is powered by Unjustness, Blasphemy, Disdain, Lust, Weakness, Impudence, Vanity, Destruction, and Selfishness. While the Darkness is not as powerful as the Light, it is easier to obtain. So the weak-minded are immediately drawn to it, consumed to it, committed to it. It is a bond that forms and almost impenetrable to disrupt."

Trium paused, finding support in his other gargoyles.

"This Darkness we speak of, though easiest to fall prey to, is not always present. It comes and goes like the waves of the ocean. It is not constant like the Light. It takes a time for it to expand, adjust from All-time to your universe and back. A time where it grows and another where it retreats."

"Is this Darkness the same I dreamed about?"

"It is."

Her jaw dropped. "I'm confused. Are you saying what I dreamed about is a prediction? You said it was just a dream."

They looked past each other, no longer offering answers.

"Can you tell me why my uncle came here?"

They could answer her if it didn't have to do with the celestial couldn't they? But the longer she waited the more the truth dawned on her. They wouldn't answer her. Not now. Probably not in a year from now. Probably not in decades. Their silence would stretch for as long as they kept it for Antonio. She wouldn't live her life waiting.

"If you're not going to answer me I don't see why I'd want to come back."

Jamie turned away from them and walked with conviction, every step releasing a burden form her heart. They didn't try to stop her and she was glad they didn't. Why should she trust in someone who didn't reciprocate trust back? Jamie snuck a final glance at Amadrius who returned her gaze solemnly.

I guess I'll never hear him speak after all.

She made her way downstairs with no intention of returning. Making sure no one saw her, she snuck into the church library and placed the diary back where she found it. Life and death. Good and evil. Nature and choice. Light and darkness. Beginnings and ends. The world was all ever dichotomy and extremes and it would continue like this until the end. She didn't wish to involve herself in them anymore. They didn't deserve her interest. Religion was only a popularity contest. She didn't want to think of their provocative thoughts any longer, force herself to think on things beyond the realm of understanding. It was too much when you were no closer to getting any answers, only sinking deeper into wanting to know more.

And with the progress she was making with the gargoyles, she'd never get any answers in her lifetime.

19

"We still"—Ms. Ava lifted her hands and waited for the class to quiet down—"we still have two weeks left until break. Don't start slacking off now. Your final portfolios are due in less than ten days."

"School days!" Alric called out.

Ms. Ava impressed a gaze unmistaken with one who'd dealt with students for over ten years. "I haven't seen much from the majority of you and so I want all of you on a computer *working*. If I see any of you messing around I will have no qualms separating you."

Three of the yearbook staff entered as Jamie headed toward the lab. It was while passing through the doorframe she overheard one of them mention the upcoming space shuttle launch. It was the first launch in over six years.

"Michaela's grandma just died," said one of the staff. "The funeral's Friday so she won't be here for the launch."

Ms. Ava made a piercing glare their way and they hesitated. As luck would have it, Ms. Ava's favorite student stepped between them and forced out a laugh. "What's with the mood?" Minjae caught Ms. Ava's gaze and clicked his tongue. "Ms. Ava!"

"Not today, Minjae."

"Is this about Michaela?"

"Yes," Ms. Ava said, looking at him with interest.

"Don't be too impressed," he said, waving his hand. "I was listening from the hallway. Don't worry Ms. A I've got no plans this weekend. I can go."

"The space launch isn't your responsibility."

"Michaela's already gotten all the info. I just need to take the pictures."

"You've already got junior interviews, homecoming, and the final football game."

"The space launch's honestly at the bottom of my list." Minjae noticed Jamie and remembered something he wanted to share with her. However she wasn't interested, turning and finding an empty chair between Cate and Ian, sliding on headphones Ms. Ava only allowed in the computer lab. Minjae didn't follow though, being summoned on a task for Ms. Ava.

Later that afternoon in the Rock Gym, Minjae leaned over the front counter and bounced his eyebrows.

"Hey . . . pal . . ." He sounded hesitant, but his eyes were playful.

Jamie had her legs crossed and a copy of *Frankenstein* in her hands when she glanced up to him, her eyebrows furrowing together. "Is there something you wanted to share?"

"Heard you've missed my company in Ava's class."

"I've actually gotten some work done."

"Am I distracting?"

She stood up and set the book down, asking what it was that he needed.

The humor began to drain and a genuine smile rose. "I'm actually here to keep you company. The gym's pretty slow today."

"It's work. I'll keep myself busy."

"Okay I was just trying to be friendly but I'll tell it to you straight . . ." He inhaled deeply and released the breath with upturned hands. "I need help with a photo project over the weekend. Care to keep me company?"

"Finals are next week. How do you have a project?"

He closed his eyes, a tense smile as he rolled his lips from one side to the other. "There are fleas on dogs less difficult than you."

Jamie wore a sour expression as she returned to her seat. "I'm working. Go away."

Pushing off the counter he turned toward the door, avoiding her eyes as he said, "Women are so difficult."

Jamie glanced over her book and sneered at him. When he reached the door he lifted a finger and raised it anticipating the harangue, catching Jamie's eyes and nodding. "I'll see you tomorrow!"

Unsure of what to make of his performance, she tried focusing on her book again before the next customer. But it was impossible. He'd made an impression.

She usually wore a hoodie to school and work but near the end of the week she wore her first turtleneck of the season. Her mother had insisted she and Aiden wear ones they were gifted with the year before. Aiden had one the shade of cool gray, Jamie's striped navy and white. Aiden didn't care for turtlenecks and yanked at his collar as he looked over his breakfast at their mother.

"The launch is this weekend, don't forget."

"*Cariño, lo sé*. I told you I'll try to get out of work early."

Jamie was removing a crumb and wiped the fabric over her skin when she overheard him. She remembered the yearbook staff mentioning the launch earlier that week and sighed. Aiden was in that phase all boys had about being something extraordinary when they grew up whether an astronaut or an archeologist or a firefighter. It might've been challenging since she'd tried not to speak to Minjae since his odd episode at the gym on Monday, but she knew she would have wanted Aiden to do it for her if the roles were reversed.

"I know some people who are going." Jamie said, attracting their attention instantly. "I can get them to take us."

"Come again?" Aiden said.

"Don't you have work?" asked their mother.

"Finals is next week. Noel's giving me a long weekend."

"Would you really do that for me?" Aiden asked, still skeptical.

"No promises," she added.

Several hours later Jamie sought out Ms. Ava and while she was hard to approach since everyone seemed to want to speak to her at the same time, her turn finally came and even then, she only had half of Ms. Ava's attention.

"I was wondering who's in charge of going to the space launch for Yearbook tomorrow."

Ms. Ava peered up to the ceiling, recalling her memory with an open mouth. "That was supposed to be Michaela's responsibility but she isn't here, so Minjae volunteered."

"Anyone else?" Jamie knew about him. She wanted to know if anyone else was going.

"Not that I'm aware of. You'd have to ask him." Ms. Ava had seen Minjae with Jamie and had even criticized him for bothering her and the rest of the class. He'd fluttered his eyelashes and said something he thought was charming which only received a backhanded comment in return. Minjae was the only one who believed Ms. Ava loved him best, though she did admire his buoyancy.

Class was starting soon and Jamie went to her seat, noticing Alric eyeing her skeptically. She ignored him and sat down, wondering how she would go about asking Minjae for a favor.

She found him walking to his car after school and stepped out from behind a column.

"*Kkabjjakiya!* Jesus . . . " He planted a hand on his chest.

She eyed him warily. "Sorry."

"You scared the Korean out of me. You know how rare that is?"

"I'm sor—"

"Forget about it!" He flashed a smile and leaned on his hip, pulling the backpack strap further over on shoulder. "What can I do you for?"

Jamie felt it best to be straightforward. "I overheard you were going to the launch tomorrow night and my brother's—"

"Aiden! How's he doing?"

Jamie nodded once as if that were an answer. "Anyways, he's really interested in seeing it in person. I was hoping if maybe we could tag along since you were already going. My mom was going to take him until she learned when it was and because of the holidays work's holding her up. She won't be back in time to pick him up and take him there."

He brushed a hand over the other arm and slid it back and forth. "I'd *love* the company." Jamie was surprised how easily he agreed to it after their last encounter.

"But," he added, lifting a finger, "I need your help on my photo project."

"I can't over the weekend. I'll be studying for finals. I'm only leaving the house to buy a Christmas tree."

He thought over something, and then returned his gaze to her. "All right, I'll meet you wherever you guys are going."

Biting back an excuse to get out of it she conceded. "How long would it take?"

"Not long. Just need simple contrasting pictures. Nothing extravagant. Nothing flashy."

"Can't you ask Emily to help you?"

"Not really. We broke up." The words were said emotionlessly like he was talking about the weather. She didn't need to know any more and simply nodded, but he seemed to want to share more. "It'd been unstable for a while but I think it's for the best."

Considering he was going to bring her and Aiden along she pressed her lips together and thought about Alric. Had he brought up his concerns for Minjae's affections with Emily?

"Was it mutual?"

He stared back solemnly for the first time and she regretted asking. It wasn't her business. She wasn't close enough to him to expect an answer. She opened her mouth to ask something else but he found his attention called somewhere else.

"As mutual as divorces tend to be. When one wants out the other can't really hold on right?"

They had dated for close to a year. Jamie was surprised how nonchalant he was being. She agreed to his appraisal and asked, "Is your brother coming for the holidays?"

Humored by something, the corner of his lips lifted as he walked around her, unlocking the car door and tossing his backpack in the passenger seat.

"I've got some stuff to do. We can talk on the car ride Friday."

With little to add he jumped into the car and waved farewell. Jamie scanned around wondering if anyone noticed how she'd been brushed aside. It was foolish to think it, but it felt like he'd just blown her off like he had Emily.

It was, in fact, him who broke it off. It didn't need to be said.

Some things didn't need to be.

The doorbell rang and when Aiden opened it, he stared up at a face he only partly recognized and a hand held in the air in a frozen wave.

"Howdy," Minjae said with a flashy smile.

Aiden stared at him for a moment then arched an eyebrow, taking in his appearance. "You're Daehyun's brother."

"Guilty," Minjae said with a wink, bringing his hand down.

Aiden drew his eyebrows together, already taking a dislike to him. "Well he wasn't wrong."

"Who? My brother?"

"Either of them. They said you were a character."

Jamie stepped up beside Aiden and wrapped her arm around his neck. "*Mira* Aiden, he's doing a kinder favor than I would've done driving us. Let's not insult him yeah? What did I tell you about being yourself in front of strangers?"

"Don't worry. I see exhibiting sassiness is a family trait." They both looked at Minjae as he smiled with closed lips, the feeling of diffusion in the air. "Shall we go?"

Neither of the Diez siblings could think of an appropriate response, none that lacked sarcasm or solecism, and followed silently to his car. The ride was exceptionally long for Jamie as she spent its entirety catching any light glint, car, piece of trash, and bug splatter that passed by. The beginning was quiet aside from the car radio, but then he began singing along with it and while Jamie didn't notice, Aiden leaned forward and requested silence. Typical Minjae, unbothered, hummed silently for the remainder of the drive. He asked trivial questions to warm Aiden up to him. Aiden either was anticipating the space launch or his sister beside him and beyond what was required of him, said nothing.

Minjae didn't need to ask why Jamie needed a ride to the space launch. However, while Jamie was far from noticing, nothing could confuse Minjae's staggered expression watching her automatically go to the rear door and Aiden climbing into the car after her.

They parked on the side of the road behind a long row of cars just as eager for a good spot for the first manned space launch in years. After the past year and the extensive budget cuts toward the space program, this manned flight was more than a miracle. To those within a hundred miles of the space coast, who'd seen the rise and fall of NASA within sixty years, this was a celebration for the community. It made up for any political grievances neighbors had with one another. Side-by-side, neighbors would look up to see the string of fire shot like an arrow into the sky, with a human as its heart and its core. No matter what, progress and man would persevere.

Aiden calculated Minjae up for a moment as the latter scrolled through pictures on his camera. "Pluto a planet?"

Minjae wasn't tickled by the question like Jamie expected him to be, speaking with reverence. "You weren't even alive when it was *officially*"—he quoted with his fingers—"declassified. I'm one of the few who remember. Of course it is."

"I was alive. I don't remember it since I was too young, but I was born a year before the IAU redefined the conditions." Aiden huffed beneath the cover of the wind. "Your brother was never condescending like this . . ."

Minjae looked over his shoulder. "Daehyun doesn't consider Pluto a planet. Is that someone who you find more agreeable?"

Aiden couldn't be sure he was buttering him up or not and eyed him skeptically before leaning back in his seat. Jamie observed them in silence, admiring how one could find the other tolerable since both were amiable in grimmer circumstances. When Minjae felt he'd won, he smiled brightly. "Come on, we'll get a better view on the roof."

It warmed Aiden up and so as not to be left behind, Jamie followed suit. Minjae swung his legs comfortably as the siblings sat stiffly, wishing the launch time to start already.

"What got you into space and all this?" Minjae asked.

Aiden's face was as impassive as his voice was neutral. "I've been interested for a couple of years."

"Was it because the last shuttle retired several years back?"

"My birthday's the same day that the *Discovery* launched. The first one since the Columbia Disaster in '03."

"Wish my birthday was special," Minjae remarked. "Nothing phenomenal about May 6th except the Hindenburg exploded. Oh and the Civil Rights Act of 1960 passed." Minjae looked over Aiden to Jamie but she was focusing on the towers in the distance, wondering how assiduously the NASA workers were bustling only several miles away. The Diez's driver smirked. "Anything special about your birthday Jamie?"

In fact, she hadn't been paying attention. She took a moment to register what he asked. "No."

"It's funny, I don't even know your birthday."

"Why's that funny?" Jamie looked to him. He shrugged and she felt compelled. "It's July 8th."

Minjae noticed Aiden was looking at her but she only looked forward. Something unspoken was eating Aiden away and he hid his disappointment poorly. "You're wrong. Your birthday was when the last manned space shuttle was launched."

"That stuff only interests you," she replied lightly. "There's nothing special about it."

Aiden made no remark when Minjae expected him to. Minjae feigned interest in drumming his thigh with some fingers when he lifted the silence again. "Shouldn't you be a grade ahead then?"

"I guess I should've been."

Cars passed at a respectful speed as the air sunk between the three. Minjae's palms brushed together as he focused on a nearby family playing badminton. Aiden had his arms crossed as he tapped his legs up and down. Jamie was the gargoyle between them. Unable to sit still she jumped off the car and turned to look back at Aiden. "I'm going for a walk. I'll be right back."

"I'll come with you."

"I don't need the company."

"Are you okay?" Minjae asked. Neither he nor her brother could avoid noting when she tilted her palm into her temple. "I have some Advil."

Jamie dismissed the offer. "I just need fresh air. A short walk will help. I'll be back before anything interesting."

Leaving them behind for a walk was an excuse to hide how the headache had gotten worse. She thought her skull would explode from the pressure that had accumulated over the past week. Every day in class she had to concentrate and study for the finals the following week but not even simple tasks were manageable. There were no hallucinations, only pain. Perhaps fear *was* better than agony. It wasn't only school. Afterwards at work she would snap at customers. Noel caught her once and let her go early which only made her feel worse. She planned on apologizing after the semester ended.

I'm sorry, I don't know why I snapped. You know me. It isn't me. People say things they don't mean when their body's fighting something inside.

Noel was more understanding than most and was too grateful for her work ethic to let her go. He was flexible with her work schedule and had covered her countless times. In over two years of working at the gym he'd only called her in twice on short notice. Both times emergencies. One was when Era had a delayed flight and was stuck half way across the country and the second was because a coworker had the flu. It was fun working at the Gym and so for most people it was worse missing a day than working one.

Jamie reached the end of the line of cars and kept walking. It was a good distance away when she picked a grassy spot to watch the launch pad. The launch was scheduled for just after sunset, when the night would become a perfect canvas for the flames' paint splatter. They were within an hour of the beginning of a new age in space exploration. The country thought it would be decades before this day would come again, if ever, and now here it was. It was a wonder there weren't crowds by the thousands here to witness it.

"Your first launch?" said a voice nearby.

Jamie noted the clothing of the passerby and nodded after calculating he was harmless. He was only a head taller than her, traces of a beard shaven close, and rather average-looking with dark skin and dark eyes. There was an undeniable kindness about him.

"First live one."

"I've seen two others. Both before you were even born." He slid his hands in his pockets and stepped beside her, looking intently onto the northern horizon where the NASA building was no larger than a thumb.

"I thought I'd be older before this day would come again," Jamie said.

"You have an interest in space?"

"My brother."

"By far one of the most amazing things to witness. Landmarks around the world will always be there, but how could one compare seeing something you know and touch and feel rise above the concept of the sky, past the clouds we hold so dear, so far we thought they'd reached the stars?"

There was something about the type of people who spoke with nothing but gratitude, as if every day they woke up without any fear.

"My generation doesn't appreciate it as much."

"I'm sure that's not true. Look at your brother."

She felt a tingle of protectiveness when he mentioned Aiden, as if he knew him. "He could be older than me."

The smirk on the stranger's face curled up. "How you mentioned your brother—*my brother*—I'd bet the stars you are the elder. Nowadays, what younger sibling accompanies an older sibling for something that doesn't interest them in the slightest?"

Jamie looked past him down the road and noticed how there were no cars coming from that direction at all. She didn't notice him as she walked past the cars, though she was slightly out of it thanks to her migraine. It had gone away once she was outside the crowd of cars. She almost forgot why she had left Aiden and Minjae in the first place. Where had the stranger come from if not from the crowd?

"I could be selfless," Jamie said lightly.

The stranger laughed in a manner so melodically that Jamie felt she was in the company of a close friend. Could a laugh do that? Were they that powerful a comfort? Had she needed comfort that badly?

"Do you mind if I ask you something?" Her eyes replied yes and he jutted his chin ahead of them. "If you could go up in space, would you?"

"I guess anyone would want to."

"If there was a chance that you couldn't return, would you still want to?"

"There's always that chance. Our technology isn't perfect."

"Then it's certain. You would never be able to return. The catch is there would never be another space launch again. Not in this country or in any other. Not in Russia or China or anywhere. But"—there was a catch and he smirked—"the universe would be yours. Would you give that seat up?"

She wouldn't. The final chance for a human to see space—who would give that up? Just to live a mediocre life? Long years passed with nothing in them but what others have done. She'd say a final farewell to her mother and brother and then go inside that space shuttle with no regrets. Her last breath would be spent seeing the star burning, if even from afar, she would be closer to the sun than she'd been all her life. And she'd look into it directly. She would never return to her life on Earth and she would die in space. She would give up her eyesight. If you wouldn't need something anymore, wouldn't anyone want to give it up to see something no one had ever truly marveled at? She could understand why her brother had such a fascination with this stuff. Even she had to appreciate the things that were bigger than her. It was easy to forget how forces more powerful than what she could comprehend existed just outside the impressions of a definitive sky.

Jamie looked above them to the clouds. "Are you always this theoretical?"

Another laugh warmed her and he nodded. "It's a rather bad habit of mine. Especially when I stare at the stars for too long and much too often in my free time. Might I recommend buying a telescope for the brother? At least 100mm. It's worth the extra cost."

Despite his obsession, Aiden didn't own a telescope. He'd always wanted to wait for one, claiming he needed to see the capacity of the universe first. With Jamie leaving after graduation, a telescope couldn't be a more perfect gift.

She almost thanked the stranger for the idea before realizing it would've been uncharacteristic of her. Aside from customers at work she never made an effort of civility with strangers. She wondered if the reason she was getting along now was because he made her feel less alone than had she been with family.

"Jamie, you've been gone a while," Aiden said as he walked over to her.

Minjae stood beside Aiden, both looking between her and the stranger.

"I lost track of time," she said, not wanting to argue in front of the man with a selfless laugh. She smiled kindly and said goodbye. The stranger nodded his head and smiled warmly at her before nodding to the others. Jamie went over to her brother and grasped his neck, massaging it lightly as she turned him around.

"I told you to wait by the car," she said when they were a distance away. She eyed Minjae who held his hands up defensively.

"I wasn't going to let him go on his own."

"What were you doing walking out to the middle of nowhere on your own?" Aiden snapped. "That guy could have kidnapped you and no one would have seen it!"

She rolled her eyes and squeezed Aiden's neck as she pushed him in front of her.

"Excuse you, who's the firstborn here?"

"Well nothing happened so no need to say things we'll regret," Minjae interjected.

"I won't regret it," Aiden said quickly. "If something happened mom would never take me to another space launch again."

"Why were little brothers invented?" Jamie said looking over to Minjae, then sighed loudly after realizing who he was. "Obviously I'm talking to the wrong person."

"We're rather adorable and protective," Minjae said. "Nothing not to love at all."

Jamie looked away. Minjae stifled a laugh, following behind.

"You left me with that sense of humor," Aiden said, looking back at Jamie when she released him. "You deserve it."

"I have no idea what you two are talking about," Minjae said. "I'm just happy."

"Must be a condition. No one's like that all the time."

"Even when I'm asleep," he added.

They reached the car and waited inside with the doors open. Aiden checked his phone and leaned against the headrest. Jamie watched as cars passed by in search of an empty stretch of grass. Minjae drummed his fingers over the side of the chair, on his lap, on the side of the door. The night settled in as the bugs descended. It was December but the bugs were not absent.

"You don't think they'll cancel the launch do you?" Aiden and Jamie looked to Minjae. "It's an innocent question."

"If they do I'll compensate you the gas money," Jamie said.

"That's not what I meant," Minjae said.

"It'll be any minute now," Aiden said, checking the launch updates on his phone.   Another pocket of silence encased them and Minjae finally allowed words to pass his lips. He mentally counted to one hundred and mouthed each numeral, unable to handle the sedentariness. "Not that I'm one against silence but perhaps a game? It'll help the time go by faster." Neither sibling responded and he lifted a leg up, leaning back to look up at the stars. "It's a pity the sky's not clear here. At least they could have entertained us during the wait."

When the time came closer to the launch he jumped down and got out the tripod and camera before walking across the street to set up. Jamie and Aiden stayed where they were as they watched him silently.

"How is Daehyun related to him?" Aiden asked.

"He's not that bad."

"How did he survive? I'm not like that am I?"

"You are far"—she squeezed her eyes shut—"*far* worse. You know there were days I looked for your birth certificate to see if we for sure were related."

Aiden stared. She'd made far worse jokes in the past and wasn't worried she'd offended him, but still, the look in his eyes made her continue. "Oh yeah. And when I found it I took it to dad to double check it. Even mentioned a DNA test here and there."

Aiden became slightly humored. "And what did he say?"

"He said, unfortunately, we were. That headaches travel in pairs."

"What! He never said that. He would've never said that about you."

Jamie stuck her tongue out. "You're right. He said something cheesy I can't remember."

It was partially true. She didn't remember what he said. It was a year before he died, but she did remember his expression when she asked. He was incredibly humored, perhaps because it was her asking it. Or that Aiden was only seven and wanting to check this late in her life was unexpected for a girl of thirteen. His expression still remained clear in her memory. He'd returned the certificate with care as if placing a precious heirloom back in its place.

"Watching him," Aiden said, bringing her back to the present, "reminds me of him. It's probably why I find his dad jokes annoying."

Jamie followed Aiden's gaze and watched Minjae spin the camera on the tripod, then begin looking through the viewfinder, adjusting the zoom.

"He doesn't make dad jokes."

"He's trying too hard. Formula for making a dad joke." Aiden rolled his eyes.

"You're a tough crowd."

Aiden turned to her and she knew he was about to tease her by the expression he wore. "I'm sorry did I offend your boyfriend?"

Jamie laughed. "Yes." Aiden dropped his expression and Jamie sighed victoriously. "You're making fun of the man I'm going to marry so watch your mouth. He may be a dad but you're a brat. Try being a little more thankful." She hopped off the car and walked over to Minjae. Aiden rolled his lips and bit them together, scratching behind his neck and checking the time.

The sight of the Space Shuttle Intrepid disrupted the night in a cacophony of color and sounds. The crowds were blown several steps back by the sonic boom, then quick to admire the fiery trail until the shuttle coma disappeared beyond the night's clouds. Miles away in every direction, the light would take time to disappear, but from this vantage point, watching the launch in its entirety within minutes. Minjae studied the photos he took for a while as the first drove of traffic began their departure home.

During the launch, Jamie had learned to fawn over the spectacular event. She marveled in it. She understood how her brother could be so interested in wanting to one day be involved in that. Both brother and sister Diez felt the world become so much smaller yet their futures so much more.

Aiden was the first to jump out of the car when Minjae dropped them off.

"Hold up a sec," Minjae said to Jamie. Aiden walked up the drive, failing to notice his sister had stayed behind. Jamie adjusted her sleeve as she turned to him. When he looked at her he forced a sleepy smile on his face, leaning his head against the headrest. "You'll help me right? You promised."

Jamie nodded and hid her hands under her armpits. "You put up with my brother for a night. You're braver than most. I'll help. I actually want to apologize for Aiden. I don't know why he chose to be like that tonight."

"Nonsense. I like him. I'm understanding of those I like."

Jamie half-turned away then turned back. "Why are you being like this all of a sudden?"

He found something of interest in the empty street, both embarrassed and unprepared for the question. She leaned against the door and watched him. Between the two of them she was very comfortable asking. She hadn't expected that of herself.

"I've heard some stuff lately. I'm curious if what they've said is true." She watched as he sat up straight. "Can you confirm it for me?"

He spoke slowly. "What have you heard?"

"Mmm," she muddled. "That you like me. I guess it's convenient for them to say that if you've broken up with someone."

"I—" He smiled shyly, though devotedly. Whether he meant to hide it or not, he did it poorly. He opened his mouth, but nothing came out.

Jamie hadn't been in this position before and while she'd witnessed it enough, it still felt uncomfortable to be in. On second thought, ambushing him with the question was discourteous. Not that she reciprocated his feelings, it was a compliment being told you were admired.

"Can you confirm it?" she asked. When his expression began to drain and turn into regret she chuckled weakly. "It's not a pity thing right?"

"No," he said vigorously, insulted.

She apologized with a smile. "Just wanted to be clear. Wanted to be sure you were sure."

It was arguably the least elegant a confession between two people but she looked ahead at the empty street before smirking, finding her way to his eyes again. "Thank you."

Disappointment in his eyes, posture, and facial expression, he looked over to her curiously.

"For making me feel like a teenager. I guess I skipped being one. My teens happened so fast I don't think I lived a teenage life correctly. The right way at least."

"What are you talking about? You're still a teenager."

"When you turn eighteen you suddenly feel like an adult then responsibilities take over your life. Maybe being a year older than most everyone in your grade does that to you. Maybe I should have been a grade ahead. I already have the college kid's mindset without the college part. Not that I'm going."

He brought his hand down from the steering wheel into his lap, and fiddled with his thumbs. "You're not going to college?"

Until tonight she figured she would. It was speaking with the stranger and watching the space launch that seemed to suddenly change that for her. She wasn't never going to college, only delaying it for a while. She was already a year behind, what would another year do? College would still be there.

"I was going to go to one far away, but I've been thinking . . ." She nodded, already decided. "Traveling the world for a bit might be what I'm supposed to do. At least before I start my life. I always hear about people traveling the world and work as they go, living life simply and frugally. I can do that."

"It seems rather lonely a commitment."

She shrugged. "I've never had a problem with lonely." She heard a noise behind her and figured it was either her mom or her brother telling her to come inside. Minjae looked to the front door then back to her, not able to respond before watching her check her phone. "I'll help you with your project. I'll let you know soon."

She waved goodbye and shut the door before going inside the house. He watched her until the front door closed and he sat back against the seat, shutting his eyes and breathing deeply. It wasn't that he couldn't confess. It wasn't that he felt cornered. It was an obstacle, finding the courage to divulge something you've grown accustomed to keeping to yourself. Some days he'd see her and wouldn't even remember how he felt. It was a sudden ambush these feelings. Senior year came and the realization of potential permanent separation made his feelings resurface and every day seem pivotal. Confessions were sneaky bastards. One felt the right moment was one day and then the day came and it suddenly didn't feel the right time after all. And then they would wait for the next best day until they procrastinated their way into oblivion. They've moved on. The feelings have transferred, disintegrated, and are, turns out: spurious. However, he had pushed his feelings back for too many reasons. Too many excuses. When the feelings remain after all this time they have to be shared. Otherwise the feelings are for an idea. And one cannot love an idea. It's as unlikely as they are to love a dissipating dream; and they weren't meant to be loved. When a person became a dream, and the dream recurred for a stretched time, then the dream had to become a reality. The idea had to become a reality so it could be loved.

20

"I think we're the only family in the world that buys Christmas trees this late," Jamie said.

Rosario had been judging the way one tree flaunted its branches and height when she responded over her shoulder. Trees bought in the past had always been bargain buys but as soon as the tree was erected at home she discovered branches scarce in the back or the spruce scent replaced by a burnt one. After several years of trial-and-error, she'd learned to judge carefully before impulsively buying. Unfortunately waiting a week before Christmas made for slim pickings.

"Analiese hasn't," Rosario said, moving along to the next tree. Riley followed behind as Victor browsed fir trees in the next aisle.

"What will you have on the top of the tree?" Riley asked. "A star? An angel? A ribbon?"

Aiden stuck up his nose as he snickered, moving along the trees, caring less about tree-shopping than Jamie. "Who would have a ribbon?"

Riley shrugged. "I saw it on TV once."

"What a poor choice for a tree-topper," Aiden said.

"Then we won't do that," Rosario said coolly. "Victor, how does your friend rate the trees again? Did he say it was by foot or width?"

If it were possible he'd been more interested in analyzing the tree than Rosario and so had her repeat the question, uncertain in the answer himself. "I'll ask him, but don't worry about the price, I'll cover it. A Christmas gift for your family."

"You do enough." Rosario smiled at him.

"Do I? Coming over every weekend for free dinners and have you pick up Riley when I'm working over-time—don't I do enough?"

Rosario rested her hand on her hip. "How many times have you fixed things in the house? And the time you picked up my mom from the airport? And when you come over to make *us* dinner?"

Victor looked into her eyes in such a way that made all three of the kids disperse and move along. Victor walked over to her, slid his hand up Rosario's arm, and soothed it from the unusual cold of the Florida winter. Jamie stole a glance in their direction.

Small moments of intimacy rarely shared in private seemed scandalous in public, however it wasn't the first time Jamie had seem them innocently touch. She studied them, unable to see how her mother could move on so quickly even after all these years. He was the first one Rosario dated after her husband's death, but was she settling? Was she so afraid of being alone she quickly moved on from Jamie's father? Jamie couldn't help wondering if she loved him the most after all.

Victor felt her eyes on them. He dropped his hand to his side, turning back the way they came. "I'll go check the prices."

Rosario watched him as Jamie watched her. It wasn't fair how instead of focusing on her two kids she looked for another life companion. Her father gave up his family to marry her. Gave up his religion. Yet her mother kept her family. Her mother kept her religion. Her mother even found someone again. Jamie resented how she seemed uninhibited. It was for something like this, such obvious indifference, that she couldn't become closer with her mother. The space once filled with warmth by her father could not be filled. It was as likely to happen as an earthquake in Florida.

They found a winner and Victor tied it to the top of his car before delivering it to its new home. Jamie made little haste to follow them as she held the handlebars, walking along the sidewalk.

Abuela was coming in a couple of days to stay until the New Year which unfortunately meant she was going to room with Aiden for over a week. The last time they roomed together Aiden was working on a project which ended on her falling on wet paint and winning a considerable amount of gum in her hair. Luckily the gum caught near the bottom of her hair and little was lost to ruin her lackluster hairstyle, but she did lose her favorite pajama shorts. She seethed at the prospecting catastrophes.

Her *abuela* was a spark of love. While Jamie's relationship with her mother was strenuous—the same strain Rosario shared with her own mother—Jamie got along swimmingly with her *abuela*. Both her and Aiden were balanced by visits of love and discipline, with slightly more weight in the love by the spoiling abundance of gifts. The weight of her spoils could also be measured by the pounds they gained from *Morcillas, Alcapurrias, Pastelón*, and *Chicharrón* by the time she left on the Caribbean-bound plane. A Puerto Rican *abuela* would never allow her *nietos* go hungry. When the *nietos* were hungry they were fed. When they were eating they were offered more food. When they were full, they were offered *more* to eat. There was no vocabulary such as "full" and "no thank you" in an *abuela*'s dictionary.

The thought humored Jamie at how much she would be pestered for looking thin and not eating enough. That's what Abuela always said every time she visited. Until Jamie heard those words, she'd expect them patiently.

A car honked from across the street, slowing to a stop until it halted. Jamie looked up and noticed Minjae waving through the open window. He checked for cars before turning around to pull up beside her. Jamie walked to the passenger side window.

"Need a lift?" he asked.

"I never do."

He seemed more timid sharing a smile as his lips remained pressed together then pulled to the side. Jamie rested her arm on the window and pointed down the road.

"Were you headed somewhere?"

"I was. Someone was expecting me. But I think I'll just blow them off instead." Her jaw dropped as he started to become himself again, a smirk on his lips as she formed words on her own. He held up a finger and then shook it. "Yes I absolutely will have to blow them off. How could I pass up an opportunity like this? As it may be, I happen to have my camera on me. Hop in. You can help me with my project."

"How can you leave a project for the last minute? As busy as you may be with Yearbook, cutting it to the last week just days before finals is careless."

"I told you, it isn't for this year. It's for next semester. I'm not that much of a slacker. Hop in."

"I'm good."

He curled the corner of his lip and looked her up and down for a moment before sighing with disapproval. He didn't voice what he was thinking as he looked down the road.

"There's the Publix shopping center a couple streets over. Let me park there and we'll walk the rest of the way. Though . . . it would be easier if we just drove."

"I could be busy today."

"So busy you're daydreaming at that sluggish pace? Please. You're not busy."

Jamie scowled as she backed up a step and then waved him on. "I'll meet you there in a couple of minutes."

Overjoyed, he bounced in his seat as he released the break, moving the car several inches before jolting to a stop again and leaning over the seat to look at her.

"You're not going to blow me off are you? Maybe I should just drive along to make sure you don't ditch me."

"I won't!" She waved her hand at him again. "While you wait you can call whoever you're standing up. I'll do the same," she added.

Minjae moved back against the seat and sat up straight. "What a gal. So considerate of others. I hope to be more like you one day."

As he drove off she watched him incredulously. "Who says gal?"

She found his car near the edge of the shopping center's parking lot and after shutting the door behind him, he gestured in the direction they'd be going. There was little to find in walking distance of the shopping center that would serve as good photo shoot locations, however she didn't protest. She wasn't anxious to go home to Riley and Victor.

"Do you know of any good places to make poster prints?" she asked.

"Nothing in Shore; in Orlando there's a couple places. My favorite can be a bit expensive, but the staff's awesome." He sized her up and chuckled. "Why? Have a magazine cover you want on your wall?"

She ignored the jest. "It's a gift for someone."

"Oh, a gift? Who for?" He watched her expression as she remained silent. "I can probably help you get a discount since I frequent them so much. It's time I.get my annual free print."

Jamie didn't believe a print shop would do that but obliged him. "They have that?"

He shook his head and laughed. "But they do have discounts for their favorite customer. You're lucky I just so happen to be one of them."

"You're everyone's favorite aren't you?" Jamie had her turn to laugh now. "Is there anyone who doesn't think of you as their favorite?"

"When you're as lovable as me, you'd have to venture to a far gone land to find such a man. If I'm not a favorite or, God forbid, not even liked, then I'll still consider myself their favorite. They just don't know it yet. They're waiting for the next earthquake to hit so I'll save them from being trapped beneath a fallen roof or stranded on a lamppost from a flood. I'm just waiting for the next natural disaster to hit so they'll know."

"You may be the only person who would wish a natural disaster just so you could be liked. Don't you find the morality wrong in that?"

"It's all hypothetical. Just a joke."

She bumped his arm and looked ahead to Embrujado Trail at the end of the road. "For someone who jokes so much, you take what I have to say to heart too easily. Is it me?"

He moved forward as if he didn't hear her and she followed behind silently. He readjusted the camera strap on his shoulder. "When do you need the print by?"

"Ideally Christmas. Since it's so last minute though, I understand if they're backed up."

"I'll give them a call later."

He stopped and looked both ways, judging if the location was good enough. The trees formed a canopy. The overcast skies making the pictures darker than normal for the time of day. The wind was strong when they were exposed, but beneath they trees they weren't attacked as relentlessly.

Jamie watched him as he started to turn on his camera. "Why Embrujado Trail? Want to catch a ghost in the background?"

Minjae snickered. "Not many bikers or runners come here. Not even on the weekend. If someone comes we won't have to wait long for them to get out of the background. Now go over there with your bike, just hold it beside you."

After he told her where to stand and where to look, she spoke up. "So who'd you blow off?"

"Hmm?" He glanced at her then focused back on changing the settings. "Oh, uh . . ." He spoke uninterested. "Jax."

"What were you guys going to do?"

"Work out some deets for the trip. My parents said they'd be all right with it—by the way did you ask your mom yet?" Jamie shook her head and he focused on playing with the zoom. "We're running out of time. You need to get on it. Jax's hoping that I can convince his parents."

Jamie muddled it over. "I think that's important."

"I'll see them later. Finding you with extra time on your hands was a stroke of luck. I'd rather not risk waiting for another day you're free than go to his place. His parents will always be there."

"And I won't be? Am I going somewhere I'm unaware of?" She laughed and he found it good enough a reason to smile.

"Well since one of us world travelers isn't going to college . . ."

They waited for a runner to pass before Jamie asked, "Where are you waiting to hear from?"

He listed them mechanically. "UCF, UM, Florida State."

"All in-state?"

"It's a lot more affordable than out-of-state. But I've applied to San Francisco State. And Columbia."

"Apparently you need to be near the water," Jamie said.

"That doesn't matter to me. I think I just need to be near a big city. I don't want to live the rest of my life stuck in a small town with nothing to do."

Jamie found the first thing they had in common and nodded silently for a moment as he instructed her again, before returning to the subject. "What do you want to do?"

"That's probably my only problem. Probably why I'm really an idiot. I applied out-of-state and I don't even know what I want to do. But they always say it's best to apply to a bunch of places. I'm expecting it'll hit me once I'm there."

He had her sit down next to the bike and moved down a ways to capture her from the ground.

"What about the Capes?" she asked. "What are their plans?" A curiosity never seen before made him smile and when she asked why, he unsuccessfully diverted her toward a new topic. She jutted her chin out. "Does it look like I hate you guys or something?"

"Sometimes we feel you do, but I think it's because of the ruckus we make. More me and Bryden and Jax and the rest of the guys than the girls but what can you do?" He rolled his shoulders. "I find your interest in us amusing. Has it suppressed itself for too long, your curiosity of us?"

"I sound like an outsider."

"I wouldn't characterize you as a wallflower but aside from classes and the gym, you don't go much elsewhere. You should check out $2 Tuesdays at Poppy's Theatre."

"I go to church." The words came out before she thought it through and yet she was the one disconcerted. "Not habitually or anything like that."

"Oh . . ." He nodded as if he understood.

"It was for Photo," she added quickly.

"There's nothing against going. Why else would people come to Shore unless for St. Luke's?"

There weren't enough days in the school year left for her to finally leave this town and never be reminded of the time wasted there. It'd only been a handful of weeks and yet she felt all the hours sitting under the spire with the gargoyles had stretched exponentially to months.

"Did you ever want to be a magician?" she asked. By his expression, the sudden shift in conversation caught him unawares.

"A magician? A comedic illusionist!" The joke landed as well as fish could land on its tail. "No. But I would have looked handsome in one of their capes. And the hat! Oh! I would have looked good with the hat." He walked up to her and removed a leaf off her sleeve, or so was his excuse. "Why?"

"Even medicine was once thought of as magic right? In any part of the world there was always magic found somewhere. People wanted to believe that there was unexplained power in the hands of someone who could outmatch their power, because doing miracles and enchanting with an illusion, whether small or destructively fatal, had to be done by someone who had a plan. When someone was saved from death or when someone was taken before their time, people had to believe that it was for a greater plan."

Minjae drew lines in the air, looking to the canopy for the answer. "Are you talking about magic or destiny because you kind of . . ."

"Everything in the world can be explained. There's nothing you can see that magically happens. Not that appears out of thin air, right? Otherwise it's just a trick."

"I guess, if not then it's part of myth. Fantasy and legend—they're the experts on magic."

Jamie looked ahead to the path and stared at the bend where the path curved. "Religion is a type of magic, don't you think? The magic's in the words. People are the still shore and their words stir the pond. They make themselves to be the ripples, but the power's in the wind. It lies outside of them."

During her homily, she scratched her hand, only for it to be taken by his as he stepped in front of her, bringing her attention to the black square centered on his white hoodie. He was a head and a bit taller than her, about his brother's height, though not as wide. There was a sense of warmth there and it was due to the fact that he always wanted to comfort someone. She felt it in his fingers and how they shaped around hers. The connection was weak and felt more gratuitous than soothing, however as her eyes met the center of the coal black square she felt it began to fade to a welcoming pearl black, the glisten of the light hitting the abyssal darkness. A darkness too familiar.

"Jamie," he said softly, moving his hand to her wrist. He waited for her to meet his eyes. He felt his breathing tremble, deepen, every cell in his body feel his pulse throb through his veins and into his palm encasing her wrist. He feared she would feel his hand begin to sweat, and dropped his eyes before she wavered.

The release of his hand caused her to search for his eyes as he stepped to the side and brought his camera back up.

"Nothing. Never mind." When she glanced at his camera he nodded, a lingering trace of solemnity in his furrowed eyebrows. "I think I got all I want. Let's head back."

He walked around her as she watched him silently. He wanted to say something but was too afraid to. She read it in his rigid stance; how he regrettably released her hand. Had he wanted to confess the feelings Alric insisted he had? She couldn't ask him about his feelings if it was even about that. To invade someone's mind and ask how they really felt, what they were thinking, what they wanted—she felt she didn't deserve to know. He was dryer warm and she was washer cold. If she knew what he wanted to say, how could she respond to him in a way that wouldn't hurt him but also wouldn't leave her uneasy?

When she got home she retreated to her room, uninterested in helping the family dress the Christmas tree. She sat down at her desk and stared at the laptop screen. She'd never had a guy linger in her thoughts for so long. Aside from the occasional handsome customer at the gym, her thoughts rarely rested on a guy. But for some reason, how he took her hand, in almost a plea for himself and not for her, she couldn't shake him off.

Her eyes wandered to her backpack where the journal remained. Who wrote it? Why couldn't the gargoyles simply answer her questions? Minjae lingered on her mind for so long because she thought of the gargoyles. She had said church but she never specified which one. Why did he have to mention St. Luke's . . .

Her fingers tickled toward the backpack and she crossed her hands together before leaning on the desk, pressing her forehead against her hands. If either her mother or brother came in they might think she was fighting off another headache. Victor or Riley might think she was praying.

The gargoyles had taken too much from her. They invaded her life of normalcy and expected her to continue without being affected. The price? A plague of headaches every other day if not every day of the week. They cast a magic spell on her and disallowed her mind from freedom until she returned. But she couldn't. That would mean surrendering to them. All she could see in yielding was Antonio's words. Imagine his spirit.

Wretched and pathetic.

Her fists slammed down on the desk, her eyes still tightly shut.

"I won't be." She repeated it again. Again for each gargoyle and one for Antonio and one for his grandson and one for every shadow that haunted her since that first night.

"Please."

The word was strained through her teeth as she opened her eyes, waiting for the film of water to dry on its own. She could almost hear the tear fall on the desk. When her vision cleared and the shadows began to tighten along the blurry bumps of the wall, she looked back down to the backpack. She paused when she heard someone walk past her door to the bathroom. Finally, she leaned over.

Out of the silence her phone rang. Tentatively retracting her hand, she picked up the phone. It was the person she just saw. Curious if he decided he wanted to tell her what was on his mind, she answered.

"How about Wednesday, after our finals? Getting your picture printed? Do you work that day?" His voice showed no sign of laconism from earlier.

"Just for a couple of hours. We can make it there and back with plenty of time. Wednesday's fine."

Their plans set, she ended the call and gently set the phone down as she eyed the backpack a final time. The only thing she could do was push the gargoyles to the back of her mind for six more months. Six more until she graduated and she left town and they'd never interrupt her life again. Six months and it would be the end. No more shadows and agony. No more torment.

There was a clatter of noise, and she stood up to investigate which one of her mother's favorite plates had her brother's name written all over it.

21

It was Era's name Jamie read on the caller ID. She had halted outside the school's registration building, wondering why she was getting a call at this time of day. She answered with a quizzical pitch her in her voice.

"Would you mind doing me a huge favor?" Era chirped. Jamie stepped out of the way of two girls walking by. "Can I take your shift today?"

Jamie kept an eye out for the cars passing. "My shift's three hours."

"My date had to work," she sighed. "I dread thinking I'll stuck sitting alone at home."

"You kill time by working? Why don't you just go out? Nothing gives you greater pleasure." Jamie corrected herself. "Except for sex. And churros. All right after *two* things."

"Love's got me blind. You going to let me work your hours or not?"

"Oh ho!" Jamie laughed, making a face. "Loverboy disappoints you—do you want your co-worker to also? Do you want the favor granted or no?"

"I knew you'd be reasonable." Era smiled in her voice as Jamie rolled her eyes. "I saw that."

Jamie expected Era and not Minjae when a car pulled up beside her, and the call ended with Era's kisses as farewell. He opened the trunk and she put her bike in as he watched silently. When he returned to the driver's seat, he noticed she was opening the back door. He looked over his shoulder and breathed deeply.

"C'mon and hop in the front." He said sweetly, however she could sense he'd wanted to ask since they went to the space launch. She'd closed the door behind her and sat motionless as she returned his gaze. He glanced at the front seat and then down to the seat beside her. "I'll drive like a grandma I promise."

She settled herself in the center and reached for the seat belt. He turned forward and waited for the seat belt to click before he put on his own. When they arrived Jamie followed him inside where the staff greeted him warmly. They made small talk and she heard her name mentioned, but she went to find a computer and begin uploading the image. She'd always been cautious showing this photo to anyone, but after some thought, she felt keeping it a secret would be paying respect to the gargoyles. She wanted to distance herself in every way, cut any tie of loyalty to them. If they didn't deserve it, she wouldn't.

The employees said they'd call her once the photo was printed and after a short struggle to convince her to sit in the front, Minjae and Jamie made their way back to Shore. After another failed attempt to grab a bite to eat before taking her home, he pulled up in front of her house and opened the trunk.

As she pulled out her bike, Minjae watched silently with his hands in his pockets. His posture suggested he wanted to offer assistance or anything that might stir an interest of her in him, however he knew it'd be in vain and she'd simply decline the invitation. He reached for the trunk door and shut it, stepping after her as she towed the bike up the curb.

Minjae felt drained by lack of sincerity in his smile, and it was when Jamie noticed it that she pivoted suddenly. "My *abuela's* here."

"Oh?" His eyes lit up. "Grandma's here? Don't tell her what I said earlier. I'm sure she drives at a perfectly legal speed."

Jamie lifted an eyebrow, noticing the mood change. "Do you know my grandma to call that?"

"No!" He corrected himself quickly. "Not personally. Daehyun met her once. Thought very highly of her. Said she was the family Cornucopia."

She looked back in her memory and thought back through the past three years. She couldn't remember a visit they were both present. "When—"

"Must've been last year. Wow! It's already been a year. Time really flies—"

The front door opened and a woman Jamie's height emerged, her eyes on the two of them. She wore capris and a loose green shirt, her sandals slapping against the ground. Even the weather seemed to bend toward her as a pocket of warm air settled around them.

Abuela waved a hand inside as she smiled. "Why are you two out there? It's about to get dark. Come inside."

Jamie hardly turned toward the sun before focusing back on her grandmother. "Abuela, it's barely five. The sun's still in the sky."

"Well the way the two of you are sneaking around out front instead of coming inside makes you look suspicious." Since the two teens weren't moving to obey, Abuela stepped beside Jamie and kissed her on the cheek before looking to Minjae. "Hello, we haven't met before. Which friend are you?" He laughed and slightly leaned forward, pulling his hands behind him as he answered her. "You look familiar."

He nodded as if expecting the sentiment. "You met my brother last year."

"I'm sorry," she laughed heartily, sparing Jamie a glance. "I can't remember. What's your brother's name?"

"Daehyun."

"*Claro!* That's right. How is he doing?"

Minjae waved his hand and pursed his lips, a hint of a smile on them. "We can't even get the crazy guy to come home for Christmas. Too busy being an adult to visit the fam."

"Listen, come inside. I've been cooking and there'll be plenty for you to join us."

"Have you been cooking since you arrived?"

"No. *Tú mother*," she exaggerated, "didn't have *sofrito* so I had to go to the store. And then when Aiden came from school he was hungry so we went out to a fast food place. *Y bien?* Let's go inside."

She led the way as Minjae and Jamie remained in place, sharing glances that read neither of them knew what to do. Eventually Jamie shrugged and gestured to the front door. "Well, she's already seen you. If you leave now she'll be insulted."

"All right!" he said, happily following Abulea inside, hesitant only for Jamie's sake.

Long before he reached the kitchen Minjae could smell cinnamon, apple, and an aroma he wasn't familiar with before hearing the sounds of a twelve-year-old randomly spitting names at the TV. Aiden wasn't as uptight as he had been the day of the space launch as he flattened plantains, standing on the edge of the kitchen and the living room, his eyes glued on the flat screen. Rosario returned recently from the supermarket after needing extra ingredients Abuela had forgotten.

"*Ay Dios mio mami*, you just came home." Rosario noticed the disarray of dishes and bowls, both filled with food and other remnants from preparation.

Abuela lifted a finger to the air and shook it. "Like I told Jamie, you never know when you'll have to feed an extra mouth or two—"

"You didn't say—" Jamie interrupted as Abuela continued.

"When you have kids you'll understand. Whether you have one or four or ten—you never *not* want to have enough."

"My grandma's the same way," Minjae said. "Both of them. Always offering my brother and I food until we physically cannot move our mouths anymore. It would be the most heavenly way to die."

Jamie leaned closer to him. "Even *while* we're eating she offers more." Abuela noticed her whispering and knew she was saying something she didn't like. She smacked Jamie on the arm before telling her to gather the potato salad.

When the dinner was finally served on the table, the family and guest sat around *fricase de pollo*, salad, potato salad, white rice, brown rice and black beans, *platanos*, and *tostones de pana*. Aiden licked his lips, strategizing which to get when. Minjae sat beside Jamie across the table from Aiden, with Rosario and Abuela at the ends of the table.

"Call me Abuela. Ah-bwe-la," she said, lifting the lid off of the rice bowl and motioning for Minjae to help himself to more.

He shook his head nervously and Jamie widened her eyes in warning. Abuela didn't take heed to it.

"So how long have you two been together?" said the star of the night, filling her plate.

Minjae choked on his rice for a moment as Jamie accidentally dropped the spoon into the chicken *guisado*, splattering some of the broth onto the table. Aiden broke into a wide grin as Rosario looked wide-eyed between them.

"We're not Abuela," Jamie said, cleaning up the mess.

"*Porqué no?* Why did he drop you off then? I thought you two were hiding outside because you didn't want me to see and get my hopes up." She giggled at Aiden.

Aiden laughed and pointed in between them. "Is that what you two were doing? Having a secret love affair?"

"*Dios mio*, no!" Jamie exclaimed quickly, resting each wrist on the corner of the table. "He helped give me a ride to Orlando."

"Orlando? For what?" Abuela eyed him particularly and he sat up straighter.

"I wanted to print a picture for Banafsha." More relaxed, Jamie scooped chicken and potatoes onto her rice as she answered. "You know she collects my prints."

"You know we have so much extra food you should invite her over. Since she helps out so much we can at least do this. As thank you. She's really helped our family."

Jamie nodded. "That's why. I've never taken a photo like it and I think she'll like it. I know her taste."

"Banafsha doesn't get out much," Aiden said, quickly stealing a *platano*. "She'd just say no to your invitation, Abuela."

"Still." Abuela looked at the food with a blank expression, slightly heedful to their reclusive neighbor. "You invite her anyways. We have so much food."

"Then don't make so much next time," Rosario said.

"Make enough for a family, or for at least two days. No one likes the hassle of cooking every day."

Minjae lifted the corner of his lips. "The part of my family that live in Korea do a thousand dishes a day. They have a set for each meal: breakfast, lunch, and dinner." He dabbed the air once for each meal time as Abuela shook her head.

"I hate dishes. The kids never want to help so it falls on me, no? That's why I love visiting my handsome helper." She eyed Aiden whose expression collapsed inward.

"That trick doesn't work anymore."

"The fact that my brilliant brother got Tom Sawyered"—Jamie said happily—"I'll never live it down."

"I know," Aiden said through bared teeth.

"*Por favor,*" Rosario said, speaking softly though everyone could hear. "Not in front of company."

"And what about me? Am I just a plant in the corner of the room, Rosario? Who made all this food for you?" Abuela waved her knife around the dishes. "Doesn't your mother deserve a little more gratitude?"

Rosario sighed deeply. *"Sí mami."*

Jamie apologized to Minjae with a side glance. If only she had known he was actually savoring the meal and the discussion with those he thought he'd never eat with.

By dinner's end Minjae had shared some of the Hispanic dishes he'd tried in the past, though none home-made, then shared some of the Korean dishes he frequently ate at home like *Japchae, Gimbap, Bulgogi*, not neglecting the Korean staple *kimchi*. While there weren't any Korean restaurants in Shore, he mentioned some in Orlando that were well-reviewed.

"Has Jamie mentioned the hiking trip the Capes are planning?" Minjae asked.

"Capes?" Abuela said.

Rosario nodded, glancing over to Jamie with a glass in hand. "Once."

"You see," Minjae said, "most of us have gotten permission already and we planned on pre-planning as soon as possible—pardon the redundancy."

Rosario looked over to Minjae as any parent would who was about to explain something difficult to a child. "Jamie hasn't mentioned it since that one time. When was it a month ago?"

"We're planning a road trip since it'd be cheaper to split gas money."

"Oh?" Rosario eyed Jamie once more.

"I know Jamie doesn't like to be in cars much and while she's mentioned getting a plane ticket—I think it'd be more fun if we all went together."

"Road trips from here to California would take two days at best—"

"If we switched drivers it could be done in less time."

"Four days is half the week," Rosario thought aloud. "Spring break isn't that long and I'm sure you wouldn't want to rush hiking. You'd also like to explore on the way there."

"Flight's aren't that expensive," Jamie said easily. "I think I'd rather wait at airports and take a cab."

"Actually Jamie," Rosario interjected, "Victor's mentioned you using his flight miles."

Aiden wasn't as interested in the conversation, but Victor's offer immediately changed that. Abuela, who wasn't even sure what the Capes were, was still catching up with the fact Jamie considered going in a car.

"When did he offer this?" Jamie asked.

"Not long after you first mentioned it. We never heard more from you so we thought you changed you mind."

The camping trip hadn't crossed her mind other than when the Capes mentioned it. It wasn't like she was dying to go and that was if they were hiking close by. But California. There was reason for her to object, though if Minjae heard her mother say it was all right with her going now then she wouldn't be able to use that as an excuse later. She and Minjae were now more or less on friendly terms and knowing his personality, and now that they had been introduced, he could return to her house and try to convince her mother if Jamie lied about her saying no.

Abuela and Aiden eyed Jamie as she contemplated, her lips parted as if ready to give her answer. Abuela felt her response too dragged out and stood up suddenly, moving out of the way of her chair toward the kitchen.

"*Mija* bought lemon cake and ice cream. Strawberry cheesecake or was it red velvet? Is there any Neapolitan?" She spoke to herself before looking back over her shoulder. "Minjae do you like either of those?"

He answered affirmatively as he turned toward her, though back at the table Aiden looked between his mother and Jamie as she finally found her answer.

"It was something I really wanted to think about before asking you again."

Rosario shrugged. "When? Spring Break's only a couple of months away. You know I think it's best to plan ahead. And you need to worry about work. Who knows if Era will request time off then or if Noel would take time off to spend it with his daughters."

"Not everyone has Spring Break at the same time. Universities and high schools have them on different weeks—"

"If you aren't serious about going then just say it. Don't drag it out. I don't want Victor to go through all the trouble if you're just thinking of a way to say no."

"Mom—" Aiden interposed quietly.

"He has to think about Riley too. He was thinking of visiting his family in D.C. during her break."

"I didn't ask for his help," Jamie said. "He can do whatever he wants. You're the one who's kept it from me for all this time."

"Not everyone's as kind as he's being to offer you a free flight. You don't have to answer now but decide soon. Before the New Year at least."

Aiden, with a saddened frown, turned toward his sister. While he jested earlier, he didn't take advantage of taunting her once their mother started mentioning Victor. He knew Jamie bore unfavorable feelings toward him, though most were unfounded. They'd never had an altercation that Aiden had witnessed and Victor never once looked badly on her. It was in the private moments Victor had sensed her discomfort with him. And it was obvious why.

Jamie had never gotten over their father's death. Aiden knew she didn't cry anymore, it was too long ago for her to do that since she wasn't a very emotional person to begin with, but there was still something in her silence he understood as a form of grieving. He knew Jamie had acquaintances, he'd seen her greet classmates and co-workers from the rock gym when they were out on grocery runs or at the beach, but he'd never met a friend she was close with like she had been with their dad.

Aiden eyed his mother as she slowly felt his icy glare. She asked him what but he simply looked back at his food. Weeks ago, he'd learned something that was beyond accepting, and now like his mother, hid it from his sister. He'd never understood why Jamie thought their mother held a bias toward him until earlier that month. Jamie thought that their mother held favoritism toward him like their father held favoritism toward Jamie. Aiden never noticed it. He had been too young. He knew their father loved them both equally. It was Jamie who loved him more that made it seem like he favored her.

He curled the fingers on one hand in between the other. If Jamie knew she'd never speak to their mother again. His mom didn't make it any better toward herself incessantly defending her boyfriend against Jamie. But if Jamie learned that *he* knew, without a doubt she'd see him as something else. A liar and something more. There was a reason his mother kept the secret. If Jamie knew she'd leave and forget them as easily as their father's family had forgotten him. Aiden loved his mom but no one understood him like Jamie. He understood his sister almost as well as their dad had. However there were things he was unsure of. This was one of them. Secrets between mother and daughter expanding between sisters and brothers divided families that, push comes to shove, cannot be mended. He loved his mom, but he didn't want to be alone. Not in the way Jamie felt alone.

She'd described it once to him a little over a year after their father passed. Not having her dad brought an emptiness into her life only those who were still grieving over a lost loved one could understand. It was expected, there was something about her loneliness that she'd realized took her a year to admit. It wasn't that she didn't have family left and it wasn't loneliness because she didn't have friends. There was something about a loneliness that thrived because she didn't want it to be replaced. He had asked her if she was afraid she'd forget her dad and she said it wasn't that.

Dad was my soul mate. I wish there was another word better suited for it but people underestimate how platonic that word is. We understood each other. Accepted all of each other. We were one spirit in two bodies.

Aiden had never heard the term used for anything than between romantic partners, but for him it made sense. She'd believed that friendships were stronger than connections based in love. She loved her dad, and it was a fundamental love most children performed out of expectation. Children said they loved their parents too easily. However Jamie valued her father more as a friend than she relied on him as a parent. Aiden never understood how and he admired her because of that. He always boasted he knew so much, but she figured out one of life's disregarded truths long before she should have. It was a realization she was born with since Destiny knew she wouldn't have time to appreciate it beyond her fourteenth year. If there was a god or deity who was omniscient and knew how things would turn out, at least he or she was decent enough to gift her with that truth early in life.

Rosario hadn't seen Aiden look at her like that in weeks. It took her several moments to realize why when she lowered her eyes and set her glass down on the table. It took Aiden days to get over his grudge toward her and it'd hardly been three weeks. She needed to mind what she said to Jamie or she'd have both kids hating her.

"Why is it quiet?" Abuela exclaimed as she reentered the room, a stack of bowls and spoons in between both hands. She set them down before returning to the counter to pick up the ice cream bucket and the container of lemon cake slices. "*Mira mija*, you don't have any Neapolitan so you need to go to the store again. Minjae, if you don't like the red velvet ice cream I can make a smoothie for you. Jamie and Aiden love the mango-pineapple I make. Or strawberry-banana. What do you like? I think there are fruits in the fridge."

Minjae waved his hands as he assured her that the ice cream was fine while Aiden quickly and silently reached for a bowl. Their mother stood up and went to take her plate to the sink as Jamie animated herself to reach for a bowl and spoon. If only Minjae wasn't there she would have told her mother to just forget the whole trip. If only Abuela wasn't there she would have avoided dinner altogether. She didn't know if she'd be cold to her mother again and decided to avoid her for the rest of the night if it was possible.

It was getting worse. Her grudges and contempt for her mother was worsening. It was contained before her uncle almost two months ago but since then . . .

She took the ice cream scoop Abuela left in the ice cream bucket and took out two scoops.

"Abuela, can you make me a mango smoothie?" Aiden asked.

"*Claro mi amor*. I'll make some for everyone."

Abuela leaned against the counter as her daughter placed a wet bowl from the sink into the dish washer then picked up one of the pots and held it under the water. With her arms crossed, Abuela looked out into the empty living room where Aiden had left the TV on. He was taking a shower. Jamie had gone outside to walk Minjae to his car. The brevity of time alone wouldn't last for much longer and Abuela wanted to take advantage.

"Every time I come here there's a fight between you two." Abuela glanced at the scar on Rosario's shoulder from when she fell on a rock after a rough wave at La Posita Beach. The scar fanned out like palm leaves but over the years had faded. She still remembered when Marcos, Rosario's older brother, carried his weeping sister back to shore and how much Rosario had cried. She'd had worse injuries, but she never cried as hard as she had that day at the beach. Once she had overcome something difficult, she had the durability and fortitude to push through future pain. Abuela liked to think she got that from her.

With a crafty smile, she added, "At least control yourself in front of company."

"We don't always fight," Rosario said under a subdued sigh.

"I see her talk to people maybe three times. Why did you have to make her feel like that when she brought someone over?"

"I didn't mean to sound critical. I just wanted her to make a decision."

"You said she hasn't mentioned it and yet you attack her like it's the *día final* to vote and she needs to decide now."

"When should I ask her then? The week before they go? A month? You don't realize how many parents outright say no."

Abuela smiled sardonically as Rosario ducked her eyes, focusing on the dishes in her hands.

"She's eighteen. She doesn't need your permission."

Rosario paused, but resumed her chore as if it didn't matter what she said. It was reasonable. Victor was doing a kind thing and if Jamie was smart about it she wouldn't start planning at the last minute.

"I'll be responsible for her until she leaves the house. Even after. My daughter doesn't stop being my daughter just because she turns eighteen."

"Either way. Don't always side with Victor. She'll think you only side against her."

Rosario slowly scrubbed the dirty plate until she stopped, looking over to her mother.

"Does she see me that way? That I'm only against her?"

Abuela softened her eyebrows, tilting her head to the side as she kindly reproached her. "There are kinder ways of asking."

Rosario gazed ahead over the kitchen sink into the night. She watched the Christmas lights on the neighbors' rain gutter that hung all year long sway softly. "Grandparents always have a soft spot for their grandchildren."

"Does she make a fuss when Victor's here?"

Rosario shook her head. "No. But she *can* be absent. I don't want him thinking she hates him."

"It isn't hate." Abuela looked toward the living room. "She misses her father. Any child that loved their parent that much would. It's always most painful for a child to lose their parent so young. *Entiendes?* It leaves a scar." Her eyes darted to the door. "The boy's very nice." Rosario nodded as Abuela reflected on something. "He's Daehyun's younger brother."

"They're both very good boys. I hadn't met Minjae before tonight but Daehyun doted on him. It isn't difficult to see why." She rinsed the plate in her hand and instead of reaching for another plate she looked through the window again. "I'm glad things turned out this way."

"*¿Qué dices?*"

"That Jamie never held a grudge against Daehyun. She seemed mindful with Minjae tonight."

"Why would it matter anyways?"

"For some reason, it gives me peace. To know she doesn't turn to hate when she's lonely, and I know she's lonely, despite how she lives."

"Make it up to her. Living the life she is—the way she is—it isn't fair to her. You need to show her you love her and don't place her second." Abuela momentarily glanced to her daughter, returning to her native tongue. *"When do you plan on telling her?"*

Rosario didn't move and with a detached voice responded, *"After she graduates."*

"Before it was when she turned eighteen. Now it's after she graduates. Are you afraid she won't come back?"

"You should tell her now," said a voice in English. Rosario and Abuela turned toward the hallway where Aiden stood with his hair still wet from his shower. He had a reproachful look in his eyes as they altered between one relative to the other. They both spoke in hushed whispers when the person they were gossiping about wasn't in the room, so both jumped when a third voice joined the conversation. "I don't see why you're keeping it from her in the first place."

"*Cariño*," Rosario said. "It isn't easy to share something after years of keeping it to yourself."

Abuela nodded as she took several steps toward him, however he spoke first. "She'll leave. You don't care, but I do."

"That's absurd, Aiden. I care, of course I care. This is only for just a little while longer. Just until she graduates high school."

Aiden's lip twitched as he glared in another direction. "You're so concerned about Victor and Riley and me but you don't care what she thinks. She's never been your first choice. That's why she can't stand being here. Always second to you. Or last." He drew his hands into fists. "I'd want to run away too."

"You'll understand why I'm this way when you have kids one day."

Aiden couldn't help flickering his attention in the direction of his *abuela* to see the validity of that statement, but he already knew she didn't agree with that. Even if she did agree it wouldn't matter, he still wouldn't. Every passing day he felt further burdened by the secret of his sister and how excluded she felt in her own house. It was worse when he knew he was just as guilty as his mother for keeping it from her. Because in truth, he didn't know what she'd do. After high school she'd leave anyways. It was when he acknowledged that reason that he realized that was why nothing was being said. Why *he* wasn't saying anything. Just a few more months. What was a few more months after already eighteen years of silence?

The front door opened as Jamie entered, noticing the tension in the room between Aiden's clenched jaw to their mother's façade of torment. Jamie looked from one pair of eyes to another, finally asking what they were talking about.

"Did he leave?" Rosario asked.

Jamie nodded as she made her way past Aiden, giving him a final glance before retreating to her room. Aiden looked to the women in the kitchen, one finding something to move on the kitchen counter while the other stared silently back at him.

If she leaves, Aiden thought, unyielding in his gaze. *I won't look to forgive you.*

22

The scarred creature pulled a pliable rope of tissue. Slender streams of red violet trickled over the stripped flesh onto the creature's fingers. He'd become attuned to the scent of blood, but there was something in feeling how the viscous ichor oozed slowly over his fingers as if gravity was as applicable here as it was on the planet. The thought tickled him.

"Fall, cry, try, die, cycle of the beasts," he sang. "Scream, screech . . ." He pulled the tissue rope and intertwined them around his fingers as he looked ahead to the heavy smoke in the horizon, closer than it was the day before and the day before. "Hear me teach . . ." His attention returned to the rope. ". . . all about the end."

The Darkness had tickled him since word first spread of its arrival. The souls never noticed it in the plains below as everything was red and full of dust. The ranks saw nothing beyond their orders and the commands of their general. The Saplings saw nothing but the fanciful promotions they'd gain centuries from now. It was the whispers in the walls, the shadows in the corners of the peripherals that had witnessed the Darkness in the distance. It was always the unnoticed that saw everything first. It was always the ones that no one expected. Even he on top of the mountain didn't notice it at first, hadn't perceived his own master.

The lord of the fortress had been causing such a stir ever since the Darkness had been sighted. Who knew how long the Darkness had lingered.

Watching.

Them.

The creature giggled, lying back in his chair as its body made the chair groan under his weight. For a creature that was a mass of muscle within and without, he weighed less than the chair had given him credit for. His sienna skin blended with the haze in the air and allowed him to slip unperceived amongst the souls and many of the Saplings below in the plains. As large as the Saplings may be they were nothing but empty acorns, the potential to be mighty oaks doomed to remain withering on the ground. Among the hollow beasts.

Such pitiful souls.

Interesting existences: souls. Built up and torn down in life to be torn and pulled down further here. For all eternity. Pity didn't exist here but if there was one who deserved it, it was them. Curious that the creature should feel such an emotion for one that was unlike him. He still enjoyed observing them. To watch them from afar like a hawk. But only to watch. There was always a glimmer in their eyes of a long past hope. Some of them perhaps saw him on the summit of the mountain, a mouse by its hole, hoping that someone who stood so far and so safe was indeed powerful and exempt from their eternity of futile slog. Prayers for someone who could spare them mercy.

Please.

One wouldn't make a difference.

Help me. I never asked for anything in my life. I beg you. Help me!

They all said it before and they'd find new ways to beg. He was numbed by it all.

The creature stood and moved to the edge of the gate post, worn smooth by the gales that rushed around the structure of the portal, much like waves on Earth wore seaside rocks smooth. Dim traces of light slipped through the portal and down the mountain to the plains, merely ants at the back of his mind.

Numb. However after centuries of mere observation, there was still a seed of curiosity within him. The state they were in was of their own will. All his insistence, it didn't stop the slither up his back, over his shoulders, and along the trunk of his neck. It pricked him, even after millenniums.

"Rephastion." There was a limited handful who would call the creature by his name and yet, the delicacy and softness in the way his caller said it made sinister lips soften into a warmer smile.

"It pleases me the way you say that word."

"Rephastion," said the caller with dire suppression.

The creature let the smile fade as he turned around. The caller facing him was of filmy matter, shimmering among the haze as water on the pavement under a sweltering day.

"Does the Lord General have a request of me? Does he miss me? Am I late for another unbearable assembly?"

"Your task . . ."

Any humor that could've been salvaged had now diminished as Rephastion glared.

"I have not decided."

"Our Lord General—"

"Is not *my* Lord General. I serve one. And that presence has not approached me in well over many years."

The caller's sight turned toward the Darkness in the horizon as it neared the Ruined Portal. Rephastion turned back toward the plains after a skeptical gaze. The caller was not intimidated by Rephastion.

"Your master is here now."

"My master does not pester me so much in three thousand years as your master in a single day." He reflected on the parameter. "Has it been a day, Iax?"

The caller, Iax, bent accordingly to the passing winds as wisps of its figure diminished in the air, a gravitational force replacing the empty space with a regenerating growth of cloud.

"It has been an interesting few days on the Rock. Those under the Lord General of the Rock have been accumulating reports of an imbalance. It is under Tier's control and yet there have been no unexpected disturbances since the Turn. Such reports cause much distress and concern for our Lord General Erus."

Rephastion dropped the rope of tissue from one hand and twirled it beside him mindlessly as he listened. It was always one thing snowballed larger into another. He knew it would never happen but a moment of peace was almost desirable.

There it was again. A moment of sympathy for the souls down below. His focus landed on the general clusters. No one ever liked to acknowledge the exhausting lights within the hollow souls, risking all of their existence to attest nothing more was there. And there he was, able to witness a trace of light, and with no fear of punishment, he kept the traitorous secret to himself.

"He wishes to support the Lord General of the Rock in his search. Our Lord General is desperate to refrain wasting any more time."

"Iax," Rephastion sighed. "Every time your Lord General hears whispers of the Darkness he finds himself with an unmistakable opportunity. One that undoubtedly and regretfully concerns me. Reports or no reports . . . Now, after a short absence of only two centuries my master has returned, and like a child with a new toy he is giddy with himself to push his plans forward. Time has moved too quickly for him, hasn't it? His plans—woe me—require me to leave my post and journey to the Rock; a task that is not mine. Inside me . . ." He shook his head with dismay. ". . . such turmoil. I am transfixed."

Iax turned to Rephastion in silence as it reached toward the creature, tendrils of smoke caressing the burnt red flesh up the chest, around the wrists and up the arms, suffocating the neck and settling around the cap of his head and around his horns. Rephastion simply breathed in as he let Iax settle, sink, and descend beneath the barriers of his flesh. It was almost intimate. Melting into the connection, he closed his eyes and extended his arms out.

"It finally happened," Rephastion murmured. "After all this time, I have finally become allured."

Iax began to pull away and only when the last tendril released itself from Rephastion did the creature open his eyes.

"No one cares to remember, but a long time ago there was a Sapling who became curious. Souls did not exist yet and somehow he had become curious. Not with your master. Not with mine. But the one above us all. I never understood how he could have been so curious as to be discontent with our new home. The haze is hard to bear and get used to for some but he rebelled against our Lord Master. What's always been funny to me is that our Lord Master simply cast him out. Disgraced him to remain unbidden to neither the Heavens nor the Crater. Can you imagine? A Sapling! Even *I* cannot attach myself to the fleeting wind." Rephastion was mesmerized. "There's an exotic appeal to him that I haven't ever been able to discard."

"And what causes your heart to change now?"

Rephastion pulled up the corner of his lip. "I've realized. Your Lord General looks at my master the same way souls ponder at the stars believing there to be something out there. There's wonder in their eyes. I saw that wonder in your Lord General during our last assembly when he assigned me a task." The creature suddenly outburst into laughter, causing Iax to stir and shift away. The creature took his time recovering his temperament, wiping his bottom lip with an elegant finger. "Forgive me. But when I think of your Lord General and how infatuated he is with my master—I cannot control myself. I feel to be watching an instrument go in circles around, around, around me."

A loud chorus of moans, cries, and jeers rose from the plains, along the incline of the mountain to the ledge, where a short distance away the Ruined Portal stood like the cross. The wave of sounds passed them as relentlessly as wind. The two made no move or sound to blanket it. The souls below were shifting further down the plains, parallel to the Darkness in the horizon, as more souls replaced them. Beside him, the Ruined Portal admitted passage to hundreds every minute. Fleeting winds themselves, the souls, slid down the mountain side elegantly and obstinately against the ferocious currents, only to settle and solidify on the plains. Here, where they would wake from their dreams of their lives, and begin their new, immortal ones here. Rephastion frowned as he watched the cycle, unmoved by millenniums of congruent repetition.

"It's all the face of a clock. Everything is new and no moment the same, and yet nothing changes behind the face. It is only a flat surface and neither the shifting dial nor minute hand suffice me."

"Your task will allow you to see beyond this sequential picture."

"Somehow, I've come to care for why the souls continue to make the same mistakes. Their programming is not like us. They have their will, we have our choice, it should be the same thing. Yet, they're so weak. They're pathetic. I cannot keep my eyes from them. I'm bewitched. My eyes cannot pull away."

"Our Lord General will be pleased."

Rephastion crossed his arms and leaned to one hip as he faced Iax.

"The Fall, our grand epoch into the Crater, created such prominent leaders: our Grand Master, the Darkness, the Seven Deadly Sins, The Four Horsemen, me, and yet no one seems to ever mention the three Generals. Why do you suppose that is? Why is it that whenever a soul is asked about the Lord Generals on their arrival they always goggle obtunded? Why is it they fear the monsters and soldiers and Saplings of Hell and yet they are ignorant to your most revered Lord Generals?"

"Human Souls do not generally know all of the positions in their governments. Such as, they do not know of our Lords."

Rephastion pouted his lower lip. "Damn you have an answer for everything . . . Answer me this, what do *we* have to fear from them?"

Iax's form shifted toward the plains and focused on the Darkness again. The creature Rephastion felt he had won and grinned mercilessly.

"We don't fear them because they are predictable. They are safe. Stuck in the Heavens, here, and the Rock. They move silently, arrogantly, and uninvolved."

"Our Lord General will change that, beginning with your assignment."

Rephastion's shoulders slackened as he cracked his neck. "I do feel like I am talking to myself. I rarely acquire company worth the conversation. Can't you make your trip worthwhile for me? How long have you known me?"

Iax ignored him. "Choose your soul. He expects you departed soon."

"I guess he'll just find someone to fill my position until I return then?"

A subtle nod. "Until you return."

Rephastion's disposition molded similarly to one of a soldier's as he responded dismally. "What disturbances have your reports accrued? What imbalance?"

"A shadow moves and it conceals something."

A wickedly intrigued smile spread over his lips. "Could it be our banished Sapling?"

"Impossible," said Iax. "Fallen from Grace and banished from the Damned, the Sapling possesses no support from either force. He is likely between the ghosts of stars."

Rephastion thought otherwise. If he had rescinded falling from Grace he could have gained favor with the Heavens again. While impossible to return, he could have acquired the alliances of the angels. The children of the Light did have a fondness for forgiving. Especially for a lone child, fated to wander the universe neither an angel nor a demon. Angels had never been demons though demons had once been angels. And yet, none of the Fallen had ever left before. It was something he never understood of the Lord Master. How he could banish the Sapling instead of condemning him to another fate? Curiosities. He felt he was the only one in all of this place who held them, who kept them as bedside fantasies.

None of these thoughts were voiced aloud as Rephastion knew that his caller would pay them no mind. He was simply a messenger, and one that easily accepted his place as nothing more. He cared little, which is why his being had begun to diminish into the emptiness of the air. Rephastion could pass his hand through his friend while his friend feel nothing more than a slight brush. Rephastion brought his attention back to the present. "Is there a particular place the imbalance is ruffling feathers?"

"There is. You will start looking around the ruins from where the Turn clinched."

"Don't waste my time. I will not—" Rephastion heard an arrhythmic beating on the ground as a hunched Sapling began to approach them. Bent over, with holes tunneling through his rheumatic spine, the ragged covering poorly concealed the scars, bruises, scabs, and abrasions fresh on his skin. Once nearby, the abused creature bowed and remained stiff as it panted. Rephastion capriciously smiled down at him. "Italus. Rest my friend. You are weary."

"A message"—he spat uncontrollably onto the ground—"a message for my Lord, our Gatekeeper has, does he not. A message?"

Rephastion rolled his eyes. "How honored I am by not just one visit, but now another. Am I to expect another party from your Lord soon?"

"Our Lord waits—waits for our Gatekeeper's message. The task, complete it will he not? The task. Our Lord General knows—wishes to know."

"Wait a moment . . ." Rephastion stepped quickly beside Italus and rested his hand firmly on his back, turning him toward the plains. Awkwardly and frightfully Italus obeyed, moving how Rephastion positioned him, barely finding within himself to peek up.

"Joy. Do you know the feeling my weary friend?" Rephastion stared over the plains. Italus didn't reply and the scarred creature chuckled, expecting this. "I see my master once every millennium and look, there he is, after only two centuries. Why? Why do you think he has returned so soon?"

"Impossible for me to know. Very unsure. Impossible. I—I cannot f—fathom why."

"I am half joy, half curiosity. I am—could you say . . ." He glanced toward Iax, who remained impassive and immobile overlooking the plains. "Utterly transfixed. My existence is to remain numb because nothing changes. Nothing is unexpected. Yet the reason I'm able to tolerate your incessant and bothersome Lord General's messages is because I allow you to. My master has given me something new. I don't care for your master or for the Seven. Command me, damn me, beg me, curse me all you desire. Look."

Italus shivered and tried to control his convulsions, bringing his melted face up to look in the direction Rephastion pointed; toward the Darkness.

"My master is waiting. No one, not even the Grand Master commands my master, least of all your damned Lord General. The request bestowed upon me has been considered, though not made, so learn to be fucking patient you eternally damned human breather." Rephastion's eyes blazed and just as quickly ceased. "And I mean your Lord General of course, my weary friend, not you. Deliver that message for me will you? As I said it. Word for word."

Italus' scowl from the viscid burns sagging his facial features dropped lower as he peered frightfully up to the creature.

"M—my, my Lord Gatekeeper!"

"*Exactly* as I said it my weary friend. I will make you my messenger when you return. After I return from my task that is. If I choose to go." Rephastion began to cackle uncontrollably again as he released his hold on Italus, stepping forward beside Iax. Italus slunk backwards before scampering away, his hands and feet stamping deformed imprints into the ground in every uneven hurdle forward.

"What is your decision, Rephastion?" Iax asked in a wistful sigh.

Rephastion dropped the rope of tissue from his hand and allowed his horns to drag the weight of his head back. "I really do love the way you say that word."

"Your name," Iax said coldly. "When you go among the humans, they consider some words more important than others. It is your name."

"I am to go to the Rock—"

"Earth."

"I am to go to Earth in search of the source of this imbalance and discover if there is base in rumors of a weapon, all so that your Lord General may implement his plan and harness control over my master and therefore dominate power over this place and that Rock." He sighed. "I don't like it. No, I don't think I will consider his request any longer. I'll just . . . stay . . . here."

"You can go and explore your curiosity."

Rephastion brought his head up and turned toward Iax, who also turned his figure toward him. The glee in Rephastion's eyes found their way into his voice. "Have you actually been listening to me as a friend?"

"One ruler. Another ruler. Nothing changes. No matter his ambition, the end will always be between the Grand Master and the Father."

"And I wondered why you seemed less present than normal. Your allegiances aren't to a new power but to none. I believe you'll succumb to my master before your Lord General sees the throne himself."

"If that is what will be."

Rephastion sighed, reaching to rest his hand on the filmy shoulder. "Don't disappear on me so soon. There aren't nearly enough Saplings to talk to."

"You don't really think I listen to you do you?" Iax didn't allow Rephastion to speak even though the latter opened his mouth. "Go to Earth. Quench your curiosity. If not here, my Lord General cannot bother you."

Iax moved past the creature Rephastion and left him alone. Rephastion picked up the rope and went to the post, wrapping it around and using it to balance his weight as he climbed. The new arrivals streaming through the Portal wailed in branching currents, shrieking and groaning in every tier on the spectrum of pitches. Once atop the lintel he sat down heartily, swinging his legs back and forth as he rested back onto his hands. The Darkness was a hint of a distance closer.

"I guess I can have some fun by the time you arrive. With you around, I guess that worm of a general will be too preoccupied to really keep an eye on me."

A whistle passed through his lips to join the choir of cries down below. It was an unfamiliar tune and with his own musical signature he structured it to go along with the ascension of the weeping chorus.

"A Fallen angel, a banished demon, cursed forever among the stars," he sang. "Alone, unwanted, ill-fated, condemned the soulless one."

His tragic lullaby stopped. A bridge formed between his thoughts and his curiosity. "If I were a man . . . Alone. What would I do? What could I do? An eternity of solitude. I'd see man die, and demons and angels live forever. Neither demon, neither angel. Neither god nor soulless matter . . ." He seemed resolved and nodded. "He'd look for a companion. Look, search throughout time and planet. Search and search until he'd found one. Someone to be his companion. Someone—so he wouldn't be alone." His lower lip pouted forward as he looked down the plains to the souls, cast down to rise then be burdened again. The Saplings barked and slashed their whips onto the backs of the souls relentlessly. Pity. Rephastion still didn't feel it.

But *he* did.

Rephastion's eye twitched as he leaned forward, resting his arms on his legs.

"Such cruelty . . . The Banished Sapling has seen it all and he wants to prevent it. He pities them. Time amongst them has done this to him. Eventually, he finds someone to be his companion. He'll protect them. He'll shield them." Rephastion began a fit of giggles. "An eternity here and I understand those I haven't seen better than Sapling spies who live among them. Sapling to a fault. Yes, I'll seek out this imbalance, oh righteous Lord General."

The creature directed his attention to the Darkness.

"When one loses all they have, when they lose their only true family, how does one go on?"

The Darkness made no vocal reply, but a wave of epiphany flooded within Rephastion. He understood, panting in a motionless breathlessness. The answer was given to him, the answer he already knew. The task given by the Lord General was to him merely a farce, but if his master let him go, how would he dare refuse?

He closed his eyes and allowed his master to communicate his instructions. The commands were shocks of earthquakes trapped within his head and he did nothing but accept how his mind and soul trembled. Responsibilities of the Gatekeeper. As of now, he'd been reassigned.

Find the source of the imbalance.

"It's closer than we think."

Set it true.

The crumbling pressure suddenly lifted and Rephastion took a long time to collect his breath, resting his hand on his chest as he looked back toward the souls. He'd never been given such an involved task. It almost tickled him with a mortal kind of thrill.

"And while there, maybe I'll get around to understanding this mortal joy. This mortal curiosity."

23

Borrowing an elf hat from Aiden and with the printed photo Minjae delivered the night before in tow under her arm, Jamie walked up Banafsha's front walk way. While she waited for Banafsha to answer the door, Jamie adjusted the bell so it hung over her left ear. When Banafsha answered, it didn't take much to guess what she thought of the costume. Jamie's smile diminished.

"I haven't seen you in almost a week," Jamie said.

"I thought you were my Chinese." She looked down to the large frame and Jamie immediately blocked it, though the entire frame was wrapped in shiny blue wrapping paper.

"It's a gift."

Banafsha rolled her eyes and returned inside. Jamie picked up the frame and followed, asking, "And when do you order from outside?"

"I don't have anything for you."

Jamie smiled excitedly as she rested the frame against the armrest of the sofa. "You've never given me a gift before."

"So then why do you still insist on giving them to me each year?" Jamie rolled her lips together and bounced her eyebrows. Banafsha clicked her tongue at her. "Don't flirt with me. You're not my type." Jamie's humor dropped as her lower lip slipped open, her face twisting in disbelief. Banafsha withheld a smile as she tossed her hand in the direction of the present. "What is it?"

The look of joy returned as Jamie stepped beside the frame, waving her hand over it. "You know how I've been gloating about a picture for months and months and have left you in an incredible amount of intriguing suspense?"

"I forgot about it," Banafsha said flatly.

"I have captured for your eyes only the single most important and unique imprint of life in all of history."

Banafsha exhaled and tilted her head to the side. "That's bold. Are you prepared for my reaction if I disagree?"

"We always disagree."

"I won't spare you your feelings. It might be best if you leave and I unwrap it without you."

"No! I want to see your reaction."

"How unique is it?"

"Only one copy in existence. I deleted the image from my SD card before coming here."

"What made you go to such a length?"

"Because I'm stripping myself of any and every connection to the subjects of this photo once you've seen it."

Banafsha imagined the words had been a burden for her to say. It was difficult to tell when Jamie was speaking candidly because she had a special way of hiding what she really meant. Unintended, but Banafsha noticed the slight quaver in her conviction. All the same, the sentiment of bringing her a gift still softened her opinion of Jamie time and time again.

"Open it," Jamie said, nodding her head to the present.

Banafsha found no reason to resist further and gripped the corner mercilessly, pulling it down to reveal under the scar of ripped paper, the photo underneath. She made no reaction until she uncovered most of it, and when she pulled the two sides apart to examine it, it took her a moment to understand what she was looking at.

Two silhouette figures. One reached out to catch a blurry doll falling from the heavens. Unnatural horns protruded from the skull and wings extended from the back of the figure on the right. The longer it was studied, the clearer the figures seemed. The doll was in fact the human and the supposed human was the statue of a gargoyle.

"Is this some sort of photo manipulation?"

Jamie bit her lip, and looking down at the photo, shook her head. "None of it. I didn't edit it at all. In a way, it would be doing it an injustice."

"I wasn't aware the church had such statues."

Jamie wrapped her arms behind her as she lifted her eyebrows. "Not many are."

"And why do want to disconnect yourself from statues?"

"Because they're a lie. This photo embodies they're nothing more than a lie."

"In what ways does a statue lie?"

Jamie inhaled and looked up to her. "Would you believe me if I told you they were alive? Not just any statue. These. The gargoyles at the top of St. Luke's."

Banafsha shook her head. "What nonsense are you saying?"

"Exactly," Jamie said through tear-provoked laughs. "For two months I've seen and heard nothing but absolute nonsense. I just needed you to say that. To hear it from you." She took the frame and held it up against an empty part of a wall. A blank expression settled over her face, then she looked to find a better place for the frame. Jamie noticed Banafsha standing quietly and quickly opened her mouth into a wide grin. "Do you want me to put it up for you? By the way, you're invited to Christmas dinner tonight."

Banafsha turned her back and went to the kitchen. Picking up a towel, Banafsha began wiping the counter. "I don't care for family gatherings."

"One of these days I'll convince you."

Banafsha scoffed. "One of these days you'll stop asking."

Soon after entering the house, the TV on and their mother and *abuela* out of the room, Jamie spotted her brother on the phone. Not thinking much of it she walked in the direction of her room, only pausing once she heard what he was saying.

"Abuela asked for you since you've recently moved here. She wants you over for Christmas dinner." He listened to the person for a moment. "Yeah. Yeah, I'm sure she'd pick you up if they couldn't drive . . ."

Jamie walked over to him and watched him with narrowed eyes, crossing her arms as she waited for him to finish the call. Aiden pivoted his body away as he looked anywhere else. "Are you sure?"

"Jamie?" Rosario said from behind her, a basket of clothes in her hands. Jamie made no response and barely acknowledged her as she waited for Aiden to finish. When he did, he stared back with wide eyes.

"What?"

"Was that Gabe?" When Aiden confirmed it, she reined in her anger, merely exhaling through the nose. "Why'd you call him?"

"Am I not allowed?" He gestured toward their mother with his chin. "Mom and Abuela asked me to call to invite him over tonight."

Their mother walked around Jamie toward their bedrooms, pausing by the couch. "What's the problem, Jamie?"

"He'll have church obligations," Jamie said. "Confessionals or vespers or tours or whatever parochial jobs they do in their day. He can't come."

"Do you want to explain why not to Abuela if you won't with me?"

Jamie ignored her as she faced her brother. "Don't call him anymore."

"Just because you have an issue with him doesn't mean you can tell me if I can see him or not."

"Aiden, you don't even know who you're defending. You've never even met him."

"He hasn't done anything wrong. He's still dad's brother."

"I asked Aiden to call him—" Rosario said as Jamie cut her off, still focused on Aiden.

"And he doesn't deserve to be! He didn't even go to dad's funeral. None of those pieces of shit did—"

"Jamie!" Rosario stepped forward and set the basket on the couch.

Jamie jutted her chin out and glared at her mother. "Yell at me all you want. I'll never not think they're pieces of shit. They don't deserve to be related to dad and I hope they all burn in hell. If I remember their faces or their names five years from now I'll know I've done dad a disservice."

"Jamie," Aiden pleaded, the intensity in his eyes instantly dimmed down. He lifted a hand to reach for her but she stepped away.

"I don't like him and I don't trust him. I've tried being considerate but I don't know why I thought I should be anymore. He doesn't deserve it. I don't see how you could forgive him. I won't respect him for it and neither should you."

"What's spurring this on all of a sudden?" Rosario asked.

"Because!" Jamie inhaled deeply. "I don't want to affiliate myself with him or that church ever again. Even hearing one of you say it—I'd rather walk out of this house than hear another word about that goddamn man or his family."

"*¿Qué pasó?*" Abuela asked as she entered the room. Aiden had begun to withdraw and Rosario was facing Jamie off as if they were quarreling again. "What's going on, Jamie?"

Jamie looked toward Abuela and tried to control her breathing. Enveloped in the argument, her hands had begun to shake and her face had reddened.

"You never forgave them either, right Abuela?" Jamie asked, with softness in her eyes reserved only for her grandmother. "After dad died, you hated them just as much as I did."

"*¿A quien odias?*"

There was no getting past her resentment. "Mom and Aiden have forgiven them even when they remained stubborn in their damn ways—never reaching out to us. Have you forgiven them also, Abuela?"

Abuela sighed and entered the circle, resting a drying towel on the top of the couch. "You don't like your uncle coming to dinner. Your mother said you wouldn't. But I think he should. He's still your family. And he's not like that part of the family, *gracias a Dios*. *Pero* we shouldn't let him be alone on Christmas. We are his family and we are here so what is the problem?"

A film blurried Jamie's vision. She blinked, but even blinking five times didn't hinder the tears. She felt them build and breathed deeply before wiping them away, searching for a calm in the ceiling. Not even her Abuela . . . Abuela always sided with her when she argued with her mother but the time she needed Abuela to side with her most, she didn't. Everyone here was against her. She just wanted to keep him away. Only those who deserved to be loved by her family should be loved and yet her mother was so forgiving, even tricking her brother into forgiving him. This wasn't the right way to celebrate Christmas, the holiday that meant the most to her father.

"Don't be mad," Aiden said softly. "It's just dinner."

Jamie nodded, avoiding eye contact with all of them before grabbing a jacket and going to the front door.

"Victor and Riley will be coming soon—" Rosario said, though on deaf ears as Jamie didn't pause to listen, slamming the door behind her. She picked up her bike and pushed the pedals faster than the chain could crank.

She didn't want to be around any of them and didn't care if they thought she ruined dinner. It wasn't like they considered about her feelings.

Wanting to feel something of comfort she rode to the cemetery. Passing the yellowed sign, she got off and pushed the bike by the handlebars. With no one present, she suddenly felt coming to cemetery wouldn't give her what she wanted.

Her feet brought her forward anyways.

The fallen leaves fluttered over the grass as each step closer to the grave was as if stepping closer to her death. She'd escaped her house so she wouldn't have to think of her family, but going where there was no one and where there was barely a noise to distract her, she realized she'd come to the wrong place. No matter how family pretended and said what she wanted to hear, they were against her. Being together in a cheerful time suffocated her. Wishing more than ever she could slip into an unknown landscape and walk straight without any necessity to know where she was going or what was waiting for her back home. The holidays became dry, a once juicy strawberry wrinkled stale from neglect. A week, three years, nothing new gave her joy.

The world became still, as if a shell had been lowered around her, redirecting the wind and blocking out any festivities from the nearby neighborhoods. The only sounds were the ones her feet created, her bike traced, her breath emitted, her jacket rustled. The cemetery was in another world.

The bike was set on its side three graves away, her eyes already on her father's name. Standing in front of his grave, she felt the visit had been long delayed; a visit that *had* been worth the bike ride, despite her fickle heart moments ago. While she felt lonely now, facing her father off in a displaced, cut-off world gave her the air to breathe. She sat down and stared at the engraving letters, studying each line as a scarred entity and not collective symbols for a person's identity. One who loved her for her scars. Who smiled away her tears.

I wasn't an easy child to love. I only needed you to be there for me. Since you can't be, can you send someone else? Tempted to touch the rocky material, she kept her hands on her lap. She waited for the wind to blow and send a chill up her spine, or a leaf to tumble along and land on her sleeve, or an ant to crawl into her shoe and bite her. Any insignificant sign that he was with her if he wasn't going to answer her.

I'm gonna leave soon. Her eyes drifted down to the boundary between rock and grass.

One day she'd be here too, buried under the ground with strangers walking six feet above on their way to visit a relative who passed away fifty years before. She wondered how many people would walk over her grave never knowing who she was. One day, would there be a curious soul who would read her name and wonder why a Jamie Diez died so young?

Her attention flickered back to the grave as if she could feel her father's eyes on her.

"It was just a thought," she said aloud. "A thought doesn't mean anything."

Following the shape of the tombstone her breathing calmed, letting the palm of her hand stray over the tops of the grass blades, as few and as yellow as they were. The tickling sensation oddly calmed her as she sighed, leaning back to look at the late evening sky. Already she could see the bookends of the sky differing, to her right was the flooding darkness of night and to the left, the drifting shadows of the sunset, a modest orange.

"Why couldn't I have gone first?" she asked. "People who want to be here should be here. I just take up air."

The sky slipped behind her closing eyelids as she tried to remember her father's face. Pictures aside, home-made videos forgotten, what did her father's face look like? How did he smell when he came from a construction site to pick her up at school? How did his voice sound when he asked her if she wanted to build a sandcastle? She remembered his face in laughter, more than its comforting sound.

An unstoppable force overwhelmed her. Her nose stung and her chin trembled. She hooked her arm over her eyes and breathed deeply. Count the stars in the sky. Count sheep. Just start counting anything for as long as you can until you forget why you were feeling what you were feeling in the first place. That was her father's trick to overcome a bad day at school or when she scraped her knee or when Aiden wouldn't stop being a little brother. She hadn't done it in years. She couldn't now.

She sat up, spending two more silent minutes in front of his grave, before standing up and guiding her bike away. Somehow coming to this other world didn't help her unblock the congestion within herself. This was the first time her father hadn't been able to help her when she needed it. She stepped past the shell's invisible boundary and didn't get on her bike until she reached the end of the dusty road.

It was in a public park near her house that she found a bench to sit on, and crossing one leg over the other, she pulled out her phone to dial Era's number. She tapped her foot as the phone rang until it eventually went to voicemail, though she ended the call before the automated message began.

Of course, she'd be with her sweetheart today. Jamie moved to put the phone back in her pocket when she reconsidered, bringing it back out as she scrolled through the short list of contacts. She found Minjae's and hovered her finger over the call button. After a good minute of oscillation, she pressed the button and chewed her lip as she listened to it ring. It rang for several seconds, on the verge of reaching voicemail, when the caller picked up. While he answered immediately, she breathed in deeply, uncertain if she'd made the right decision.

"I called you on impulse. It was a mistake." However, she didn't hang up, staring at a gyre of leaves swirling past her.

A chuckle passed from the other end of the line. "Wrong number, huh?" The voice suddenly rose. "*What!* Do you *not* see me on the phone!"

Jamie yanked the phone away as she hesitantly returned it to her ear. She already heard Minjae apologizing before her hearing returned to normal.

"Family dinners, am I right? Christmas is a big one for us and oh my god nieces and nephews are pestering." He altered his voice slightly. "*Minjae what are you doing? Minjae what's that?* Like you can clearly see I'm in the bathroom. Was the door *not* closed!" He sighed quickly. "Let me tell you. I have learned my lesson, whoo wee! Always lock the bathroom door or you *will* be pestered with fifty million questions which more than not inhibit you from doing what you need to do. I'm used to being the baby of the family. Clearly. No one ever *ever* did this in my day."

Jamie had never heard Minjae genuinely angry and to hear him babble on and on about the invasion of his privacy actually bothering him made a small smile appear on her lips. If it hadn't been him, she wouldn't have smiled so easily.

"*Anyway!* What are you up to? You having a family dinner too? Any more family members come after Abuela?"

"No, just my mom's boyfriend and his daughter, but I'm at some park now. Couldn't be around them earlier."

"Oh? Something going on?"

"Just family bullshit." Jamie tried to pass it off as nothing. "The usual nonsense."

"Mmm, need a distraction? You can come over to my house. I promise you you won't be thinking of your family." Jamie considered his offer and when she was quiet for too long he revised it. "It'll distract you better than an empty park will."

Noting how peaceful the park had been with no people, squirrels, insects or even the winter wind to distract her from her issues, she took him up on his offer. The park only served as a reminder of pleasant childhood memories. She waited for him to text his address before jumping on her bike.

Minjae was waiting on the hood of his car. He smiled brightly as she slowed to a stop.

The smile he wore subsided as he nodded and greeted her with closed eyes. "Welcome"—he opened his eyes—"to the crazy house. You'll want to escape once you see what's inside." He jumped off the hood and extended his arm toward the front door. "After you."

The dramatic performance couldn't keep her from smirking. Before they reached the end the front door suddenly opened and two kids, both a girl and boy about nine years old, stared at them.

"Linnie, Ozzy, I said I'd be right in," Minjae said. "You couldn't wait another five seconds?"

Both kids stared at Jamie for a moment before the girl focused on Minjae and spoke loudly. "Auntie was wondering where you were."

"Then you should have told her what I told you. Remember what we talked about? Anyways, I'm coming in now."

"Who are you?" Linnie asked, placing her fists on her hips and staring at Jamie. A sinister smile spread over her lips as her eyes curved. "You his girlfriend?"

"Minjae has a girlfriend," Ozzy sang, running back inside. "He has *another* girlfriend!"

Jamie waved her hands to deny the accusation as Linnie waited patiently for an audible answer. Minjae laughed awkwardly as he turned to Jamie, a slight pitch in his voice. "Oh my god save me."

After looking back to Linnie, Jamie forced a smile as she held out her hand, gesturing for her to give her something.

Linnie curled her lip. "What?"

Jamie shrugged her shoulders. "I guess now is as good as time as any. I'm not Minjae's girlfriend. I'm his betrothed. We expect the wedding immediately after graduation. Presents are given by the youngest family members first. Since you've learned of us first, I'll expect yours shortly."

"That's a lie," she said quickly, judging the hand held out to her. "Minjae said he wasn't dating anyone anymore."

Jamie dropped her arm. "Exactly, we're not dating until after we get married. It was supposed to be a secret but since you figured it out ahead of everyone else I won't lie to you. You have such an honest, sweet face. You remind me of my younger brother. You should meet him. I guess we'll all be family soon anyways, you'll meet him later. I think you'd like him. How old are you? You two look about the same age. Should I introduce you? You don't have a boyfriend right because my brother doesn't have a girlfriend yet and honestly he's a little short but that's just now he'll grow up to be really tall, so if you can just wait a couple of years—"

Linnie started walking away as Jamie's smile widened, nodding as the back disappeared behind the front door. She turned to Minjae, staring at her in disbelief.

"I shouldn't have invited you just now." A smile appeared on his face. "I should have invited you hours ago! Oh my god." He hooked an arm around her as he leaned his head on her shoulder, walking them inside. "Never leave me again."

There weren't many cars in the front of the house so Jamie thought there might be at most ten people at his house, but the further into the house she went the more and more people she had to make her way in between. There were the immediate members of the family, but then extended relatives. Almost every relative he passed, particularly the elders, Minjae bowed his head after acknowledging them. Jamie kept an eye out open for a familiar face. Ironically, the one person she knew wasn't present.

"Daehyun went to visit his girlfriend's family over the holiday," Minjae said, pointing in general over a group of adults in the living room. "All aunts and uncles and great aunts and even I can't keep track."

"You have so many relatives. Do they all live in Florida?" Jamie smiled politely at the faces that looked her way and like Minjae, bowed her head to those who made eye contact.

"No some flew from Korea, but most are from out-of-state. Texas and California mostly but . . ." His eyebrows drew together as he thought harder. "One couple is from Canada, and another couple and their kids are from Paris. Oh! And another from Australia. We're a diaspora clan. Please don't ask names I met most of them for the first time today and I'm iffy on the faces. I only know them from pictures. I'll just introduce you to the important people. Mama!"

They came to the kitchen where his mother was surrounded by other cooks and hungry stomachs and kids trying to snatch a sweet. Minjae's mother was tall, only slightly shorter than her son, with warm motherly eyes and an inviting smile. Her hands were the hands of a woman who'd had to endure many hardships, but were strong and reliable. Her straight hair was picked up by a clip, some strands sliding in her face to which she pushed aside at the sound of her son's voice. Her eyes widened asking what he wanted, then turned to Jamie when he gestured toward their new guest.

His mother looked at Jamie for an immeasurable amount of time, standing still and forgetting the tumultuous world around her. People noticed her immobility and glanced at Jamie before moving around her or continuing their story with someone else. Minjae wasn't expecting her reaction and looked between them, the smile withering away as he lightly touched her arm for her to greet Jamie. And Jamie hadn't ever been received so cautiously. When a smile slowly began to show on her face, Jamie smiled merely in relief.

Minjae's mother reached for a towel, wiping her hands as she stepped closer to Jamie, then pausing several steps away.

"Ma . . ." Minjae shook his mother's arm softly as she continued to ignore him.

"I'm sorry," his mother said, the smile weakening for a moment as her eyes studied Jamie again. When their eyes met, she nodded to ensure her she was sincere. "It will never be enough, but I'm so sorry. I was never brave enough to tell you that. Or your mother or your brother."

Jamie drew her eyebrows in, shaking her head. "I understand. I know what that feels like."

With her lips trembling softly, she stepped forward and hugged Jamie, holding her tightly. What surprised Jamie more, other than the fact that she didn't pull away, was that she didn't want to. Despite her being Daehyun's mother and despite the fact she had never come to her family to apologize for her son's accident, Jamie welcomed the affection of a woman who had no reason to give it. It was unusual for someone to want to be in the company of the family who indirectly made her world upside down, who made every day meaningless and any small amount of joy a quest to fulfill, but never once since her father passed away had her mother held her like this. Jamie wrapped her arms around this woman and held her tightly.

"I wasn't brave either," Jamie said.

His mother's hand came up to Jamie's hair and stroked it tenderly. While everyone ignored the scene and enjoyed their selection from the holiday buffet, only Minjae watched solemnly as the two embraced. When Minjae's mother stepped back, she slid her hands over Jamie's shoulders and rubbed them comfortingly.

"I don't deserve it, after all this time, but I want to say how sorry I am."

Jamie hadn't realized it but a tear fell without her allowing it and she wiped it away behind the façade of a laughter. "Let's not think on it anymore."

Minjae's mother nodded as she turned to Minjae. Jamie saw in the way they looked at each other that it had been an apology long in the wait. If only she'd listen to her son before, her heart would have settled a long time ago.

After dinner both Jamie and Minjae went to the backyard. His relatives were watching a ping pong match, whereas others relaxed in lawn chairs by the pool. Minjae pulled a chair near an empty one that was apart from the rest of the relative's conversations. During dinner Jamie met Minjae's father and while he didn't say it, she saw it in his eyes how grateful he was that Jamie helped his wife overcome the guilt she'd been too afraid to confront.

Jamie relaxed back in the chair as she leaned her head on her arm. "I'm surprised you never mentioned how your mom felt. You or Daehyun."

Minjae tapped a finger under his nose as he shrugged. "How could we say anything? She'd been too afraid to go to your family after the crash and even after every anniversary she couldn't." The corner of his lips lifted. "I'm thankful for what you did."

"She said she wasn't brave enough," Jamie said. "I can understand that maybe it was too hard for her to come to us—maybe after a couple of years she would have been able to one day but, your mom isn't a coward. She still smiles and loves everyone so much. I noticed it watching her for two minutes. I envy her. She's able to put on a happy face as easily had she been putting on a mask. When I was speaking to your dad I noticed her happiness faded, but when she saw me again she smiled like I'd given her the best present."

Minjae weighed Jamie's words. "It wasn't just overcoming it for herself. She's still trying to forgive Daehyun for what he did." Jamie's eyebrow arched up. "It's probably why Daehyun rarely comes home anymore. He went to visit his girlfriend's family for the holiday but even if he wasn't going there I'm sure he would have just stayed in California. Every time he comes, it's harder for him to face my mom more than it is to face you. He feels more welcome at your house than he does here."

Amazing, Jamie thought, *how mothers can make their kids feel they're not at home when they are.*

"He told you that?"

"Your family forgave him. Whenever he'd come home, he seemed to be picking up the burden he left behind when he went to see you guys."

"I never realized," Jamie said, shaking her head lightly. "I thought your parents just wanted to disconnect any part of yourselves from us. If what happened to Daehyun happened to me I would do that. Or if it happened to my kid. I don't know if I'd be able to continue to make contact with them." Jamie tilted her head to the side. "Why do you think he does it?"

Minjae tapped his hand on the armrest. He'd thought it many times, Jamie figured, but never asked her and probably never asked his brother either. Ultimately he glanced over to her and shrugged. "Daehyun's just Daehyun. He's the world's biggest pacifist. He doesn't want to weigh the experience too heavily on his heart or your family's, but for some reason, revisiting you guys shows that he didn't think the accident was just a tragedy for you. It was tragic for him too. Even after you've accepted it he'll still carry it with him."

The ping pong match ended with a chorus of cheers as a new opponent approached the table.

Minjae suddenly added, "At least that's what I think. I think it's more or less close to why."

While Jamie didn't fancy her own family, she enjoyed being surrounded by Minjae's. Perhaps it was easy because they weren't hers and it was nice wondering what lives they lived. Minjae had mentioned that most of the relatives came on vacation to go to the Disney and Universal parks but considering how many relatives came at once, it had to be because they wanted to come together for this family reunion. The family collective came for the grandparents from Korea but also for Minjae's newest cousin, recently born in October. Celebration of family and life and holiday cheer ensured they would enjoy themselves even if there was reason for them not to. Somehow, in the presence of strangers, Jamie felt at peace.

"Can I ask you something?" Minjae tried to pluck up the courage to ask before slowly looking back to her eyes. "What happened at your house?"

"What always happens," she said, resting her head back. "I felt like an outsider."

"Does it have to do with your dad?"

"It has to do with my family. I wish I was you and actually liked them."

"That can't be true. I only visited your house once and it didn't look any different than the way my family behaves. It's only hard to see that when it's not your own family."

Jamie sighed. "My *abuela* visiting and tonight my mom's boyfriend and his daughter were coming to dinner. Nothing extravagant. Everything was fine until I caught my brother inviting my uncle. He moved to Shore last month. He's my dad's younger brother, and one of the people I hate most in the world."

"What'd he do?"

"I don't want to get into the drama of it all, but he's one of the people I wish didn't exist. You weren't there but when my dad died—after he died, at his funeral, we invited his side of the family. We hadn't spoken to one another in years and yet even after he died, not a single one of them came. Not a word after the funeral—for three years—until this year when my uncle spontaneously decided to move to St. Luke's. Now, why do *you* think that is?"

Minjae thought how to answer carefully. "Maybe he wanted to reconcile."

"That side of the family's intensely religious. I wouldn't doubt they're heads of their own cult. Out of all of them his younger brother was the only one my mom and I expected to see, but even he didn't come. You never knew my dad but he didn't deserve to have his back turned on. How could someone have a family who pretends to care so much for the weak and needy, turn their back on someone—just because?"

"It isn't fair." Minjae agreed, then shifted in his seat. "But if you're going to turn your back on them, then I don't see how you can forgive my brother." When that caught her attention he continued. "Don't get me wrong I'm glad you did, but while they're in the dark about your lives so are you on theirs. Maybe this uncle is in the dark in their eyes too. I don't know the reason why your family split from your dad but your uncle came here for a reason. As great as St. Luke's is Shore is hardly impressive a place to live at all. Your family must have been part of the decision to move here. It's hard for you to see a redeemable quality in him because he hurt you, I get it, but your family wants to give him a chance anyways. It's what I admire about them."

Jamie didn't speak for a long time. "I was hoping that you'd be on my side. If *you* can't . . . Maybe the problem is me."

"I didn't mean it like that."

"It's true. Though whether it'll change anything before I leave—I need to look at it from a different perspective. I've only ever cared about my own. Be honest, is that how you would've handled it?"

"I haven't lived your life. I'm far from the right person to ask."

"People normally pry into each other's lives. I'm asking you. What's your opinion?"

"I don't think we need to judge each other. Or hate anyone. I think if people's first thoughts were to behave with compassion then there'd be less hostility between each other." Minjae looked ahead to his family. "Between strangers and families, it's easier to attack the ones you're closer to."

Jamie followed his eyesight as she looked from the grown-ups to the young adults to the kids to the two golden retrievers wandering around aimlessly.

"In any case, if I hadn't stormed out of my house like a grouchy Scrooge then I wouldn't have come here and saved you from your cousins."

Minjae realized the validity of that fact and bowed his head, bringing his hands together and lifting it up and down. "I take it all back. Thank you for saving me. You're welcome here anytime you like. Anytime!"

Jamie snickered as she watched the Jang family, the uncles and aunts, nieces and nephews, kids and grandparents, gossips and drunks, pious and agnostic, foreign and English-speaking weave between and around one another as if they were all protected under a charm, blocking all hazard and all misfortune.

"Where did everyone park?" Jamie asked. "There's only like four cars outside."

Minjae pointed a finger at himself. "Five bucks per trip. Don't quit my day job, am I right?"

Jamie was several houses away when she passed by one of her neighbors. It didn't hit her for several seconds but it was the new one. The one Banafsha bore toils to trust. A flood of questions prodded her to slow her bike and stop in front of his house as she examined him in his front yard. He stood by a telescope, craning his head back as he surveyed the stars. An elementary curiosity seemed to possess him that she rarely saw in young adults, and the unusual sight persuaded her to stare in wonder.

A sense of eyes on him, he looked in her direction. She'd only met him once a month ago and he seemed friendly enough, but they weren't acquainted well enough for her to stare at him in the middle of the night. Collecting herself and clearing her throat, she adjusted her posture, leaning from one leg to the other.

Ethan, whose name she finally recalled, watched her for a moment, recollecting when he'd met her before too before suddenly smiling and waving his arm.

"They're brighter than I thought they'd be," he said.

Jamie glanced up to the stars before pushing her bike up the driveway. He watched her for a moment before tilting his head and torso back.

"Wow."

"Could you not see the stars where you used to live?"

He nodded. "But you can see them here even with the street lamps on. I always heard you couldn't see stars in the city. But I don't even need this thing."

"I wouldn't go so far as to call Shore a city."

"So involved in work I never cared to appreciate them."

Jamie searched for the night sky he saw. She knew his type. The ones who suddenly felt meaning and purpose in the passing wind and the ant on the ground. He must've survived a life-or-death situation recently. She'd approached him first, so it'd be rude if she backed away pretending she hadn't seen or heard him. She tried to think of a way to escape.

"Come on over," he said cheerfully.

"I can't . . ."

"Allergic to grass?"

"No . . ."

"Keep me company. You're already out. Five minutes. I promise. You can even time me if you want." He had a charismatic dimple in his chin when he smirked like a young Josh Holloway.

He seemed oddly upbeat. It wasn't like she was anxious to be reprimanded at home. She knew never returning the ten missed calls, her mother was going to give her an earful for ditching the Christmas family dinner. Let alone a dinner that involved her boyfriend. Unable to find any more objections to his request she set her bike down and walked over the grass.

"Did you learn their names? Apparently you guys are big on naming things."

"You guys?"

"The world. I never cared for studying when I was younger."

And yet he was able to afford a house at his age, presuming he lived alone. Not just anyone could move into this neighborhood. While houses weren't luxurious or elaborate, Shore was a very popular beach town in Florida, therefore real estate costs were higher.

"Nothing beyond Sirius," Jamie said. "They don't interest me enough to learn their names."

A shock possessed his fascinated disposition as he immediately sought the reason in her eyes. Impulsively he grabbed her arms, then just as quickly gave up on the idea, dropping his hands and folding them behind him. Jamie felt the pulse up her arms.

"You know," Ethan said. " All I ever hear is that people spend so much time and have so much trust in the stars. Ancient sailors depended on them, risked their lives on them to cross oceans. And now countries spend millions to send satellites out to study nearby planets and galaxies. I never understood why. The known is safe. The Earth is home. Why go out? There are enough problems here to worry about without looking up. Incurable maladies, decrepitude, discrimination, dishonesty, trickery, war, bigotry. The stars are only innocent lights in the sky. The world should fix itself first. Can't even crawl and they already want to jump. Unbelievable, don't you think?"

Ethan turned back to Jamie after he'd gone back to stand by— though not look through—his telescope. Jamie mirrored the curiosity in his eyes however the curiosity was for him. Who was he? Had something happened to him that he suddenly felt a need to share his existential crisis with a stranger?

She thought an honest question deserved an honest answer. Troubled or not, someone on the brink of a crisis or someone with a lot of free time must have a reason for sharing his thoughts with her. The only reason she could think of was because he had no one else to share them with. Maybe he had a friend or two or a coworker he bonded with but maybe he already knew what'd they say or maybe they'd dismiss him. While Jamie considered herself far from the consoling type, being unloaded a wealth of ponderous thoughts somehow resonated with her. She'd never been able to do that since her dad died, though she'd tried to be open with the gargoyles.

A slip from her new staunch way of life. She allowed it. It was only Day One. It would get easier with time.

She smiled and looked up at the night sky. "I never gave it much thought. I don't really care what goes on up there."

"But—" he struggled to find the best way to say it.

"It's just a pastime. Like all subjects of school they tried to teach us as kids. A little about astronomy, a little about the ocean, a little about politics, a little about our biology." She noticed his gaze, and nodded. "Back in the day they didn't have schools so people studied it on their own. Ancient sailors studied the stars because their culture and their stories were their technology. Astronomers have the technology now and they're still curious. What for? Maybe looking out is more fulfilling than looking in. Maybe the answer's out there. As much as our world provides maybe the true answer is somewhere we have to reach for. Beyond our limits. Beyond what we know and feel within our grasp. I've never been curious about the names of stars like my brother but they're still nice to look at. Who knows, the world may destroy itself before we find the solution to all our problems out there, but in the meantime, just looking up kills time. It eases our minds. We admire them until it's time for bed and then another day of work comes. I think the stars are up there just to satisfy us until the next day begins. For all those inquisitive minds and tired minds that don't otherwise give two cents."

Ethan faced his nemesis up above once again. "So we look up to we settle for its beauty or because we want answers." It wasn't enough for him and his head shook. "The possibilities seem too limiting."

The night filled the space between them until Ethan broke the silence.

"What might someone do if they are alone? No friends to call. No family left. How do they go on?"

She shrugged. "I guess, they'd look for a new companion. So they wouldn't be alone anymore."

"A companion?"

Jamie tilted her head so she could get a better view of his face without moving from her spot. "Does the urge to answer the mysteries of universe come along often or is this a first?"   The joy in his face subsided as it flattened, facing her with a new sense of curiosity. However, the small smile on her face made him mirror her as he brought his hand to his neck. "You could call it long-held; suppressed."

Jamie nodded, taking out her phone and showing the screen to him.

"Not to run off on you . . ."

He waved his hand back to her bike. "No of course. You're young. You probably have"—he tried to remember the word—"*school* tomorrow."

Jamie laughed as she slid the phone back in her pocket. "We're on break."

"Oh, really?" He followed her with his eyes.

"Make sure you don't accidentally fall asleep while pondering. Shore's relatively safe but you don't want your telescope gone in the morning. Looks fancy."

The consideration tickled him as he chuckled. When she had the bike up next to her, she waved a final time before resuming her journey home. He returned to his telescope, setting his hand on the eyepiece as he looked up and tried to connect the bright stars to one another. Eventually he gave up, realizing the absurdity in the attempt, and bent down to look at the stars closer through the eyepiece.

The porch light was on as she slipped through the front door and shut it quietly behind her. As bright as it was outside she expected it to be darker inside, and paused when she noticed one of the living room lamps still on. Her mother was beside it, her eyes blinking open at the sound of the front door. Jamie lost the will to make her way stealthily through the house and shrugged off her jacket, tossing it over the top of the nearby armchair.

Rosario stood up as Jamie waited to be scolded. Mother and daughter stared in silence as eventually mother lost the will to confront her.

"We'll talk tomorrow. Get some rest." Without another word she turned toward her room and quietly closed the door behind her.

Not thinking the event would pass without blood, Jamie turned off the light. Once inside her room she shrugged off her shoes and fell into bed, leaning over to turn off the light when she spotted her camera on her desk. Releasing an internal groan, she stood up to pick it up, then scrolled through her pictures quickly in search of a specific one. Once found, she stared at it and tried to memorize every aspect of it. It would be easy to remember it tomorrow and even a week from now. But in a month, in a year, the picture would begin to blur and this nightmare would step in line with every other nightmare she'd had. Eventually, the time would come when she had forgotten which way they faced and if there was even more than one figure in that picture. Her thumb hovered over the delete button for a moment before she pressed it. Another hesitation when the camera asked if her decision was certain. Any images erased could not be recovered.

Her thumb went down again. There would be no more shadows to haunt her at night.

24

Jamie stretched her arms above her head after helping a patron, watching him pick up the climbing equipment and leaving to find an open wall. After yawning, she sat down and rolled closer to the desk, scrolling through the check-in registry to kill time. Noel and Era were working on the floor. Even with the holiday over they worked in a light-hearted mood. Jamie shared little, mindfully eluding she'd spent some of it with one of the gym's patrons, and to her relief neither asked further.

While checking the drawers for a pen that worked, the front door open. Minjae's wide smile and waving arm greeted her as she glanced behind him for the rest of the Capes. Alone, and proudly so, he leaned over the front counter as she wondered what he was doing at the gym on a Wednesday.

"So I have a question for you." Her expression asked the interrogative. "I know I shouldn't ask but that picture I helped you print up for your neighbor, what was it?"

While a number of people had seen the photo by this point, she didn't feel the need to hide it anymore. She'd borne a grudge against the gargoyles but now she could treat it like any other insignificant thing from her past.

"I took it at St. Luke's. Why, you like it?"

"I just thought it was curious. How'd you make it look like that?"

The urge to lie arose—then abated. "I didn't. The statues did all the work themselves."

Where did the cathedral come from all of a sudden? She'd deleted the picture over a week ago. She was past this.

Expecting a follow-up question, there came a sigh. "I just know someone who's interested in the church too."

Jamie nodded formally for the sake of the customer's interest and not her own. "That's nice. I recommend if they're interested to check it out for themselves. They won't be disappointed."

"Would you mind showing me a day you're free?"

The thought made her laugh but she kept a composed face. "A day I'm free?"

"Yeah, you must have time off too."

"I thought you were going to be busy with Yearbook."

"My friend has history. Interested in the cathedral for years and of late it's become one of mine. Call it interest of association."

"That's great." Jamie nodded, noticing Noel's gaze over to them and why she wasn't helping him get his equipment. "Let's talk about this another time. Later tonight—or better yet, tomorrow."

"I won't have time tomorrow."

"Then any day after that. Listen, I'm working now so before I get in trouble—"

His hand came up and he closed his eyes. "Say no more. We'll find a day."

As soon as he arrived he left, and Noel came by the front desk, a look reading he wanted to know. Jamie almost lied and said it had to do with school, but he had an ability to tell when she was lying by omission.

"He wanted to check out the cathedral by the beach."

"St. Luke's?"

Everyone knew the cathedral by the beach. The only church anyone ever mentioned visiting was St. Luke's.

Noel rolled a rope around his arm. "You know I have an uncle who lives there."

Jamie's eyebrows quickly furrowed. "Come again?"

"I don't keep in contact with him much because he's so invested in the church and I have my two girls at home. I haven't seen him in nearly a year or spoken to him in months. Crazy how we live in the same town and never cross each other." Noel lifted the corner of his lips, as if a distant relationship between families was funny.

"Why are you mentioning it now?" Jamie asked.

"In case your friend had a question about the church. It isn't like having a friend who works at an amusement park, I can't get you any good deals but if he's interested in its, my uncle is probably one of the ones to go to. Once he starts talking—well you know how they are.

He may be a little difficult to talk to but I'm sure if I asked he wouldn't mind—"

"Who's your uncle?" Jamie never thought of it before but now she wondered if she should have pieced the two together.

"Elias Dauve."

She'd known Noel for years, and not only would she never have imagined he had a relative at the cathedral—one he ever failed to mention—but for that relative to be one of the reasons she disliked going in the first place; more than the long bike ride across town though not to the extreme as the gargoyles, was too coincidental. Jamie would admit Elias was communicative, if not frank. He never let the opportunity pass to show he disapproved of her presence there.

"I've met him," Jamie said. "Cheery sort of fella."

"My girls don't take to him much either. But family's family."

Jamie rolled her eyes and Noel spotted it, pointing his finger at her. "Not everyone shows it well but it's true. Even if the relatives hate every ounce of the other's being, the blood doesn't lie. Nothing can change that."

"Maybe if you spent more time with him he wouldn't be so grouchy."

Noel crossed one arm over the other as he leaned on his hip, tilting his head. "When did I start allowing my employees to backtalk? Who's the owner and who's the part-timer?"

Jamie lifted her hands and pressed together, as if in prayer, then shook them. "Apologies."

"Get back to work," he said turning away, muttering under his breath. "Try to help and get disrespected. This is what comes of being friends with your staff. They walk over you and a high schooler too— she doesn't even drive. What's becoming of my life . . ."

Jamie failed to hear the rest of his grievances, and made sure he was across the room before she chuckled.

The handlebars under her fingers, she glanced at the flat tire. A criminal had punched a hole in the front one and now she had to make a ten-minute bike ride into an hour's walk home. She'd texted her brother about the delay and while her mother had texted back that she could pick her up, she'd pretended she didn't read it. While the journey home wasn't as expeditious as she'd have expected, walking Shore's hushed streets was soothing. The post-celebratory merriment due to the Christmas and New Year's holidays had passed, and while the prospects of new adventures in a new year lingered, so did all the reminders of her responsibilities.

Her final semester in school would begin the following day and while she'd be working most of her regular hours, she'd spoken with Noel about cutting them down. He'd ask why she didn't do that before she started applying to colleges in August but all she said was she wanted to finish her academics with commendable grades. A lie, since she'd thought a lot since Christmas with Minjae's family. She decided she wanted to spend as much time with Aiden before she left.

When she did leave, she'd miss Shore. Not the people so much as the feeling of walking down these streets. Despite being a respectable distance from St. Augustine, Shore wasn't the oldest city in Florida; therefore what Shore lacked in age it made up in charm. The street lights were still winged with bells and mistletoe decorations. There was the occasional Christmas tree still proudly flaunting its jewels and sparkles in the windows of small shops. Every other lamppost tailored a vine of lights snaking its way to the lantern. Once, and thankfully only once, did she pass a store with Christmas songs still playing. Shore was not unlike every other city that drowned itself in the festive craze of the season.

A sudden silence settled around her and she paused, glancing around like a paranoid character in a horror film. Slowly, she looked forward again as if the real monster waited for her relief to settle before springing itself on her. The night around her had frozen. No sound, movement, or presence existed but her own. There were none, and yet, there was something she couldn't place that would suffice the tremor in her heart.

"No." Her teeth were clenched. She gripped the handle bars tighter, dragging it closer to her body.

A soft whisper, breathing warmly over her ear, caused her to yank her head in the new direction.

Not done.

"No," she said with conviction. Her eyes stretched as her neck twirled around, from the road ahead to the alleyway to the trees to the far side of the street. Nothing. Nothing was closing in on her.

She'd gotten better.

The hallucinations had gone away.

"They're still gone," she corrected, shutting her eyes and forcing her words to sound calm. "No one's here. I'm alone."

No.

She flinched, but kept her eyes closed.

Not alone. Never again.

"I'm going home. Don't follow me anymore."

Not allowing the whispers to respond, she pushed forward the moment her eyes opened. Whatever ill-wisher—hallucination or not—causing her to resort to paranoia would remain here. For her sanity, she couldn't believe anything more. Six months. That's all the time left for her in Shore and she wouldn't let it be ruined by the quicksand, by the vines, by the churning mud; whatever immovable, impenetrable force that had slithered its way into her mind. And all of this started because her uncle came to Shore. She'd abandon it as he had them.

Forbidding whispers to spook her again, the rest of the journey home she had her shoulders hunched and her eyes alert.

A figure with dark eyes hidden below a midnight hood watched silently from beside a lamppost as Jamie walked away. Warnings, any messages sent to her, were returned and blocked. She wouldn't listen. After a moment, the figure realized she couldn't. Like a cup with no bottom, she couldn't grasp anything, and it all went through her as if it had never affected her in the first place. There was something blocking her.

They took a step after her as a car's headlights shone over his form. When the driver drove past the place where the figure stood, they looked over an empty space.

As if there had been no one.

****

Ms. Ava stepped next to the white board as she watched the syllabi passed around the classroom. Sad that it would be her last semester with the seniors, she wouldn't deny being happy some in particular were leaving. "We'll have a good semester this semester, right?"

The room mumbled as they looked over the schedule for the year. Ms. Ava clapped her hands together. "While Advanced Photo isn't a college credit course, treat it like you were paying for it. Now, you've developed a lot since last semester, so we've reached the point where you understand the demands for the basics like composition, lighting, subject, et cetera. You know what I want. You've critiqued your fellow students works, so you know what you all want. This semester you'll explore that."

"What?" Alric said. "We don't have any criteria to follow?"

Ms. Ava nodded once, folding her arms over her chest. "Yes, you'll be forming your own assignments. I want to get to know what types of photographs you like to take. Photography is a branch of art no matter what the critics say; disregarding how many you take on your phones. It's an art that deserves respect. While pictures may be duplicated perfectly, no one can replicate why that picture was taken at the moment it was taken, and no one can know what you were thinking when you clicked the shutter. So this semester you will be exploring what you think is worthy to be photographed." She cast a side glance at Alric. "Aside from the explicit and graphic subject matters you all know is prohibited in high school, your projects will be designed and formed all on your own. Which means that your projects will be completely unique. *Which means*, if you try to copy the project of a past student you will automatically fail."

Alric and others snickered at the unimaginable as the details for the project were elaborated on.

Jamie had spent the night with her eyes closed, though not asleep, never risking to check the time as the hours of the night passed. She would wait until her alarm. Only then would she get up. She had work after school and that would afford her time to waste until she'd go to bed again. By the end of the day she prayed she wouldn't be visited again.

A body slumped in the chair beside her. Alric leaned his head on his hand, his arm bent over the table as he looked at her with innocence. Treasuring every second as another second undisturbed by a breath over her ear, she hadn't noticed how twenty minutes had passed since Ms. Ava had left them to brainstorm for project ideas before Alric invaded her concentration. Jamie stared at him as he continued to gaze silently at her. They watched one another in an impasse. Eventually, it became too unnerving for Jamie to sit still and allow him to remain staring at her transfixed.

"What?"

"Have a nice break?"

"I'm not in the mood."

"I'm only curious what you're planning on doing for the final project."

"She *just* sprang it on us. I don't have any ideas."

"Think you'll get help from a friend for it?"

Jamie looked him up and down before parting her lips, though saying nothing. She had a feeling since the last semester that Alric had a thing for Emily and that somehow he'd managed to pin the blame on her. The more he bothered her the more she figured that was it. Why else would someone who had no interest in her before suddenly find it his new life mission to aggravate her every time the class was left to their own devices?

"I was thinking of asking Jay," Alric mulled over, his eyes rolling to the ceiling. "Since he's in Yearbook and might be able to give me some tips on what Ms. Ava's looking for. What do you think? Think he'd be able to help?"

"That's an excellent question to ask next time you see him."

"Well I figured since you were so close—"

"How about you ask Emily? She's *a lot* closer with Minjae than I am. Even broken up she's the perfect choice to go to about him."

Alric shut his mouth and stiffened before relaxing again. His hands came to his knees as he leaned his chest a hint forward.

"You know you're cute when you're like this." He lifted a finger to her chin and tilted it upward as she tugged her chin back out of his reach. He smirked coldly as he stood up and returned to his table.

Another bother in her life. While it was annoying she preferred something tangible and manageable like a high school boy. They were much easier to handle.

Noel set the box of harnesses down beside Jamie as he took in her expression.

The gym was absent of any customers for the time of day and the quiet room was a party for the staff. A CD by one of Noel's favorite indie artists hummed in the background as the three staff members did inventory. Era was taking out the trash as Jamie and Noel were overlooking the used equipment from the day before. Noel's hands were on the box as he leaned on his hip.

"You all right, hon?"

Jamie looked up from the harness she was inspecting, puckering her lips as if she'd been caught breaking the equipment on a dare. "Do I look not all right?"

"There's somewhat of a depression in your face. Is it because your hours are about to change and you're regretting it?"

She shook her head. "No. This semester's going to be unrelenting. I'll need more time to study for final exams and work on Photo."

"Gotta admire a student who goes strong until the end, particularly when they're dead set on avoiding college. I still think you should go."

"You and my mother both."

"You can do whatever you want afterwards. Go for the experience if not for educating yourself."

Jamie snickered, looking to the equipment in her hands. "Sure, put myself into fifty thousand dollars worth of debt for experiences I don't even care to have."

"It won't be that much if you work. And if you go to one in-state—"

"I'm gonna have to stop you there."

Noel shrugged. "Fair enough. I've lectured you enough."

Era returned and noticed the box of harnesses in Noel's hands. "Is that yesterday's equipment?"

He nodded and left it for her to take care of. Jamie tossed the harness she finished inspecting into a new box, grabbing another.

"How are things with your boyfriend?" Jamie asked Era.

Era beamed. "Fantastic. He's a gem. I think things are getting serious. We both came into this casually but I think he's seeing what I'm seeing."

"A dancing fish wouldn't impress me as much."

"You're such a poor liar. You might've well have said you can't wait to go on your first road trip." Jamie ignored her and Era spotted something in the window. "So, what about you? Any men you have a thing for? Or them for you? Casual or no? One of the gym members from your high school? What do they call themselves, the Capes?"

"No," Jamie said flatly.

"Not any of them? There's a couple cute guys. *None* of them interest you?"

Jamie eyed her for a moment. "What's with you today?"

Era gestured her chin behind her and Jamie noticed the Capes coming inside. All the members entered as Jamie set a harness down, already preparing to check the members in. Vienna handed her membership card over first as the others leaned by the front desk, their cards ready in their hands.

"Jay's at Yearbook today," she said, noticing Jamie scan the members' faces.

Jamie checked them in, and after handing over their equipment, the first thing Era did when they made eye contact was bounce her eyebrows at her. When Jamie asked, Era merely shrugged and took the box of harnesses to the back. A chime at the front door rang and two more customers entered. Jamie rarely spoke to the others, focusing on the tedious tasks around the gym.

When her shift ended, she spotted Minjae hanging by the front of the gym. Jamie was more interested he was standing by a bike than the fact he was outside and so after she greeted him, she couldn't help looking to it. He noticed the focus of attention and patted it.

"I don't usually ride but I wanted to ask you about St. Luke's. I figured you wouldn't want to talk if I offered you a ride home."

Like dark clouds before a storm, Jamie sensed a wind forewarning the approach of the unnatural silence she felt the night before. Without waiting to explain or for validation that she was right to be paranoid, she grabbed his arm and suggested to start riding. Only when they were safely on one of the main roads did she ask. "What's your interest in the cathedral again?"

"A friend of mine's the one interested."

"Then what do you call what you're doing?"

"Mmm, doing a favor?"

"Okay," Jamie said. While he was shocked she agreed she had her own reasons. So far, the day was a success from hearing any whispers. Almost an entire day. Having a companion for the ride home would distract her.

There was a fair amount of traffic on the road tonight. While the cars were in the lane farthest from them, the calmer of the riders focused on the cars behind, the other focusing on the dark road ahead. Minjae rounded his bike so he was closest to the street, forcing Jamie to ride in suddenly, instigating a perturbed glance his way.

"Who's your friend?" Jamie asked.

"Her name's Penelope."

"The one in our class?" After Minjae agreed Jamie looked his way. "Vienna's mentioned her before. Jax was making fun of her. Apparently she's strange."

"She's quiet," Minjae said. It didn't escape Jamie's memory that Vienna described her the same way. "If everyone who's quiet is strange then you're the strangest of them all."

Jamie ignored the tease. "Why is she interested in the cathedral?"

"It's something of a family hobby. They've researched a lot about it and are the biggest experts on the church aside from the priests themselves."

"How do you know all of this?"

"She's a friend." The answer wasn't enough and when she was about to ask for more he said, "You haven't heard anything lately about the cathedral have you?"

Jamie looked to the rider beside her. He was already watching her for her reaction, waiting for her response before he'd even asked. It seemed the cathedral was haunting her. Every time she swore it off somebody mentioned it. Every time she thought it was gone from her life, it snuck back in. She'd lived in Shore all her life and the cathedral was mentioned less than ten times on its own, but in the past few months she'd never heard anything mentioned more. Not about graduating or college or money. They rode past two streets before she answered, "I haven't. But what does it matter if I have?"

"That picture . . ."

Jamie lowered her gaze as the two entered her neighborhood and rode to her street.

"The statue—I've never seen anything like it. I could believe you Photoshopped it, but I'd need to hear it from you."

They stopped in front of her house, the lights from the front porch on. While she hadn't worked until closing, she knew when her mother was home. For the first time in a long time she wished that she were inside, suffering from her mother's droning then continue their discussion on the cathedral, even if it was with Minjae. She liked him. He made air breathable for those around him. He was himself at school and at home, with friends or surrounded by family. He was a lot like Daehyun, who despite having an opposing personality to hers, somehow managed to mold their dispositions around her. She wasn't the outcast with them.

But she'd had enough of the cathedral; with the flying buttresses and stained glass windows, the statues in the galleries and the details in tympanums, the enormity of the bell towers and the pride of the transept spire reaching high like the Tower of Babel. Everything under the roof of the greatest cathedral in the world was beautiful. Everything the eye could see was a treasure in the New World's most respected church.

The Poison Dart Frog is beautiful. The Box Jellyfish is majestic. Neither nonetheless venomous.

The Sirens and the Lotus of Greek myth were no less intoxicating though their beauty and aroma were undeniable.

The building that the town and nation revered was no different to her eyes. Even though she'd been captured by the impossibility of the gargoyles, she'd woken up.

Jamie would have to lie. A lie could be believed if colored with enough details. She had only to be mindful of anything which would disprove her when a quick trip up the bell tower would expose her.

"I worked for a long time on that photo. I stemmed the inspiration from a painting I admired a long time ago, of an angel falling from Heaven and a mud monster on Earth catching them. I took a bunch of pictures so that I could manipulate the texture and face of the gargoyle, and then darkened it so that you couldn't tell off the bat. I did a good job didn't I?"

She watched her words slowly sink in and when he nodded, she knew she'd fooled him.

"You can't really tell since it is so dark," he said. "Only just. I guess I didn't see it like that. I must've thought . . . I don't know."

Jamie knew it was dangerous but couldn't help herself. "Thought . . . what?"

"I thought you saw something you'd never be able to prove otherwise."

"A moving statue?" Jamie asked, looking ahead to the empty street.

"A glimpse behind the curtain. A hidden El Dorado behind the waterfall. A buried Fountain of Youth."

She snickered and he cast his gaze to her. "A living myth living in one of the most iconic buildings in the country. What deceptive skill the church must have to keep such extraordinary things secret. For none to have ever crossed paths with them. Never chancing on them. Ha! I'll leave the fantasy to the zealots and filmmakers."

He slowly began to smile as he relaxed a foot onto the bike pedal, moving it forward then backwards before it caught and stopped, then moving it forward again.

"Wouldn't it be something though?" Minjae said. "If you did chance upon something like that?"

Jamie nodded, walking up the driveway. "If I ever do uncover the greatest secret of all time, I'll be sure to give you a call."

Minjae nodded contently, readjusting his stance on the bike. "Share the glory huh? None of the explorers in the past were famous on their own. Sure their *names* are famous, but they didn't do it on their own. Don't stand on the little guy. We're very sensitive people."

Part farewell, part dismissal, Jamie waved as Minjae waited until she went inside. He couldn't hold back a grin as the front door closed and he turned back the way they came.

A sigh.

The figure under the hood watched as the boy on the bike rode away then looked back to the house where the girl lived. The curtains were closed so he didn't know what was happening inside, and yet he closed his eyes and imagined. Inside, the girl answered her mother's questions about her day emotionlessly before going to her room. She returned to collect her dinner and eat quietly as her mother and brother watched TV. She'd do the dishes as her family went to shower before taking one herself, followed shortly by going to her room for homework and turning in for the night.

Routine. Life of a normal family.

However, she couldn't afford a life of normalcy anymore.

The figure crossed the street and stepped onto the driveway of the house, looking at it for a long time before slowly lowering his head and muttering several words.

25

A man, hunched over a thin mattress spread on the floor, controlling the unstoppable writhing bubbling inside him as best as he could. His hands bent inwards like gnarly claws. His breath emitted clouds of frost into the air. The robes over his body, wet from sweat, blanketed over him in hopes it would protect him from the coldness sourced within. Somehow he'd survived the arctic dungeon better than the chill in his body. A dim light shone through the crack of the high wall, traces of the moon on this clear night.

The door to the cell opened. A soft orange light approached the bundled man. Soft whispers of encouragement fell on deaf ears as a sympathetic hand rested over the blanket shell. The man continued to shiver as no blanket, companionship, or fire could feed him comfort.

He was alone in this cell, with no future and no morning to hope for.

Metal holds clamped on the walls. Heavy chains hung loosely. The wind whispered through the window above.

"Morning's soon," said the source of warmth. "Just a little bit longer."

The bundled man shook under the soft words as if they'd been drummed and echoed throughout the gloomy cell. Piercing, his eyes suddenly flashed open. Streaks of red and purple struck over his sclera like jellyfish tentacles. Hoarse and raspy, the man on the floor inched his chin up slowly to the candle beside him. "The pain's everywhere."

The visitor nodded with a somber frown.

"I can't stand it anymore. It's never enough. I think I can handle it but it always overpowers me more. Stretching, twisting, suffocating—all at once."

The man standing soaked in the suffered's words. "I understand."

A pitiful cry escaped and reverberated in the small room as no tears fell. No tears for a man who hadn't truly cried in weeks.

"I can't do it anymore. I've had enough. Tell them to stop now. I want it to end."

The visitor lifted his hand under the man's cheek and shepherded him to look up.

"That's fine. Just endure until morning and I'll do that. I'll take you out of here. You've suffered enough."

The man cried out again and felt the soft hand on his cheek be no less cold than the floor, walls, or endless midnight cold pumping from within him. Each tick of the clock was an age as every second meant another lifetime of night. And in the night were no stars and no silence, only a cascade of crackles and jeers as shadows of darkness surrounded him and struck his body with their clutches, sucking into his skin like burning acid. He suffered no deformity from the phantom grips and no physical mark was ever seen. However, it was not undetectable. His body temperature decreased and the trembling within his heart was inconsolable.

The screams of the man began as darkness' Never-End consumed his mind. There was no finish line. It would be this dark night no matter how many times the visitor assured him. He was no more than a figment of the imagination. There was no truth there as there were no truths in dreams. He couldn't hope to wake up. Waking up didn't exist. Only pain and only darkness. Nothing more. Numbness by the cold made every pain a degree more striking. He'd finished crying tears. He would cry blood before crying until his last breath. All for hope.

Even on the edge, his mind hung onto it. Despite it all he had to hold onto hope when truth was forfeit. He thought he'd never last another moment. It was the same thought he had an infinity ago. And the infinity before.

The softness of light slowly overcame the night as the rising sun began to claim its authority over the Earth. Songs of birds arose as the dim, bleak cell welcomed the new day. The waves of the ocean less than a mile away were gently embracing his ears as the rhythm of the water slowly rose—not drowning, but melting into the warmness of the waters on a scorching day; basking under the shade with cool water rushing over his skin and down his throat to cool the inflamed fire inside. He rested on a plump cushion in the skies as he watched clouds high in the atmosphere gracefully pass by. He watched for hours until night came, only to be welcomed by the stars and vibrant moon. Streaks of light passed as if the eras of time backtracked altogether at once, until he came upon the creation of the universe. The sun, a pulsing heart in the expanse of the endless, grew larger and expanded whiter until the star became the only light in the sky. The other stars were overshadowed. A lovely young voice began singing in a language and tongue he couldn't recognize. Sitting up, he felt wisps of warmth from the cloud he rested on as his eyes took in the majesty of the sun and the melody of the universe. The child's voice was joined by a chorus equal in heart. Complete souls glorified the sun, celebrated its birth, exalted the existence of the tiny life in the new universe. The man felt a tear on his cheek and he touched it with a light hand. Every movement he made, even to breathe, was not gravitated toward anything around him. He simply existed and floated in the good Never-End. He looked to his tear-stained fingers and smiled, looking up to admire the sun. And he appreciated the warmth and light the sun embraced him with. Never before was there this truth that lacked the necessity to be told, shared, or hoped for. It was before his eyes. The impossible in all enigmatic glory before his eyes.

The cell lightened, and the faces of the men became known. The visitor had a kind face in despair or in glee, as the man he looked upon had an agonizing expression turned painless. The claws, pulled tightly against his chest, relaxed and flattened against the mattress as he moved to sit up, supported by his companion. The man leaned his back against the wall and lifted a hand to his shoulder, rolling it as much as the sore muscles would tolerate.

"It is passed," said the visitor, resting his hand on the man's shoulder.

"It didn't seem possible. Every night's becoming longer."

"That's all right. You won't have to worry about that anymore. You're done, no longer needed for this. You will rest easy from now on my friend."

The man looked up uncertainly to the kind eyes. "Ended? No."

"You have begged this many times before but there was more this time. When you pleaded—"

"I beg you, do not to remind me at this moment. I want to enjoy the songs of the birds."

The visitor kept quiet as the cell lifted in the birds' song and the ocean's orchestra. He leaned against the wall beside him as the man on the mattress calmed his breathing, his eyes closed as he let his ears fill with the refreshing sounds of the new day.

"Regardless of what you and I want, your body cannot suffer for much longer."

"My body's fine."

"We need to speak with them. Beg them to help you fight off the worse of the nights."

"Do not seek them out. They are waiting for her to return. Do not give them unwanted news."

"Gabe," entreated the visitor, a plea in his eyes. "If you wait without doing anything . . . Nothing will change. For your sake, we must ask the messengers to guide her back."

"Three-hundred-year-old statues are masters of patience. They will not be prodded by a single man's pleas." Gabe exhaled deeply. "I'm sure they are working on something themselves."

The visitor lifted his eyebrows. "And if they are not?"

"Then each sunset I will return here to suffer the wrath and torment of the night."

"It is not the night—"

"The day is just beginning, Edgar," Gabe said. "Come, let us find breakfast."

Edgar helped Gabe stand, serving as his crutch as they slowly crossed the room. Reaching the door post Gabe rested his hand on the frame, glancing over his shoulder to the cell, wishing it farewell until sunset; where he'd be beckoned to return.

26

Six weeks of the same dreams. Either of a man Jamie initially thought was her dad—realized to be her uncle—hunched in a cell, or of a robed creature. Always a man in a cell or a creature walking through dimly lit halls and conspiring in phantom chambers. What were once mornings shedding silent tears now were minutes in catatonic immobility, followed by a stirring remedy of rubbing her face to prepare for the day. Nights spent avoiding nightmares were mornings flaunting dark circles. In time, she accepted suffering the nightmares. Occasionally she dreamt of nothing and woke up by the bliss-induced emptiness, but these occurred rarely if at all. Of late, she'd had a new subject in her sleep.

The Partner.

It was a recurring theme in her dreams. Nightmares were dreams of fears and worries and awful memories, however everything she'd dreamed was set in a new world with people she'd never met, heard of, or imagined. It was difficult finding the common denominator aside from the unending darkness, the rumors stirred by whispers. The only face she recognized was her uncle's, bent and twisted into agony she couldn't help but feel pity for, especially when that face resembled her father's.

She'd seen her uncle only once, yet she could easily recognize the curves of his tight cheeks, the line of his nose, the darkness in his eyebrows and hair, the clenching of his jaw, and the desperation in his eyes shut tight or stretched open. It was a premonition and only that, but weeks of nightmares changed her. She had to see if he was all right.

Stepping upon the darkened steps of the cathedral, she felt no differently than had she stepped onto the main road of a ghost town. Millions of people had passed under the archway to see the skyscraper vaults and mammoth columns. Millions more in years to come would praise acclaim on the condition and upkeep of the country's treasure. But past and future souls gave her no comfort as she looked upon the building, affording her the same chills Poe's narrator felt as he approached the house of Usher. It was neither a stormy day nor an ominous night, yet she couldn't help feeling as if someone was watching her. Not from in front of her. Behind.

A half-mindful glance over her shoulder, she trusted there really was no one. She'd checked multiple times, every day for six weeks, and like then this time would be no different. Fear orchestrated terror too beautifully to be real. Her assignment called her attention back forward.

Slipping through the narthex and stepping silently up the stairs, she found her uncle's room and knocked on the door.

She called his name and identified herself, waiting. She tilted her forehead near the door. "Are you in there?" Another set of knocks.

She stepped back and rested her hands on her waist. The journey seemed in vain. If he truly was unwell then the priests would have kept him in his room or taken him to the hospital where her family could've been notified. The reason she decided to stay and be sure he was healthy was because she needed to see it herself, with her own eyes. What was happening in her dreams need to be proven beyond fantasy and the sufferings of a seer.

She glimpsed over the mortal and heavenly statues below in the atrium, both types evoking an internal suffering in their uplifted eyes.

Back in the main gathering of the cathedral, not far from the baldachin, she was spotted by one of the clergymen. Wide in the shoulders with wavy brown hair, a serene aura moved about him much like she'd seen in Edgar. He asked her if she was there for a tour when she shook her hand. "I asked my family and they said Gabe hadn't called in months," she easily lied, not discouraged by the location. "I wanted to make sure he was all right."

"That's peculiar he wasn't in his room," said the clergyman. "I'll inquire upon his whereabouts."

"Cadogan."

When Jamie turned to the speaker she was immediately disappointed at the sight of Elias. He looked no different than usual, with a fixed scowl and a mirrored disappointment in his eyes, but for some reason she had the impression he wasn't as disinclined seeing her today as she thought.

"I can help her," Elias said, stopping near them.

"She's looking for Gabe," Cadogan said.

"I understand."

Cadogan read his eyes and knew his departure was being suggested. "I'll leave her with you then."

Elias nodded his head slightly as his fellow clergyman departed, wasting no time to focus on Jamie. As she opened her mouth to speak he began walking past her. "Follow me."

Not questioning, she obeyed, assuming he was going to take her to her uncle. She didn't want to be there longer than needed so it worked in everyone's favor.

They passed one column after another, past vaguely familiar faces, then down a quiet hall. She passed the entrance of the library, lingering for a moment before following after Elias' shadow. He seemed unconcerned, let alone aware that she had fallen behind, and moved at a smooth pace.

"I recently learned you're related to my boss," Jamie said.

"Is that so?" He didn't mean for his rhetorical question to be answered and yet Jamie felt the cold shoulder ought to be met with some form of affability.

"Noel. He mentioned you two don't talk much."

"As often as you reach out to your uncle. I noticed your visits have lessened in the past months."

"What can I say? I got bombarded with homework."

Edgar approached them and looked alarmed at the visitor's presence beside Elias, unable to maintain a composed face. He questioned the parson.

"She's inquiring on the condition of her uncle." Elias cocked his head to the side, his eyes on Edgar. "I was simply taking her to him."

"Gabe must be in his room."

"She's informed me that she's already checked."

Jamie noticed Edgar send a silent message to Elias before he looked at her with a regrettable expression. "I'm sorry but if he isn't in his room, then he must have gone out. He and another of the clergy were headed out to the grocery store and other stores for supplies."

Elias inhaled deeply. "It was a sincere gesture coming here. Perhaps she should wait for him."

"He has many responsibilities to attend to once he returns." Edgar pivoted his body to face Jamie. "I'll be sure to tell him you came, and call you as soon as he has completed his duties," he added.

Jamie knew they were keeping something from her, but she couldn't understand why they lied when it was obvious. And Edgar, she assumed he would be the honest one. Casting a glance to Elias, who kept his hands held behind his back from the moment he approached her, Jamie looked back to Edgar with a defeated expression. "I won't take up his time. I just need to see him really quick."

"Is something going on, Jamie?" Edgar asked.

"I want to be sure he isn't unwell. I haven't heard from him in weeks."

Edgar placed his hand on her shoulder and turned her away, leading them back the way they came. "I completely understand. You're welcome to wait in the seats of the nave." Edgar spared little of a glance to the other in the passageway. "I will take her back, Elias."

Elias had something to say but didn't have the chance to voice it as Edgar led her far from hearing range. Elias left the opposite way of them as Jamie looked back to Edgar.

He was keeping something back, she had no doubt now. If he was going to keep secrets she would play behind a mask as well. A corner of her lip pulled up in a teasing smile. "My trip really was in vain, wasn't it? I'm just being silly."

"Of course not. Of course you have every right to visit your uncle. Anytime you wish to see him you can come. I'm sure it will please him very much to see you. It's been a long time since I've seen your face around the church. While it may not be for service, a visit from a friend is always welcome."

"Edgar, you'd tell me if something was wrong right? Like if he'd gone to the hospital . . ." She hesitated. "Or if he was holed up in his room or something?"

Edgar grinned with the same effort as a royal. She sensed the lie and like earlier said nothing, only waiting to hear what lie would come from his lips next. Everywhere she turned there seemed to be someone lying or keeping a lie close to them.

"Your uncle. Hmm . . . Your uncle is the most committed man I've ever seen. Well I'm sure he's told you why he came. Personally, I'm glad he chose our humble family."

They approached the sanctuary. She'd been too concentrated on hating and despising her uncle's choice to live there she never learned why St. Luke's was his choice. After months lying to them, saying that she was meeting with Gabe when she'd been with the gargoyles, it was assumed Gabe would've told her why he came by now.

It was tempting for Jamie to risk it. She believed Edgar would remain entirely unsuspicious. Taking a good glance at him, one could know his life.

He'd been raised by happy religious parents for years before another sibling joined the family. The family of four prospered well until the father passed away just after Edgar graduated from high school. Working a wide range of jobs from milk delivery to shipyards to mailman to second assistant set decorator for a major Hollywood film, he could never maintain a relationship to give his mother a grandchild. In fact, so content with his simple life he worked only to get his paycheck at the end of two weeks and go out for a night on the town. He didn't find comfort in his faith until decades later when he witnessed his mother surviving a miracle operation following a despondent dive in her cancer treatments. She'd gotten better until a decade ago when she passed peacefully in her sleep. By this time, his faith had long past settled him underneath the cathedral's roof. He'd resided in two churches before he transferred to St. Luke's, where he'd been for almost two decades. In his aged eyes, Jamie could see a soul completely satisfied with a life of prosaic routine.

"He never told me," Jamie said.

Aged. Secretive. Edgar had more to him than the common sexagenarian. Out of them all, he was most gracious.

Edgar couldn't believe she'd asked, however the tension in his eyebrows softened as he folded his arms behind him. "He came for you. And your mother, and your brother. You were his family. He said he'd been misguided."

The uncle she knew was a creature in a children's book. There were creatures you knew from a distance because of the stories you'd heard, but then the book cover would close and the creatures would remain safely tucked away until the book was brought out again. Always a distance away. Never too close. And the story never changed.

Somehow, for some reason, he'd left the world he belonged to. He approached her, said hello, tried to reintroduce himself, become a part of her life. She couldn't give him a chance to become the flawed human being because he could only ever be the twisted creature in a story. A creature that would never change his being as any living thing in fiction couldn't. Once written in ink it couldn't be erased. Once acted in the real world, it was impossible to go back and change its past. Gabe didn't side with his brother when his family ostracized him and he couldn't keep in touch with his sister-in-law's family after his brother died. It was fixed.

Her anger at her uncle was stretched to a degree she wouldn't allow to be changed. She wouldn't allow it because she couldn't accept that father, who loved his younger brother as much as he did, could love someone who turned their back on him. All in the name of faith. Religion split her father from his family, and ever since she was five and was told why her father's parents wouldn't come to her kindergarten graduation, she never forgot it. She'd never loved anyone more than her father and mother. She'd have nothing if it wasn't for her family at home to comfort her when she struggled to find a friend or kindness at school. Her family's love is what replaced the inability to function well with others. It replaced that peculiarity she didn't understand about herself. It's what made spending more time with Minjae easier. After Christmas with his family and after the weeks together during her slow hours at work, she'd discovered why Minjae could be so open and friendly. He'd gotten enough love at home and now as a mature adult could spread it.

It unexpectedly wasn't difficult for her to swallow that warmth could be found in people you wouldn't expect and coldness where you needed it most.

"Misguided?" Jamie's voice was thick. "A grown man?"

"Everyone is capable of living under control. Everyone grows at their own pace. When he'd learned to follow what his heart said over what people said, it was the right time for him to seek your family out. Some just need more of it than others. After he'd found himself, the person he had wished himself to be, it was too late. There's no mistaking the regret he feels for it."

After taking in such high praise, there was a softness in her voice she'd never thought she'd have when speaking about Gabe. "It sounds like you've spoken to him many times about this."

"Learning to accept and move on from the guilt one has for the passing of a loved one is a meditative practice. It isn't something one moves on from one day then they're fine the rest of their life. For some people, for those who care the most, they need to relearn forgiveness within themselves. Your uncle is incredibly sensitive. It is like the world's griefs are on his shoulders and he needs someone to share the burden with, if not unleash his concerns on. Members of the congregation don't only listen to the laity, they need counseling and shepherding as well."

"Gabe came because he wanted to make up for not showing for my dad's funeral."

"When your father passed he was remiss," Edgar said unfazed. "When years of guilt due to one's negligence hounds down on the mind, it can have a rather scarring effect."

A muffled, familiar sound filled the space between them as Jamie's phone went off. It was a message from her mother asking her to come home. She silenced it as she slipped it away, as if it never made a noise.

"Then can I ask you a personal question?"

"Of course."

"What do you make of dreams? Do you think they're tied to reality in anyway?"

"In some way, yes. The mind is too complex to disregard such an idea. I believe the mind is capable of many things we haven't yet discovered."

Jamie arched an eyebrow. "That sounds incredibly close to evolution. I thought you guys didn't believe that."

Edgar let out a heartfelt laugh and stretched his neck like an accordion. His bright brown eyes shone back to Jamie's as he waited for the humored ripples in his chest to settle. "I think it's possible to believe in many things. Evolution can be as flawed as religion may be. All was written and studied by man and what is man but a walking flaw? Scientific theory is accurate until new instruments discover new discoveries and then theories become tiny paragraphs in history books. I believe evolution's still occurring and it isn't something that will end until man knows everything. Until man has developed a way to become perfect. But, I think the world will end before that happens."

She smirked. "I'd never heard of a Catholic priest believing in evolution. Do the others know?"

Edgar glimpsed one way then the other before leaning toward her, beckoning her closer with the flutter of his fingers. "I am the master secret keeper. And . . ."

"And?"

Edgar's cheeks rounded to plump red hills. "It's always healthy to believe anything is possible."

27

At the end of February, the Kennedy Space Center held its first event featuring Scott Kelly, where patrons could spend half a day touring the facility and share a lunch with the astronaut. Jamie paid for her and Aiden to be part of the exclusive meet-and-greet, and while offering to pay Minjae's general admission ticket, he insisted on taking the trip to the center he'd protracted visiting long enough. The Diez siblings arrived early, as per Aiden's request, and listened as the astronaut shared his experiences during his space missions, as well as the effects of his time there since returning and comparing the results to his twin brother. Jamie glimpsed at her brother multiple times. The glow in his face never faltered. There was nothing Aiden wanted more than to one day become an astronaut, to look out a window and see forever, as it continued to form and unravel and expand. To look left and see our star (from the Earth's perspective, a rising sun). To look up and remember it wasn't really up and affirm that what was once a map had suddenly become a globe.

The three returned to Shore and when parked in front of the Diez residence, Aiden jumped out of the car. An early spring wind slipped inside and rushed into Jamie, almost causing her to sneeze. Covering her mouth, she leaned over the vacant seat to call his attention.

"Whoa! Has meeting Scott Kelly destroyed your manners?"

Minjae chuckled. "He's fine."

Jamie widened her eyes the way their mother did when she expected a specific answer.

Aiden rolled his eyes. "Many thanks and you'll have good fortune in the near future."

Jamie disputed the weak show of gratitude and out of habit, Aiden slammed the car door in his sister's face.

"Little brother's never say what they mean," Minjae said.

Jamie moved the seatbelt out of her way as she took her bag in her hand, scooting toward the door.

"Another way in which I owe you," she said. "After taking me to Orlando and then to the space launch in December, you do too much. My mom's off but Aiden would've preferred to go with you. I haven't seen him get along so well with anyone outside of the family."

"A friend of yours is a friend of mine."

"If I must call my brother my friend," Jamie said, scooting to the door and opening it.   "Um, Jamie . . ." He was half-turned in the driver's seat and fumbled with his fingers as he swallowed nervously, a chuckle slipping though his lips. She'd seen Minjae passive on rare occasions at school, and disappointed when his house was out of stock of caramel corn, but never nervous and never at a loss for words. It was Minjae after all. He was the type of person who would keep going on with his Oscars speech, unaware the music started playing telling him to wrap it up.

She waited as he slid his palms together, noticing how he avoided her eyes that made sitting in the standstill car increasingly unbearable. She resisted fanning her face as she cocked her head to the side. Before she could speak and before he found his courage, he chuckled once more before looking at her with a bland grin. "Tell Aiden I'll take him next time he wants to go to the space center. Anytime."

Jamie felt the offer insincere but didn't call him out. "What do you mean anytime? Even I don't want to go anytime."

"It's a favor. From his *hyung* to his little bro."

Jamie laughed. "His what?"

"His big brother. Could you not get that from the context? It's Korean."

"Ah!" Jamie nodded. "I think I heard it Christmas at your house a couple times." She drummed her fingers on the headrest of the front passenger seat. A moment before she moved her hand over the door handle their eyes connected. "Is that all?"

He forced the last ounce of sincerity in his smile as he finished yet another perfect performance.

Minjae sank into the driver's seat after he watched the front door of the Diez house close, then leaned over the steering wheel as he hung his head down. A perfect opportunity to confess—but once feeling the jitters all over his body, backed out. He tapped his forehead to the wheel several times as he lambasted himself for being a coward.

It was late in the morning the next day when Jamie, at her desk in her room, heard her brother in the living room. She yelled that she couldn't hear him and he repeated himself only to suffer the same response.

"I said!" Aiden boomed, suddenly opening the door and staring at her. "That Jay's outside."

"*Minjae* Jay?" Jamie asked.

"The only friend you have Jay." He rolled his eyes, closing the door behind him. Jamie made a face as she mocked him, then went to see what he was doing there.

Minjae was standing in the driveway, his hands in his pockets when he noticed the front door open. He lowered his gaze to the front lawn then returned his wary gaze to her when she neared him.

"Did you forget something yesterday?" Jamie folded her arms over her chest.

"I, uh, forgot . . ." He lifted a hand to rub the back of his neck as he leaned to one side, looking away again.

"Yes. You were going to say something else last night instead of offering my brother rides to the Space Center."

"How about a walk? I need fresh air."

She could see he wanted to unload whatever was on his mind. As they walked toward the neighborhood park she brain-stormed what it was. Their relationship had been good so far. He'd helped her way more than she did in return, but he seemed absolutely willing. Occasionally she'd bring up his responsibilities with Yearbook but every time she did he assured her he was ahead of his work. It could be about Emily. The two broke up months ago and Alric had never let it slide. He was long past mentioning it to Jamie at this point however there was always the lingering glance after Photo; blaming her. Emily was a nice girl and if she was heartbroken Jamie could understand why her friend would become protective, but Jamie was not involved in their breakup and had no influence over Minjae's continual presence around her. Almost all the time they spent together, they were either in Photo, or with Aiden, or at the rock gym with the Capes.

After two months, Jamie had become closer with them. Vienna in particular would come to console her grievances about Jax and Jamie listened with an open ear. Surprisingly, it didn't bother her as much as it did when she overheard strangers complaining over the phone or while people were climbing a wall. She could only credit her transition because of Minjae. If he wasn't somewhere in her life at least every other day then she would've remained the same practicing nihilist who abhorred any contact with people outside of work. She had acquaintances but she'd never had friends before. Not one like her father. Now she had Minjae, and Vienna, and on occasion Jax. Most impressive of all, her change had prodded her to check if her uncle was okay.

She'd received a call from him thanking her for visiting and inviting her to come back, but she never returned the phone call. She kept the call short before her mother or brother heard the conversation in the first place.

Her progress with her uncle was still transitioning. All those years of hate couldn't be worn away so quickly, nor so easily.

Unbeknownst to her, Minjae was fixing that.

On one trip to St. Augustine in late January, Minjae was waiting for Jamie and Aiden to use the restroom at a Publix. Jamie returned before Aiden and spotted Minjae comforting a reunited child with her parent. He was rubbing her arm and complimenting her on her outfit, a print with black penguins over the blue tights and a matching white and blue shirt with one large smiling penguin. The little girl stared timidly. Whatever he said—it didn't matter what he said, this was Minjae—made her smile. The parent thanked him again as Minjae wished them farewell, focusing on the girl and causing her smile to break out in a perfect laugh. Jamie saw it with friends and with strangers, the kindness and love Minjae uninhibitedly shared with everyone, and wished that somehow she could be like that.

The souls of her father and Minjae were of a similar likeness, as if their souls were taken from the same source, one loving and rich in kindness. Her father didn't just love her, he couldn't help loving and smiling and being thoughtful to everyone. Strangers were just lost relations, until he said hello and wished them a good day. All the good she saw in her father, she saw in Minjae.

After witnessing the scene at Publix, Jamie was drawn to Minjae. Some days he'd just hang at her house while she made dinner and waited for Aiden to come home. Aiden didn't spend every day at Banafsha's house anymore. Jamie didn't see her neighbor as often and she was sure that Banafsha was thankful for the peace and freedom.

Aiden had noticed a change in Jamie's demeanor and he hinted at it once, though Jamie construed the comment as an immature jab from one sibling to another as kids in elementary school tease when they see a boy and a girl share a snack. Aiden only wanted to remark on the shift and Jamie gave him the cold shoulder for it. He never mentioned her change again and from then on watched in silence.

And he and Minjae had a good relationship. Minjae did his best to get on Aiden's good side (taking him on drives to the space center always helped). Whenever he visited the Diez house he tried to update him on something new relating to the space watch. Whether it was about an astronaut or events at the space center, he used what he could to gain Aiden's favor. It took Jamie some time but one day Minjae was actually interested in bringing the news to Aiden. The Tesla Roadster launch was a big day for both of them. Learning as well as sharing. Jamie wanted to try that. Take something that someone else loved with a passion and let it become her own. To see why they loved it. To understand for herself. It had to be the secret formula for why Minjae was always so happy.

Not today though. Something was off today.

Combing her fingers through her straightened hair, she slid her fingers to the tips and held it down until the wind settled. The park hosted families enjoying the late February weather, more appropriate for a spring April day.

"Oh, there's people here," Minjae said suddenly.

"They won't hear us from over there," she said, pointing to the far side of the playground where benches bridged to an open field.

Uninterested while unwilling to refuse, he walked rigidly beside Jamie and settled himself on top of a bench table. Jamie folded her hands together, leaning over her legs as she glimpsed over to her nervous companion.

"I'm usually patient in these types of situations," Jamie announced, smirking before leaning closer to look into his downcast eyes. "There's too much suspense though. *From you*. It's better if you just say it."

He sat still, shutting his eyes before making a decision and standing up, twirling back to look at her. However the courage in his eyes crumbled once they made eye contact and he spun around again, huffing out a breath as he shut his eyes and rested his hands on his hips.

"Okay. Just a minute. Pull yourself together Minnie."

Jamie thought the self-given nickname cute and held the amusement in her eyes.

The courage returned, he looked at Jamie deeply as he took her hands, and then dropped them again. "I'm sorry. It's just not easy. I can't get it out." He opened his mouth to spill but only resulted in shaking his head. "God! Why's it so hard just to say it?"

Jamie stood up and gestured her hands in a way as if trying to persuade him to inhale. "Let's just breathe in. Everything's good. Your friend won't think any differently of you."

A flash of shock spread over his face when she stood up and he pointed to the bench table. "Actually could you sit down? I don't think I can tell you if you're standing."

"Okay," she said, surrendering her hands as she sat back down.

He cupped his hands around his neck like a shackle as he hung his head back. "Do you know what's the worst thing to fear?" he asked it more to calm himself.

I'll bite, Jamie thought.

"The one you never knew you were afraid of. You're standing in front of it for the first time and it hits you, I've never been more terrified in my life. I've never known fear before." Minjae disconnected their eye contact to study the ground, then inhaled a final time before looking her straight in the eye. "There's something you don't know about your dad's accident."

A winter chill shot down her sleeves and over her arms. This hadn't been what she expected. All the same, she'd listened to what he would have to say. She owed him that much. For all he'd done.

"Three years ago," Minjae said, "when my brother crashed his truck into your dad's car, he was on his phone. I know you won't remember but that year he'd gotten the latest smartphone, and if you remember anything about that phone it had the most obnoxious ringtone—some alert noise every time you got a notification. Like some warning about UFOs—it's not important." Minjae closed his eyes as his lower lip trembled. "My brother was distracted by his phone, because— it was because he was answering my texts. I had sent a flood of them. Some as short as a word or a punctuation. He'd been ignoring them until it got too much and he picked it up to see what I was fussing about. He was going to see me soon, bringing home a bouquet of flowers. But I'd been insistent."

Chrysanthemums. Jamie remembered. She despised the flower now.

"I was going to ask you to the homecoming dance the next day with them. But," he paused, his lower lip trembling as he covered his mouth, "after that day I couldn't. I couldn't approach you without the accident coming to mind and seeing the way you hated me and my family. Even if you didn't hate me, you'd only think it was me pitying you and I didn't want you to think that of me. I've never pitied you and I didn't want you to think I did anything for you because it was me feeling bad or being forced into it."

The confession became a river bulldozing through a dam. Now that'd he started he couldn't stop. Jamie simply listened with her poker face, Minjae oblivious to everything around him as he only heard the words he was saying echo in his ears.

"When Daehyun kept in touch with your family I became selfish. I thought maybe if you kept in touch then it was because you'd forgiven him. And if you could forgive *him*, then maybe it was possible you could believe me when I told you how I felt. It had nothing to do with the accident because you hadn't done anything. It was me. Only me."

Minjae patted his chest, resting his hand on it as it rose and fell. He felt numb and vulnerable to whatever her response might be. On Jamie's end, there was only an empty mind.

As time passed and nothing was said, the numb feeling in his heart began to thaw as panic replaced it. It unsettled his stomach first. He began to pat his fingers against his chest next, pulling his lips into his mouth and exhaling through his nose. Cautiously, afraid what it would set off, he said her name.

She registered her name and suddenly a pressure compressed within her chest stole her breath. In hindsight, she had a blank mind, but there was a very small hole in the back of it, slowly streaming all the emotion of that day three years ago. When he said her name, it suddenly ripped open and all the emotions poured out.

It was unavoidable that the way to the hospital was past the crash site. Images flashed over her eyes. A severe dent in the door where her father should have escaped from. Shattered and sprinkled mementos of the accident cast around the site in grave concentrations like stars clustered in the sky. What were once stray pieces of trash were substituted as petals of the Chrysanthemum flower. Red and blue lights redirected traffic. These images from the road, then the ones from within the car. Her mother fighting temptation to not see what her fears painted for her. Her brother asking questions, questions, questions. A muffled sob from the front seat as Jamie could only stare through the window, praying it all to be a dream. She'd willed herself numb to believing it could possibly be true.

"I—" Jamie focused on him as her calm flipped back. "I need to go home."

Unable to control the tick he nodded rigidly as Jamie walked past him. His breath was held for as long as it took for the sun to set; until he felt his muscles cringe under his exhale. The air through his nose suffered as his chest began to shake. He knelt down. He covered his face. Two drops fell and slid down the inner lining of his forearm as he cried silently. He wasn't allowed to cry. Not after keeping silent for three years. But finally telling Jamie didn't appease him like he expected it to, like it usually did when you got something off your chest that you'd kept deep down. Something he'd never confessed to anyone aside from his brother and his mother. He had a new expectation now.

Jamie would never speak to him again. It seemed like the past months were for nothing.

All of it, for this.

Lying in bed, Jamie heard Minjae's voice over and over. It was her name. Over and over. She heard everything before it but the way he said her name . . . Tentatively. Fearfully. He kept this back for years and now after years, more than anything, he needed to hear her say something and all that existed in her mind was a leaking emptiness. Once the nothingness emptied then it would be full again, of a new nothing.

Not only was it a struggle to fall asleep but the darkness seemed more colorful than usual. It was supposed to collapse as she fell asleep but she noted rings of dull colors pulse and shift as if it were a caterpillar. A weak beating yellow outlined by a dark violet. Maritime blue melted into a dark wood black. No reds or oranges. No greens. The only traces of definition was white. The caterpillar inching across the globe. She pressed her knuckles against her eyes as the night drifted away.

A soft rap at the window and she was awake. She'd been dozing off somehow after hours of thinking of her meeting with Minjae, now to go through it all again. Only, the noise at her window returned and her head shot in that direction. Knowing it was foolish, she got up to get the interruption out of the way. The sooner she saw it was nothing the sooner she could fall asleep.

Taking the curtain loosely at first, she pulled the material into her fist and moved the shutter out of the way, just enough for her to glimpse through. There was a figure with electric eyes, a white so bright it looked blue, staring at her, gazing upon her, unforgivingly. All she could do was scream. Frozen in place, stunned in shock. She screamed as the eyes and her voice had a standoff.

Here, there was no time.

No time was why suddenly the world outside of her window fell backwards, the world inside of it collapsing away from the figure. A flush of heat soared up her body as violent winds propelled around her.

Jamie shot up from her covers, heaving as lines of sweat slowly scaled down her back and linked her shirt to her skin. Calming her breath, she waited until the heart under hand established a slower rhythm. She turned toward the window, absent of any noise, and eventually lied back down. If she couldn't get a handle of it soon, then she'd have to talk to her mom about seeing someone. She didn't want to talk to a doctor but they'd have a solution. Yoga? Meditation? More walks in the morning and evening? By this point, she'd do anything to be rid of the nightmares.

28

All members of the assembly were agitated as if they were in a subterranean crypt and not atop the edifice overlooking vast plains and deserts. The robed one, Erus. His tail, Acario. The seven clouds closely reminiscent of malfunctioning siblings. Ill-conceived demons standing at attention around the room. The only one composed, the scarred demon, an ill-amused titan of burnt sienna skin and horns of a mountain animal: the Gatekeeper, Rephastion.

This was to be the last meeting.

Erus scanned the room like a predator, spending little attention to any one member before moving on. Rephastion, in turn, paid special attention to Erus. Before they made eye contact, Rephastion lowered his gaze to pick dirt from underneath his claw-like fingernails. He'd been on the Rock for barely a month when he had been summoned back.

"My brothers," Erus said. "Dear sacrifices of the cause have delivered us worthwhile rewards. After centuries, the struggle has proven to not have been in vain."

From the rumbling chorus Erus knew they were pleased. They wanted results, and he didn't even need to provide them with any details. How beautifully simple the heads of power could be.

"There is a concern that has always bothered me," Rephastion said, focus remaining on his nails.

"Shut up Gatekeeper!" screeched one of the smoke shapes. "We'll all benefit from none of your sarcasm today."

Rephastion stood and slipped out a rusted blade, digging the tip further into the nail bed as he continued calmly. "No, no sarcasm. I simply wished to point out something that's been weighing on my mind."

"It's best kept to yourself," said a smoke shape beside Erus.

The Lord General clenched his teeth and glared as the spawn of inconvenience interrupted what would otherwise have been a smooth meeting. However, he needed the Gatekeeper's presence to ascertain the loyalty of the smoke figures. They might detest his personality at times but they would not have considered Erus' plan without him.

"Conspiring against the ruling power is always a delight, however, I think we've reached the point of the plans many of you have overlooked. You see there . . ." Rephastion pointed the tip of his blade over his shoulder toward the Darkness. A sky-encompassing ghost, it lingered beyond the plains, swallowing the hues of the distant horizon. "That cloud of Darkness your Lord General so wishes to harness and unleash upon the world of souls is the most powerful dumb beast you'll ever lay your eyes on." He glanced up to the smoke shapes and flicked his fingers up at them. "Not that you'd know anything about that."

"We lack the necessity of eyes," spat a smoke, the remnants of its outburst lunging toward Rephastion. The Gatekeeper avoided them effortlessly. "We are beyond human senses. Eyes are for the diseased—"

"You see," Rephastion chuckled. "I'm an abomination who knows my master is a dumb beast of immense power because clearly *anyone*"—Rephastion glanced at Erus—"can overtake him. If you have the brawn and the foolishness to try." Rephastion stopped and lifted his gaze to the smoke closest to him. "You wonder why I would serve such a disgrace—well, why would you?"

Erus hissed as he leaned over the table, setting his hands on its surface and digging his nails into the rock. "Make your *point*, Gatekeeper."

Rephastion smirked as a loathing glare settled on him. "I mean, my irascible ally, to say that whoever takes over my master will be incredibly powerful." He waved the blade to one side. "Congratulations to them."

"I would fear whoever overpowered your master as well," Erus said. The closest he could get to an appeased admission.

"The Lord General is not taking control over your master just to control you," voiced one smoke across the table from Rephastion. "No one would go through so much hassle just for you."

"Obliged," Rephastion said. "All of this I mention as context for you in case you have forgotten. While you havoc your time on the Rock I fear you have forgotten what life is like here. I should know. You see, I leave almost as often as your Lord General. However, never have I once forgotten who the Grand Master is. Perhaps he's slipped your minds." Rephastion wiggled his fingers at them again. "If you had any."

"Never!"

"How could we!"

"Impossible!"

"Precisely," Rephastion nodded contently. "He is not my master but master of my master. He does not command but is above the Darkness who commands me. As I am before you all shows clearly by right my master is not always with me. Do you realize that I, in turn, have realized something all of you have not?" Rephastion stepped by Erus and looked down at him, towering at over twice his height. The Lord General waited to be enlightened as Rephastion permitted a minute for the smoke figures to ponder. "This is all in vain."

Erus didn't call his bluff and Rephastion glared until the idea began to form in Erus' mind. It wasn't a bluff. Everything he said was true. It was a bird's egg trying to fly. Flapping when it didn't even have wings.

The Gatekeeper stepped backwards and looked among the council of traitors. "The Grand Master will realize that one of his Lord General's has plotted against him—*again*—and he will not remain still. He is not forgiving. Between the two, what makes Lord General Erus a greater match against the Grand Master? The Rock will remain as it has until the end, where only there will remain the Grand Master and our *former* Father."

"Whispers say two will remain until the end," spoke a cloud, considering Rephastion's words. "Two that are not alike."

Panting like a dog Italus skidded then slipped after losing traction on the floor as he attempted to slow his anxious sprint into the meeting room. Sliding against one of the smoke figures and staring up frightened at the drowning cloud, he quickly shrunk away to nearby Erus. The Lord General lowered his ear slightly as he listened to the message. It didn't make a difference if the news had been good or bad, the cheekbones and eyebrows would not budge or twitch or betray him to either.

"It seems you are wrong," Erus said, looking over to Rephastion. "Already your master is collecting offerings by the whale. Thousands upon thousands of souls: accepted. Your master will have swallowed an ocean by the time you've returned to the Rock." A hint of amusement seeped into his voice. "Have you accomplished the task I have given you? Have you discovered the source of the imbalance?"

"There is something for you to fear still?" Rephastion arched an invisible eyebrow. The clouds of smoke billowed with interest. "After harvesting the most powerful force there is, you still quiver at an unknown *imbalance*? Even the other Lord Generals are not weary for it—let alone the Grand Master. How are you to conquer if you tremble upon trinket rumors? Surely living here has accustomed you to the lies the souls embellish. Imagine a Sapling, or another Lord General, or the Grand Master lying to you. Your kingdom will crumble just as soon as you've built it. All in vain . . ."

"Enough!" Erus slammed his fists against the table under the shake of his howl. Italus shrunk inwardly as he backed away. "No! Era after disgusting era *I* have been the one whom he had forgotten. The Lord General of the Heavens is at the Father's front door while the Lord General of the Rock is constantly praised for seducing and tempting and making all the souls of mankind fall. And the praises do not end with the Grand Master! The souls of the Rock fear Tier themselves. They don't know it but every shadow they see, every chill down their bones when they sense an evil near, every damn prayer to save them from death is all to glorify the workings of the Formidable Lord General Tier! All of the righteous armies of Heaven and Rock are commendable but mine. What about the souls *after* they have died! This fiery hell would be nothing to fear if it were not for me! No longer will I remain unacknowledged. I refuse to sit here and be forgotten like a king of dust and ghosts. I can rule the living. *I* can ruin the souls! I can do *more* than just tempt them! I will create savagery in the womb and nest hatred before they've open their eyes. The Rock will not simply go on as it has for millenniums. I will establish a new planet. The end is now and *I* have brought it."

Rephastion watched as the dark mouth of Erus began to spew wisps of shadows, hideous and possessive, lifting his hands up as the smoke figures around the table began to thunder.

"No more order!"

"No longer indentured slaves to meager souls!"

"Treats us worse than smoke! The Deadly Sins deserve respect by *all*!"

"May the end be delicious and dreadful. Burning eruptions and spasms!"

"Give us rivers of weathered bones and wet dust!"

"Give us eternal moonless night!"

"Light the fire!"

"Let us soar!"

"End!"

"End!"

"End!"

While the chorus of accumulating mayhem applauded louder, Rephastion waited for them to settle and his voice to be heard. "Your mistreatment will not assure you success. You may obtain power, however you need more followers than just Saplings and the Sins. Even

I and my master are not enough to combat the Grand Master. He will have the armies of Heaven and the Rock by his side. What is your secret weapon?"

The last spills of shadows slipped from his mouth as Erus straightened, then looked at Rephastion with a morbid curiosity.

"My Gatekeeper will see, dear sentry of the mortal bridge, upmost respected servant of the Darkness. My wait is not futile. You will cast yourselves into the arms of the souls in repentance for ever having issued my plans in vain." As Erus spoke he rounded the table to approach Rephastion, growing in size and mass with every step. What before was face to belly was now equally face-to-face with the Gatekeeper. A narrowing in the eyes had slipped into a twisting of the mouth as Erus suddenly slapped Rephastion. Unlike Acario and Italus, and the countless Saplings and messengers before, Rephastion growled as he glared back to the Lord General. However he did not strike back. The Lord General would soon control his master and undeniably control him. He could not act now.

The Lord General's lips trembled as an expression of glee began to shapen. "Prove yourself to me, Gatekeeper, and I will unbind you from your perennial leash." Erus lifted the back of his hand and brushed it against Rephastion's cheek.

Over Erus' shoulder Rephastion spotted Iax, a shimmer at the entrance of the meeting room. Unknowing to how long his friend had waited there, the amber eyes of the Gatekeeper slowly refocused on the Lord General before him.

29

There were three reasons why Jamie wanted to confront Minjae the next day. Firstly, despite how she felt after the confession she knew it wasn't his fault. Daehyun didn't have to pick up his phone and look away from the road. He could have easily ignored it or raised the volume of the radio to silence the alert sounds or just switched his phone to silent. Blaming Minjae for Daehyun's error was like blaming a drenched person on the rain and not on the fact they neglected to bring an umbrella when there were stormy clouds outside. Secondly, she needed someone like Minjae in her life. He'd brought her out of a slump she'd always pictured was her life. Unintentionally, she always lived each day hopelessly as if there wasn't anyone who could give her a reason to smile and want something to look forward to. Lastly, the nightmares were weaker after spending a day with him. She believed over enough time they'd leave altogether. She needed him.

It was when she opened the door to her new neighbor with an apologetic expression on his face that she forgot every one of them. Ethan had lost his dog and wanted help from someone in the area since she knew the neighborhood. Relaying the message to her mom, she and Ethan spent the Sunday wandering around the neighborhood and nearby parks for a russet brown Havanese. Unsuccessful after four hours of searching, Ethan walked her home, sharing he'd update her if he found him.

Returning to school, Minjae was nowhere to be found. Vienna informed Jamie he had called in sick and wouldn't be coming in the following day. Expecting to see him in Photo, when he never showed,

Jamie planned to intercept him sometime after school since he usually worked on his Yearbook tasks in the photo room. Meeting Jamie for the second time that day, Ms. Ava relayed that Minjae had planned to work from home that afternoon. It was unfortunate for Jamie since she would be working the rest of the week and wouldn't have time to go to his house until the weekend. She didn't want to wait until the weekend because finally speaking to him after a week made it seem as if it had taken her that long to realize that she was okay and she didn't blame him. And she certainly wasn't going to tell him this over the phone. She couldn't get the expression out of her mind even when his voice from that day had faded. He'd never suffered from a trauma than when he learned about the accident. For three years he'd blamed himself. She couldn't properly communicate that it really was all right unless she looked him in the eye and assured him with word and heart.

Whether she wanted to or not she would have to meet him on the weekend or sometime over spring break. While the Capes had planned on hiking on real mountains for months, in the end Jamie couldn't handle the thought of being in a car with a stranger while he drove her from the airport to the hiking site, let alone a road trip with seventeen-year-olds. Even if Minjae would've driven the entire way she would have just gotten carsick and they would've reached the mountains the day that school had resumed. Anyways, she'd be better off saving that money for after graduation. No matter how close she'd gotten to Minjae and Vienna since the New Year, she'd be leaving the start of summer.

Returning to the Jangs house for the first time since Christmas, she rubbed the arm hairs down as she walked up the driveway to the front door. After a set of knocks she pressed her lips together.

Minjae's father, a kind man who lent his taller-than-average height to his sons, opened the door. After nodding that his son was there, he welcomed her inside and led her toward the living room. "I'm glad you stopped by. He's been rather down for the past couple of days and I figure you might be able to bring him back to normal. He's been happier these past months than I'd seen since Daehyun left for college. I'll bring him over."

The soccer match between Orlando City and the San Jose Earthquakes was on TV. Since she didn't spot Mrs. Jang anywhere she suspected she was out and it was just the boys in the house. While she knew Minjae loved soccer and the Orlando City team, she didn't understand why father and son weren't enjoying the game together. She'd seen him around school so he wasn't sick. She looked toward the direction where his father left as she waited.

When the two returned Minjae seemed surprised what his father said was true. He shared a glance at him before his father returned to the sofa. Jamie knew he wasn't kicking them out and presumed since the TV stayed on it was a polite request.

"Can we take a walk?" Jamie asked.

Minjae nodded slowly before gesturing toward the front door. The two made their way in no particular direction. Neither spoke as they walked, ignoring the pernicious storm clouds in the distance. They came upon a kid's playground and sat on the swings, weakly swaying against the upcoming winds.

"I can't know how you've been feeling but I can guess," Jamie said. "I wanted to see you the day after but something came up. And then the week flew by. You weren't in school and if you were I couldn't find a time to talk to you. It's almost like you were avoiding me."

Minjae swayed on his swing, studying the rain clouds so intently Jamie almost thought he was ignoring her.

"I needed a moment to process what you said but seeing how you've been this week, I regret not staying and comforting you. You've carried this guilt around for three years and when you needed me to tell you it's okay"—she tugged at his swing's chain—"*it is okay*, Minjae. I'm sorry I left you. After all you've done for me . . ."

"I didn't do anything for you." One of his eyes twitched as he exhaled through nose. "You reacted exactly as you should've."

With both of her hands around the chains, she leaned forward and tilted her head. "And I regret it." He tsked. "I've always worn my heart on my sleeve. Why would I spare your feelings unless I was being sincere?"

"It's unfair for me to think of being forgiven so easily."

Jamie pressed her lips together as they heard the storm clouds thunder under the strengthening wind. Jamie moved a lock of hair in her face out of the way.

"My family has a bad relationship with my dad's side. We don't speak to them. There was a falling out when my dad decided to marry my mom." Minjae looked up at her as he listened, while she couldn't be as courageous and look back. "Something ludicrous. My mom didn't want to go to the church they went to or to any church at all. My dad married a woman like that. All of his family decided to disown him and all my life I never had a real relationship or memory with them. His younger brother came to the hospital when I was born but he rarely kept in touch after that. Even when dad died he never came. None of them did. Up until a couple months ago my uncle decided to move to Shore and I hated him for it. I hated my mom because she welcomed him and because she forgave him. It's funny how easy it is to hate someone who makes the hardest decision. Any time he came up I would leave the room or start an argument."

The distraught expression on his face had eased slightly. "Why?"

"I might've forgiven him. I might've pushed aside he'd ignored my family and never showed up for my dad's funeral, if it wasn't for when I went to see him he couldn't remember when he last saw me. My dad praised him for his intelligence and potential but the first time I meet him and can actually communicate with him as an adult, he became the stranger I've always known. Family isn't who is related to you by blood. It's who's in your life. I hated him, his name, and everything about that family until a month ago. A month ago I worried if he was all right. If he was sick. Within a span of four months I'd rethought that the man I thought I hated most in the world was actually a decent human being who deserved to be looked after."

"What changed?"

"Me." Jamie steered her attention to him. "Because you've been in my life. Ever since the space launch, every time we were together you've made me happy—even when I thought you were weird as hell, which is too often. It's the same feeling I had whenever my dad showed me he loved me. I know people at school and at work but I never considered anyone a true friend aside from my dad. Except you. You've made me reconsider what I've been mad about and who I've been mad at. I think of you as close a friend to me as much as my dad. When I think about how intractable I was to the world when I was beside you, I imagine being that way beside him. And my dad was the kindest person I've ever known. I didn't want to be like that anymore."

He blinked repeatedly as a layer of water settled over his eyes, closing them as he leaned his head against the swing chain.

"Minjae, I don't want you to think I hate you."

Ignoring her, fighting her, he responded with closed eyes. "Deep down you do."

"I don't."

"I took away the person you loved most in the world. I would hate me."

Jamie stood up and stepped in front of him, taking the chains in her hands. "You gave me a good replacement."

His eyebrows came together as he managed his eyes open to her.

"My dad would have loved me and I would have never looked to find a friend in someone else. It was you who gave me someone to smile with, someone I'd want to be my family and never lose. You helped me want to forgive my uncle."

"I didn't."

A smile bloomed over her lips as she walked to one side and hugged him around the neck. His face dropped as his hand slowly lifted and held onto her arm. He cried quietly for a minute as she rubbed his back in circles, as if she were comforting a baby taken from his mother. While he didn't unload his sadness onto her arm, she tried to lighten the mood, chuckling as she turned her face toward him.

"Silly boy. With how much you love the world, how could I hate you? How could I even dislike you?"

He didn't respond and she began to lean away when his other arm came up and kept her there.

"No. Don't look at my face. I'm ugly when I cry like a man."

Jamie smiled as she began to lean away again, successfully as his hands dropped. "You're ugly anyways." He frowned and she bounced her palms against his cheeks. "But not as ugly as my brother when he cries." She wrapped her arms around his neck and hugged him again, giving him all the time in the world for his emotions to normalize. It was when the thunderclouds were joined by lightning that the two stood and ran back to his house.

Before the rain came, he believed her.

The children of the storm shook the trees and bushes as Jamie and Minjae sat in his back porch, watching its ferocity behind the safety of a screen. The water in the pool thrashed as mini waves cascaded over the edge and spilled onto the ground, reaching as far as the grass and joining the puddles quickly forming together under the deluge.

"I can't take all the credit for you being able to forgive me," Minjae said. "What I always admired about your mom was that she forgave Daehyun right after the accident. Not many would have. Do you know how many lesser grievances I've done that have gone unforgiven? The fact you can forgive me in so short a time may be hereditary."

"I think it's the people. Your brother and you deserved to be given another chance."

"Like your uncle."

Jamie nodded once. "Even him."

"It's hard to give him another chance, but after all he's ignored in the past eighteen years of your life I'm sure it's just as hard for him to try and reconnect. I could barely stand properly when I had to tell you and it had only been three years. He deserves some credit for trying when his family hasn't."

Jamie slid her fingers over the inside of the other palm as she meditated on a thought.

"If I asked, would you come with me to see him. To apologize?"

"To see your uncle? I would. Whenever you want." She nodded as he turned over in his seat toward her. "I'm curious. How is it that I'm the one who could barely sleep all week and yet you're the one with dark circles under her eyes?"

Bringing her fingers up to hide them, she blushed at his frankness. "I've been having nightmares lately. Especially when I don't have a stupid joke you told me to laugh at before going to bed."

Minjae bent his arm over the chair and rested his head on his hand. "Think about me before you go to bed huh?" Jamie covered her face as Minjae laughed. "I knew you girls thought about me just before you go to bed . . . That's quite intimate. *Ooo* I feel so giddy just thinking about it."

She lowered her hands. "You really do just pick and choose what I say don't you?"

The two teased one another until Jamie felt compelled to ask. "Can you tell me why Alric has it out for you? Why does he hate you for dumping Emily? It isn't like you were a bad boyfriend, were you?"

The subject change stirred Minjae in the wrong way as he stared back. Jamie didn't want him to misunderstand so she explained.

"Yesterday Alric mentioned he saw you a couple of months back stealing a picture from my computer." Minjae's expression shifted. He'd been caught and he hadn't prepared how to talk his way out of it. "The reason I'm mentioning it now is because it was around the time he started making a fuss about it and unloading his aggravations on me."

"He's been bothering you about Emily?"

"I know he's known her for years now and has had a crush on her for who knows how long. I never mentioned it because I didn't care at first. But I'm curious now."

"Why now?"

"Because I know you now. I'm curious what the reason could be that you dump a sweet girl like Emily and have a brute like Alric get on my case."

He adjusted his position in the chair to look over the backyard as he fought within himself if and what he should share. Enough time had passed that she figured he would change the subject. Instead when he shrugged, she felt he didn't have a reason after all.

"I liked Emily, but as time went on I realized it was more as a friend. And, it was coming to the time that I didn't want her in my life like that. I wanted to start spending my time with you instead. She understood."

It slowly made sense. Alric didn't blame Jamie for them breaking up, he only bothered her because he couldn't bother Minjae. Because then Emily would know. She wanted their break-up to be on good terms.

"Why was it time now?"

"I couldn't bring myself to talk to you after the accident—despite what my brother did. I thought maybe a year, but when it came to it I chickened out. So I said another year. But then I still couldn't. I knew our senior year was the right time. It would be three years. Plenty of time for you to not hate Daehyun's family."

No one could expect to be close friends after a tragedy, let alone when the perpetrator was in his family. Anyone would have just given up at the thought. He had to have really liked her for him to wait years for the right time to approach her. Jamie reflected on the event Alric witnessed.

"Why'd you steal my picture?"

Minjae leaned forward to adjust his sitting position. He seemed unable to sit still while she remained comfortable in her seat. "I mentioned it to you before. My friend was interested in the cathedral and the picture was affiliated with something she's mentioned before. I'm sorry, I shouldn't have taken it. I only assumed you'd say no if I asked for a copy."

"Penelope?" Jamie asked after digging in her memory for the name. "Did you show her the picture?" When he nodded she asked, looking ahead at nothing. "And?"

"She said it was Photoshopped."

The corner of Jamie's lip went up as she felt like the rollercoaster of the past few months hadn't resulted her in betraying the gargoyles. Their secret was their own. The only one she'd ever revealed the truth to was Banafsha who she knew would do nothing. The woman never left her house.

Their Spring Break was spent in central Florida while others left the state, went on cruises, or drove to Miami. The Capes flew to California to spend an extra day exploring the mountains, Bryden and Jax sending short videos to Minjae whenever they had signal. Several days into the week when they returned to school, Jamie and Minjae went to the supermarket for ingredients for *Tembleque*. Minjae and Jamie had been visiting one another's houses often and began a habit of treating one another to a dish they'd grown up on. Other than the *fricase de pollo, tostones de pana*, and *platanos* Minjae had tried when Abuela visited, they'd made *empanadas de yuca* and flan. When the two went to Minjae's house, his mom helped them make *bibimbap, dak galbi*, and the dessert *hotteok*. Jamie preferred the simple *bibimbap* to the spicy *dak galbi*.

Minjae had run out of his home supply of caramel corn and obliged driving Jamie to the supermarket. She still refused to sit in the front seat, but her disinclination to ride in his car gradually lessened.

Optimistic of her growth, Minjae suspected he would have her sitting at least in a window seat by graduation.

Jamie tagged along as he contemplated buying his favorite brand of caramel corn with another brand almost as good with a holiday two-for-one deal.

"They're smaller though." Minjae frowned as he balanced the caramel corn bags in his hands like hacky sacks.

"Good, less fat. You'll ruin your teeth if you keep eating this when you're under twenty."

"Ruin my teeth," he scoffed, concentrating on the candies, oblivious to when she rolled her eyes. "Please! If I could ruin my teeth I'd actually be worried."

Jamie leaned away from the shopping cart and snatched a bag from his hand. "Together they're more candy than if you'd've bought the other brand."

"I don't know." He shook his head. "How could there be more? With air space they had to have ripped me off. Why else would it be on sale? You know candies and cereals are making boxes smaller and bags bigger so that there's more air in the product and on top of that increasing the prices so you feel like you're getting gypped when you're actually getting gypped . . ." Minjae paused when he noticed the drab way Jamie was staring at him.

"I'm like eighty percent sure you're lying."

"I'm not."

An emphasis in her blink, she nodded once. "Eight-five percent."

"I'm only saying you can't take these purchases lightly. Do you know how much you could save if you micro-managed your purchases? Compare the price to the weight. Sometimes you gotta be careful of these things or you'll lose maximum money-to-purchase benefits. You know"—he laughed—"I once scored a steal of a deal when—get this—in line with my bag of caramel corn a kind mother of two mentioned there was a discount with my favorite brand at Walmart. Same weight and everything!"

"Minjae, do you call your brother *hyung*?"

"Dae? Not since I was ten, why?"

Jamie went on the tips of her toes to compare which check-out aisle was the shortest.

"Oh, no reason. I only wanted you to stop talking like a mom of four. I figured if I didn't say anything you'd talk about financial planning until we got to my house . . ."

Minjae steered his attention to what Jamie had stopped talking for. There was a commotion escalating as a customer at the cash register was waving her hand at the cashier. He didn't think much of it aside from the normal dissatisfied customer experience until he noticed Jamie suddenly leaving the cart beside him and rushing over. He never saw her so affected by a person's affairs unless it was at her job, and remained immobile watching her stand beside the customer and face the cashier. When he recognized the cashier as Caprice he figured Jamie was going to her aid, however Jamie turned to the customer to be told the problem. A Middle Eastern-looking woman he'd never seen before. She had to be his grandmother's age.

"No! I won't stand for this prejudice any longer!" barked the woman. Minjae caught up with Jamie, standing by the woman as if she were her granddaughter, waiting for her grandmother to release her frustrations before poorly convincing her to let the matter go.

"She always comes in and does this," Caprice said. "Starting a fight like I did something wrong."

"Every customer she offers to get someone to help them load their car and never once has she done that for me. Or she makes *me* go back to exchange a food item from the shelves when she gets a staff member to get it for others. I won't stand for this discrimination anymore. If not that then she bags my food poorly they bear too much weight and the handles rip apart. Or she gives me incorrect change on purpose!"

"She's lying!" Caprice said.

"I'm sure none of this was intentional," Jamie said.

"No! Every time I come and she's here she does something against me. I never made a fuss because I didn't want to be the reason she lost her job, but I've lived in this country longer than any of you have been alive. I'm a citizen of this country. I don't deserve to be treated this way!"

"Banafsha," Jamie pleaded.

"If you have a problem with me you don't have to go in my check-out lane," Caprice said, noticing Minjae for the first time.

Minjae and Jamie stared dumbfounded as Banafsha waved her hand again. "I shouldn't have to avoid anyone for any reason!"

A man not unrecognizable as the manager arrived and faced Banafsha after glancing at Caprice. "Can I help you with anything, ma'am?"

Banafsha eyed the manager as she nodded unreservedly. "I have come to this store for years and my experiences have been intolerable this past year whenever this cashier checks out my groceries. I never complained before but I've had enough. I've had enough!"

"What did she do? Perhaps there's been a misunderstanding?"

Banafsha stared at the manager for a moment before chuckling sardonically. Jamie took her arm as Banafsha shook her head, laughing at the cruel joke.

"A misunderstanding. It's always a misunderstanding against me . . . Like it's always *random* selections at airports."

The manager noticed the attitude shift and licked his lips before opening them, preparing to rescind his statement and apologize. Before a word came out, Banafsha took the wallet she laid on the small counter beside the credit card terminal and stormed past him. Jamie immediately followed her as Minjae studied Caprice. She looked embarrassed as her manager folded his hands over his waist and then nodded his head for her to return to work. Tossing his bag of caramel corn on the conveyor belt, Minjae ran after the two women.

Jamie was keeping up beside Banafsha as they walked in the direction of her car. He lightly jogged behind them as he noticed Jamie reach for Banafsha's arm.

"I can come with you from now on," Jamie bargained. "No one will make a fuss when there's more than just one person."

Banafsha disregarded the offer immediately as she pulled from Jamie's reach. "I shouldn't have to! I'm a grown woman. I've never had to rely on anyone else to do something for me, ever since I came to this country thirty years ago. I won't start now."

"I don't mean it like that."

"Of course you don't! You saw her in there. Pretending to be in the wrong as soon as she saw I wasn't going to be quiet anymore."

"I know her. I'm sure it wasn't how it seemed."

"You're just like them. It's *me* who was wrong. But I only saw her more the deceptive bitch as she played innocent. She'll deny left and right that *I'm* the nuisance. That I'm the instigator. No . . . I've had enough. I don't need this in my life. I'll take my business somewhere else."

"Banafsha," Jamie said, watching as her neighbor opened her car door and sat inside.

"If you think I'm making it up then I don't know you like I thought I did. I'd appreciate it if you didn't visit anymore."

The door slammed shut as Jamie watched her car back up and drive away. Banafsha never noticed Minjae behind Jamie and Jamie had forgotten he was there at all. A minute passed after the car drove away until Jamie turned and finally noticed her friend waiting patiently.

"Who was that?" he asked.

Jamie slightly frowned as she pressed her lips together. "My neighbor. I didn't mean to ditch you I just never see her outta the house."

"Is she someone important to you?"

Jamie nodded, folding her arms over her chest. "She's mentioned having bad grocery shopping trips before." She slid her hand over her face. "I've done it before. Not be considerate toward her. After watching Aiden every day I should be on her side even if she's wrong."

"You should go and make it up to her. If she rarely leaves the house she mustn't have a lot of friends. I doubt she'll want to lose you."

"I'll give her a day to cool off. We're very similar. I'd want to sleep on it."

Minjae wrapped his arm around Jamie's neck as he towed her in the direction of his car. "I'm here if you need me. But since we ditched our food back there, we might need to stop at another store to pick up the ingredients for the *Tembleque*. And more importantly: my caramel corn."

30

Caprice stopped visiting the rock gym and the times Jamie did see the Capes, the only one who treated her differently was Bryden. Jax sided with Vienna, by then officially a couple, and she had already begun to drift from Caprice since the return from their hiking trip. Jamie never learned the details and while she'd grown closer with Vienna, she elected never to affiliate herself with anything concerning Caprice after the incident with Banafsha.

Armed with a flan she had made with Minjae, Jamie coaxed her way back into Banafsha's good graces. The afternoon began with their intentions of making only one, but after considering Minjae's suggestion that she get ingredients for two, it became worth it when instead of getting the door slammed in her face, Banafsha allowed her entry—not without the requisite snort. The cold shoulder, but she left the door open. A fireplace crackled. Onions, nutmeg, pepper, curry, chicken, cooking oil, and other aromas flooded out.

"You're cooking now," Banafsha said, neither question nor observation. "You have a boy now?"

Jamie closed the front door behind her and followed her down the hall. "A friend."

"Girls don't cook for friends."

"This one does."

Jamie set the flan on the kitchen counter. Banafsha glimpsed at her face and then down at the aluminum-covered dessert. "Are you trying to bribe for forgiveness by making me gain five pounds?"

"It's not five pounds . . ." Jamie suddenly smiled under a mask as she walked over to Banafsha to hug her. Jamie underestimated how well Banafsha knew her which is why as soon as she stepped closer to her, Banafsha arced around the kitchen to the living room to turn on the TV.

"Well I won't forgive, because you have no reason to apologize for." Banafsha set the remote down and returned to the kitchen, safe from any eighteen-year-old Puerto Rican rock climbers trying to coax her into consolation. "I don't want to hear another word about it." She went to the stove where she was frying balls of dough, picking them up one at a time with a soup ladle and setting them on a plate. She set the plate of hot and cooled snacks beside Jamie as she finished frying the others.

Jamie took a bite into one and noted a spicy flavor she'd never tasted before as she looked inside the stuffed ball. "What is this?"

"*Gol Gappa*," Banafsha said with her back to Jamie. "Street food."

"Why have you never made this before for us? Have you made this for Aiden?"

"Many times."

"The only thing you've ever cooked for me was chicken *karahi* which tastes too close to *guisado* so it doesn't count."

Banafsha looked up to the corner of the wall where mahogany wall met white ceiling, thinking. "I've made you *kheer*."

It was a tasty dessert Jamie'd forgotten. She tried it at the beginning of their relationship. It was easy to forget such a small detail in a big moment of her life.

Banafsha had just moved in next door. It hadn't been a month since the funeral and Jamie left home not unlike a zombie. Voiceless. Aimless. Rosario had introduced herself to Banafsha with a pumpkin *budin* in hand, and the next day their new neighbor returned the favor supplied with a tray of dessert bowls filled with coconut white cream topped with sliced almonds and pistachios under sprinkled brown spices. Jamie didn't remember her mother coming to her bedroom and putting the bowl in front of her but she did remember looking at the bowl as if it had been a trick. How it appeared from nowhere. She tipped the spoon in the pudding and when the texture of the rice pudding and cinnamon settled in her mouth, she heard her family's voices for the first time. She returned the tray and clean bowls to her new neighbor and began what became a friendship rooted in understanding. It seemed her dad didn't leave her without someone to connect with for long.

"It was so long ago I didn't remember." Jamie ruffled her shoulders. "You know, I've known you for years and I rarely see you leave your house. Seeing you at the grocery store was bizarre."

"Just a quick run to the store after my walk. Which reminds me, that new neighbor is ruining my peaceful walks again."

"The one you said smiled too much?" Banafsha nodded and Jamie examined the *Gol Gappa* in her hand. "I wonder why he hadn't told me he's found his dog. Anyways . . ." Jamie licked her lips as she focused on the *Gol Gappa*. "I wanted to know when you'd share with me what your life was like before."

Banafsha turned hard face to Jamie. "Before?"

"You mentioned it in passing at the store. Your life before you came to the U.S." Jamie moved her hand as if it would help remind her. "In Pakistan . . ."

"Jamie, when have I ever made you think I wanted to talk about that?"

"It just doesn't seem right how I can say I've known you for years and you've helped out my family so much but I don't know anything about you other than you came from Pakistan decades ago."

"Because it isn't anyone's business."

"Banafsha," Jamie said, trying to gently coax her to the idea. "You know me. What do you fear of me knowing about your past?"

"You don't understand." Banafsha shut off the stove and placed the frying pan on a cool stovetop. With her arms settled comfortably over her chest she concentrated on Jamie with an elder's plea. She needed Jamie to understand. "My past is my shame. No one shoves their scars in a passerby's face. You wouldn't do it here and you don't do that there."

"I'll understand."

Banafsha and Jamie both were resolved to stay silent until the other spoke but as the heat from the stove began to fade, the women began to understand.

"Jamie," Banafsha said with unforeseeable initiative. "The reason why I hold back on my past is for the same reason you do."

"I don't know what—"

"The only difference is I've adjusted myself. I know I've failed in many things and regret them. I choose not to talk about it. You don't acknowledge it even in your heart."

"What do you think I'm not acknowledging?"

"The fact that for three years you've lived without living. You go through school and work with no spirit. And it's because of your father. He meant everything to you and when you lost him you lost your spirit. Your mother has shown me home videos of you before your father passed away—not long before he died. You were nothing like that before. You loved life. I never knew that part of you but I know you loved everything about life. When your father died, so did that part of you. Now after three years are you ready to talk about that?"

"I don't live without spirit—"

Banafsha lifted her hand. "I know why it was sucked out of you. You only understood one person. Just one. And when that was gone, everyone else became part of the background. Even your family. Everything became gray what was once colorful. I collect your photography you know. Each picture: remarkable pieces of your soul. The little passion you share with your family and with the world you put into your art. It's why I admire you. Why I can tolerate you and your brother and your mother. Some of the few people in the world that I can stand seeing every day."

"You say I'm just getting by but so are you." Jamie stood up, halting by the counter and resting her hand on it for support. "Never meeting anyone. Never accepting, barely tolerating the people who are different from you. I was like that. It's why our relationship worked so well. Why me and you found comfort in one another when it was impossible with others."

"No. We're not alike. Not even close."

"How?" Jamie lifted her chin. "How not?"

"Because what made you give up to life was because something was taken from you. I gave up life because I gave up. *I* gave them up." Banafsha lowered her gaze and shut her eyes, flexing her fingers as she pulled her sleeves closer to her. Drawing power from herself. That was the source of strength and even with a friend, she needed to pry strength with her fingers to let the words come out. The strength and will Jamie thought was Banafsha's disposition was a mask. A well-worn mask even in front of people close to her.

"I was born in the birth of a new country. Pakistan was still discovering what it wanted to be. Everyone still wasn't sure if they belonged. All I knew of the world was that people could only live one of two lives: one where you would die in poverty and one where your life meant something. I was a middle child of three and while we knew our lives would never grant us access to a world with new shoes or to have a home we didn't need to share with other families, we had Allah. We had a new future with possibilities. Pakistan was the symbol of freedom. We'd gotten there by will and so much loss and we couldn't let it go to waste. It was the spring of childhood before the winter of adulthood. I'd fallen in love with a boy when I was seventeen. He was intelligent, a man of potential. He received a scholarship and went to university to study then forgot about me. Heartbreak was something I thought would never leave me. I spent a year crying over what I had lost. Years later when I was a beautiful young woman in her twenties I fell in love again. This time to the right man. He was intelligent too. He was a doctor who visited the poorer districts and helped them. I loved his compassion and wanted to become a doctor just like him. After time, he realized that our mutual drive to help people wasn't entirely unselfish. I wanted to spend time with him. Eventually he understood that my feelings meant something more and soon he began to feel more too.

"While the name of the country's leaders changed often with little mutual agreements between each succession, nothing really changed in our everyday life. After almost two years with the doctor I learned I was pregnant." Banafsha held a distance in her eyes. Banafsha rarely reentered her memories and the fact she was sharing this with Jamie now proved she never revisited her past—even in private.

"An unmarried woman pregnant in Pakistan made me far from safe. Not only in society, but it was the year Zia-ul-Haq claimed his presidency. Politicians used Islam as a weapon. My love for Allah had been taken long ago after loss and terror and heartbreak. Before Zia-ul-Haq I could live freely as an apostate, but now politics affected me because I forsaked Islam. When you questioned Islam you questioned his rule. Prayer times became strongly advised at work. Clothing for both men and women were altered. Men and women were divided further apart than they already were. Damn I couldn't have even have a drink because we started our own era of Prohibition. I had suddenly become trapped."

"What did he say? The doctor?"

Banafsha reflected on the memory of the man she loved. "He was a good man. A man of some faith. To not shame me he wanted to marry me. Pretend the baby was legitimate. However the world's never as good as you hope it to be. I had many scares during my pregnancy. Some from my mutinous anti-Islamic sentiment. Most from terrorist attacks in the city. Karachi was unstable and every time I heard about a bombing I would just prepare myself with the news that my doctor would never come back. And then it would just be me and the baby. My heart stopped at every ambulance siren. I couldn't handle being a mother despite having a man who cared for me."

The soft smile Banafsha had for the doctor faded away. "After my baby was born, I came home from the hospital. And I fed her." Banafsha paused. "And I put her to bed. And I watched her sleep. While I felt every day was the last I would see my doctor, I would stay home with the baby and pray that nothing would happen. No bomb. No accidents. Nothing. It was when my brother was stabbed and my mother became sick that I knew that there was nothing to save me from more heartbreak. My baby had caught something and I knew it was a matter of time before I was left behind. It was then I knew the love lost for Allah was lost love for a figure of fiction. He did not exist—could not. And neither would they. No family on this Earth and no Allah in Heaven."

Banafsha blinked suddenly and turned to Jamie, a layer of tears refusing to pour out of her piercing stare. "And so. I kissed my baby on the forehead one last time. Looked one last time into her light eyes, and I left.

"I stowed away on a train to East Pakistan—by then a new Bangladesh—where I lived near a Christian church, discovering the language to the world. Many times it was told once you learned English, you owned the passport to the world. I knew I must learn. There was nothing in Bangladesh for me and I had to go where no one knew me. Where I could live without any heartbreak.

"I cared for children of the missionaries and they taught me English. One of the women who worked with me had connections to helping me obtain a passport. I applied to move to the U.S.: the land where opportunities were endless for people like me. Someone who wanted a fresh start. Those years were the hardest because I saved everything I could to pay for my passport and then for my passage to the United States. When I finally stepped off of the ship, my baby would have been seven."

"Your baby." Jamie had to clear her throat. "What's her name?"

"Hina."

Jamie said the name as if an amnesiac had finally recalled their memories. A smile rose on her lips. "It's a beautiful name."

Banafsha considered something for a moment. "All my life lived, I only care if she had hers."

Jamie came beside Banafsha and held back the hand wanting to take Banafsha and hold her close.

"You left them. That's why you've never shared this before. You're ashamed to share that."

"Whether it was the best thing after all . . . It is done."

Jamie swallowed as she avoided Banafsha's eyes. "Haven't you ever wondered how she is? If she's married and had children? How your husband is?"

"I *don't* want your pity!" Banafsha said, stepping away with an outstretched arm. Her eyes were pinned on the floor. Her voice on edge and desperate. She exhaled in a huff. "This isn't how life should be, chosen or not."

"It isn't about pity, Banafsha. I only think it's natural to be curious. She was your child. Still is. Haven't you ever wanted to go back, to learn what kind of life she's living?"

"A woman who abandons her child has no right to ask such questions. To be given the answers to those questions. A mother who abandons her child in any way should live the rest of her life in shame and misery. As I have."

Jamie shook her head and stepped close to her, taking her arm and squeezing it beside her. "You were scared. Walls were collapsing around you. You fought for any way to lead out, even if it meant leaving someone behind."

"I'm a coward."

Jamie didn't refute it. She abandoned the family who never learned what had happened to her. Who had no idea if she was living in the slums in a district on the far side of town or who had died years before as an anonymous immigrant. However, Jamie couldn't hate her. Because while she wasn't meant to be a mother at the time, it didn't disprove she couldn't have become a mother later. She'd taken care of Aiden since he was nine. And it was no favor and no obligation that she did. What led Banafsha to make three bowls of *kheer* and offer it to her new neighbors—neighbors that had recently lost someone important— was a calling. It was a family who had rarely known sadness that needed to be mended by a woman who had almost always known just that. Ironic that it was the broken who could mend the wounds best.

"You weren't ready." Jamie looked from Banafsha's cheek to her pinned-back hair. "If you place a child with no ability to swim into a pool, is he a coward for not trying to reach the land, or is he simply not ready? I don't think you failed as a mother. You are a wonderful mother to me and Aiden. And probably to other kids I never knew."

"I'm not a mother to you both."

"You feed him. You help him with his homework— sometimes. You teach him your language, your culture. You take care of him after school. You take an interest in my photography. You're there for my family whenever we need you."

"That's not what makes a mother. A mother is one who loves her baby. Who stays with them and sees them grow."

"No you didn't see your daughter grow into a woman. You don't know if she learned the alphabet or went to school or became a doctor like your husband. But you helped watch my brother grow. You help me grow."

Banafsha departed from Jamie's consolation. A handful of kind deeds couldn't eliminate the shame in her heart that she'd carried for over thirty years.

Jamie knew it might take years to help her overcome that shame and to help her accept the mistake she'd committed years ago. It would not be easy. And it might never be possible. But she'd fight for as long as she knew her to overcome it. The world had changed over the past decades. She could even help her to reconnect. The world had been brought closer by the internet that it ever could before.

"Because you know the truth now doesn't mean you understand. Like I said, I've accepted it."

"There's more for you Banafsha, then living here at home, never speaking with anyone aside from your neighbors and the cashiers at the grocery store. You've accepted your grief and your past, but you haven't accepted your future. What it could be."

"Don't make my mistakes, Jamie. Don't be like me. Hiding away. Afraid to love anyone because you're afraid it will hurt if they're taken from you."

Jamie walked over to Banafsha and hugged her tightly around her back, pressing her cheek against Banafsha's tough shoulder.

"I love you Banafsha. I don't know much about your past and your life is the biggest mystery to me—and I've had my fair share of mysteries, trust me. But for the bizarre, cynical woman you are, I love you."

"Be careful. Loving a person like me. Having pity for someone like me."

"I thought you said it wasn't my place to pity you?"

"I lied," Banafsha said mechanically. "Don't you know me by now?"

"Even for the bizarre, cynical *liar* you are, I love you."

Banafsha shrugged out of Jamie's embrace and pointed a finger at her. "If you say you love me one more time I'm never offering you food again."

"I'm more worried about something else." Jamie's eyes had been looking over Banafsha's shoulders, scanning the walls of the living room and the hallway in search of a photograph. One, in particular. When she didn't catch sight of it, she looked down at her neighbor. "Where's my photograph? The one where I fall?"

31

Jamie handed climbing equipment to several college students as Minjae leaned over the counter. Noel and Era were spotting for a family as Jamie manned the front desk. Normally it would be Noel at the front desk and Jamie working with Era, but once the parents learned Jamie was still a high school student they asked for the "more experienced" employee. It wouldn't have mattered if Noel had mentioned Jamie had worked at the gym longer than Era, so Jamie assumed the desk job. Minjae had come to the gym after working on Yearbook for two hours. Eventually Ms. Ava kicked out all the yearbook staff and while they wanted to be grateful to start the weekend, they were still stressed about completing the finishing touches. Deadlines for yearbook weren't enough. Most of the seniors had AP classes. April was when prom, Grad Night, Grad Bash, and AP exams clashed. While the natural case of senioritis pumped through their veins, these final weeks of March and first ones in April would be most dire for them; and that wasn't mentioning any college acceptance strays slipping into their mailboxes.

"You look worse than I do," Jamie said, glancing up at Minjae's dark eyes as he checked his phone.

"Yearbook's kicking my ass. I regret, I regret, I *regret* taking three APs my final year. I'm an idiot."

"Are you worried about them?" Jamie rounded the counter, wiping it clean.

"Not English but Calc and Biology. I'm ninety percent sure I'm going to confuse one for the other and talk about Hardy-Weinberg law in my Calc exam and Euler's Method in Biology. My mind's going to explode next month." He slid his hands through his hair. Jamie patted his back as she moved around him. His head turned. "Any suggestions to help me relax? Take my mind off of my responsibilities . . ."

Jamie registered the chaff and glanced his way, noting the way he bounced his eyebrows and pouted his lips. Jamie slowly walked back to him.

"I know you're not hitting on me right now. Because then I'd have to kick your ass." Minjae lost bravado as Jamie withheld her laughter. "You see, I know you're not serious because I know you wouldn't hit on me while I was working. Which, by the way, you should be thankful my boss isn't kicking you out right now since you're not actually here to climb and there's other benignant patrons present. And, I *know* you're not serious because that's not how you'd *entice* your girlfriend. I don't know Emily very well but she doesn't look the type to go out with a guy like you. And you guys went out for a year or so right?"

Minjae frowned as he dragged a finger over his lips, lowering his gaze before flickering his attention back to her.

"Damn, I meant distract me not hurt my feelings."

It was continuously a struggle to keep her laugh down and have a reason to keep her back to him. She managed to walk around him to return behind the desk. Minjae didn't hold ill will against anyone, let alone her, the exaggerated frown on his face melted into an innocent smile as he watched her rearrange the office supplies. His head rested on his arms as he silently counted to ten.

"So . . . Any more reasons you can think of?"

Jamie shook her head and he muddled over asking. The gym phone rang and Jamie answered, listing the hours for the weekend before hanging up. Minjae didn't know how to subtly steer the conversation back, ultimately deciding to be blunt.

"Is there a reason Emily came up all of a sudden?"

Jamie didn't turn from the paper in her hands. "No."

It was a lie, but not one that made her feel guilty. Earlier that week Jamie came across Emily for the first time. While it wasn't a moment she intentionally avoided, it was one she wished she had taken greater heed to avoid. As she wiped the cloth around the computer monitor screen, she remembered the brief encounter.

Jamie had jumped at the chance to escape a debacle in the computer lab and had been returning from an errand for Ms. Ava. She had the copies of yearbook sale tickets from the front office in hand when Jamie noticed another student in the empty courtyard. She'd seen Emily in passing, but had never faced her alone. With the past months spent hanging out with her ex and no security cameras to serve as witness, Jamie felt incredibly vulnerable. Being in high school, people often wear a mask when others are around and shamelessly take it off when there's no one around. So hoping for nothing, Jamie walked forward and—not after more than a two second pause to acknowledge the other person in the courtyard—was approached. Anxiously, Jamie swallowed quickly.

Emily held her hands together, fiddling with her thumbs as she smiled with her eyes. "We haven't actually spoken before. I hope it wasn't because you were avoiding me." Jamie felt as if a source of sunshine had slowly slipped through her lips and breathed easier. "I'd understand. The past couple of months haven't been fair to you. I just learned Alric's been bothering you."

"I get the guard dog façade. I was annoyed sure, but I didn't give it any more thought."

"He's a good friend. I have to take some of the blame. I knew he liked me but I always treated him as a friend. I don't want anyone to think I was leading him on. I was still hoping that someone would know I hadn't moved on."

Jamie nodded once with tight lips. Minjae. "Since you two went out for so long I'm sure he's told you about the accident. What he was ashamed of for so long." Jamie muttered further, "And everything."

Emily dodged her eyes as one hand took the other arm, rubbing it around the elbow, smiling shyly. "You should've known first."

Jamie stepped up to Emily and while she couldn't look her in the eye, she patted the hand over the elbow. "I'm just a friend."

There was something that stopped Emily from refuting, perhaps because Jamie was partially the reason that they broke up or perhaps because Minjae didn't look at her that way anymore, but it was why she merely smiled kindly in turn.

"You don't believe that." The two girls stood quietly as the abnormal March heat cocooned around them. "Neither do I."

Jamie watched Emily walk away. Neither allowed Chance to force them to meet again.

There was a slip of paper in the crack of Jamie's front door, an address scribbled on it. The street name looked familiar but she slipped it into her back pocket to look up later. The smell of *arroz con salchichas* filled her nostrils as soon as she entered the house, and she spotted the bowl of rice set beside *amarillitos* and salad on the dinner table. All but Riley were in the living room watching whatever show was on TV when they all suddenly stood up in staggered unison. Taking half a step back she looked from one face to the other.

"Am I in trouble?"

"*Por el contrario, niñita*," Rosario said, walking over and kissing Jamie on the cheek. As she wiped the spot with her thumb she took Jamie's shoulder and smiled brightly. "We have good news to share with you."

"Good news?" Jamie lifted an eyebrow, looking around her mother to the guests and Aiden. "Mind if I change first?"

Settled into something comfortable she found everyone getting ready for dinner as they'd waited until she got home before eating. Usually they ate and saved what was left over for her, so to see everyone unnaturally happy made her more than wary. It was only on rare occasions they behaved so uniformly. In the moments when she didn't know what to expect of her mother and Victor, Jamie sought aid from her brother. However his eyes offered nothing as she sat in the empty chair and brought the attention back to the news.

"So whatever it is must be big if all of you waited for me. But the food smells good and I haven't eaten since lunch . . ."

"We'll share with you after then," Rosario said, glimpsing at Victor before taking Jamie's hand and shaking it.

Not wanting to complain after almost eight hours of no food, she began to fill her plate and watched as the others followed suit. They must have already talked about the insignificant dealings of the day since they seemed inclined to find something new to talk about.

"I was thinking," Victor said, crossing his hands together over his plate, looking over to Aiden. "Since you already know so much, we should enter you in the Kids Jeopardy Tournament next year. I've no doubt you'd be qualified to enter and go all the way to the top."

Aiden squirmed his lips as he rolled a sausage over the rice as Rosario waited for him to answer. When he didn't seem ready to anytime soon she jumped in for him. "You know it's something you're passionate about. There's no doubt you're prepared. You watch Alex every night like he was your religion. You know so much I know you'd go far." Aiden looked over their faces blankly as he shrugged. "What's wrong? Do you think you'd get stage fright? I know you don't like presenting but I think once you're in the room with Alex you'd forget all about everyone else."

It was far from public speaking that made Aiden reluctant to reply.

"I'd prefer to enter it when I'm older and I know more. The Kid's Tournament, as great as it is for kids my age, isn't impressive. I want to wait until I'm older and can win more."

"I completely agree." Jamie nodded. "You should wait. With you in the mix, it isn't a competition." Jamie winked as Aiden took comfort in his sister's support.

Victor nodded along and looked down to his plate. "Of course, if that's what you want. That's very mature of you. Planning so far ahead."

Rosario cast appreciative eyes his way. "It's sweet of you to suggest." Her attention turned to the food. "Riley, does the rice taste fine to you? I know you said it tasted off last time. You haven't really eaten any."

"It's fine," she sighed.

Jamie knew once her mother started knit-picking on why someone wasn't eating she wouldn't stop, which is when she decided to interject.

"So, I think my stomach content's enough. What's the big news?"

Rosario grinned with tight lips at her kids as she stood up and went to the counter. Jamie hadn't noticed before but a stack of mail was sporadically spread near the edge. Rosario found one and held it up, then walked over to Jamie and handed it to her.

"A letter from Florida State came."

Jamie took it but looked at her mother. "Why are you smiling? I haven't opened it yet."

"We already know you got in. Deferment or no, your grades and accomplishments speak for themselves. Besides, they sent an envelope. Rejections don't get envelopes." She smiled around the table and folded her arms, returning her focus to Jamie. "Go on, open it. Let's celebrate. I'll make your favorite *Piña colada*. Not as good as Abuela's, I know, but I went out to the supermarket the moment I saw it in the mail. Listen to me, I keep blabbing. Open it *mija*."

A rush of hesitation. Jamie exhaled, lowering the envelope onto her lap. She tilted her head to the side, slowing finding the courage to look up to the over-excited being before her.

"Mom, I know you're excited your oldest child's applied to college and getting responses, but I'm not going to college."

Rapture slowly drained from her face, Rosario's smile waning as she couldn't find a reason to doubt the expression on her daughter's face. Her body stiffened when the words came out, but she forced the words out regardless.

"Not going? What do you mean not going? What are you going to do?"

Jamie stood up and shrugged. "I don't have a concrete plan. All I know is I want to travel. See a bunch of places around the world I'd never even heard of. I thought I'd start in India."

"How can you possibly travel when you can't even stand being in a car?"

The question hung in the air as each person took their turns glancing up at Rosario. The disappointment was one thing, but the cruelty and insensitivity was another. Rosario had said it as if she'd kept it in her arsenal for the day that Jamie chose to be recalcitrant.

"Mom . . ." Aiden said.

"*Por favor, cállate la boca,*" Rosario said, lifting a finger to one child as her eyes drilled into the other's. "If you are not going to college, what are you going to do? I want a serious answer from you. Not some *non-concrete* plan."

"College isn't for everyone."

"No, that's an unacceptable excuse."

"I don't know what I want to do in my life. Not enough for me to waste and invest my time and money into."

Rosario disregarded it. "Your first two years are general classes. You'll have two years to think about it and be exposed to careers and majors you didn't know were out there."

"Dad didn't go to college," Jamie offered.

Mother and daughter held a connection. Victor stood up and motioned for the two kids to follow him out of the room. Mother and daughter were blind to the movement. They remained cold and stared down one another, refusing to accept and yield to the wishes of the other. Daughter wanted freedom. Mother wanted security.

Safe from exploding, Rosario widened her eyes slightly. "Your father didn't have the opportunities you do. You know his family wanted him to go into the church. They never helped him go farther than that. They wanted to keep him ignorant so he would do what they want."

Jamie scoffed. "And in an ironic way you're not?"

Rosario froze, but continued to keep her voice under control. "I want you to have an education and be qualified for any job you want. I want you to have the choice to be something, not be forced into a job because *at the time*"—Rosario air-quoted—"you didn't *feel* like going to college."

"Well college will be there for me if I decide it's time. But it's not what I want."

"Jamie, what is this really about? Are you worried about money? Or about how you'll get there? If you go to Tallahassee I'll make sure you live on campus and have meal plans so you never have to worry about getting food. Or even if it's not there, it can be anywhere you want I'll make sure you don't need to worry about transportation and food."

"That isn't it."

"What? Is it because it isn't out-of-state?"

"That isn't it. I'm"—Jamie emphasized her hand out to her mother before coughing out a laugh—"I'm actually trying to tell you for the first time in my life what I want, and it's budding heads with the only thing you want for me. I want to travel the world, see some part of it before I decide what I'll do with my life."

"Legally considered an adult or no, you are my child and I want a bright future for you. Eighteen, thirty, fifty—I don't want *my child* to ever look back at where she could be in life because she didn't make the tough—though *right*—decision at the time."

"You don't know. What if just a couple of months in South Asia or in South America I find my calling?"

"*After* you graduate. After you have your degree you'll be free to roam the Earth. Just get it over with and you won't regret waiting. You'll be more learned and prepared to face the world then."

"What is it!" Jamie suddenly yelled. "Why are you so fixed on treating me like I'm not responsible or ready for anything in this *goddamn* world?"

"Lower your tone! You will not speak to me like that!"

"Then tell me why you're being so iron-willed about this. Why won't you let me go and fail on my own?"

Rosario held a cynical smile on her lips as she readjusted her stance on her hips. "Should I watch you ride your bike over a cliff into a river and just let you learn on your own—you'll struggle to swim and make it to land, but hey, I *let* you go and fail on your own."

Jamie bit her tongue as she shook her head, clenching her jaw to restrain from unleashing a myriad of abuses. "I don't need your approval. It's my decision. Maybe it's best that we get this out in the open now. I've saved money from the gym and since I don't drive it's all just sitting there in the bank."

"I won't let you waste your life like that."

"You do realize you have no legal authority over what I do."

"I told you—"

"Unless you want to kick me out over this."

The words so willing to spill out before were suddenly blocked. Mouth hung agape, Rosario's eyes widened, then narrowed. The thought had never crossed her mind and the implication that their argument would result to that hurt her more than she thought it would. After all the years of ill-fitting against one another and all the discrepancies in their everyday lives, Rosario never thought her parenting had resulted to her daughter thinking that she'd rather kick her out of the house because she wasn't getting her way.

It was just Jacob's family all over again. Ever since she met them and knew who they were, ever since they disapproved of her and Jacob's marriage, she thought she lived her life exactly the opposite from them. After years, it came around full circle. Her nose was pointed so high, she failed to see the throne she was sitting on had been sinking into the mud, and now her nose was eye level with the weeds, bugs, and dirt of a rotten human being.

She'd forgiven Daehyun after the accident. As Jacob would have. She had coped with Jamie's further retreating personality after Jacob had died. As Jacob would have. She'd tried so hard to focus on loving and raising her kids the right way and instead, months from her elder child's graduation she was slapped with the realization she had hoped to never be insulted with. She was as bigoted as Jacob's family. While they might have been steadfast about religion, she was the same about education. She needed them to grow up in a normal household and develop into normal adults with experiences and memories that everyone else had. They were exceptional and spectacular to her, but she wanted her kids to hold onto memories that would connect them with others. She didn't want them to only remember the sadness of their childhoods where there should have been cheer and fondness.

What if Aiden's devoted commitment to Jeopardy was because she wanted Aiden to grow up to be as intelligent and aware of the world she wish she could be? What if Jamie's reclusive nature was due to her always pushing to meet other people and make friends her own age when in truth she'd only been shy? What were supposed to be natural and adopted traits of her kids felt stamped into them. She needed to let them find their own passions. Accept them. As much as her mother did for her when she decided to become the first college graduate in their family. Even when she had to wake up three hours before class to get ready and take a public bus across town. Even when she had to get a part-time job to help her mom pay the bills and take care of her siblings. She chose that challenge for herself. She needed to let Jamie choose what was best for her.

It was only how to get the words out . . .

How incredibly difficult it was for a mother to confide in her own child.

"I just want release," Jamie said. "To feel it now, when I'm young and immature and know when I'm old and withered that I went out and I embraced the world. Felt nothing and everything all at once."

Rosario still felt heart-broken over her daughter's suggestion to leave the house. So instead of approving or disapproving, she walked around her and retreated to her room, closing the door silently. Unmoved, Jamie closed her eyes.

It was too much to ask to a single parent who had provided so well for her brother and her, to give up an opportunity when it was given. To surrender the chance to do bigger and better things. However, she needed to say it aloud. What she wanted. To the person she was most afraid of disappointing, but the person who mattered the most. With her father gone, it was her mother now who mattered. Aiden might or might not understand one day. What it felt like to be unsure and lost, almost stuck in this world with no true passion or compassion for anyone. It was why Jamie needed to go out and find it. Empathy or sympathy, treasure or morals, something she could feel heavier in her heart than in her hands. Something that would make her life mean something. To make her heart feel destined for something beyond the love she shared for her father. Because it had to be possible for her to love a stranger the way her father loved a stranger. If she wanted it enough, she had to discover it in her life.

Jamie crossed the living room to the front door. Walking down the front sidewalk she found Victor, Riley, and Aiden on the driveway, searching for celestials beyond the evening clouds. Victor was pointing toward a cluster of dimly lit stars as Aiden scratched his nose and informed them of the dominant star's name and the constellation it belonged to. Humoring him another moment for an accomplished erudite address, she invited them back inside to finish their dinners.

32

Mother and daughter didn't speak. The only contact they made were brief glances passing one another in the kitchen in the mornings. This lasted a week. Jamie found distraction studying for classes and working after school, but it couldn't be like this for her final two months in high school. After getting better at the start of the year, she didn't want to end like this. The hope she'd had for the end couldn't have been taken from her so easily.

"Just give her time to cool off. No parent wants to hear their child chose not to go to college." Vienna had become a good substitute for Minjae as he began finding less and less free time to hang out with Jamie. The two girls were at the rock gym at the beginning of Jamie's shift and since there were no customers at the time, Noel had no complaints. In fact, Jamie wondered if his reserve about her impending departure from Shore was actually because he was really sad to see her go. Occasionally she'd glimpse at him sulking whenever he went over something Jamie had done though she'd made no mistakes. It was a week or two before Era confided how he was troubled having to find a new replacement for Jamie. While there were four others who worked at the gym, Noel really became attached to his employees, and had a difficult time letting them go.

"Enough about me," Jamie said. "What happened after lunch today? I noticed you and Jax got at it again."

Vienna bit her lip and made a face at the floor as she skidded her foot, bringing a hand to her neck as she looked past her brown bangs, her short hair falling in front of her eyes.

"Jax being Jax. I don't know what him and Bryden have against Penelope but I swear it's always about her."

"Is he," Jamie said with a nod, hoping the gesture implied enough for her. "You know, cheating with her?"

"No. Thanks for having so much faith in my boyfriend though." Vienna rolled her eyes. " Jax's being the douche he always has to be in front of Bryden. They made fun of her because she was weird and part of the strange family in the neighborhood, you know, whatever. But the past couple of months I've been getting the impression that Bryden actually kind of likes her."

Jamie had to stop sweeping and laughed, her brush-off not paralleling the way Vienna took it.

"Bryden's a dick—we know this—but he's also immature and I think all this tugging at her pigtails and taking off her glasses to call her four eyes is because he wants her to notice his interest in her. Like he likes her."

"Doesn't he have a thing for Caprice?"

Vienna scoffed. "Caprice has a thing for him."

"Ah," Jamie acknowledged, but then realizing what she said muttered, "Oh . . ."

"Yeah, so prom will be interesting, right?"

Jamie pulled the dirt and bits of trash into the trash scoop as she glanced over to Vienna. "Let me guess, she hasn't been asked yet."

Vienna finished the thought for her. "And she's waiting. Patiently. Irritatingly so."

"I don't know Penelope that well . . ."

Minjae had mentioned her in regards to the cathedral and that he was friends with her. Vienna had mentioned they were friends a long time ago. Jamie was just uncertain why Penelope kept being mentioned around her. It wasn't like they hadn't attended the same school for almost a decade, but for her name to be incessantly hinted at her from the depths of dark memory felt apposite.

"The three of us: Minjae, Penelope, and I live in the same neighborhood, down by the Bilem Site, so we were closer back then. Well, me and Penelope at least. Minjae's still friends with her though."

"He's mentioned her," Jamie said lightly.

Vienna misunderstood her remark. "He's just friends with her though. You don't have to worry."

Jamie knew why she explained it but said nothing. "I think you should get Jax to get Bryden to fess up about Penelope. Find out if he really likes her or not. Because if he does, then you'll have to deal with Caprice. And if not, then get him to back off being a jerk. He's a senior. Needs to act the age he is instead of just looking it. We're legal now so it isn't funny anymore."

"It wouldn't surprise me if he was drinking some juice every morning." Vienna caught her hand over her mouth as she giggled then lowered it. "Oh, who am I kidding? He definitely had something to bulk up so much in the last two years. Puberty my ass."

The street address popped in Jamie's mind after Vienna mentioned the Bilem Site. That address was near the new home development. "Does Ash Lake Road sound familiar to you?"

"It's a couple of blocks from my house. Why?" Jamie relayed the address and Vienna mused for a moment. "That's Penelope's address. I'm 90% sure."

Without an idea as to why someone would leave her address at her door when she'd never spoken with Penelope, she dismissed it as simply an odd prank. If Penelope was the one who left it, she would've confronted Jamie and not led her on this wild-goose chase. The two girls said little more before several customers entered the gym. Despite the slight shift in atmosphere, Noel only gestured for Jamie and Vienna to talk elsewhere from the rock walls. They decided to empty the trash bins. They tossed the bags into the bulk container the rock gym shared with the neighboring dry cleaner business when Vienna pointed two fingers to her eyes, leaning forward to reexamine Jamie.

"Is it AP?" Vienna asked. "I didn't want to mention it but . . . the dark circles."

Jamie hadn't been sleeping. It seemed the less time her secret weapon Minjae spent with her, the more she began to feel small waves of nightmares again. The night before last was unusually unsettling as she witnessed skin being flayed by the demons in the plains. Hoping to avoid it, she stayed up most of last night.

"Yeah," Jamie said.

"I didn't know you were so passionate about English." It was Jamie's only AP class. She forced a convincing grin on her face as she focused on the ground where they were stepping. There was a plastic drink lid torn through near an open Snickers wrapper. Vienna picked up the trash. "Animals. We're literally ten steps away from the dumpster. We'll probably drown ourselves in trash before the rising ocean levels do." Vienna glanced over her shoulder as she tossed the trash away. "Well if you ever want help and want to cram together let me know."

"Will do." Jamie suddenly had a thought and looked over to Vienna. "By the way, are you decided on UCF?"

"My eyes are set there. Go black and gold."

"You know, after we graduate I'm gonna leave Shore for a bit. My job will be open. I can give a stellar recommendation."

While Vienna wasn't sure if she would want to work at the gym, Jamie had an inkling that ultimately she'd take it. The pay wasn't bad and Noel was flexible with hours. And Jamie was the shoe-in for her getting the job since Noel wasn't advertising for new hired help yet. She was ahead of the curb and could take advantage of the opportunity. The little Jamie had spent with Vienna, she knew she was very resourceful and conscientious of her time and money. In a couple of days she'd agree to do it. While it wasn't much, it did make Jamie feel better she was leaving Noel with a good substitute.

Although she had no reason to, she walked her bike once she entered her neighborhood, taking every opportunity to avoid being home as soon as possible. It was late and by now her mother would have picked up Aiden from Banafsha's house, so she passed on dropping by. She always had tomorrow.

It was when she was walking by Banafsha's driveway she spotted Banafsha's form walking up the sidewalk to the front door, smoothly slipping in. Unaccustomed to seeing her neighbor outdoors she hesitated for a moment, reconsidering dropping by when at the same moment a feeling inside her told her not to. Banafsha had to have seen Jamie coming from down the street and didn't want to speak with her. For all of her charm, she was direct in her feelings. Jamie respected that of her. Her feelings weren't complex. If she didn't want to do something she didn't want to. There wasn't much more needed to be known.

At the end of her driveway, Jamie cast another glance toward her neighbor's front door, waiting to see if her neighbor's eyes would peek back at her from behind the curtains or maybe just to see her come back outside and acknowledge her. Unsure what she was expecting, she walked up the driveway.

It was one of those feelings where you feel eyes on you for no reason, but Jamie looked over her shoulder. There was a man walking away down the dimly lit sidewalk across the street. She wondered if maybe he was the reason Banafsha had left her house. Though it would be strange since, one, Jamie had never seen Banafsha visit or invite . . . *anyone* into her house; and two, who could he be that he walked and not drove? If it was someone in the neighborhood then Jamie had to have seen them sometime in three years, so why now? What phenomenal event conjured such a change?

Accepting she wouldn't know tonight, she set her bike against the house and went inside.

33

They were having lunch the Monday after prom, Vienna playing with French fries more than eating. Jamie chewed on a burger, studying her downcast companion. Returning to school after the weekend was less and less appealing the closer to graduation they became, but Vienna seemed unwilling to share the concerns weighing on her.

There's no prom without its own moments of drama and for the Capes, it escalated beyond repair when Bryden insisted dancing with the girl Jamie felt like she couldn't get away from. It started off innocently enough—for Bryden's standards—with him simply asking Penelope for a dance. He'd had enough of his date, Caprice, and while she left to get drinks, he slipped through the crowd and found Penelope—who he hadn't let too far out of his sight all night. Penelope had never given him any indication she wanted to dance and it only worsened when Jamie, Minjae, Vienna, and Jax tried to settle the destabilizing ruckus. Spiteful words were shared, several shoves, until Bryden suddenly revealed he and Penelope had had multiple trysts during the fall. While Penelope had withstood him boldly and tenaciously, the leaked scandal destroyed her ego and the old camaraderie Vienna shared with her from their youth resurfaced. Jax was forgotten by Vienna for the rest of the night as she stayed with Penelope to support and ward of any future advances by Bryden. Caprice had witnessed the scene and didn't return to her date. Aside from Minjae who stuck near Jamie, everyone scattered apart for the rest of the night.

Jamie was never skilled at initiating conversations, let alone trying to counsel a weary heart, and swallowed as she forced the words out.

"Is it final exams? AP?"

It was mid-April and the exams were less than a month away. All concerning seniors were already suffering from the colliding feelings of relief from graduation and stress from deferred college acceptances, but AP exams were the final hurdle to overcome.

Vienna's chin rested on a form-fitting palm. Blankly looking at her French fries, she shook her head. Jamie read her mind.

"It's Jax. It's always Jax."

A reluctant frown formed on Vienna's lips. "Do I always complain about him?"

A rush of guilt flooded Jamie as she quickly rejected it, flapping her hand as if the movement could erase what she said in the way she said it. "It's only I've noticed how you and Jax enjoyed yourselves a lot less that night after the Bryden incident." Jamie remembered she hadn't seen Penelope all day. "I thought you weren't that close with her."

Vienna let out a breath and shrugged, her shoulders slouching as she thought back on prom. "We're not what we used to be but she didn't have anyone else to defend her against . . . Bryden." She said his name with inflection, then sighed. "And Jax didn't say anything at the prom but when he drove me home we argued. He said he felt like I stole his prom from him because I didn't spend most of it with him. Which isn't true, I was with him for most of it. It's just, Penelope froze up when Bryden broadcasted their affair."

"I noticed."

"I mean she's quiet for a reason. She's incredibly private. Her and her whole family. She can't hold a tough façade up for long, regardless of how good she holds her ground." Vienna washed her fingers of the salt from the French fries. "It was out of the friendship we had when we were little. Or maybe for anyone Bryden sets his sights on."

"He must like her. Why else make such a big deal? At least we all can breathe easier knowing the end of the year is upon us."

Vienna pursed her lips together. "What about you?"

Jamie cast widened eyes to Vienna. She read the question in them.

"You don't look like you've slept well again. Did you get in a fight with Jay?"

Without thinking about it Jamie lifted a hand to cover her eyes, smoothing the skin as if she could wipe the darkness away. The nightmares were the same. Always the same. Tiringly so. She'd had enough nightmares, hoping it was something different so she could feel a new type of fear.

The fear she thought would purge her sanity like an emetic virus had been worn dull by its recurrence.

Yet she still hoped it wouldn't happen. Every night. That was the sting. Jamie searched for a distraction. She didn't want to think about the nightmares until that night.

"Have you made up your mind about working at the gym?" Jamie asked.

Vienna began to smile timidly. "Yeah. I was thinking I might do it."

Jamie smiled at her. "Good. No rush of course."

"Why? Did you already suggest me to your boss?"

Jamie feigned flattery with a hand to her collarbone. "I wouldn't suggest something to someone unless speaking to the party involved first."

Vienna couldn't be sure if Jamie was lying or not. But she smiled down at the cold food, minutes from being tossed into the trash by the sound of the bell. It was a smile Jamie had felt she had seen somewhere before.

****

Any building west of St. Luke's Cathedral was shielded against the fierce ocean winds as Shore's first real thunderstorm of the year boded on the eastern horizons, bringing with it the lowest temperatures of spring and the last before the caresses of fall. The end of April sent the insects back under the rocks and chilled the squirrels and birds for a day of rest, if not coverage, from the storm. By Noel's dismissal, Jamie had ridden home early to better avoid it, as the occupants of the rock gym heard the first signs of thunder. Storms like this were bad omens, Noel cautioned, followed by a reassuring pat on the back.

"I was thinking of making your uncle a visit tomorrow," Rosario said, putting dinner leftovers into Tupperware. The storm had lasted the dinner but by now the last of the storm's hostile threats were faintly heard under the hum of the fan. Aiden was turning off a game on his Xbox and put on a movie they'd rented from Redbox. Jamie was sitting on the sofa, her arm wrapped around a leg when she looked over the top of the sofa. Rosario lifted her eyes up to Jamie's, sensing them on her. "Can I mention him? I've yet to have him over for dinner once. I'm a poor sister-in-law. I've haven't spoken to him five times since November. It's been six months."

"You don't think something's wrong, do you?" Jamie asked.

The question, unanticipated, stirred Rosario to connect with Jamie's eyes again—this time for longer. Concern? It couldn't be that since Jamie had never shown a sliver of concern for Gabe all her life. Even when she went to the cathedral back in February, it wasn't a worrisome heart. Only a simple consideration. Nurses did it on their rounds at the hospital, cops did it in residential neighborhoods in the late hours of the night, a courtesy. A kindness. It didn't count.

"No," Rosario said slowly. "Nothing's wrong."

"Well, in any case"—Jamie turned back to the TV, the previews for the movie appearing on the screen—"the priests would call if anything was."

"You've been saying that for months," Aiden grunted, sitting on the far end of the couch from her.

Jamie stuck her tongue out at him and Aiden ignored her, as he'd grown used to ignoring her every time she ridiculed him. With a smug shake when her taunt wasn't reciprocated in turn, Jamie looked back to the TV.

"Not like you'd know who he was if you passed him on the street."

"I've seen pictures!" Aiden contended. "He looks like dad. I'd recognize him."

"But he isn't, now is he? He's different from the pictures."

"Why do you two always fight?" Rosario sat down in the loveseat on the end nearest to Jamie.

"You haven't seen him either," Jamie said coldly to her mother. "Everything's just been on the phone or in short messages you've left with the priests." Rosario dismissed her with her silence. Jamie felt her point unmade. "You've forgotten. Here, I'll get a photo and show you a picture of dad and Gabe side-by-side. I know the perfect picture too." Jamie stood up and went to the bookcase where the photo albums.

Rosario lifted her voice in Jamie's direction. "The movie's going to start. Leave it for later."

"You'll both be asleep by the time the movie ends."

Sliding her index finger over the spines, she couldn't spot the album of her father's side of the family. Even their wedding photo album wasn't in the bookcase. Her mother must have moved it. She went to her mother's room and looked in the small bookshelf by her nightstand. Unsuccessful again. There were only so many places her mother could've kept her photo albums and doubted she kept her father's album in her closet. Either way, she stepped inside and scanned the shelves above her work clothes and spotted it. The worn red spine had yellow ribbons striped over the curvature. Exactly as she remembered it. She reached up and slid it out, accidentally releasing unclipped papers loosely placed underneath.

"Shit," Jamie muttered.

She set the album on the bed then reentered the closet, kneeling down to pick up the papers.

"Jamie, what's taking so long?" Aiden yelled from the living room. "Mom said to leave the album and show us tomorrow."

"I'm coming!" Jamie called back, gripping the papers together, straightening them on the floor and then reaching on her tip toes to set them back on the box. It was in the shadows, but a box behind the papers had a reapplication of tape, slightly misaligned with the darker impression left behind from the old piece of tape, contrasting the lighter tone of the box covered from dust. There was an inkling of intrigue in her which made her have a double take. It wasn't hidden away and she didn't know everything that was in her mother's closet, but she never remembered seeing this box before. Using a step ladder she reached over and brought the box out. Quickly uncovering the top, the first thing she saw was a plain blue album cover; the blue seen when balloons are brought to celebrate having a baby boy. She picked it up and opened the cover, passing over the birth certificate to see the first pictures taken of her after being cleaned up, moments after delivery. There was a clean white outfit slipped over her small form with a bracelet around her wrist.

With pursed lips and furrowed brows, she analyzed the photo a moment longer. Moving on to the next photo, she noticed something wrong about the shape of her nose. She knew her baby photos; she'd looked over them with her father countless times. In her baby photos, her nose wasn't so narrow and small. And her eyes hadn't opened for a day. Yet there they were. Open. It must have been incorrectly dated. The photo must've been taken several days after her birthday.

Only, it wasn't just the day and month wrong, the year was way off. It was three years before she'd been born. She turned the page and saw another photo, of her mother and father holding her for the first time, together for the first time as a family. However, this baby gazed absently past the camera.

She scrutinized the picture longer, finding more and more wrong with the setting, the date, the people. The color of the walls where she was delivered was a light green, and in this room it was a drab beige. Her mother had a disarray of bangs in this picture when she never had bangs in her pictures. And her father had short hair when he was meant to have long with an unshaved face. Uncertain as to why there was so many discrepancies with these pictures, and knowing for a fact that these weren't her brother's pictures, she flipped to the front of the album to the birth certificate. Her heart had never pounded so hard.

Not since her mother got the call. She read the name over and over and it still didn't answer the question her eyes asked.

James Axel Diez. To Rosario Joelys Diez and Jacob Manuel Diez.

Her eyes drifted downward to the date: Born June 21st, 1996.

A memory suddenly rushed to mind. It was a summer day. She was celebrating her fourth birthday. Aside from her uncles, aunts, and Abuela, several of her parents' coworkers were there. They brought along their kids as well. She didn't like playing with anyone outside of her family, silent every time she was alone with a stranger, even a child, and escaped from the party in the backyard to look for her parents. She spotted her father walking inside from the back door and followed him, stopping at the doorframe when she noticed her parents standing by the kitchen counter, heads bowed in deep conversation. From a distance, she spotted how her mother had another cake reserved, and she planted a candle on top. The number 7. She watched as her father softly rubbed his wife's arm, leaned close to her ear to whisper something, then kissed her hair before reaching around her toward the cake reserved for Jamie. As Jamie stepped back toward the backyard, she briefly watched her mom reluctantly push the cake to the back of the kitchen counter. The unlit numbered candle being slid into a kitchen drawer.

So it was for you, Jamie thought, her eyes flickering down to the birth certificate. She flipped the page to examine the baby picture again, an involuntary tear falling, landing on her forearm. She'd never met him. An older brother she had never known about. Why?

Jamie returned to the living room, shuffling her feet as she held the album in her hands. Aiden was walking to the living room from the kitchen with a bowl in his hands, picking pieces from the top.

"You took so long I made popcorn," he said, concentrating on the TV. "Mom, you can start the movie now." Aiden didn't notice the album in Jamie's hands and neither did Rosario as she reached for the remote.

"Who's James?" Jamie asked, her voice subdued and tremulous.

Both Rosario and Aiden noticed the delicate conviction in her voice and turned to her. Aiden glanced back at Rosario. Their mother never unlocked eyes from Jamie. Until, that is, they flickered down to the album and the birth certificate being shown to her.

"Why is there a birth certificate to a *James Axel Diez* that I don't know about?" Jamie reiterated as the pairs of eyes did nothing but stare.

There was little to know in her family. Despite their petty arguments recurring daily, they were a rather open family. Devoid of the gargoyles, Jamie had hidden nothing from her mother and brother, and before this day could be certain her family reserved the same courtesy to her. They didn't lie. Not to each other. They didn't hurt one another. They didn't hold onto faded memories. These past six months was a test to how Jamie had begun to move on from a memory long dead. She loved her father, but she wanted to find something else to devote all her love toward; not let it sink and be wasted into the void. It didn't have to romantic, only something to care about that would last a lifetime. Just one thing. Just long enough.

Rosario struggled to speak as Jamie's eyes descended uncertainly on her. It was with a last push of strength that she explained.

"It was something your father and I decided."

"Decided," Jamie exhaled. "Decided what?"

"That we wouldn't tell you until you were older. After you graduated and left the house."

"It isn't news like I'm adopted. Why did you want to wait *until I was legal* to tell me I have an older brother?"

"Had." Rosario stood up and approached Jamie slowly. "He passed away a week after he was born, years before you were here."

"It doesn't discount the fact that I had an *older brother* you didn't tell me about."

"Because it isn't something I knew how to tell you. What age is the appropriate age for that information? Honey, you were an exceptional child and I couldn't bombard you with that sort of news. I didn't know how you'd handle it and how you would look at your father and me."

"Why do you have this perception that I'm fragile and will crumble at any type of bad news?"

"Jamie, you were"—Rosario searched for the right word—"I wanted you comfortable. Happy. You didn't befriend others. The only comfort you took was from me and your father. Mainly your father. I didn't want to upset you. I didn't want to make your life unstable."

"Jesus, what are you talking about?" Jamie found her voice again. "Is there something I'm missing from my childhood? Did I have breakdowns every week I couldn't handle anything even remotely heavy?"

"No!" Rosario couldn't hide the suffering in her eyes.

"Was it this? This whole time? This reason deep down why I've felt you loved Aiden more than me. That you looked out for him more than me. That you cared for him more than you did for me. It was because he was the son you lost and you were able to do it over. Do it right."

"*That*"—Rosario lowered her voice and jabbed a finger in the air toward Jamie—"is *not* true. Nowhere near true."

"It isn't the type of love babies of the family always get. One of the reasons why I was so close to dad was because I saw how you always tended to Aiden first in everything. Always had one eye on me and another out for him, when otherwise it would've been both eyes on him."

"I'm sorry—" Rosario's voice broke, tears coming down her face, taking hesitant steps toward Jamie. "—if for all these years you've felt that way. I'm so sorry you felt that way for even a moment. I never wanted you to feel like you were second to anyone. You're my baby and I love you both so much. You, Aiden, and your father. I loved you more than anything. No *one* over the other. You didn't take a portion of my heart. Each of you helped it to grow and love you all so it would be equal."

Jamie exhaled through her nose, her eyes flickering to Aiden. "Why aren't you saying anything? You have an older brother you never knew about. Why aren't you as mad at her for keeping this a secret?"

Aiden shifted his eyes to their mother as Rosario closed her eyes, waiting to be scolded. Aiden's eyes returned to Jamie's as they shaped to windows of repentance; pleas kept restrained from an unknown amount of time.

"You knew?" Jamie's voice cracked as she felt a betrayal worse than the one she felt by her mother. While she might've been harsher in her words toward him, she'd also been more honest.

He nodded with a heavy heart, his eyes faltering from her gaze for a moment. "Since December."

Jamie felt the taste of the month's name for the first time. Then, a smile formed by iniquity, dropped as the corners of her lips turned down. Aiden let out a breath before using the voice he made when defending himself against something he hadn't done. "It was an accident. I was upset with mom for weeks after it."

They never *didn't* get along which is why Jamie remembered. Aiden rarely spoke to their mom all week. It was by her advice that he forgive her for whatever she did.

"I knew you'd be upset," Rosario said. "I was prepared for that. I'm sorry I kept it from you and you thought it was meant as a secret from you."

A cruel expression twisted on Jamie's face. "A secret implies it was never meant to be shared with those who don't already know. You were never going to tell me."

"I was." Rosario might have been uncertain about everything else but this. "After you had graduated."

Jamie looked down and flipped the pages of the album, stopping at the one where it was her parents and the newborn together for the first time. The boy was innocent and if he couldn't live a week, he had to have been inordinately weak. She should ask what had happened. Why it was that he lived less than seven days. However, eighteen years of unfulfilled love and suddenly the exposure of a secret crashed over her. She felt unloved. Even her younger brother knew before her. Why couldn't she have been first? Now she wasn't even the oldest child. She was the second. The child to make up for the one lost. Her mother probably didn't even want a girl and kept trying to have a boy again. Her parents never tried for another kid after Aiden was born. Was it this? Was that why?

"It should be asked," Jamie said coldly, her emotionally driven eyes guiding their way to her mother. "But I won't ask it."

She set the album on the coffee table and moved past her mother, as she said Jamie's name, and past her brother, as he lifted a hand to her as successfully as grasping an aberration. Outside she grabbed her bike and rode away. No direction. No destination. Her mind was blank as it automatically halted at red lights and noted oncoming cars. Never once had she been so daring to ride among cars without full awareness and now cars were an arm's reach away. There was no awareness because she didn't care if she got hit. There was no pain to be had in a being where there lacked a heart to be hurt.

Her bike led her east, past downtown Shore and the suburban neighborhoods, past St. Luke's and the division where concrete met sand. When the front wheel got caught and she was lunged forward, her senses snapped back, demanding her leg jut forward and catch her before landing on her face. Her hands slid through the top layer of sand as she supported her weight under the bike, crawling out and in a stupor, stumbling forward toward the water.

The moon peeked out from behind the straggling clouds chasing the westward storms. The Earth's only satellite brightly illuminated the black ocean and calm waves, struggling to form like a toddler struggling to walk on its own. It was in the presence of the strongest force in the world that she looked at its master and screamed, clawing her hands by her sides, arching her head back, demanding to be heard. She yelled so that the moon would look down on her and illuminate the answers that she needed.

Why do I own a life lived alone?

Why did the only comfort in my life have to be taken from me?

Was there no pain to replace her loneliness? Even pain could be treated. No one could give her the warmth that she felt when shown kindness by that stranger. Not even her family could do that. Not after her father died. Not Aiden. As disillusioned as Jamie was toward her, not even her mother.

I didn't even get my own name.

Jamie lied back on the sand, her hands burrowing under the cool sand, letting the night's icy breezes numb her mind. If not where she had needed it most, at least let the bitter temperatures still her mind so there'd be pain. Or no pain. No feeling at all. She closed her eyes and remembered a life with love. A life where there was someone for her.

Her father taking her to school. Her father picking her up from school. Her mother and father in the audience as they watched her play Mice #3 in her elementary school's production of *Cinderella*. When she fell from the top of the monkey bars and her father rushed her to the hospital, the arm fractured though quickly healed by ice cream trips every Friday. Her father riding the Ferris wheel at Shore's July Fourth Festival despite his fear of heights. Her father driving four hours each way to pick her up from her uncle's—Rosario's older brother's—house because she was homesick. Her father reading her *The Ugly Duckling* and *Corduroy* and waiting by her bedside until she fell asleep so the monsters wouldn't come. Her father going to the park with her to build sand castles until it was too dark to see. Her father who taught her how to ride a bike. Her father who gave her her first lesson in driving two months before he passed. Her father who spoke to his wife in the night about giving her time to open to others, that she'd meet people at her own pace. In her own time. Someone who looked out for her more than anyone.

She heard footsteps not far from her and when opening her eyes, there was a man looking down on her, his silhouette almost completely dark but for his eyes. Starlight white. Frozen or in deep serenity, she watched the man smile kindly with those eyes, kneel, then reach a hand toward her shoulder, supporting her up. Closer, she noticed the man had a familiar face. A beard closely shaven and while his eyes were white and reminiscent of the gargoyles, they looked warmhearted and open. Like an altruistic stranger.

"You'll always have him," said the stranger.

Jamie knew she'd heard his voice before, uncertain as to when. There were some people with a voice no one else could have.

The corner of the stranger's lip pulled up. "For ever longer than you need him."

The stranger rested his hand a moment longer on her shoulder before nodding once and withdrawing. Suddenly, the world twisted and gravity was not below her but behind her; the waves of the ocean suddenly rushing around the man to crash through her.

Struck by the force of the waves, she felt her center suddenly pulled back as her mind lost sense of everything below the neck. Her eyes shut just before impact. While she tried to hold her breath, her lips were no match against the pressures molded around her, tumbling and rolling her along the waves. Her breath was held for as long as was possible as she desperately sought air, heaving an intake of air as nothing entered her mouth.

Suffocating on nothing she lunged her chest forward to sit up, shooting her eyes open and gasping as she quickly established where she was. She had fallen asleep and couldn't guess for how long. Even with a soft wind, she wasn't buried too deeply into the sand. With sand as a glove, she wiped her forehead with pressure before reaching for her phone. She didn't remember she had it on her when she left the house but it didn't matter. Her mother had called several times, once every half an hour until she gave up an hour ago. It wasn't the missed calls or curiosity of the time that drew her phone out though. She went into her contacts and called a number, waiting for the ring when she brought the phone to her ear.

The caller picked up. "Hey, you all right? I called you a bit ago. Your mom called asking if you were at my house."

"Minjae." She pleaded, resting her temple on her palm and staring up at the moon, far from where it had been earlier. "You're on my side? Right? You're the only one I can depend on right?"

"Yeah, I'm on your side. What's going on? Did you get in a fight with your mom?"

"And"—Jamie exhaled as a drop slid down her cheek—"you like me for me. Not because you want me to be someone else."

"Of course, Jamie. You know I do. You're really freaking me out. Are you all right?"

Jamie closed her eyes, ducking her head and pinching the bridge of her nose with two fingers.

"Are you at the beach? Do you want me to pick you up?"

His voice brought her back to the present and she brought the phone back to her ear.

"No. I just need someone on my side."

She hung up and stood, realizing where she was for the first time, then turned and picked up her bike.

Returning home, she didn't answer her mother when asked where she'd gone and made no noise other than what her feet made. Inside her room she locked the door and shut off the light, dropping on her bed and staring into the dark. The hours into the night passed. Every tick of the clock passed quicker in each second. It was when Jamie had

begun to drift to sleep that she discovered that she had a new nightmare
to fear. One with a young boy. Much too young. Smiling a cruel curve.
With vacuous eyes.

A light tap was made at her window, followed by a whisper.
Jamie ignored it. After all she'd heard noises in and out of her sleep for
months. It was the persistence of the taps that alarmed her. The sounds
were done to unnerve her. First it would be sounds and then she would
descend through a thin barrier where her nightmares would resume, and
she would walk, shadow upon shadow, descending no further into hell
and yet no less unraveling. Here she would see mammoth demons
abuse hollowed slaves, with cavities as eyes and sagging wrinkles as
their tears, burdened and unburdened, hunched and misshapen, under
the crackling of the whip and the strike of a quarterstaff. Jamie would
be with them in the fields staggering behind the misshapen creature
Italus, or up in the fortress with the robed demon Erus, even on the
hilltop beside the Empty Gate and its river of souls where Rephastion
guarded ever-present, never seen. Jamie hadn't seen Rephastion in
months. However on the hilltop, the dark storm in the distance was
unequivocally alive. Across plains and beyond mountains, without
voice or facial features, it was unquestionably aware of Jamie's
presence. As if she had overstepped the rules which bound the living to
Earth and the dead to the Afterlife. As if having the nightmares was in
her control . . .

The taps continued. The whispers grew slightly louder. Her
name. The whispers called her name.

Wanting to face the ghost for the first time since last seeing the
man with the white eyes—a white so bright that she thought they were
blue—a sudden burst of courage pushed her forward as she tugged the
curtains aside with enough pull that a repeat performance would bring
the rod down. Only it wasn't white eyes she met, but a rather alarmed
face, one not expecting a sudden appearance despite his persistence.

"*Kkabjjakiya*!" Minjae rested his hand on his chest.
Embarrassed, Jamie tore her eyes from him and turned the window
switch. "Jesus . . ." Minjae released under his breath as he snuck in,
turning around as Jamie closed the window. "Good thing you don't live
on the second floor or you'd have to explain to your mom why there's a
Korean kid with a broken spine outside your window." He whispered
beneath a crooked smile as if the injury would've given him a scar he
would've been proud of.

Jamie snapped at him. "What are you doing here?"

"You think I haven't noticed your raccoon eyes these past
weeks?" He pointed two fingers at her eyes then slid off his backpack,
shaking his head as he dug inside to find something. He pulled out a
flashlight and turned it on underneath his chin. "I'm here to protect

you." The deeper voice he borrowed for a moment trailed off as he suddenly chuckled.

Jamie looked at his backpack, wondering what he brought as he misread her eyes.

"Don't worry. I sleep anywhere. I'll just be on the floor. All I need is my Woody blanket. Got a pillow you can spare?"

"Won't your parents be upset when they learn you're not at home?"

"It's the weekend, they hardly bother me. And I've been working a lot lately. They know I need my beauty sleep. I left a note I went for a bike ride to destress my mind. You should be more worried if your mom catches me."

Jamie moved around him and took a pillow from her bed, handing it over to him as she let out a breath. "I doubt she'll bother me."

Minjae looked at her. "Why?"

Jamie pointed to where he could sleep. She shut the curtains then settled into her bed. Once Minjae found a comfortable position, he shut off his light and brought an arm behind his head.

"What happened?" He treaded carefully, quickly adding, "We haven't seen much of each other all month aside from prom. Yearbook's done so I can be a good friend now."

"You were always a good friend," Jamie said softly.

He chewed his lip for a moment before prodding her again. "Does it have to do with leaving after graduation? You said she didn't take it well when you told her college wasn't for you."

"I just found out today—a secret she'd been holding back from me all my life. She hadn't cared."

Chancing it wouldn't spark a reaction, he spoke cautiously. "I'm sure there was a good reason. It wasn't for as long, but you forgave me."

"Your secret was nothing. You wanted to be honest. You gained a reassured heart. My mom, she kept it a secret. Not only that, she kept it a secret and so did he."

Minjae meditated on it for a moment. "You mean your dad?"

Jamie nodded, frowning again as she ignored how a tear rolled down her temple, not caring if it would leave evidence. She thought she'd cried it all out at the beach.

"All my life I thought I was supposed to be the good older sibling. If I did something wrong then I would be a bad example. I'd be kicked out of the family. For a long time, I thought that was why my dad wasn't in contact with his family. They had disagreements and they thought he was a bad example. He was the worst of the family and they didn't want anything to do with him. No association, even through mutual friends or emergency phone calls. My uncle who moved here last November, he broke that rule and now he doesn't have his family. He turned to the church and eventually came here. That's all a tangent, though. I had to be the good sister. And then," Jamie paused, "being the good sister wasn't enough. I needed to be responsible. Now I feel that was taken from me. I wasn't the first child my mom and dad had. I wasn't the first one they chose to love."

"You have an older sibling?"

"Did."

Jamie closed her eyes and tried to imagine had he lived, what he would have looked like. Would she have been so different from him? Would he have known loneliness as intimately as she had?

"He died a long time ago. Before I was born."

Minjae fiddled with his thumbs. He knew she must still be tormented by her mother. He was still curious. "Why do you think they kept it from you?"

"Some bullshit about protecting me. Since I had no friends at the time she thought something was wrong with me and was worried the wrong word would set me off."

"I understand why they did it."

Jamie let out a breath, perturbed by the lack of support. Minjae anticipated an onslaught of expletives but when they never came, he looked in the direction of the bed. "You were too young to understand. And when you were old enough, you had a little brother. While you may not have had friends, you do care a lot about your brother. You must've shown a connection with him that was enough for them. They didn't need to tell you, because what would it have changed anyways? For whatever reason that your older brother died, it didn't happen to you or your brother."

Silence settled between them.

"They named me after him."

Minjae flattened his hands on his chest, searching for an explanation that might be adequate, if not acceptable.

"James Axel Diez." Jamie weighed the name on her tongue with much more delicacy. As if the name deserved respect. "They loved him so much, they wanted to hold onto him so much, they decided to erase the person the next child was. Every time she looked at me, she was looking at James. What he would have grown up to be. What he wanted. It wasn't of me."

He leaned up and reached for her arm, rubbing it with his thumb as he rested his chin on the bed. He couldn't see her face, but he could see the outline.

"It's just a name."

"You don't understand. You're not the oldest. You're not named after someone else."

"Actually, I am." Jamie looked at him and he sighed. "Daehyun and I are named after two musicians my parents loved."

"Parents name their kids after artists and peers—even fictional characters they love all the time."

"Not when they're your uncles. God there's a reason why their band never became famous. They were *horrible*." A shudder ran up his spine in the way he said it. "I love them but they sucked *so* bad."

"Why did your parents name you two them?"

"God it's so cheesy." Minjae fought within himself whether to share or not. "They met when the band was playing at some club. You know when you love a song even though it's really bad but you love it anyways." He tilted his cheek to rest on the bed. "So don't think being named after someone else is a sin. It isn't like they named you James. It's a praise. Besides, girls have guys' names all the time."

Neither spoke for a long time. "All I am. For eighteen years . . ."

"Listen, at first, it might have been about your brother. But over time, they would have forgotten. If they hear James, they might've automatically thought the person meant Jamie and thought of you. You. Responsible, sarcastic, awesome big sister Jamie. Fast climber and aspiring world traveler. Who has the cutest friend Minjae. Who, shall I say, is incredibly, incredibly adorable."

Jamie pulled her arm from out of his hold and after palpating the darkness for his head, found it, then pushed his forehead back. Chuckling, she took his hand and pulled him on the bed beside her, switching to rest on her side and follow the line of his silhouette. The two rested quietly as they studied each other, unable to fall asleep.

"Jamie?" Minjae said gently. "Why don't you sleep at night?"

The answer came easily. "I have nightmares."

He chewed over the thought of asking, and then did. "Often?"

"I can't help it."

He reached for her arm and rubbed it again. "I'll be here. As long as you need me."

It was more than because he was a friend. It might have taken a while to notice, but she appreciated him. More than she thought. Even when he didn't side with her, she felt satisfied that he was there. Interestingly, that was enough. Nudging closer in small increments, she lined herself next to him, feelings his arms go around her, and tucked her forehead against him.

"Minjae?"

He sighed contently. "Yeah?"

"Where did you leave your bike?"

His eyes shot open.

34

A week after the night with Minjae, Jamie ventured up Ash Lake Road. She did a double take of the crumbled piece of paper in her hand and the number on the mail box. Jamie took one glance at the house and immediately understood why people regarded the Varanos as the neighborhood Boo Radleys. Not only did she struggle discerning the color of the house beyond the serpentine vines scaling up the sides of the house, the exterior seemed to be in a dilapidated condition, nothing exceeding utter shambles. The house seemed a shrine to all of nature; the cobblestone driveway a path of fallen twigs and all stages of leaves. Closer to the house she was overwhelmed by the smell of rain, glancing up at the sky, expecting a heavy shower to descend upon her. While there were no clouds, far to the east she noticed hovering storm clouds. Setting her bike against the house, Jamie heard a distant roll of thunder.

The door opened to a girl with loose pigtails, dark freckles under her eyes and around her nose. It was taking a second glance at them Jamie realized they weren't freckles but paint splatters, another take at her arms and apron confirming it.

"I'm a friend of Penelope's," Jamie said.

"We don't get many visitors," said the girl, sizing Jamie up and down. "Come in."

Following the brazen guide, Jamie was in disbelief that the house inside was roofed under the house outside. The walls were lined with memorabilia from their family's history. Not only photographs on the wall, but tokens from an array of countries. Masks, candle holders, fans, shelves, table stands, and flower arrangements lined down the hall alongside photos blanched white or tarnished yellow. Photographs dated from the early twentieth century with its first cars cruising up downtown Shore's oldest streets. Vases and candles embellished table stands. The dark hardwood floor shined as if they were walking toward the last sunset of the earth.

"It's certainly different from outside," Jamie said. The girl snorted under her breath. When the two reached the end of the front hallway and came upon the living room, it opened to a congregation of nature. "It's like a greenhouse."

While there were common furniture items like a TV set, couch, loveseat, coffee table, and table ends, almost every visible surface was covered with magazines, newspapers, school and work papers, and canvases freed from their wooden frames. Used candles, abused lamps, and a small stone fountain were in the corner. The room opened to the kitchen on the left and the backyard through the glass doors, home to a vast garden maintained daily by its worn dirt paths and vibrant flowers, ubiquitous though fastidiously placed. The openness of the space reminded Jamie of the Carousel of Progress at Disney World, meant to accommodate many people.

"You sure are perceptive."

"Fia!" Penelope barked. "Go back to your painting—if that's what you call it."

Fia snorted under her breath and walked past Penelope.

"You're welcome for bringing your friend in too."

Penelope gestured for Jamie to sit and sat on the couch beside her. "I've been mulling it over for a week and decided I was unable to keep it to myself any longer. I messaged you since I felt that most of the pieces were already there. It just made sense."

Jamie nodded as if she understood what she was talking about and ushered for her to continue.

"Jay told me you've had nightmares for a while now. Nightmares that slip into reality. It doesn't take a blind man to notice the circles around your eyes. It's that, plus the fact you took an interesting picture at St. Luke's—"

Jamie unconsciously froze, keeping her eyes open as if blinking would betray her.

"But since you've neglected to tell anyone about the moving gargoyles . . ."

"Wait, what do you know about moving gargoyles?"

"Me? Not much. Only what my *nonna*'s told me. The seven gargoyles of St. Luke's, guardians of the church until this supposed battle—"

"Wait, wait, wait. You know? I mean you *know* about them?"

Penelope nodded seriously. "My family's obsessed with the church. How couldn't I?"

"You—I mean, Minjae said he showed you my picture and that you said it was Photoshopped."

Penelope rolled her eyes, then looked over her shoulder toward the backyard as if her name had been called. Taking another glance over her shoulder and making up her mind, she stood up and beckoned Jamie to follow. They walked through the glass doors and struck an invisible wall of saccharine aromas, the truest nature could produce. Penelope called out *nonna* several times until they finally came upon an older woman, hunched by a flower bush. There were many surrounding a small pond, a fountain at its center. She wore a white sports visor and green gloves with pink flowers, her white Bermuda shorts and green blouse having seen many days in the sun and rain, with light dirt and grass stains. The woman hummed a tune softly as she moved the dirt with a trowel.

"The reason I called you here was because you need to know. What you're really up against. But I don't think I have the patience, and honestly, it's better my grandma explains it." Penelope folded her arms and leaned near the woman. "*Nonna*. The girl I told you about is here."

Fully engrossed in her work, the elderly woman jumped forward at her granddaughter's sudden declaration, turning over and glaring at her before leaning over to stand up.

"You think maybe next time you'd give me a warning before blasting that trap at me? Oh, look. A guest. It's been over a decade since I've seen a new face in my garden."

"*Nonna*, Jamie's seen the gargoyles."

The woman cast a fresh glance at Jamie as she folded her hands on her hips.

"You've seen them move?" Jamie nodded sheepishly as the woman stepped closer. The '50s schoolteacher glare melted unmistakably into eyes of a child with joy. "What were they like?"

Jamie studied the two women, speaking about the gargoyles as if they had known them all along. Of course they *knew* about them, but they had an intrigue in their voices as if they'd encountered them before.

"How do you know about them? They never mentioned your family."

Nonna flickered her gaze to the sky and let out a breath, taking off her gloves. "It's more interesting and far more important how *you* came to know them."

Jamie and Penelope followed Nonna back inside while Jamie explained her uncle's move into town and living at the cathedral, then their introduction, followed by her first encounter with the moving statues, followed by a terse anecdote about her investigation into their creation. Her relationship with them lasted less than a month, however she'd never been able to move on, although not for lack of trying. She'd been incessantly plagued with nightmares and paranoid by shadows ever since leaving them in December. While her relationship with Minjae had cast them away when they were together, when she felt alone, they returned as if patiently waiting in the wings.

"Well," Nonna said reluctantly, "that isn't the way he lived. He had nightmares constantly. There was no cure to assuage them."

"Who?" Jamie asked. "Is there someone besides me who's seen the gargoyles breathe? Who's had nightmares constantly? Do you think they're connected?"

"Don't be naive," Nonna said with a shake of her head. "They *are* connected." Without missing a beat she turned to Penelope. "Get some tea. Chamomile."

Penelope stood without complaint, though there was dispute in her eyes. She wanted to stay and listen, curious to how Jamie would react to the stories she'd heard ever since she was a child. She'd heard it many times, however the family's stories were rarely shared with outsiders.

"I doubt you know much more about the gargoyles aside from what you've read in the journal. Well that journal had belonged to my great-grandfather, around thirteen times great—I don't remember—who was the sculptor of the gargoyles. You noticed the initials? AG." Jamie remembered and shook her head. She wasn't sure of the name and so the woman filled it in for her. "Antonio Gallo. He was instructed to create symbols of the church. And was never the same man since."

Instructed, Jamie wondered. "By who?"

"He claimed it was by a voice in a dream. But first, he would have to find the right tools. On a fool's chance, he traveled to the Middle East, and within a month from arriving was already on a ship returning to Italy. The reason for the brevity of his excursion was because the item he was looking for was where he dreamed it would be. The mission successful, he believed to have passed the first test."

"He passed a test finding something in the Middle East?" Jamie asked skeptically.

"No," Nonna giggled suddenly. "It was a test for the giver of the dream."

Jamie looked over to Penelope as if she could better explain and Penelope, who'd been watching them rather than focusing on preparing the tea, met her eyes.

I'll bite, Jamie thought. "Who gave him the dream then?"

"While afterwards everyone considered him crazy, people thought he had begun around this time. It's impossible to say who—it might've been no one, however, he began the gargoyles immediately upon returning."

Jamie struggled to believe the luck of the man, though was humored by the elderly woman. Sometimes, in the eyes, people emitted a joy from storytelling—even if they've regaled a story a hundred times. It was an adventure relaying it.

More for the storyteller's benefit, Jamie asked, "What did he go to the Middle East for?"

Penelope returned to the living room, handing her *nonna* a teacup and saucer and placing another near Jamie. Clearly Penelope's grandmother wasn't meant to have her mouth busy with anything; to be free to ask and to answer. The consideration was merely a pretense.

"A carpenter's chisel, the very one used by Jesus Christ when he was young."

Jamie scrutinized the woman, her forehead scrunching and her eyebrows coming together.

"I understand your skepticism—" Nonna began.

"Because it's impossible."

"Improbable. Not impossible." Nonna smiled excitedly. "Incredibly improbable sixteen hundred years later such an item could be rediscovered, guided by dreams. All the same he found the chisel and took it with him, to use for the gargoyles."

There was no certainty in Jamie's mind that what she was listening to was true, however the creases from Nonna's smile made her reconsider. These stories weren't just family legend to her. She'd come to believe them as essentially as gravity.

Nearly a week had passed since Jamie had spoken with her mother. Between them were a total of fourteen sentences dispersed between five encounters. It was a grudge refusing to let go. And now, this story. One after the other. Jamie felt all of life's impossibilities crashing down on her.

"How can you be sure the chisel had belonged to Jesus?"

"It was where he was told it would be. Things like coincidence don't happen." Nonna clasped her hands together. "Not with a man with faith."

Jamie turned to her tea and picked up the cup, taking a sip. The action was to give her a moment to swallow what was being said. How did Penelope and her grandmother expect her to handle this news? Did they actually expect her to believe it? Just because she saw the gargoyles become what they shouldn't have?

Nonna misunderstood Jamie's diversion as a polite indication for her to continue.

"Antonio obeyed the dream maker and began with *Trionfante*. The others followed."

"I know," Jamie interrupted. "And when he was finished, he believed they could become shields against his nightmares. He spent the rest of his life believing that. Living in fear. And then his grandson came here and built the cathedral, to clear his deranged grandfather's name, bringing the statues to guard and protect people against evil and nightmares. The rest of their lives—wasted." Jamie said it distastefully and Nonna straightened her back. "For what? Something that would never come."

Nonna sent Penelope off to retrieve something from a room down the hall. When she returned, she offered Jamie a decrepit frame.

"You know a history." Nonna looked from the frame to Jamie. "You don't know his story."

The picture was of a man standing before the skeleton of a cathedral. He wore no smile and squinted against the iridescent sun. Men moved behind him unaware of the moment being captured, forever frozen. She didn't recognize the bones of St. Luke's without its spires and bell towers, though Foley Avenue hadn't changed in over one hundred years. The same palms that lined up the street, years before it would be dwarfed by the church, towered over the workers, the working ants still in the process of building.

"Who is he?"

"My grandfather, as a young man. He did not have Ricardo's gift as an architect, but he was an avid follower of the church. And when it burned down in the 1890s, he and many other members of the church volunteered to help rebuild."

Jamie studied the toil from the day's labor on the man's face, offering the frame back to its owner.

"I don't understand."

Nonna took the frame extended out to her gently, though her eyes never wavered from Jamie's. "You learn the story and history from books and you think there is nothing more you need to know. You learn the secrets to life's mysteries and think because they do not quench your curiosity they are not as mystifying as they were before. But you don't understand the story because you only know it by one source. You never felt a connection to something more than what words on a page told you. The truth isn't something you learn by reading a book. You need to hear it from someone's voice and see it with your own eyes, because if you go through life only listening and reading and understanding through one source, through one news channel, through one radio station, through one newspaper, through one other person out of the seven billion people in this world, then you will only ever be lost. You've listened to the gargoyles. You've read Antonio's journal. Now you've heard what I've told you. Someone who doesn't listen to a story, whether it's true or not, because they *already know* what happened, will always only ever be impassive. And a life spent chained inside a cave, satisfied watching shadows on a wall instead of leaving to see the torches and wagons and flesh of animals and people, will truly be a life wasted."

Jamie never realized how much hypocrisy she'd spat out in the past months until that moment. She wanted to see the world. She thought she needed to see it to understand it better. To learn to sympathize and empathize with people. To learn who she was in the world. And yet here in her hometown, not ten miles from her house, she wouldn't listen to a woman share a family memory—myth or not.

"*Allegory of the Cave*," Jamie said, a hint of a smirk on her lips as she remembered Aiden. "Professor to ignorance."

"Jamie, there is little time. The Battle is almost here."

"It's just a tropical storm—"

"Jamie," Penelope said. "The gargoyles came alive. For centuries my ancestors have never seen the gargoyles move outside of their nightmares, but they did for you. It isn't something that was coincidence. It's time. Not in a hundred years like you think it will be . . . now. My family's always been here, waiting for something to happen. Some of us even dreamt of the Partner, heard whispers of them being unlike any other in all existence. Generations of us, planted just a few blocks from the church that we should hate and spit on. That church was designed and built to restore my family's name—because those gargoyles are what destroyed it in the first place. Even after the cathedral was first built, and as small as it was compared to how it is now, it was still impressive. That still wasn't enough though. A superstition still lingered around the gargoyles and it took generations and a fire to erase it all. So the gargoyles could finally be looked on with respect of an artist and not the remnants of a deranged man. Not a mistake for his grandson to have to make up for. All that, and my family stuck through it. We stayed here. On a fool's hope maybe. On a precarious conviction that the Partner that Ricardo briefly mentioned would come. That they'd find the gargoyles and they'd help them win the Battle."

"Against all of evil? Come on, even that's a stretch for the imagination," Jamie rebutted as Penelope left the room. Jamie turned to Nonna. "And I didn't find them. My uncle brought me to them—up all those two thousand steps."

"Find them," Nonna said. "Stumbled upon them, introduced to by a third party—you met them. Fate or not, it's you who woke them."

Jamie sought help from the wrong person as she only met Nonna's tired eyes—one who had truly waited all her life for this Partner, since the first time she'd heard it.

"What do you expect me to do?"

Penelope returned with a binder, handing it to her without a word.

Nonna sat forward. "*Meet* with them."

"I won't learn anything new. I'd go and they'd only tell me what they told me last time."

"You're not the Jamie they saw last. I believe that unprepared before, you're the person they need now." As if holding the Gutenberg Bible or handing over the keys to the city, she displayed the binder to Jamie. Inside were many plastic sheets filled with hand-written, weathered pieces of paper. Nonna brought it down to her lap. "These are the only entries of Antonio Gallo that we have. Written before the gargoyles, during, and after. All that is left of his hands work aside from the gargoyles. Insanity made him repeat himself. Document everything again and again."

More family heirlooms, Jamie thought. What else would they bring out to try and convince her?

"He began it shortly after first having his dreams. It is in Italian and dated, but I will translate it for you:

"It has been two weeks from my travels to the East. I have discovered a relic. I dreamed of it and when I traveled, I found it. I could only believe it to be a trick. It could not be true. The tool was a legend and for someone like me to find it . . . Why me? But I know from my dream that it is no trick. It is real. I do not feel worthy to use it as I have been told to. I cannot look at it. I will not tell a soul of its existence."

Nonna turned the pages until it was close to the end, the pages of different paper material. She found a marked spot, clearly read multiple times, then handled the thick binding with heed.

"Antonio was told to use this tool from the East to make the gargoyles. When he did they became alive in a way he couldn't explain. He never told anyone of its existence until he was on his deathbed. He told my father, who was sworn until his deathbed. I shall take it with me to the New World as a reminder for who I am working to restore. To be kept safe, until the gargoyles wake again, and for their reason."

Nonna closed the book and looked to Jamie. "And on every deathbed, from father to son and father to daughter and mother to daughter, this message has been passed. In the chaos of the New World, our family feared the chisel would be discovered and stolen. And so as they buried Ricardo, they slipped the tool into his casket. And there it remains. In a mausoleum in the cemetery across from the Bilem Site. We have never told anyone outside of the family. None outside of the Gallo bloodline."

Penelope stepped forward and took Jamie's hands in her own. "Our family may be outlandish but we don't reveal our secrets to just anyone. We're not wrong. Not about this."

"And has your family ever gone to see if it's really there or not?"

Nonna scrutinized her for a moment, as if they'd already succeeded in convincing her and shouldn't have to prove themselves further. "When a person you love tells you their dearest secret on their deathbed, you tend not to be skeptical. We never looked because we don't need to see."

"Then how can your family know about this Battle for generations and not one of you be the hero?"

"Our family was just a piece of the puzzle. One of the first pieces to create the image. But not the last piece. The last piece was someone worth waiting for."

Jamie's eyebrows lifted as she rubbed her forehead. "It can't be me."

"You've spoken with the gargoyles?" Nonna asked.

"Yes."

"Then that is enough. You made them come alive."

Jamie stood up. "Why me?"

"Well, why not?"

"Because I'm empty. Someone who's going to be your Battle's champion will be someone who has allies and a heart open to loving, if not someone who actually believes in something after this life."

The old woman stood up and came to Jamie, closing her hands around Jamie's cheeks. "That makes you more fitting, doesn't it? Without you, whoever would have won would not have been a true victor. The world needs to see someone who struggles to believe, so that as impossible as it is for them, one day, they might as well."

The two Varano women watched as Jamie shook her head. "I just don't want to feel alone anymore."

Penelope smiled kindly for the first time and stood beside her *nonna*. "That's the beauty of a partnership. You're never alone."

"So who's the Partner then?" Jamie looked in turn at both of them, only to be returned with a shake of the head and a somber smile.

"He'll be someone not of your kind. Someone different in every possible way. But someone who you won't feel any disconnection from. Someone who will feel closer than family."

The thunderstorm had neared as winds shook the house. The three women looked to the ceiling as if expecting the floor to collapse and furniture, wires, tubes, and other inhabitants of the house to fall on top of them.

"You need to go," Nonna said.

Without a word, Jamie was guided to the front door. Penelope watched her as Jamie took her bike and began walking away, pausing and turning back. "Penelope, I'm the last person to be giving advice on it, but don't settle to be normal. Not for the likes of Bryden and even for the best. You're too good for that."

After a perfunctory nod, she pushed off on her bike, leaving Penelope to watch as she rode toward the oncoming storm.

Jamie couldn't believe the things she'd heard. Regardless if the gargoyles came to life, she needed to hear it from one more source. If he said it . . . well, she'd decide then. Despite the ferocious appeal of the clouds, she headed east.

To the cathedral.

35

The wind fought her as she rushed up the steps of St. Luke's. None of the clergy were in the narthex, the side corridors, or the staircase. Stomping past cold passages and exhausted candles to her uncle's chamber door, she banged on it with the discretion of lightning striking the earth. His name became an anthem to her impatience.

"Your niece is here for some long overdue answers!" She slapped the door with a flat palm. "I'm coming in."

An empty chamber. Then, the inexplicable feeling that it hadn't been occupied in months. She scanned for a sign that her suspicion was misguided. The room seemed to be in the exact state she'd left it last November. A hiss escaped her teeth and she turned over her shoulder to look over the courtyard. The immobile figures.

If I'm not available, I encourage you to come up here, her uncle had said.

Jamie flickered her eyes up the bell tower.

She descended down the hall then ascended the steps.

Less than five paces from the door of the roof she stopped, turning to rest on the top step. Her mind told her it was from climbing over two thousand steps. She did everything she could to ignore her heart. *Shame*. She wore it. Three weeks, and her relationship with the gargoyles severed. Her temper had turned her from them. They had made the world alive, something unreal, and life more of a beautiful mystery than it deserved to be. It should have been monotonous. With no kindness but from the memories of a happy daughter. It was unfair of them to show her that something she had closed her heart and mind to was more than stone walls. Magic. Power. Faith. A Light drifting into the air like jellyfish in the ocean, smooth and mindlessly. And suns. Incandescent universe eyes.

You were asinine. An impertinent teenager. So self-defined and mature for eighteen and you couldn't even listen. They never asked to be believed. Only listen.

Jamie stood up once her breath returned. The gargoyles were there. Where they always were. Stagnant and majestic under the shade of the canopy. The thunderclouds, a bark without its bite, had blown over Shore. Far into the eastern horizon Jamie could see the formation of a hurricane. The storm wouldn't be patient for much longer. She needed to find her uncle soon and make it home before it was more than just wind creating an obstacle for her. She ran down the aisle and shuffled the last few steps to Trium . . . breathing.

Jamie turned each way to notice all gargoyles breathing.

"You're already awake."

"You did not waken us," Silas said. Jamie had almost forgotten how their voices were of another universe and lost her balance, catching herself quickly in hopes that none of the gargoyles noticed.

"Not me?" Jamie said breathless. "Then who—"

"You have come late," Cato said.

"Not too late," Marius said, "The storm is nigh only . . . there." He pointed an expenditure toward the hurricane.

"I'm—I'm here for my uncle. And . . ." She licked her lips, turning from one pair of eyes to another. Their wings jolted suddenly. The forms stepped forward to huddle in conference around her. "I want to apologize for not trying to listen. I came because I wanted something from you. Answers for pain. To make me believe in something I could see. But when you reached too deep, I thought it'd become a game to convert me into some disciple of the church. To cozen a girl who had turned her back on anyone who tried to get to know me. Be there for *me*. I should have listened."

"It isn't the mind that doesn't want to listen," Marius said, "but the heart. The heart had trusted before. It formed a barrier. Away from any voice—malicious, compelling, and honest alike."

"We can only implore"—Trium breathed in heavily—"that you listen now."

"I will." Her eyes darted around them as if he were there. "But you haven't by chance seen my uncle? He wasn't in his room. I had a feeling he might've come here."

"They won't tell you," said a voice behind Sidra. "But I will."

Sidra and Marius separated to make way for Jamie's uncle, dragging one leg behind. Focused so much on the gargoyles, she hadn't seen her uncle leaning against a pillar. Even with the light, he seemed to walk under a draped shadow. It was when he was closer that she saw what creature he'd become. Deep impressions below eyes and cheeks. Chin sharp with angular premeditation. One hand, brutally scarred, curved inward as if to hold himself together. His skin was merely a sleeve over bone, muscle, and veins. Shaggy hair poorly hid the scabs and abrasions across his forehead, skull, and face. One injury in particular stood out, from temple to nose, as if one nail had attempted to pull off the mask of his face.

"It's for that very reaction I don't go out." Gabe meant it as a joke. When it wasn't well received, he grimaced. "None but the clergy have seen me for months."

"What happened?" Jamie's voice cracked.

"Is there time?" Gabe asked, briefly glancing up to the gargoyles. Jamie thought he avoided direct eye contact out of reverence, unable to look up to the heavenly beings, however it was in the way he bit his lower lip that she understood. Whatever caused him these injuries sunk further than the surface. All the gargoyles turned to Trium, who looked down on Gabe with a motherly gaze, nodding. Sidra confirmed, and Dominic stepped around Marius and leaned down on one knee, offering his hand for Gabe. Without giving it much thought, Gabe extended a hand out to Dominic's finger, using it to lift himself onto his palm.

"Are you all right?" Jamie asked, the way it is asked in hopes that the person will answer in the way they want.

"It looks worse than it is."

"You look like you haven't eaten in months or seen real light in years. Gabe, why didn't you call us? "

He seemed determined. "I'm stronger than I look."

"Stronger than most," Sidra agreed proudly.

Gabe pulled up the corner of his lips, intending a smile, however Jamie could only see it as a reaction against the pain.

"The months have been stretched. It was as if I was pulled in all directions, disabling me from breathing. And to breathe had never seemed so important. We all forget how important breathing is. You asked how these past months have been? Before I tell you, believe me when I say it was my choosing. It was not requested of me. Others frequently advised me to end the torment. Madmen always forgo generosity."

While Jamie could only sympathize with his condition, there was a meditation in his gaze when he pushed past the pain and settled his eyes over the gargoyles, as if not only was he relying on the gargoyles for strength, but on someone who'd undergone what he had;

an unspoken camaraderie between beings of light who had yielded to the temporary darkness.

"It began the night they presented themselves to you. When ran from what'd you seen, you saw shadows running alongside you. I know because I watched them chase you. It was the first night I saw them, too. The demons were unnerved by your recent discovery. They knew if they frightened you, you would choose to stay away. Had you done that, they might have left you alone. They desired for none to communicate with the gargoyles and your heart was not strong enough to fight them." Gabe moved his wrapped hand up and down. "When you returned, you continued to see them, yes?"

Jamie nodded. "How could you see them though?"

Gabe made an expression of discomfort as the corner of his lip went up. "Family connections, perhaps?"

It wasn't acceptable enough of an answer for her. "Then why didn't they torment my mom or Aiden?"

"Clever girl." Gabe exhaled. "The gargoyles had never revealed themselves to anyone before. Only to you. And, unbeknownst to them"—Gabe chuckled lightly—"to me."

"You were there?"

"I had a heart attack watching you fall at that height, but before I'd taken a step, right before my eyes, he caught you."

Jamie looked up to Trium, his wings upright and animate like a fish's tail in the water, not colossal rock, obstinate against wind.

"In shock by what I'd seen, I couldn't move until you were long fled into the bell tower. You were far down the avenue when I reached the cathedral's front steps, demanding for them to stay away from you and the church. They did not like that. They did not like that at all. You see, I didn't know then, not until I spoke with the gargoyles and they told me of the shadows. The demons. They shouldn't be seen. By none. None that isn't already like them"—he gestured toward the gargoyles—"or was like them. No matter how high or low in faith. It was a rule they had existed by for all of time and the fact that it had been broken intrigued them. They began to abuse the fact that I could see them and decided to have fun with me. They came that first night. First it was nightmares, their faces tormenting me, soon torturing me, soon transforming me. I'm ashamed to say the only way to escape was to kill myself and wake up.

"As the weeks passed, it began to all blur together. What began as only nightmares reserved in the nighttime came about in the day. They'd crawl from under my door and become shadows out of nothing, beginning again. I could not perform my votary duties, and the others noticed. It was impossible to tell trick from nothing; if I was still dreaming . . . There was no line. And it all became real. It was a month after they started that I tried to kill myself. I hadn't known I was still awake. It was all the same air of vividness. The others feared for me, so they began to lock me down in the crypts. I could no longer feed nor groom myself. Though none of the clergy will confess it, they were unfortunate to become my caretakers."

"They were not ashamed and neither should you be," Marius interjected. "They are your family, caring for one in need."

It must have been said countless times and Gabe smirked, lowering his gaze in chagrin. "Well . . . perhaps." Returning to the story he looked away from all eyes. "I was locked down there for hours every day. I'd begun to forget the beauty of the wind and the color of trees; what it meant to have light. Too dangerous to be near walls, I was chained to the center of the room. My hands were shackled toward the corners of the walls and eventually my knees would buckle from exhaustion; I could barely stand on my own. They still came. Though I spent my time in the darkness, they came, which unhinged me further to insanity. Their voices screeched in my ears. I screamed for them to stop. I am weak and soon begged. Their laughter was worse than their voices. I'd tried to imagine happiness and could not. How many hours did I pray for help? Eventually it came that I prayed for silence. All my world was noise and torment and hostility. I was powerless. All I could do was wait for time to declare them finished.

"I lost sense of time. The concept foreign to me like a fish understanding the universe. There was no measure for it. But silence came. The clergy would save me from my shackles and bring me to the light. And I became"—Gabe cringed—"blinded. By such beauty—the delicacy and subtlety of daylight. I crumbled at the sight, too etiolated to embrace light. But it was light. Warm light! My eyes burned at my refusal to blink. Just finding and feeling daylight. I'd been told I'd been below a month and that I had finally stopped screaming. They believed my torturous depression over. And they brought me to them: the gargoyles."

Gabe paused, holding his breath as a pain overtook him and he fought to suppress it. Jamie reached to cradle her hand under his arm, embracing him as if she could hold him together long enough to outlast the pain. After it passed, he looked down to the foreign hand and noticed it was hers. Comfort appeared on his lips as he took her hand with his free one, the one not scarred or broken. The hand beneath hers was altered by a tremendous force, uncorrectable. In her arms was a creature marked by debility, and she could only hold him.

"I had told the clergy what I had seen and they brought me before them. The gargoyles told me much of what you already know. Not everything, but enough for me. They told me of the dark spirits sent to me, for they could hear them and see them. They knew of my state and wished to help me, but could not. They told me that one day you would know of the truth and be a part of the Battle. Their brave Jamie.

"I knew peace for a short time before the evil spirits returned. I had to be taken below again. Whenever your mother would call, another priest would cover for me. We feared she would notice the lies and be suspicious, but she never did and never became. I was never strong enough to oppose them on my own, so some days the deacons would bring me here, to where for a short time, the gargoyles might protect me. Merely their presence kept the shadows at bay. Those were my best days, when unable to see, I could hear the world. The gulls. The waves. That was when I truly knew I was on Earth. While I didn't live down below for months at a time, I had come to live in the dark. Awake. Asleep. It soon became the only way I saw to live."

Jamie closed her eyes and held herself together as she struggled to say how apologetic she was. When the apology came, she couldn't look him in the eye to affirm if he believed her. How mortifying that it took someone to go through pain for her to open her heart.

He shook his head and took her hand, meaning to squeeze it in reassurance, though patted it instead.

"It was the shadows. No one else. No one, you hear?"

"Why didn't you call me? Tell me what you were going through?"

"You weren't meant to have your faith defined by guilt, by obligation. It had to be your choice. Decisions made by someone else's words or someone else's pain is not true faith and we needed you to be true in your faith. Above all, that was most dire."

"I hear you now. I see you in pain now. What faith do they think I answer to now?"

Gabe shook his head. "It wasn't me that brought you here. It was truth. Your desire for truth."

Jamie didn't understand. How could the shadows have physically tormented him and only come to her in her dreams? She voiced it.

Gabe released a chuckle under his breath. "You must have a guardian angel."

Angels, demons, guardian angels, shadows, unprecedented battles, pain, loss—their lives encompassed and defined more by pain and loss. Jamie examined his form. "What will you do now?"

"I am still here. From what I see in the horizon, the Battle is anon. I must prepare."

"Prepare," Jamie scoffed, "you can barely stand." Nevertheless when he got to his feet she supported his weight. Like an old man in denial he began to walk.

"When you lose the will to fight with your strength, fight with your words. Words are unforeseeably powerful weapons." His seemed final as he lowered her hand from his arm and walked away. Jamie made a silent prayer for him, turning back to the gargoyles.

"What do I do?"

Trium stepped forward and knelt on a knee, reaching a hand out to her. Unsure what he wanted, she stepped forward with a wise man's trepidation. She lifted her hand to his, a small distance between them before he murmured something deep and foreign. The small suns in his dark eyes expanded slowly until they replaced all of the darkness. A stream of light expelled slowly from his lips, wrapping around his arm, trickling into a swirling pool in his palm. The luminous pool shined brighter as if mirroring an afternoon sun. She covered her face as the pool dimmed down and Trium brought his other hand over to cover it. Flattening palm against palm, no light seeped out. Whatever he'd done was complete as he leaned forward and revealed radiating white stars dotted across both palms, constellation lines connecting the tips of his fingers to the edge of his wrist. Jamie stared in a daze as he enveloped his hands around her. She thought he meant to cage her in the stone until the last moment, where he extended the pressed fingers apart, revealing the outside world as if she were safe behind a glass and outside was the lie. When his words restarted, the stars and lines and dust in between began to pulse brighter. As the light intensified, she didn't think to shield her eyes again. Instead she felt the light pulling her away, until her perception of the present separated from her body and she stepped into a new present. One where it was safe. All troubles of the past and future gone.

It was a white space, the air soft like feathers. If she stepped forward she knew she would've stepped on a fresh bed of grass. Nothing bad existed here. A calming rush lightly pushed and pulled from her side, the soft currents of waves on the shore. Home. All her life had been by the waves.

A child's laughter broke the meditating rhythm of the waves and Jamie opened her eyes to search for the source.

He was young, younger than Aiden by a couple of years, running back and forth along the shore, jumping and hopping, chasing a butterfly. He jumped in the air and hovered for a moment before coming back down. She walked toward him, feeling warm sand under her feet, and neared the edge of the retreating water. She stood and watched him for a long time, simply at peace with the happiness of the child. When he came to noticing her, he smiled in such a way she felt that the world had just been born. Something so bright and so innocent had to mean the start of a beautiful life.

The boy ran up to her with his hands cupped over one another, slowing down several steps away. He had bright brown eyes and curly hair reaching over his ears. Strands which were once dark had lightened under the sun.

"I haven't seen you before."

A warm blanket suddenly encased her at the sound of his voice. She'd never felt so full of joy. She had no relation to him and it didn't matter. She'd never loved anyone more. Not even her father. Because back in another present, he'd left her with sadness. She grieved for him when he died. But this boy wouldn't do that to her. He would always be there for her. It was undeniable.

"I know you though," he said, a curiosity spreading over his face, his smile never relenting. "From a dream."

Jamie worked the courage to speak in the strange boy's tongue and was surprised that she could sing as joyfully as him. "Am I the first you've met?"

He shook his head, opening his hands to reveal a hue-shifting violet butterfly, its wings trimmed with black and dotted with white spots. The insect crawled over the tip of his index finger as if to show them off.

"Everyone comes and goes except her." He spoke grateful for what was, not dismayed by what wasn't. He lifted the finger the insect was on as if preparing her for the stage. "She's my oldest friend."

Jamie looked on the boy with a tenderness she'd never felt before. It was almost like he was her child and she had never loved anyone more. "Are you an angel?"

The boy giggled and Jamie smiled in response; it had been a silly question despite however possible it seemed.

"Who else has come?" Jamie asked, wanting to hear the ringing from his bell-like laughter and song of his voice.

"Tall men, pregnant women, young children, people in the wrong body, people in the wrong time. Smiling faces and scared ones. I've seen them all. Lost and those still looking, and those who don't want to look anymore." For the first time, his smile began to wane and Jamie wanted to reach out and console him.

"Don't you get lonely?" Jamie asked. "Everyone leaves."

The two had begun walking along the shore as the butterfly walked across his palms. It seemed to be the one directing the boy, in turn directing Jamie, though side-by-side she failed to realize.

"My friend never leaves me. Everyone that comes leaves like the wind. You don't miss the wind when it leaves, do you?" Rhetorically meant, he looked up to Jamie and smiled brightly again.

"Won't you miss me when I go? You said you knew me."

The boy looked down and took Jamie's hand, smiling at her when she looked down at their interlocked fingers.

"I won't miss them, but I loved them. I didn't get to know them for long, but I loved them."

Jamie and the boy walked down the beach for a long time in silence, until they came around a bend and stood under the shade of palm trees, looking ahead to the shore snaking north—what Jamie believed to be north—in the distance. There was a mountain to the northwest of where they stood. She wasn't sure if they were on a tropical island or on the edge of great continent. All she knew was that she was on the beach, with an angel in denial holding her hand. All of this, on the precipice of the unknown, and she'd never been happier. She only wanted to walk forever with this boy holding her hand. It was the dooming thought, that what she wanted was only an illusion, and that eventually, she would join the countless others that had come and gone, that surfaced within her.

"Why am I here?" Jamie asked aloud, the boy looking up at her with widened eyes as if hearing the question for the first time. "Before Here, I was"—she struggled to remember— "There."

The boy giggled again and the butterfly on his hand flew off, flying around their heads and then up beyond cover of shade. The sunlight seemed to pass right through the insect, although the colors of its wings only saturated brighter.

"You are very silly. You'll be my silly girl."

Jamie lost focus and looked down at the boy, smiling as if the would-be memory was nothing. "What does it matter? I'm here. Your silly girl won't leave you alone anymore. I'll be with you when others come and go."

The boy didn't forget for her. "Wherever There is, needs you. You don't want to look anymore but you need to. You do." His hand slipped from hers and she felt such a flood of emptiness she reached for him again, only to slide through his hand as if he were as tangible as a ghost.

"Perhaps it was to meet you," she said. "Just to meet you." They looked at one another for a long time before the boy reached for her hand, taking hold, and suddenly becoming overwhelmed with emotion, wrapping his arms around her and hugging her tightly.

Jamie slowly felt the inevitable departure coming and hugged him back, then reluctantly released him, one finger at a time. With his shoulders beneath her hands, she rubbed them up and down as if to reassure him and not herself. She was suddenly feeling overwhelmed. It wasn't farewell forever. She would do everything to return.

"Before I go back There," Jamie said, forcing a smile on her lips. "I want to make sure I left you with your friend. I don't want to leave you alone."

"My partner is never far," said the boy, wiping her fallen tear away with a soft stroke. "She always comes back." Jamie took that hand and kissed the palm, reaching to hold his shoulder again.

"As long as you're not alone . . . You're happy . . ."

The boy smiled like he had when he first saw her and any traces of gloom within her vanished. There was no need to feel like that when a boy as precious as the one in front of her smiled.

The butterfly flittered down from the heights, a humble subject to the winds, finally finding a pocket of still air to settle upon Jamie's lifted finger. Their touch elicited a spark, a firework catalyst, shocking and igniting until bolts of lightning extended from the where the butterfly touched her skin up her arm to her chest and the furthest edges of every extremity. She felt powerful. She felt . . .

Purposeful.

He cradled her cheek and looked up with ancient eyes, much older than his body made appear. "I do know you."

Everything began to blur, like water over windows obscuring the world. All that was clear was his face smiling, forever smiling at her. The mountain in the distance disappeared first, the jungle below, then the shore and the waves; everything but their sounds. She felt white light overpowering her, then from nowhere pulling her back. While she shouldn't have been able to move her arms, they came over her eyes to block the growing luminescence.

When Jamie lowered her hands, the stone cage around her drifted away. Trium's palms glowed white, only just, then softly diminished away. It was impossible for her to know if time had passed, she could only assume that it hadn't. All of the gargoyles stood where they were before. The clouds in the distance the same. All that had changed was instead of her arms by her sides, they were lifted before her face.

"What was that?" Jamie asked. She noticed her arms were lined with white dust, fading slowly. "What did you do?"

"The Turn occurred because the general could not succeed on his own. He met a force as resolute as him. This time, he has an army to stand by him. To succeed, the Partner cannot be alone."

"The Turn?" Jamie looked up from her arms. "You mean what caused the destruction of the cathedral over a century ago?"

Trium nodded. "He will be looking for you. The mark will make it easier to locate you."

Jamie struggled to believe it. "What I saw—it wasn't real? The boy . . ."

Cato stepped forward. "Everyone who moves on experiences it differently."

"Are you saying that I died?"

"A temporary death," Marius said. "One in which you simply looked through an open door. We did not send you through it."

"Branded with the mark, you will see things you thought were unnatural," Sidra said. "What comes with the storm will test what you know to be true. And few will believe you."

"Be resilient, young Jamie," Silas said, suddenly landing beside her, pointing out to the storm. "For they feed from fear. It is wily. It transforms itself as easily as you blink."

"When afraid, use our prayer," said a voice. Jamie didn't recognize the speaker, and when she turned, was in awe by the speaker. Amadrius. He stepped forward from behind the pillar, saying, "When you do not know how, use our prayer."

"Amadrius—" Jamie caught herself.

"Punctual," Dominic said with a grotesque smile.

"We have a prayer," he said, his hands curling around the pillar, his eyes drifting upward. "When we feel His Light beyond us. We say a prayer. And He listens." Amadrius walked out from below the canopy, followed closely by Jamie and the others. He turned to look at the storm, already noticeably closer, though still miles from the shoreline. It seemed restrained. Out in the ocean deep, a nest of darkness pumped, branching out like coral into the waters. Amadrius turned his head up as the others followed suit. Marius recited the first line.

"Our Father, for You are just. For You are merciful. For You are love."

Silas spoke next. "We pray that in times of need, in times of trouble, in times of marvel, and times of farewell."

"Our faith," Cato followed, "will be as strong as the power You hold in us. The Light that makes us."

"That the power that flows in us will be untempted," Amadrius exhaled. "Untouchable."

Dominic opened his wings. "As our faith and hope and love and devotion is in You."

"Through You we are unconquerable," Sidra meditated. "Unwavering."

"In You," Trium finished, "there is all. In You, is the Light."

Amadrius let the words run through him before he turned to Jamie. While it was easy enough for her to remember, she didn't see how words could do anything. She needed the assurance of something physical.

"Shouldn't I be armed with something? A weapon? Even Antonio had the chisel."

Trium extended his wings and they suddenly stiffened. "The chisel? A weapon?"

"Saying it aloud," Jamie recounted. "I'd heard mention of a weapon last year when I started having the nightmares. *Rumors on the Earth.*"

Sidra stepped forward and kneeled down, looking closely at Jamie. "Do you remember who spoke of rumors?"

"No. Only that it was mentioned. But the guy who was in robes disregarded it. That the weapon was an old wives tale."

"The rumors hold It is the Tool," Sidra said, looking at Trium with a light in her eyes.

Trium looked from Sidra down to Jamie. "The Tool. You know of it?"

Jamie nodded. "The architect of this cathedral, he was the grandson of your creator; the sculptor who made you. His descendants still live in Shore and they told me that he brought it here, and supposedly they buried it with him. Ricardo that is . . . not Antonio."

Marius' smile brightened. "It is here?"

"There is a chance," Sidra said.

"Very slim," Dominic reminded them.

"There is little time to spare," Trium said, turning to Jamie and kneeling onto one knee. "Do you know where he is buried?"

"In the cemetery by the Bilem site."

"You must retrieve it," Trium said, "and return here."

"Me?" Jamie said incredulously. "Why don't you go? No one will fight you if you have it. You're the perfect guardians for it."

"No," Trium declared. "We cannot touch what the Son has touched."

"What am I supposed to do with it? If it's even actually there. You know the *abuela* sounded kind of off."

"You must take the chance. There is something that it can destroy, and only the tool."

"What?"

"We wouldn't have told you. Not if you were unarmed. Not if you were void of faith. In the church there is a tunnel which descends deep. It reaches a portal, one that bridges Earth to the shadows."

Jamie meditated on the description for a moment and her face dropped. "You mean at the bottom of the cathedral is a gate to Hell?"

"It is a link for shadows to come, created by the Lord General who initiated the Turn. And, is the source by which your uncle suffered for months—"

"As well as one of the sources of your nightmares," added Dominic.

That caught her attention. "One? What do you mean one?"

"The Partner has kept an eye out for you. Ever since you came to us, he has carefully watched you. When your path diverged, he brought you back."

Less in anger and more in shock she said, "So you're saying the Partner who's supposed to have helped me is the one who's given me nightmares for months?"

"While his methods were fallacious, he needed to be sure you were the one: the Partner. Only they could turn the Battle in our favor."

"Wait, wait, wait—now *I'm* the Partner?"

"A Partnership constitutes of two," Cato said.

Jamie looked at him and processed something late. "The Partner—he's a shadow? He's a demon?" No one corrected her and she squeaked unintentionally. "How are you in communication with a demon?"

"We could not tell you before," Sidra said. "And we cannot explain it to you now." Her attention had been most on the fast-approaching storm as the others were on Jamie. She joined the others as she said, "The time has come. Jamie, you *must* retrieve the Tool and destroy the Gate."

"That Gateway had been swung open by an inattentive force," Cato said, "and it needs to be closed permanently. It can be destroyed, and it can be by you."

"If I hadn't mentioned the Tool, how were you expecting me to destroy the gate? Pray to it?"

None responded and the cool reserve she was holding slipped.

"Really! You actually expected me to just talk to it and hope it got destroyed."

"Power is in words. In feelings, in believing," Trium said. "Not always in the fist. There is always a way."

Jamie closed her mouth. It was true. What need was there for angels to fight? She remembered all the psalms they told her. Angels had a proclivity to praising and using their voices. Only in matters of importance did angels come to Earth and actually change things by force.

"Why couldn't you get a priest to do it or the demon you mentioned? I figure you need someone to fit down the tunnel."

"It needed to be one who changed," Trium said. "None of the others could. Their faith was certain."

"Perhaps we should have told her sooner," Silas said, eyeing the darkening sky.

Trium was reluctant to agree. "Perhaps."

"There is no time for regret," Marius said.

The gargoyles looked down at her face and how she was beginning to second guess, and Trium spoke carefully. "Jamie, think of your family."

It was too embarrassing to admit that she hadn't thought of them. She hadn't thought about all the other residents of Shore. All her panic had been for herself and yet she had to do something to help the gargoyles. To save her family. They were the only way. But after another moment she remembered Minjae, and Banafsha, and Vienna, and Penelope and all the Varanos. It had to be done for Noel and Era, Ms. Ava and even Ethan, the neighbor she knew for less than six months. It was for all the people who came before her. And for her father. His grave was here. She wouldn't see it destroyed. Even if it happened after she died, she couldn't imagine his grave being destroyed.

"That's it," Trium said. "Your center."

Jamie nodded, uncertain as to what was. "I'll do it."

"When you have found the Tool, you must be quick," Dominic said. "Once the Fallen see it, they will be quick to destroy it. It is the key to permanently closing the Gate."

"How will they try to destroy it?"

"With forces you mustn't dwell on," Marius said. "Remain clear of mind for your task. Do not become distracted. Reach the Tool as soon as you can. Once you have found it, immediately get to the Gate."

Her hands slid over her face. "I still can't believe the gate to Hell is below a church. Isn't that some form of religious irony?"

"It was there," Trium said, "long before the church."

"Rather ill judgment in location . . ." Jamie muttered.

Trium smiled, as much as a gargoyle may, measuring Jamie's eyes and holding them. "It was luck that you found him."

"Who?"

God?

"Minjae."

Jamie eyed the gargoyle's eyes. She's never mentioned Minjae to them. In fact, she hadn't had the relationship she currently had with him when she last saw them.

"We were told by a friend," Trium answered. "We knew one would come and we would help them learn what they needed to know. However, it was the change the boy made for you. We never thought we wouldn't be the only ones. To help you."

The storm was there. She needed to leave now. It was a lingering thought she didn't want to ask, always keeping silent until next time she visited the cathedral. It was the storm to the east which contested there being a next time.

"I never asked," Jamie said, treading carefully. "But my dad was a believer. He had faith and when he died—can you tell me if he . . ." The turmoil she suppressed for three years couldn't make its way out. How could she say Heaven when it was still an uncertainty to her, and Hell seemed only a dice's throw more likely. Despite the magic of the gargoyles or even the foreboding storm stretching from the shore to the horizon, she still needed something to suffice as proof. That there was really something good or bad after death. Even if they were just words by the gargoyles, at least their answer would reveal how she truly felt about them. How much she actually believed.

There was a terrifying crack in the air and the cathedral suddenly trembled below their feet. The gargoyles shook their heads and their wings rose. They looked to the ocean when another thunder clapped. The clouds undulated from the horizon to the shore at a quickening pace, racing in command by a force greater than Nature and all her power combined. The ocean's dark well unleashed a slate viscous substance toward the tempest, spewing greater volumes by each passing second.

"You must go," Trium said.

A moment later, an orb of fire crashed through the spire two feet from where they stood. And it wasn't the only one.

Over the ocean, they fell from the sky like meteors.

36

The pandemonium of clashing metal and billowing shrieks were far from what the robed creature of the fortress heard on any other day. Drums of mirth beat against the clamor of the Saplings on the plains. Weeping choruses lamented a past life as faded as the memories of an elder's childhood. Erus stood by the ledge, staring over his army with an expression, the closest to buoyancy he could muster. The time chad come and he couldn't have hoped for it to be so abrupt.

It was just recently—between an hour and week before—he had been overlooking the plains, his eyes staring into the Darkness on the horizon, searching for the source—the weak spot—where all he had to do was reach out with his hand, curl it in exactly the right spot—

"My Lord General."

Acario.

Erus hissed. He hadn't finished.

The Darkness had swallowed his arm while wisps of the beast devoured him further and further. No longer was it just his arm, it stretched up his shoulder to his neck and crept down his chest. He had been submerged in a fume of ash and metal; his throat inflamed and his veins clogged. His face had shifted from dark ochre red to a bruised purple; cups of boils bubbling from his skin—doses of poisonous sins seeking to be exhausted from the host—only to gurgle and burst. Sins of black pus emitted into the air, only to be sucked back through his mouth to be recycled. He had screamed, as he had seen the souls on the plains scream. It was lacerations, burns by flames, organic melting acid, strikes by lightning, and skin torn apart cell by cell—and it was too much. Only then, he laughed. His eyes, desperate for relief, became windows into a deeper abyss of hell than in the Darkness beast consuming him.

In an instant, a twisted power summoned him and his hand knew, without doubt, where to reach. His palms cupped a material of bark, thick enough to demand two hands to strangle it, and dug his nails in. The texture of bark was like steel as the nails reversed their penetration, digging deeper into his nail bed and out through skin. The prickling of pain only sparked his laughter to extend from beyond the screams, and his fingers squeezed further.

The bark beneath his fingers shuddered, grew rigid, then fell limp. Erus pulled the bark closer, only it was he being pulled closer to it. The distance between them had only been a body's width, but *now* he saw it. The bark to which his fingers clung onto, as if off a cliff side, encircled the neck of a baby, its eyes still unopened. It didn't cry, though its mouth was agape. It didn't attack him, though its fingers desperately clutched onto his arm. Looking in, it would seem both refused to be separated from the other.

Erus studied it, never seeing such a creature before. It was plump, ribs stretching through skin on the brink of ripping through. It had no hair. By all appearances it had to have been too young to have suffered any abuses, however marks and ridges in the skin inferred the baby had to have been as old as the Earth.

Only . . . human, thundered a voice in his head.

The voice brought Erus back to the present as his body had never suffered a moment of leniency by the beast; the eruptions on the skin's surface and below continued its looped series of torment. The manner of pain he'd seen for almost all time.

And I deserve it, Erus cackled.

His eyes dug into the deformed and quickly jerked the head up, the baby finally releasing the cry it couldn't before. The pain on his skin began to subside until it had depleted.

"M-my Lord General," said a quivering voice. Erus flashed his eyes open and turned cruelly down to the shaking figure. Italus, hunched over and his cheek to the floor, had one eye turned unnaturally up to his master.

"Eons have I suffered this crueled position. My rallying forces combined and I have learned the way to command the masterless Darkness, untaught and unprepared. On the eve of my usurpation, I take a moment to glean over my servants intel and reminisce on my deserved victory. I have no worries. No fears. No fears left for me to fear. And yet . . ." He heaved. "You call me . . . And *demand of me* . . . *Your. Obsequious. Succor!*"

The hand of Erus suddenly gripped Italus' neck. Tendrils of Darkness sunk through skin; they caused terrified eyes to burst. Italus' tongue stretched outside of his mouth as he shrieked. Italus' hands reached for him in distress.

Erus leaned close to Italus' ear, furrowing his brow and borrowing an empathetic voice. "Yes. Scream. As I have screamed." An invisible hook pulled up the corner of his lip as he suddenly dragged the pitiful creature toward the parapet, hurling him over edge of the precipice into the abyssal chasm below. As Italus cried while desperately scraping the chasm walls for hold, Erus scoffed under his breath. "Damn sycophant."

The most his strength had demanded in centuries, his chest took several breaths to regain a calmed composure. The Lord General Erus turned back to Acario, who had witnessed all with no movement, and even less impassiveness.

"The Seven," Acario said, "await *your* orders, Lord General."

"The Darkness is a product of man," Erus spoke stiffly. "So for man it shall return. Oh, I will collect in full. And more. I will return first to where it ended last. To the place of my defeat. Where I left my child, my first perfect creation."

"Aside from the Gatekeeper, the Seven know the Darkness— *most* intimately. They will know where best to strike." Acario felt his master's eyes come hard on him, however he continued. "There are places where casualties will be much higher and your victory more renowned."

A hand lifted to strike Acario, his eyes dropping a degree before unexpectedly, Erus became still. His hand slowly drifted to Acario's cheek.

"No servant has been more constant. Your counsel's given in vain, Acario. The Lord General Tier will be pending to those cities and the other portals. I don't want him to know yet. I want it to come to him in whispers. Soft. *Intimate* . . ." Erus passed the back of his fingers against Acario's cheek, before digging his nail in and slashing through. "Until I come upon him, and burst through him, and make him *remember* . . . who . . . I . . . am. Who I am to him. Who I am to that other Lord General. That I am *not* to be forgotten. That it will be *them* to sink into oblivion."

Acario lifted his eyes to the burning whites of Erus' irises.

Holding Acario's eyes, Erus lifted fine fingers over the laceration. Tendrils of mist finer than smoke were drawn to the injury and healed it.

"Am I not merciful?"

In place where there should have been softness, Erus' eyes hardened.

"I've depleted my patience. Go."

His servant bowed his head and backed away. Erus looked to the wide Gate, open and unprotected from seizure. That was the entrance to the world. No longer a one-way avenue. From there, the world would suffer. By forces of nature they would think—only by forces far crueler.

A tickling feeling stirred Erus to look at the corner of the balcony. A shadow. There a moment . . .

Then gone.

37

The flaming missiles shot down upon Foley Avenue like a volley. Jamie had to actively remind herself she needed to move forward to draw her attention away from standing fixated on the impossible. The massive storm hadn't deterred people from stepping outside to witness the chaos raining down on them. Several cars sped past her as people scattered and ran in panic. She'd been warned of the Battle and even she had to not give way to panic. She could only grind her teeth and focus on running forward. Overly focused on simply moving, she wasn't aware of a car quickly turning, inches from hitting her. The last thing she saw was the front of the car before she was suddenly yanked back and tossed like a doll.

The car's horn drifted away as she sluggishly opened her eyes. Sitting up, she felt her forehead burn and brought a hand to it. It'd been scraped, not yet bleeding. A hand came to her cheek and someone spoke in a muffled voice. Her eyes came forward to a man, kneeling in front of her, eagerly seeking her attention as he continued to mumble. Words, incomprehensible at first, until they became English.

He said her name. He uttered something further in an accent. Another language. He returned to English. "Ground yourself. Focus on my eyes."

Her eyes wandered but then obeyed the stranger, finding irises of brown. Eyes of kindness. She settled her eyes on him until she heard a crash twenty feet away as if it were right beside her. She gripped onto his arm and stood up, his arm supporting her as she moved her palm to her temple.

"Now would be a good time to start believing in the gargoyles."

She blinked hard and looked up to him, her head almost falling back. She had regained consciousness but needed to place herself; remember what she'd been doing. Trying to reach the cemetery. The stranger's words rang through her head.

"You know about the gargoyles?"

"It's started. And it's here. I've just returned from the fortress. You need to go to Trium. He will explain what is going on. You will believe him. I swear it."

Jamie took a languid step forward. "I just came from there. I need to go to the cemetery. Inside the grave—I need to find it."

"What?"

There was no reason to hide it. "Jesus' chisel."

The man turned statue. "The Tool?" He smiled. Hope. "It still exists?"

She'd heard "the Weapon" mentioned many times in her nightmares. Why was it that everyone was getting worked up about a "Tool?" Questions she'd have to ask *after* she reached the cemetery. "I have to go."

"Can you walk?"

She stood straight, releasing him. At the same time his hands dropped from her sides.

"It was shock. I'm okay now." She looked up to see how much the sky had worsened. It was as she looked up, she noticed one exceptionally large mass of fire descending toward the Earth, crashing through the transept spire into cathedral; a mini explosion suddenly bursting and lighting inside. Jamie could see the light of flickering fires through the windows. She didn't even know where to look to find the tunnel in the church—if there even was a church by the time she returned. At the top of the bell tower, a dome—an orb of light—began to expand, spreading over the canopy, then the spire, then the bell tower, then expanding over the entire cathedral. She had seen that light many times. When the gargoyles shared their stories with her. When Trium showed her through the door. They would use the power of the Light to protect the cathedral. They'd protect it until she returned.

She couldn't waste any more time. She waved for the stranger to follow. "I need an extra pair of eyes."

By the gloom of the cemetery and small clouds of smoke, the graveyard hadn't been hit hard. The currents of wind charged the storm forward. Both Jamie and the stranger approached the dilapidated entrance. The longer they ran together and the more her mind spent thinking on it, she realized the man wasn't as unfamiliar as she'd thought. She'd seen him before when she, Aiden, and Minjae went to the shuttle launch. She didn't have time to ask him how he knew about the gargoyles or what the fortress meant. All she needed was help. And judging by the good fortune of him saving her from getting crushed by a car, he would be more help than harm."

"Do you know the Gallo family?"

He squinted his eyes and lowered them toward her, having constantly been checking the skies since the moment they left Foley Avenue. "The grandson is the architect of the cathedral. He's buried here."

"So his grave—" Jamie began.

He pointed to the southeast. "His body rests in a mausoleum." He led them across the tombstones to where the structure stood, a commanding body. A St. Luke's Cathedral of Halcyon Cemetery.

Jamie put her hands behind her head to help her breathe. "How'd you know?"

"I know many secrets of Shore. Including the gargoyles. Including the family line and their *peculiarities* in society."

"But you didn't know about the chisel?"

He closed his mouth a moment. "I never said I knew them all. Now . . ." The two approached the mausoleum, a solid structure of marble with a circular walkway running around the quadrilateral tomb. Two prominent columns stood on each side of the entrance with weathered Corinthian capitals. Below the name of the tomb's inhabitant were two statues of monsters, their legs hanging over the doorway. Stationed under trees, their bodies faced each other, but their heads craned unnaturally toward the viewer.

"Is that meant to be a gargoyle?" Jamie asked. The stranger swung the lock against the door, then kicked it a flurry of times. It faithfully served its purpose as Jamie began to scan nearby for an abandoned worker's hammer or garden scissors. No scissors in sight but she spotted a shovel thrown aside on the grass. Returning with a vengeance, she smacked the shovel head against the lock twice, the chain slipping after the weight of the lock. The doors creaked as they opened, Jamie covering her mouth as she looked around the dilapidated chamber. As expected, every surface was covered in dust, and in some areas, several layers of it. Spiders had found corners to peacefully live in as they lingered out in the open, in lieu of any predators to swat them away. The four walls were covered in cubbyholes containing sundry, save for the far wall with deep impressions, holding simply a flashlight, hammer, and a bust. Taking into consideration whose tomb it was, the bust had to have been of Ricardo. She'd never heard of architects receiving such dedications and one look at his likeness, accurate or not, he could have had much more. There was more to a face than it being handsome. Something regal. Divine. While born under a family curse, God granted him striking looks so that he may succeed even with the world against him; a visionary who would contribute to one of the modern age's greatest wonders. Ricardo Gallo: immortal beyond name.

But at the center, the sepulcher dominated the room. The coffin was encased underneath its mammoth shell, and Jamie calculated for a minute before leaning against a nearby column and fixing her feet against the its edge. After commendable failure, she gathered the shovel and set it against the end, grunting as she used all the muscle strength she could exhaust, her feet sliding on the marble floor further from the sepulcher. She leaned next to the wall and pushed her feet against it again, grumbling when she made no progress.

"How . . . am . . . I . . . supposed . . . to—ahhh!" Dropping to her feet she glared at the stranger. "Aren't you going to help?"

"The family designed this on purpose. So not anyone could just take it."

Jamie regained her breath as she watched the stranger close the doors, hoping for a hint or a trigger on the back and when finding none opening them again to light the room. He went to one wall with cubbyholes, Jamie following behind, catching onto his thoughts. A hidden catch, perhaps? The two scavenged through each of the myriad of slots. The two came to the last wall, the almost empty, together.

"A lever," Jamie said. The stranger set the flashlight and hammer down after looking around them, and Jamie approached the bust. She tried knocking it back, but it wouldn't sway. Neither could she rotate or press it down. When her hands went under the mouth to open it, her hands slipped. Her thumb pushed in its right eye, and while it resisted at first, it ceded to the pressure and a puff suddenly released behind them.

No sign, but whatever kept the lock in place released, and the cover of the sepulcher slid just enough. The puff of air visibly released a combination of dust and dirt into the chamber. Excited that opening it was easier than expected, she quickly walked to the center, only to suddenly step back and cover her nose with her elbow, waving her hand and blinking up at the stranger. He squinted as the rotten stench erupted from the thin opening, waving the dust away before pushing the cover aside. Jamie held her breath helping him push it three-quarters of the way off until it fell under its own weight. There was a wooden coffin inside and the stranger already had the shovel in hand, breaking through the cover. The real division between the stench and breathable air was unleashed as the last wave of stench rose and Jamie forced herself to suppress vomiting. Wanting to get it over with, she stepped forward and began combing around the withered fabric of clothes and frail bones, doing everything she could to look away from the skull. Hollow sockets would haunt her if she gave it a chance. She patted down the pockets of his jacket, over his pants, then below his rib cage before hitting on something harder than bone. Quickly, she rushed the fabric aside and grasped the handle, bringing it out to examine it in the light.

The chisel.

Unable to look away, Jamie marveled at the object. It had to be impossible, but there was no denying it belonged to someone long ago. Further back than centuries could dictate and by someone notable beyond myth. A tool for which he crafted important furniture and unimportant toys. It had lasted all that time, to be discovered by an Italian sculptor creating the most impossible creatures in all of humankind's history. It survived the Atlantic Ocean to reach the New World and become entombed in a crypt; buried below contested legend. Until now, where it rested in the palm of a rock climbing, amaxophobic Latina.

"All this time," the man said, looking at the chisel in Jamie's hand with a mesmerized smile.

An innate feeling of possession made Jamie suddenly alarmed by the stranger's presence. She had completely trusted him because he saved her from the car, however she knew nothing of his intentions. Why would he help her with not even a single question? The fact he knew so much should have set her suspicious from the start. It was the pressure and anxiety from the world coming to its doom that she wanted nothing more than to hide the chisel from his sight and make him forget he'd seen it in the first place. The shovel set on the marble sepulcher cover only a few steps away seemed unreachable.

"I've heard of whispers of the Tool for so many years. I never thought it would end up here, of all places."

The focus in his eyes were not made by surreptitious lust, but of a historian rediscovering a long lost artifact he hadn't been searching for in the first place. Realizing that her lapse of judgment had been misplaced, she brought the hand with the chisel inching safely behind her back to her side.

Albeit a stranger, he was a harmless one.

"Who are you?"

"A friend," he said.

"A friend I don't know. And don't say mutual friends, that doesn't count."

"I *will be* a friend. You can trust me, Jamie."

"There you go again knowing more than you should. You knew my name—you said it before when I was almost hit by that car."

"The gargoyles told me long ago—"

"How do you even know about them? You're obviously not from St. Luke's. Even so, how could you speak with them? Only me and my uncle—

"Jamie"—he surrendered his hands—"I promise to answer your questions but we must return to the cathedral." He begrudgingly conceded to the inevitable with a side-long glance and tilt of his head. "If it's still there."

A stampede of thunderous clouds shook the room like a child with an ant farm. The storm wasn't coming anymore. It was there. Any last chance to safely escape would only ever be a memory. The rolls of thunder reminded Jamie of the beats of drums; ones she'd heard weeks ago. Or had it been more recently? She struggled placing when as she looked at the man beside her. His face was turning back to hers when a horrific sound ripped through the air. The stranger ran out through the entrance. With a hand clenching around the chisel, Jamie followed.

Both looked to the east, the smoke coagulating into a thick murky mass. Miles away under overcast skies, there was no mistaking the wisps of ash and embers. While the flames couldn't reach high enough to hedge over the treetops, the destructive light echoed a dreadful red and orange against the tsunami wave of smoke. The white light Jamie had seen the gargoyles cast was deep beneath the fumes. She prayed that they still were there, and it was while making her silent prayer that they first made their appearance.

They seemed to have been waiting for Jamie to be in that exact spot watching the anchor of her hometown fall into ruin. Beings that she'd seen countless times in her nightmares; beings she could see so clearly at night but became without true form once her eyes opened suddenly burst from her memories as they emerged from the poisonous fumes, twirling through the contaminated air north to the woods, west toward downtown Shore, and blood chillingly southwest to her.

There's so many.

The fear wasn't just in seeing them. The gargoyles entrusted *something* in her. They had to have taught her something in those few weeks she'd spent listening to them.

Think, please Jamie think.

In the very least, it had to have meant something she had an item they revered and believed belonged to the most famous religious figure in the world. They sent her here to get it and now she had it. Only . . . what if *they* knew too.

If not seeing the demons in the flesh was enough to be revolted, the emetic air was beginning to overwhelm her. Their oozing skin of sores and pesters long forgotten reflected the dim light. As if they had been sweating, the infected liquid slid off and fell to the ground when they extended their wings and patagia of sewn-on flesh and flapped, swerved, banked, and glided toward her. Was it her imagination or were they all coming straight for her?

No, not her. For what lay in her palm. Marius said forces would be sent to destroy it.

She wouldn't allow it, above all she wouldn't. However fear had still obtained possession over her feet and she hadn't been able to move.

"They are drunk on the human air," said the stranger beside her. It was oddly comforting at least one of them knew what was going on. His assurance released her from the invisible hold. She tumbled backwards a step while he continued watching the skies. "They might be distracted enough for us to get back. Just keep it out of sight."

"They won't know," Jamie whispered, a tear falling over her cheek. "You didn't even know. They won't know it exists."

While he'd been a comfort a moment ago, the expression masking his face begged to differ. "The Shadows are everywhere."

Opening her mouth to ask what that meant, the reason to fear manifested itself into the air before them. It was a moment of free static air until a cloud circumvented around an empty space. No breeze or flash of lightning like stage cues to lift the curtain and reveal an embodiment of tremors and foulness; he was suddenly there and that was truth. Truth—no matter how unbelievable or unrealistic—was truth, and could not be deluded. And there was the absolute certainty that a figure she feared but never imagined would be real was in fact there, not fifty feet away, floating in open air.

Fabrics of nightmares blended with reality and began to bend physics; establish its own rules. One new law was such:

A figure standing over nothing, with clothes that did not bend to the wind around them, and a strangely commanding persona that acquired immediate obedience by forces like lightning and gusts of air, was real.

And from human brown eye to supernatural black, there was no mistaking he was the reprehensible, the abhorrent robed creature.

And then the entity did something that clouded her mind's capacity to choose what to believe. The creature smiled formidably; foreboding what was to come. More dreadful than when his eyes narrowed over a tormented demon or glared into the open air at nothing, or simply glowered into the vacuous air whenever he was in a meeting with the Seven. She remembered Minjae's confession to his involvement with her dad's accident and he admitted: *You're standing in front of it for the first time and it hits you, I've never been more terrified in my life. I've never known fear before.* It was only a smile, but there was never-ending torture in it. There was the approaching destruction of a town and then a nation. Never stopping until it trounced the world populace. There would be the genocide of people, and then the extermination of the animal world, eradication of plant life. Next would be history, all the cultures bled and carved and designed into buildings, sewer systems, power lines, caves, rivers, museums, historic land sites, homes, and sidewalks. The world would be flattened to a wasteland, not even embers to live in the acrid air of death and lost memory. There would be nothing. He would only then return to where he came and continue his rampage, twisting and tearing apart all souls, millennia and seconds old. Not a moment of victory to be wasted in the hustle and drive for desolation. All of this, in a single smile.

And the robed demon knew. What she saw in his smile, he saw in her eyes. He saw everything he planned to do and not even the tip of the iceberg. Because how could a mortal possibly comprehend?

Not long after his smile stretched across his face, a horde of demons accumulated behind him as though rushing in last minute before the show started. Their raucous chants and dissonant taunts rose to a muffled roar as the stranger suddenly reached over to lightly hold onto Jamie. She thought it had been out of fear, only to find when she glanced at him from her peripheral, that it was a touch intended to move her in case something unexpectedly happened. He was already leaning just an inch in front of her. Unsure for only a moment what inspired another moment of chivalry, her attention returned to the robed creature. He had lifted a hand for the crowd behind him and they silenced.

"It's laughably absurd how easy it was," said the robed demon, in a skeptical voice so strangely human Jamie let her guard down for a moment to register that the creature from her nightmares was still the supernatural demon in front of her. A voice of a human did not make a human. "Centuries and centuries of imbalance and I smell it all within minutes of fresh air. You don't realize how clean your air is. I can smell charlatanry, fornication, avarice, and hubris all within a thousand steps. A single step outside your precious cathedral and I had already inhaled the scent of a Loyal . . ." Amusement. " . . . and one not so loyal."

Jamie wanted to respond but was unsuccessful with the delivery. What could she say? She could only stay still and hope that he couldn't read her mind. The stranger beside her didn't seem as swayed, speaking for her.

"Erus, this is a mistake."

It was odd that he narrowed his eyes on the stranger as if only then just registering him. After all, the stranger was mostly blocking Jamie from the creature; and stood half a head taller than her; and simply had a more imposing bearing than her. Erus studied her rescuer for several moments, searching for the truth in his stoic face. When the truth came to him, he didn't show it, only tilted his head just slightly.

"We meet at last."

"Again," corrected the stranger. "We've met before."

"You keep your humor when the world comes to an end." Erus' gaze was relentless. "I cannot decide if I am intrigued or impressed."

"There are many reasons to be light of heart here on Earth. Perhaps then, you would reconsider your plans . . ."

"A jester. An optimist. A fool all the same!" Erus lifted his hand to dismiss him. Wiping his hand through the air as if swatting a fly away, the gesture was meant to do more damage than it did. Which is to say, that whoever he was, the man shielding Jamie from the oncoming evil was commendably resilient. What Erus meant to do was burst the mortal flesh, explode the blood within the veins then detonate the veins up against the skin until it couldn't contain the pressure anymore, ultimately smearing the girl with tissue, metallic blood, and dust particles of bone. Instead, the skin over the left half of his face and stretching down that side to the elbow merely eroded away to reveal bone. Underneath the bone, instead of reddened muscles lay black masses of unidentifiable tissue. Jamie leaned forward instinctively when he leaned toward her at the brush of the impact, noting the organic corrosion, and flashed wide eyes up his form. He scowled in momentary discomfort as he looked back up to Erus, witnessing the skin being replenished.

Erus muttered a curse of disbelief in another language as the stranger straightened, already mostly healed. Jamie exhaled an interrogative sound as Erus collected himself again.

"All this time you've been here. Of course it was you."

Jamie darted between one staunch pair of eyes to the other, wanting to ask but knowing if she broke the illusion of her invisibility then her quest to the cathedral would be forfeit.

"The Gatekeeper cogitated vacuous theories, his favorite: the source of the imbalance being the one cast from the Pit. The one. So long ago damned into the emptiness."

The stranger lifted the corner of his lips cruelly. "Finding a new Earth was a stroke of luck."

Erus already seemed weary of their conversation. "You are of no consequence. What are you to the Generals of the Damned?"

"What are you to the Master?" the stranger rebutted. "If I'm correct it took you two millennia to create a plan and two centuries further until the Darkness returned for a second chance following your last failure. You're indebted to luck. The Darkness shouldn't have returned so soon. And Earth time is not the same as—"

Erus' eyes flashed orange as he cascaded a booming voice onto them. "No one can compare to me! No one has my strength, my forces, my might! None possess my patience!"

The stranger softened his expression. "Brother, that is a virtue as well."

One might think he'd been cursed and damned, Erus swung his arm aside again to obliterate the stranger; deteriorating all of his face, down the arms and over the legs until just above his knees. The stranger cringed and grinded his teeth as Jamie caught him, having to bring her hands beneath him to support him. Unfortunately, the act required quicker instinct and slower thought processes. The hand with the chisel came up under his armpit and around his front. Realizing her mistake, she pushed him up and tried to discreetly hide the chisel behind her before . . .

"What is that?" Erus asked, his eyes darting to Jamie. He jolted forward twenty feet in a blink as the stranger held up his arm. Erus refused to look away. "Guilt is one of the easiest to smell and mortal you reek of it. What is that in your hand?"

"Erus!" Jamie suddenly yelled.

The name registered a nostalgic feeling inside him, which is why he paused, though he continued to stare toward her hand and then glare straight into her eyes.

"You should be appalled to learn that when a soul says that, it is utterly revolting."

Jamie's brows came together as she forced baring her teeth, threatening behind a mask until she could scrounge all the last bits of courage she had within her. "He isn't going to be happy with you. Once he finds you, he will destroy you."

Erus suddenly chuckled into a fit of hysteria as he leaned back. "You are but a soul. You have no idea what he is like. What he is *really* like. But then again, you have seen me—thanks to some." He darted his eyes to the stranger beside Jamie. "Why yes!" He exclaimed as if answering a question. "The little filth gave you a look into Hell. Were you honored by that? Not many glimpse into the Pit that continue to live on this pest-infested planet."

The little filth?

"It is an honor, but not for me," Jamie said. She needed to prove to him that she wasn't afraid; let alone buy time. Though now that she was having a stand-off with him, there was even less of a chance for her to reach the cathedral. It didn't escape her notice that the demons behind him had begun to circle them, already closing the path back to the mausoleum. Jamie felt a tickle down her neck and after looking up, noticed a demon slide a twisted finger down her neck and smile disgustingly down at her. She twisted her neck back to Erus already laughing at her sudden bravado. He *smelled* all her emotions.

"You will be wise to remember that you do not hold the power here. I can end you almost too easily." Erus cast an unfortunate glance to the stranger beginning to straighten himself up again, returning his icy glare at her. "Watch your tongue."

Afraid to test him, she said nothing.

When she didn't reply, Erus chuckled suddenly again and covered his face, as if he could be modest. "I never understood how the Gatekeeper could cluck so much but for the first time, I understand!" He continued to chuckle and spurred by it, the demons echoed him in a discordant roar.

"You know it was really becoming stuffed down there," Erus continued. "If not the demons then the souls! Alas! I truly believe I will enjoy fresh air."

"Power that is not rightfully yours will not be yours for long."

"So she speaks?" Erus pulled up the corner of his lips. "I was beginning to become disappointed."

"If not the Devil, someone else will intervene. He's not going to just let you annihilate mankind."

"I am interested young soul," Erus humored her. "You lack any testimonial praising him within you, so why should I fear someone you do not even believe really exists? Even now, with the waves of hell flooding in."

The words out, she knew that she'd meant them. It was all denial before. As her grief had been denial that her father was still with her. The fact was that Erus, a creature from her nightmares, existed. So did the demons. And so will where they'd come from. The bad and the good. Which meant there was a deity up there that he feared. Who knew even creatures of the supernatural could be in denial.

Whether she'd forgiven the deity didn't matter, only that he wouldn't let everything he'd created get destroyed by someone like the robed creature.

When her faith in that knowledge strengthened, her skin began to blaze as though she were unstoppable. A shape descended from the sky and flew toward them, landing hard on the ground several paces behind Erus. He towered over everyone, even larger than the gargoyles. Hideous, and a manifested nightmare, the figure looked like none of the others. Most notably was the hideous scar running down along his jaw. He had the same horns, the same mark, the same supercilious smile. The Gatekeeper, Erus called him. Known by another name.

"Overworked yourself already, Erus?" Rephastion asked, looking at Jamie for a moment before his eyes were drawn to the man beside her. In amazement, he uttered something in another language before smiling. "I should've brought you back years ago if this was all it was going to take."

Erus looked confused as Rephastion tilted his head enough to show he was talking to him. "Why . . . I came so close as the girl and even then I didn't see. Even marked, the girl couldn't reveal him to me. Standing before him now"—Rephastion's eyes looked deliciously over the stranger's form—"I think I've never been more roused."

"Rephastion," gasped the stranger, "if this continues any longer, there won't be a way to reverse the damage."

The light in Rephastion's eyes which brightened when he said his name dimmed as he gave a perfunctory nod. "Irrevocably."

"My dear Rephastion played a pivotal part in my victory today," Erus gleamed. "Due to his following, many souls have assimilated nicely into the volley of vices you see before you. It is the least I expect of the Pit's shining knight. Alongside the Seven and the Darkness, my army and I are unstoppable."

The stranger tilted his glance over to Rephastion, smiling with the gaze of a Balinese mask.

"The Darkness does not bend to one power."

The Lord General Erus interjected. "It did to me!"

The stranger grimaced as his gaze shifted. "It isn't natural for an ant to demand of the sun."

Erus' eyes enflamed. He flew to the stranger and grasped his neck, tendrils of smoke beginning to sink into him. Jamie jerked back as she saved herself from tripping on the mausoleum's bottom step.

"You human damned Sapling! *I* am more than the sun."

No one noticed his quiet steps as Rephastion put a calmed hand over the one choking the stranger.

"Rest yourself, Erus. What is he but a Sapling?"

Resolute, the Lord General ignored the Gatekeeper. The long-held restrained anger seemed desperate to latch onto any hindrance or nuisance in his imminent victory. "If but to damn you from where you came."

"It's . . . not . . ." gasped the stranger, his hand pulling at the vice grip. Rephastion lowered his hand and sighed tiredly, almost as if the game had lost its fun.

"What?" Erus asked, his head tilted up and his lips open, prepared to swallow whatever answer he was given.

"Not . . ." The stranger's skin deteriorated the longer Erus held him, and Jamie watched as the man's skin burned away, revealing another form inside. His human skin seemed only a shell. The dark mass inside began to deteriorate as the smoke from Erus' hand pumped something ruinous inside.

Only small patches of skin remained on his body when Erus suddenly released him, letting him crumble to the floor. Erus concentrated on the hand that held the vermin; wiping away the remnants of the dissident as he said, "I'd have you witness the destruction of your precious world before I give you what you deserve."

Jamie had frozen. She didn't reach for the stranger when he expelled the smoke in a fit of coughs and gags.

"If only it were possible to condemn you a fate worse than banishment in a time where there are only two places to go. And you have already forfeited your right to one."

"There are more," said the stranger, already collecting the strength to look up. "Many more."

"Dear—" Erus' eyes lighted up suddenly as it came to him. "*Me*. Ha ha!" He began a fit of giggles as he laughed unabashedly, the army surrounding them joining him.

When he'd had his full of humor, Erus' eyes lifted to Jamie and a genuine smile became haughty. "But, oh, how could I forget? How rude of me. Human girl, what are you hiding behind in your hand?"

This is it. No more buying time.

"Nothing," Jamie lied through clenched teeth.

"Lie better," Erus instructed.

"I have nothing, Lord General Erus."

He began chortling again as he stepped forward, a demon coming behind her to place a firm paw on her back and push her forward. When Erus wrapped his hand around her neck, being within a foot of her worst fear, she lost all of her breath. It was staring into the endless black of his eye she realized . . .

"No."

"No?" Erus said through thin lips.

The expression over her face suddenly passed an understanding of peace. "There are worse things to fear."

Not what will come . . .

But what won't.

Erus smiled as if the insignificant mortal could only amuse him. "I wouldn't be so sure."

He suddenly released a volley of smoke tendrils her way as they immediately slid down his arm and over her skin, digging into her neck and crawling further to sink over her chest and shoulders and arms. They didn't burn and they didn't bite. It wasn't a sudden blanket of numbness or a fragmenting collapse of bone and muscle. As the smoke dug through her, reaching high up the neck into her mind and her eyes, she suddenly felt all of her past sins coming upon her. All her sins and the sins of her brother. Then her mother. Then Minjae. Then Banafsha. One after the other, spreading and collecting all the sins of one connection to the other as if branching from a person's interaction tree. She'd accumulated all of the sins of three thousand people, spreading from the Caribbean to South Korea to Pakistan. Then places she hadn't known people from: Morocco, South Africa, Brazil, Indonesia. When she hit India the sins suddenly rocketed and again when she hit China. England, Germany, then France. To the far-reaches of the world: Ilulissat, Tristan da Cunha, Aitutaki, between the dunes of the Sahara, and deep in the Amazon. From the melting northern ice caps to the southern polar deserts. All the sins of the world began to weigh on her and she suffocated. The asphyxiation was spreading throughout her face when Erus released her.

Sin refused to let go.

The chisel fell from her hand as she reached both to her neck. Oddly enough, Erus was easily forgetful when the thrill of agonizing was involved. Glancing at her empty hands over the tendrils, Erus was reminded why he was interested in the human. His eyes cast themselves down to the hidden object on the bed of grass. He had begun leaning down when a bright spark diverted his attention. The spark was oddly close, as if coming from the girl. And when his eyes lifted, he wasn't wrong.

They outburst sporadically—no larger than the size of a closed fist—then grew into masses that connected and overlapped until the light shined brightly underneath her skin. There was something below; obstinately fighting.

A look of disbelief crossed Erus' face. He opened his mouth to voice it when Jamie began screaming. The tendrils of smoke expelled from her body; the light wholly expunging all traces of affliction from deep within.

When the screech ended, Erus continued to stare in confusion. It refused to ebb. When Jamie looked back at him, with something in her eyes she didn't possess before when she was afraid, when she was helpless—hopeless; it enraged him more than anything to have ever happened to him. More than when Italus delivered news late. More than when he was delayed for an appointment with the Seven. More than when Rephastion said—anything. Above all, more than when he failed last . . .

The girl, the first human he came upon, and she resisted him. She had stood tall, eyes ablaze in a marvelous light, before falling over onto all fours where the cool grass caressed her hot skin, gasping. The fact remained. She had resisted him. She would be normal in minutes.

Uplifted, she had been. Triumphant.

Over him.

Impossible. He snarled and lifted both hands to deliver twice the destruction when someone yelled "Sapling" and he found himself suddenly surrounded inside a sandy cage, coiling further in to constrain him. Encased by distraction, he didn't notice a shadow slip behind the mass around him and abscond into the mausoleum, the light trailing with it. Demons suddenly untethered to provide succor for their restrained commander. By the time Erus had flung Rephastion off and cast him sailing into a copse on the edge of the cemetery, both pests were gone.

Settling in his pool of disappointment, Erus failed to sense seven incandescent lights flying in the direction of the cemetery.

Jamie couldn't process the stages her body had gone through. Utter failure, to hope, to triumph—she was suddenly catapulted from the darkness by an embracing light. It caressed her cheek, then took her shoulders, and violently gravitated her through level after level of endless darkness. There was an abrupt flash, subsequently followed by a sporadic show of sparks as concomitant as gasoline to fire. She thought she had witnessed the beginning of the universe. Not just suddenly there but a foreordained explosion. Life had to have begun with a show. A celebration. Her body wasn't celebrating the start, but the end. It would be victorious to a fiendish attack. And there would be such light. Not only for her. Those in another realm would see how victorious the warm light would be. In glee, she stared awestruck.

"We don't have time," said a voice near her; hoarse, though resolute.

She found herself back inside the mausoleum, the doors melted shut. She needed to blink several times. The metal scab which seemed to have been a result of hours of cooling had only taken moments. In her hand: the chisel. When she fell to the ground, moments before she felt hands yank her away, her fist had tightened around the wooden handle.

"There's no other way out," Jamie panted. "We're trapped."

"The Gallos were incredibly prepared."

She focused her attention on the stranger, already heading to a specific spot by the bust. He pressed in the left eye and suddenly the sepulcher gasped, sliding to the side. Jamie and the stranger pushed it as far as it could go, waving their hands to blow away the dust and calculating how far the drop went. The slams and beats upon the mausoleum walls only escalated after a momentary pause. Marble was strong against mortals, but the hellish from below possessed a strength beyond par with humans. They would come through.

Soon.

"Down there," Jamie said, unafraid. "Where does it lead?"

"Far from here." He extended his hand to her and she took it, glimpsing only once more toward the endless darkness. He released her and she landed lightly, looking up with wide eyes. He had his hand reaching across the hole to support himself, making himself comfortable. He wasn't planning on jumping down after her.

"Keep running. No matter what. Even if you look back, never stop. Always move forward."

"Are you not—"

"I'll hold them off for as long as I can," he said quickly, then uttered, "Go."

His eyes suddenly brightened into stellar white dwarves. The sepulcher closed before her and she looked down the avenue of the darkening tunnel. It was impossible to know how far it went, and with no light it would be unnavigable. Her fist clenched around the chisel as she bared her teeth and did what the stranger entrusted her to do. She sailed forward into the unknown, a hand outstretched; a blind courier into the darkness.

38

Once, Aiden had told Jamie he'd tried adding vanilla extract to his oatmeal and accidentally poured too much. Curious, he'd insisted on tasting it anyway. While the aroma filled his nostrils before he'd even lifted the spoon, as soon as the oatmeal touched his lips, vanilla tainted his mouth. He gagged and spat for a minute until the vanilla taste was gone. He avoided the flavoring ever since.

Running down the tunnel spurred the same reaction out of Jamie.

The tunnel had been undisturbed for decades, not even rats or moles to infest its corners. The taste of the earth was on her lips and in her mouth, like the smell of rain on road pavement, a soft burning odor filtered through the dead leaves and soil, encasing her in a hot, familiar embrace. The idea of blindly running somewhere that no one had visited in years haunted her. The idea of going on faith that she would find the next tunnel—the one the gargoyles mentioned—and she would be successful in destroying the gate appealed to her. The idea of not failing . . . it was almost too good for words.

Forward. That was what the stranger had told her. The task required nothing less.

She couldn't help looking over her shoulder though, her feet never giving way, and discovered just as much as she saw forward. Hearing was another matter. Whatever the stranger was doing, he was doing a good job of it. What weapon, she wondered, did he possess that could keep the offspring of hell at bay but not strong enough to destroy the gate that the gargoyles held in such high esteem? Returning forward, the bones in her wrist collided upon one another as the tunnel made an obtuse turn. Not wide, but enough that straight forward was no longer an option. She soothed the aching wrist with the hand with the chisel as she stumbled onward.

How had this tunnel never been discovered before?

Someone ought to have found it; she couldn't imagine herself being too deep underground. Her throat ached after biking across town, climbing countless steps up the bell tower, then running through neighborhoods to the cemetery. All this, and several explosive outbursts in between. The chisel in her hand popped back to mind and she knew it didn't matter.

Please, still be there.

Not long after the bend in the tunnel, she spotted a feeble light far, far into the distance. A smile spread over her lips.

At the end of the tunnel, she found the focus of the light spotlighted on a raggedy ladder. Wondering why there wasn't a ladder at the other end of the tunnel, she quickly dismissed the thought and began climbing it. The light snuck through the cracks of a wooden hatch, heavily overrun by vines and decayed foliage. Jamie bared her teeth as she pushed upward with her shoulder, the wooden hatch resisting not by a lock, but years of accumulating debris.

"Damn . . ." Jamie grunted. " . . . gravity!"

Nearly upside down, she lifted her leg from the step with the intention to kick, but didn't get so far as the level of her hip when she paused. Her eyes studied the indistinct shape of the chisel for a moment. Not thinking it possible, she slid the chisel in her back jean pocket and pressed her hands under the hatch, baring her teeth again.

"The . . . Light . . . is . . . my . . . strength . . ."

The hatch continued to resist but with one burst of force she nudged it just enough, and really pulling a strength from somewhere she'd never felt before, the hatch lid lifted, the debris sliding off.

"Holy shit that worked."

It was a sudden collapse of earth and stone far behind her that unsettled her. The voices she had temporarily escaped from had returned. She only prayed they couldn't see in the dark.

She quickly pulled herself up and flipped the hatch back down, quickly kicking a pile of mud-fused leaves over it before darting away. When she heard a booming sound from the skies, she thought it had been the demons already down the tunnel and up the ladder; too easily and too quickly caught up with her. However, in the next moment, the earth became unstable. Nearby trees cracked and lumbered over. Power lines wavered. She struggled to move forward over the shaking ground, intent on reaching her nearest neighbor.

St. Luke's.

The cathedral was easy to spot looming over the nearby forest. The ocean waves wrestled under the tempest and along with the missiles of fire striking any target below, chaos seemed to be a song too horrible to listen to. She could only hope to reach the cathedral before the demons reached the end of the tunnel.

Fortunately, the cathedral was very close.

Before the earth finished shaking, she reached the cathedral. She'd never entered from the back gardens before and chose this entrance as running to enter through the front doors a half mile away was moot. Moments from reaching the street adjacent to the cathedral, a discomforting crash exploded from the forest behind her.

Cavities scaled the sides of the bell towers. The roof over the nave and transept had mostly crumbled in. Fortunately by innovative engineering, the weight of the cathedral still held steadfast. The ingenuity of design clearly predicted a vicious unworldly attack. St. Luke's held strong.

And if a *building* could . . .

Once entering through one of the lesser entrances, she had to follow several corridors before placing herself. While familiarity immediately eased her, it diluted quickly.

"Where would you be?" she thought aloud, glancing into rooms as she ran past them. "Somewhere at the bottom," she surmised contently with a nod. "Where's the lowest level of the cathedral?"

The crypts.

It was ages ago, but she did remember the declivity of the halls when she was led to the church library.

Rounding the corner to the last hall, only steps from the library door, she bumped into Elias, his expression of disbelief overpowering her as he snatched her arm.

"You can't be here. The cathedral won't stand for much longer."

Jamie shoved his hand off and narrowed her eyes on him. "Get yourself out of here."

She had taken a step when he grasped her arm again and refused to be shoved away. "We need to evacuate! *Both* of us. I'm not leaving you behind."

The skeleton of the cathedral shook around them, high above their heads and in the walls around them. Both Elias and Jamie cast their eyes up and waited for the unnerving trembling to diminish. Jamie didn't have time and reached for her back pocket to exhibit the object. Elias examined the chisel for a heavy second before looking up with wide eyes. Jamie searched their dark depths, finding no concern for it.

He must've known what she held, how could anyone in the church *not* know about the infamous relic, yet there was no doubt in her mind that he didn't care.

"I will never be forgiven if I don't get you out."

She rose to protest when he began pulling her back the way she came. Back to the surface. Middle-aged he might be, he was a good head taller than her and had a wider girth. He continued to reiterate loudly that they must leave and there was no time to go back for anything when half way up the hall a member of the clergy came running.

"Elias is that you?" Jamie noticed the voice belonged to a friend, and through the haze, hadn't seen her yet.

The interruption caused Elias' attention to lapse. Jamie took the opportunity to yank her hand free and slip past Elias. Burly he may be, fast he wasn't.

She followed the hallway to its end. The undercroft was a wide open room spaced evenly with crypts. Jamie counted seven doors each leading to a private chapel, save one, with a DO NOT ENTER, WE'RE RENOVATING sign over it. Inside blankets and chains were cast across the floor. Above there was a window. Jamie took a moment to appreciate what her uncle endured for her in this room, then closed the door.

There were no more exits. But it had to be here. It was most logical for the lowest part of the church to be where the tunnel began. It was either here and she rushed past the entrance or it wasn't and she had to move forward.

Always move forward.

The answer wasn't here. It wasn't right. She ran back to the church.

When she came upon the library, she slammed the door shut behind her and scanned the room. The answers to her questions before had been in this room. What she needed was here. The tunnel led where no one would go; the entrance needed to be inconspicuous. There were rugs on the floor and she began flipping one after the other, finding nothing but solid ground.

"Come on!" she whimpered, raking her fingers through her hair. Her eyes fell on the bookcases. She leaned against the wall looking for an opening but it was too dark to see if they were connected to the wall. She wiggled bookcase after bookcase and from frustration kicked them on their sides when they revealed to be nothing more than humble servants to their purpose.

Standing at the back wall before the last of the bookcases, she noticed this one was closer to the wall than the others. It was the one that held the hidden diary. In her urgency to find the tunnel, she'd forgotten this was where the answers were. The bookcase was so close to the wall it almost seemed attached. She leaned against the wall and snuck her fingers behind, coming upon nothing until almost two inches in, her fingers crammed and she met a solid wall. It was all hidden in shadow, discreet and invisible. She began to shake the bookcase from the floor, as successful as if she'd been trying to shake the wall itself. The books tumbled from the shelves and she ignored when the heavy tomes landed on her toes. The shelves came out next, as the shelf in the middle remained anchor. Her hands slid over the back of the bookcase, meeting no obstruction or indication of passage. When she bent on her knees, scanning the back of the bookcase below the middle shelf, again she found no hole or sigil. Only, not in the middle. The answers were always discreet.

A mark was engraved in the corner, one she'd seen many times before. The profile of a hood, a covert wing in its fold. She whisked the chisel from her back pocket and leaned to one side, remembering by the cracking screen that her phone was in that pocket. Disgruntled by the ill-timing discovery of it, she brought her foot forward and kicked hard. The wood cracked under the force and after several thrusts, the panels caved into an empty cavity. Knowing there was something past the wall, she kicked with more fervor until there was room enough to sneak in.

By the aid of her phone's flashlight, the cave behind the wall revealed to be nothing impressive. While she could stand straight, had she been six foot, she would have needed to hunch her shoulders. The room extended out far enough for there to be another element in the space: a hatch, once opened, revealing a spiral staircase of stone and earth.

The chisel firmly in her grip, she descended.

She counted the steps at first, coming quickly upon one hundred then two. However somewhere in four hundred she stopped, as the narrow staircase suddenly overwhelmed her with a wave of claustrophobia she'd never felt before. She tried counting again but didn't make it past forty before feeling nauseated. It soon became a headache thinking about finding the end and wondering if there ever really was one. What if it had all been a trick and at the end of the tunnel was merely a wall?

When they said the tunnel went deep below the Earth, they weren't kidding.

At first the staircase wound counter-clockwise, then it seemed to turn and descend clockwise, then straight for a bit until it began a dizzying spiral again. The tunnel would play games with her. The steps would lead back up before spiraling downward again. Her palm around the chisel began sweating as she tried counting for the third time. Convoluted mind tricks flipped order, inside out, backwards and forwards, time and structure, chaos and paradise. She'd gotten as far as eighty when she came upon a fork in the tunnel.

The gargoyles never told her about a fork. They just said it was at the bottom. Both of the paths seemed much wider in comparison than the staircase well. Uncertain which was the right way, she took the left turn. She silently prayed she hadn't taken the first wrong step in a maze.

This path wasn't as criminal as the stairwell. It led straight and not for very far because after a minute of walking, she came upon an open cavern. It stretched for farther than her flashlight could reach. Less than twenty feet away from where she stood lied the docile bank of a lake. She scanned the shoreline but never found anything but chunks of rock. This wasn't where she was supposed to go.

Returning back to the fork, she took the other path and began another, although short, decline. The game finally ended when she reached the bottom.

All of her worries seemed obsolete as she flashed her light into the smaller cavern chamber and laid her eyes on the gate. The portal was grand even though it rested embedded into the sloped rock. It was made of iron with an emblem cast in the center, a fissure in the middle where the doors opened. Spirals like the ones in Norse art outlined the perimeter of the large gate and similarly around the perimeter of the emblem insignia. Closer, she found the insignia to be of a fruit resting at the base of a great tree, a snake wrapped around both, its mouth open in anguish. Holding it in its talons was a vulture, its head craning at an odd angle. When she focused on the eyes, deceptively empty holes, she noticed they were peering at her.

Ready.

Out of everything that had happened in the past hours: from witnessing the cathedral be bombarded with fiery missiles, to confronting the most frightening unheralded being in myth, to forgetting what her last encounters were with her family, she was most scared of this moment. Whatever was about to happen, the thought of it made her immobile; purloining her ability to think.

No fear, a voice soothed her.

"No fear," she repeated.

She brought the chisel up from beside her and looked it over slowly, knowing what was coming next. Because after all this, she knew it only led to one end.

She remembered the boy from the Light and used his smile to remind her what it was to be warm, strong; to remind her even now when things were hopeless, she was safe. He probably wasn't real, but she wanted him to be. And she loved him. For that brief encounter on the beach.

"We say this," Jamie repeated. "When we feel farthest from the Light." She inhaled. "Our Father, You are Just . . ."

Their words didn't taste right in her mouth though. Because they weren't human. And she could never be a gargoyle. She could only say what she knew was true.

"Whether this is for a god of mankind or for a good person. Whether this is for someone I love or a stranger. I will keep you safe. I will protect you. I'll make sure you never come to harm. I'll make sure you're never lost. I'll be here so you're never alone."

She cried. Because who could see her? Who could save her?

No one.

Aiden. Mom. Minjae.

Jamie closed her eyes.

Dad.

In one quick motion, Jamie set her hand on the relief and lifted the chisel back, striking it down onto the beak of the vulture. As if it had belonged. As if it had been the key.

On impact Jamie was tossed across the expanse of the chamber and crashed against the wall. Earth walls and cave ceiling shook, chunks falling—blocking her only exit from this black pit. There came an explosion she'd recognized from the frequent thunderstorms of central Florida. All leading her to this unmistakable fact:

She was trapped.

Her lungs gave out first. The oxygen vacuumed out quicker than she deserved. She wasn't being given enough time to cry and regret and wish. Soon, nothing would remain and she would still be there, one without last wishes.

She clutched her throat out of reflex, then slowly set it down.

All she expected of her last moments seemed to fly away from her.

In truth, when within the clutches of death, there wasn't time to wish for all the things one wanted.

All she could do was start.

She thought of her brother. How he'd become an exemplary astronaut one day. A future role model for another child who would live dazzled by the stars.

She thought of her mother, and wish she could've told her that she didn't hate her. Let her *know* she didn't hate her. Anything to go back and let the last thing said be that she didn't hate her.

She thought of Minjae, and how she wished he would move on with a heart at peace. So he wouldn't feel guilty. That he would know she loved him as a true friend.

She thought of Banafsha, wishing she could know that good people make mistakes and shouldn't be defined by them. They outshine their mistakes in other kindnesses.

Finally, her father. The one she loved most in the world. It felt right, knowing her last thoughts on Earth would be of something from happiness. There was no greater way to go than to think of the one you loved most when you were more alone than ever before.

An evening on a swing set with her father flashed across the earth sky.

Rising and falling.

She loves as much as me.

Rising and falling.

More.

Rising and falling.

Do you doubt me?

Rising and falling.

Demasiado imposible.

The cave had begun to collapse when she closed her eyes, her lungs desperately taking its last contractions for air as it found none. Her throat closed. Her body tightened, and while she couldn't feel it, her arm reached out to grab—anything. Her eyes flashed open as a final tear escaped and the ceiling lost to the weight of the earth.

Black spots. Rings of white.

Gravity pressing down.

The walls collapsing in.

And then

scorching

39

The white wisps in the air glowed, foaming away from an iridescent center. They were headed to Erus. The will to command spurred a reaction from him too late. The gargoyles dropped in front of him heavily, as if the substance they were made of resembled and behaved organically in a similar function as skin, muscles, and bone. Erus didn't need to look at all of them, just the one they surrounded. Their leader. This would only be his first test; as annoying as it may be. Erus clasped his hands behind him.

"When I crawled out of the Pit of Hell I never imagined I would have to worry about the cockroaches too." Erus tilted his head. "Well, when conquerors reflect, they don't care how many cockroaches they had to squash under their boot."

"Erus," Trium said. "It will not matter how far you wish to go. You have already lost."

"Against, who?" Erus' eyes flew over the other gargoyles. "Your army of seven?"

"We are not made of stone."

Sidra extended her wings out to the demonic shadows hovering nearer to them. Dominic lifted his arm and one wing reached high behind him as the other wing enveloped him in a cocoon. Amadrius noted the shadows reaching to hang on his arm, and with only a flare of his fangs, the shadows scattered away.

Erus huffed a bubble of disdain. "One thing I know I can always count on: human expectations. You see, in this world—in all the years of your world—the children of the Earth pray for miracles and for blessings. And only by *their* matter of science, they occur. But, Loyal

Ones, have you actually, with your own eyes"—Erus glanced into their white suns and decided it was best not to debate too much into the literal sense of the word—"witnessed a *true* miracle? Like, a woman regenerate an arm that was cut off? Or watch a child who coughs up blood live to an old age? A suicidal walk away after falling from a high-rise? For a world to witness a catastrophe like the world's end, and pray, and hope, and wish that their mighty Savior would send a multitude of hosts down to Earth to rescue them and *actually* be saved?" Erus studied Trium, immobile, and smiled.

"Not even in the Son's death," Trium said.

"Why?" Erus asked, the corner of his lips risen high into his cheek.

"Because, the Son was not fighting a force from the Pit."

"Oh!" Erus spat. "Call it Hell you sanctimonious Loyal."

Trium smiled, the kindest he could manage with his gargoyle mask. "The humans name us angels."

Erus rolled his eyes and waved his finger. "No less sanctimonious."

Behind Erus, the demons that had been fighting to get inside the mausoleum finally broke through, not expecting the fight waiting for them inside. There were small firecracker explosions as demons suddenly vanished on account of white bursts, removed from this life into another. The being inside let out antagonizing jaunts as demons flocked inside.

"However," Trium continued, "the world did not need to prepare itself against a chaos beyond their aid, beyond their understanding. The Light and the Heavens above will not merely watch you tear this world apart."

"They did nothing last time. I have no fear for what will not happen."

"We knew you would fail last time."

"And not now?" Erus smiled again. "You *do* fear me as a threat."

"Not fear," Trium exhaled. "Recognize a dog off of his leash."

"A dog?" The word was repeated in a cough as Erus' eyes enflamed, a burning amber ignited to a fervid orange.

"When the other two Generals see that you are outside of your yard and in theirs, tearing through the grass and scratching up the fences, they will attack. You will become no more a danger to them as your followers to the humans."

Erus had been growing tired of the intrusion. His hands had fisted and unclenched, then fisted and unclenched, repeatedly.

"They do not harness, do not dream to possess the power I wield."

"Your power is limiting—"

"*My power*"—Erus expanded to twice his size—"is beyond anything even your Light can persuade. You see, I *know* your Light. How it makes one feel whole and lack nothing else. But as, *an angel*," Erus said with a bitter taste, "you understand nothing about the Darkness. I will remedy your innocence."

The hand that had begun to unclench suddenly lifted, palm faced toward one of the nearby gargoyles. A swirling ribbon of shadow struck it in the upper left chest, immediately scattering tendrils of evil waste all over until the white that had begun to radiate from between the cracks instantly dimmed, then sunk below the surface until the center could no longer hold. All the gargoyles watched as Marius lifted his hands, looking down his body, uncertain as to what possessed him. Marius lifted his eyes—no longer white but matte gray—to Trium, aghast, and unprepared.

"It does not end here," Marius said, the last of the tendrils plugging in the final crack of white light. All encompassed, the Light and the Darkness within reacted against one another. At first, slowly, then it happened at once. Marius' form expanded with undulating motions, a power within wanting to escape the form it was trapped in, until it became desperate. The stone which coalesced the gargoyle shattered, multitudes upon multitudes of tiny fragments hovering in the air in a form similar to the amalgamated solid it had been before. Every eye on the dissipating gargoyle witnessed a volatile spark resist a looming darkness; watching as the spark lost its vitality. Until the darkness swallowed the seed of light. It soon exploded, and the traces of Marius floated softly as dust in the air.

Trium lifted a hand to the drifting fragments. To no avail, he brought his eyes down to Erus.

"Impressive," Erus sighed, indifferently. "You see, with mortals, there's no show." A thought occurred to him and he fiercely cast his gaze on the lead gargoyle. "I defeated a Loyal where I failed with a mortal. How?" Trium was far from accommodating.

"Lay your mark on the world, but you *will not* have them." Trium clenched his gnarled fingers as he squatted down, his wings behind him preparing to ascend.

The Lord General Erus laughed. "Again, with what army?"

"No army," Trium said. "But me." He launched himself into the air, beginning to utter words of another time, soft rivulets of white Light slipping from his mouth, down his arms and down his legs.

"And me," Sidra thundered, launching after Trium. Dominic, Cato, Silas, then Amadrius. One after the other, muttering prayer after prayer. A patois of freedom, a language of knowledge, for love, and immersed in hope. Surrounding each form, wisps and rings of light, first white, melting into other gradients of color, easing back to white.

"How fruitless," Erus uttered, lifting both arms up to the sky, spewing cascades of sin. High above, the Darkness had been waiting and in a cruel manner, formed resemblance to a distasteful mask, an unforeseen gargoyle. However, the gargoyles made no note of it. Neither did they make note of the demons surrounding them, flying to them and reaching past the rings to them, ultimately failing and being flung away. And neither they, nor Erus, noted how Rephastion gathered himself up to run and intercept the direct path of the dark waves, becoming struck with the force of waterfalls on stone.

He collapsed, his body shaking as he collected his arms and hands inwardly. Erus lowered his arms and looked down the Gatekeeper, a wave of disappointment passing over his face as he knelt to one knee.

"You were never more powerful than your Master," Erus said, allowing a disgusted gaze over Rephastion's body. "And now I am its Master." He pursed his lips and clicked his tongue. "You never can trust a traitor. Such fun we will have when we return."

Erus rose, the hem of his robes stretching out to blanket over the colossal demon. Rephastion spat at Erus, or perhaps the tendrils of Darkness snaking up his body. Snapping his maw at one, the tendril sprouted another, thicker and more tenacious. Rephastion snapped wildly until he began giggling at the contest. Laughing and laughing, until all Erus could hear was the Gatekeeper's blithe hysteria.

Leaving the wriggling and tortured demon behind, he returned his attention to the gargoyles, who were now collecting a substantial amount of white brilliance, tempting too close to outdoing the dark atmosphere around them. Almost as if creating their own sun; one of warmth, and safety, where strength could be pulled from.

"There is no power that can defeat mine." He gritted his teeth as he lifted his hands out again, sending large bands of Darkness out into the sky. Once the ribbons found the Darkness in the clouds, it shook the air, causing a massive wave to suddenly ripple down to the earth, shaking older buildings and causing them to dislodge and collapse while the robust newer buildings stood a chance, only severe cracks fissured in their frames and foundations. Trees bent. A spine-curling snap and eucalyptus and slash pines fell like dominoes, only oak trees enduring a significant breach in their trunks. The roads crumbled with sinkholes and crevices captured unfortunate passersby in depressions as deep as fifty feet.

People were at a loss as roads were now unsafe to drive on. The demons had not been enough, now their earth had turned on them, making any potential refuge a risky venture. They couldn't stay in a single place as the ground might concave below them. Crevices and deserted vehicles formed barriers between a field of abandoned corpses. Outside of the cemetery, demons had been having their long-awaited fun as Erus and the gargoyles remained in conference. They would ravage a face, digging their fingers into the eyes or the mouth, or through the ears and nose, or simply disengage an extremity from the body, then abandon the soul to deal with their newfound panic on their own. Others were less violent, indulging in inspiring fear and chasing souls down the roads. They sneered and they laughed and they sang while they havocked, shadow into and through air, discovering tunnels through space and breaking physics laws.

Cato was the first of the gargoyles to desist praying, suddenly flicking his wings at approaching demons, slicing through their shadowed forms and expelling them from this life. He collected tufts of white light from the ring that connected each gargoyle to one another and flew through the crowds of shadows. As he whisked his arm, the light in his hands formed medieval weapons. He flung a double headed battle axe through a demon lunging toward a fleeing Shorian.

Next, Dominic dislodged from the white ring, instantly dispatching the nearest demons. As the servants of the Lord General fell, they cried and pierced shrieking waves through the air until their cries were all that remained; first shrill, and then faded into the air as a dissipating ringing. Dominic chortled, collecting weapons of his own from the light and charging into the battle.

Sidra followed suit, followed closely by Silas, as they linked a tether of light between them and used their connection to glide and eradicate the demons that passed between them. Severing the tether, the two gargoyles launched away and began to pummel through the ranks, then fight to obstruct any demons from reaching Trium and Amadrius. Sidra barked just as loudly and snapped just as detrimentally as the demons that outranked her in brutality.

When she turned to the side and cheered as her brothers continued demolishing the army, her will remained steadfast when a peculiarly deformed demon, half the size of most others, suddenly latched itself onto Silas and implanted a suckling Dark bug onto his neck. It happened much quicker than it had with Marius, as his eyes simply matted stone gray before he turned his head skyward, releasing a final breath and solidifying immobile before the Darkness dispensed of the spark within. The gargoyle became fragments of dust in the polluted air within seconds. Sidra roared before forthwith overtaking the responsible demon, obliterating him into nothing and inflicting vengeance on the unfortunates nearby.

Trium turned away from another fallen brother down below as he looked across the ring to Amadrius. Both of the gargoyles' wings flapped unwavering, knowing they were protected by the other gargoyles. Cato and Dominic had stretched the outer limits of their dome of protection to beyond the cemetery, across the street into the nearest neighborhood where frightened children and disbelieving parents stared petrified. One father brought arms of iron around his young children and covered their eyes, though they had gripped his hand to look up anyways. At another house, a mother clasped onto her grown son as he failed to lead her away. Down the street, panicked teenagers and adults slowly ran, as if hindered by their nightmares of real. Behind closed curtains, an elderly couple grasped onto each other on their living room couch, the third they'd owned since they purchased the house forty years ago. The roof which had never failed them from hurricanes to Florida thunderstorms, now shook unsteadily from the explosions above and the earthquakes below.

The ribbons stretched from Erus' hands and reached at its thickest a width of a sewer pipeline. Although instead of sewage, the black muck of smoke drained out into the cloud of Darkness, recycling the matter into a dark murk that returned down the ribbon back up Erus' arms and neck and into his mouth. Erus swallowed the matter, seemingly choking him, until the matter filled him. His eyes cooled from flaming orange to glossy black. His arms dropped down to his sides and he breathed heavily. His eyes sharply twisted around toward the mausoleum door.

"Where is the girl!" he roared in a voice not his own.

One of the demons, not expecting the attention, cowered against the mausoleum, bringing up one distorted arm to shield his gaze.

"The tunnel leads to the cathedral."

"Well?"

"L-l-lord General . . ."

"Has the cathedral been destroyed yet?"

"W-w-we aren't sure what she has is the Weapon."

"She will have sought safe haven in the cathedral. If there's no cathedral . . ." Erus dismissed him as the demon lingered.

"There—there will be no girl!" Desperate to please his master, the demon twisted his face into a grotesque smile. Erus turned back to him.

"Then go. Or there will be no you."

Like an abused animal, he scampered off as soon as he was released from Erus' gaze. Away from the demon, Erus was reminded of Rephastion and caught his eye. Rephastion's spasms softened. He drew his eyes upward.

"Do not look at me like that," Erus said.

"My Master never lingers for long. You will not possess a tenacious grasp on It. You know this."

He drew his upper lip back and snarled. "I wanted you to witness it. My victory. But I no longer have any need of you." Erus gripped the Gatekeeper's neck and lifted him, emitting Dark tendrils to choke him high enough until he held the colossal demon at twice his height. Rephastion's feet were forty feet above the ground, his slouched form an arm's length from Erus as the Lord General leaned forward, whispering, "You can wait for me back in the gutters of home."

Erus scowled as his attention was drawn behind the Gatekeeper, high in the sky where one of the two gargoyles in the ring departed. It was the fierce one, the grotesque. He snarled and roared into the sky before spinning, spreading bits of white frost and sparks off his wings, arms, and legs. When he stopped, he withdrew a whip for each hand, cracking the air with each flick of the wrist. He lifted one arm and charged into the folds of Darkness, bringing down two shadows to every one the others brought down. While Sidra was the fiercest, there was a natural catastrophic fury to this grotesque's mission.

"They are only seven and you fear them," Rephastion chuckled, then wheezed as Erus squeezed tighter. "Imagine the force of Heavens. They are only the emissaries. But then there is Tier's army. And Paxiphen's." Erus said nothing, only quickly looking between one eye to the other. Rephastion's eyes widened to its borders. "You don't truly believe that even my Master can withstand all those forces."

"You still haven't learned. So be it, my Gatekeeper. Sit down. And *watch*." Erus swirled a tether around his neck and flung him down, tightening it so that Rephastion was forced to look above. "I'll obliterate them so you will see. With the Darkness at my disposal."

A roaring shook within Rephastion's ears, the sound swelling to break past his shell. His horns bent in pain. He drew his fingers across his face and screamed. Jagged lines sunk through his skin. Welts appeared near the red lacerations. Erus heard the roar too, however ignored it with a twitch of his neck. He returned his focus to the sky, where the final gargoyle finally finished his prayer. He opened his eyes and looked around him for them. The other four.

Sidra had landed on the ground and was digging her wings into the Earth, using them as stilts as she swirled and kicked through the shadows cussing and provoking her. Amadrius was leaping backwards off a smaller mausoleum on the far side of the cemetery and flew up before spinning, forming a white enveloped bullet through the shadow multitudes, the whips extending past his wings and stringing behind like tentacles of a jellyfish. Dominic was strenuously flapping his wings as he ascended up, staring down to the Earth, using his wings as a weapon before bringing his forearms together then suddenly opening them to release a wave of white Light. Cato was the furthest away, implementing his medieval weapons, flinging one to the enemy before summoning another from the infinite supply of light on his arms.

Cato bounded over roofs, hurling shields between frightened humans and hungry shadows. From above Dominic spotted Cato and flew forward, sending a white wave upon a demon preparing to lunge against the unsuspecting Cato. Sidra heard a man's screams, her wings beating like as she soared through the torturous demon. Amadrius pulled from the Light on his arms, growing, extending, snapping and slicing through a giggling demon preying on a pair of twin girls separated from their mother in the chaos. Amadrius scooped the two girls in his arms as his wings shielded them, expansive gray filmed and textured in Light, averting two missiles of mayhem, screeching at the touch of Light and being cast away into the sphere.

When Trium separated from the ring of light, the others drew back to him. He had said nothing. They knew.

Erus soared up until he faced Trium, staring him down as the four gargoyles came beside him. When they assembled their ranks, Trium and his four against Erus and his forces of shadows, they looked hopelessly unbalanced. Erus would crush the gargoyles with only just the right amount of force. However, there was just a small part of him, all that he would deny, of trepidation. Of still feeling he was about to fail.

"No," Erus said with a quick shake of his head. "Not this time."

Trium's jaw parted as he studied Erus. "You have never been alone."

Erus laughed and those behind him joined in. Trium continued to look with peace in his eyes. "Even if we fall. Even if you succeed, you will be no less lonely. Until you accept. Until you turn from the way you have gone."

"You'll have better luck bringing back that girl's father."

Trium nodded, looking to Cato and Dominic on his left, then to Sidra and Amadrius on his right. Trium found Erus' eyes. "At least . . . he is safe from you."

The Lord General scoffed, exhaling sharply through his nose before lifting his hands. "Enough."

The hordes of Darkness charged first. The messengers of the Light flew forward. At first the statues glowing in white disappeared in the fog of shadows, soon shining through. At the darkest of the evening, the light had shone; far more radiant than the afternoon sun, far richer than a summer sunset, far worthier than the lights in the gargoyles' eyes.

Each shadow struck down was replenished by twice its placeholder, multiplying like parasites. The gargoyles did not waver. They continued to expand their light.

The first to fall was Cato. A giant shadow had wrapped its arms around the gargoyle, encasing him in a Darkness that only layered itself thicker and thicker until it had laid the appropriate damage. He fell from a soaring height, though before reaching the ground, a flash ignited. The light slowly ebbed before succumbing completely. The shadow responsible jumped off of his host of dust and swerved before reaching the ground in search of new prey.

Dominic stopped a nefarious missile aimed at Amadrius from the Darkness, but was ambushed by a multitude of shadows, never standing a chance.

Sidra was next, though she relinquished her place in the fight valiantly as a parasitic flurry rushed upon her.

Trium found Amadrius as his final comrade and flew to help him.

Trium gripped tightly onto a shadow planning to latch itself onto the grotesque gargoyle's back and hurled it. Amadrius smiled at Trium, noticing two shadows intending to ambush the nescient Trium. He spun and cast one of his whips across them, obliterating them from the battlefield. Unfortunately for the gargoyles, who could only focus on so many at a time, were negligent to notice the others. They clasped onto Amadrius and brought him down. He thrashed as they fell thousands of feet. Trium chased after Amadrius, slashing at the shadows. He destroyed two and they were replaced.

Too late.

Only when feet from the ground did Trium pull up, softly landing with the dust of Amadrius lifting around Trium's face, blanketing him with final farewell.

The lone gargoyle closed his eyes and bowed his head. The shadows had begun whirling in toward him, but were blocked by a film of light encasing Trium's form. The last gargoyle prayed silently as the wind blew away the final traces of Amadrius. Trium opened his eyes and looked forward to Rephastion, several feet from the white film boundary.

"You are restrained," Trium said softly. "Why?"

Rephastion, a floating head above an undulating mass of empty Darkness, kept his face serious, the longest he'd ever been before. "I protected the balance."

Trium nodded, needing no further explanation, then cast his face skyward, looking past the dim shadows to where the ring of light still radiated exquisitely.

"I've bought time. All that I could pray for."

Rephastion stretched the Darkness from him as far as he could manage, breathing in once, exhaling, "It does not end here."

Trium looked back to Rephastion and smiled kindly, nodding once. "So not."

The film of light dissipated and the shadows charged.

"Father," Trium said, so softly Rephastion couldn't have heard from three strides away. Trium closed his eyes and lifted his arms.

Rephastion watched the gargoyle become swallowed in darkness. Slender trickles of light escaped through the wispy smoke until it collapsed and dimmed. When the shadows abandoned their quarry like predators, they left the bones behind. Trium's outer shell had ruptured and the fragments of stone that remained softened in the light of the darkening day. A sphere of Darkness gnawed at the orb of Light and while the white flashed and thrashed out, the Darkness continued to prevail. Eventually, the orb became too small. The spark within him vanished. Once the energy had gone, the fragments of stone withered away in a breeze, floating over to land on Rephastion's face. He inhaled the essence of the statue.

Erus rejoiced when he observed the devastation. Finally devoid of hindrances, he cast his eyes toward the city center. Forgetting the restrained Gatekeeper, he soared through the sky to the fleeing mortals. He imploded one after another, again and again, then left the advancements of his war to the soldiers. He enjoyed the view. Watching was pleasure enough.

He wanted to see more. Own more. Dominate everything he saw. Everything he couldn't. So he rose higher. He pushed the Darkness back with an intense glare and examined the destruction below. The cathedral, by far the largest structure in the horizon had collapsed within, and Erus felt especially proud of that accomplishment. If something so great could fall, the mortals below would truly fear him.

Not only in this pathetic town which in another time had conquered him. Beyond. Further. Further. Farther than he could grasp. To every end of this detested planet until he arrived where he started. The metropolises. Take them all. Peel them, strip them, smote them, consume them. Leave nothing but dust. Dust! Not even the wind! Nothing would exist unless he deemed it. Not air. Not memory. Not light.

Victory belonged to him.

No one could look down on him.

After all this time.

Down below, the ring of light that had continued rotating slowly and expanding outward suddenly flickered. Erus ignored it at first, but it flickered again. A glittering pool began to fill within the boundary. Now that caught his attention. His eyes narrowed.

One after another, iridescent forms of Light poured out from the pool inside the ring. At first it was one at a time, until they began lurching out at a rapid pace. One hundred quickly became a thousand in a matter of seconds.

Erus chuckled as he began muttering under his breath. Commanding. And the Darkness obeyed. Turbulent bands of smoke from the Darkness cloud swirled around to form a tornado, arcing out toward the ring and expelling more shadows.

The forms of Light resembled humans in gigantic measure, as they bore small tusks from their jaws, tails in singles and pairs, arms from two to eight, and anatomical feet like the planet's ostrich. There were beings with wings and those with patagia between arms and the sides of the body. There were beings with beautiful faces and others with grotesque masks. Some aged in warfare and other small like children. Some looked no different than mortal humans on the planet.

All mighty.

All resolute.

Erus had begun smiling, knowing the army of Heaven could not stop him, when his attention was drawn away again by a nudging stir. Familiar, though long forgotten. He hadn't felt this way in eons. He knew who it was and scowled. It didn't matter who came and whoever was against him. He had the Darkness in his grasp. It could defeat them all.

It was a great shadow, not Sapling, not Loyal—just like Erus. A shadow which controlled a mighty force. A shadow who only responded to a selected few. The shadow formed a dark portal of his own into the air though it was not nearly as daunting as his Darkness. The thought tickled Erus.

His Darkness.

"Tier," Erus said, stirring a weak smile onto his face. "Welcome."

"You bastard!" Tier spat, tempted to lunge into him, though keeping a tolerable distance. While enraged, he was not amiss to noticing the Darkness above them.

"Why, it has been years my brother. What has changed in the past two centuries?"

"You behave no differently than a mortal baby," Tier barked. "No one gives you attention and you throw a fit, hollering until someone gives you a pacifier."

"Well, while you have been having your fun down on Earth, I have refused to sit idly."

"Your job demands more than sitting idly."

"Well, there it is, my brother Tier. I tire of work. I think I have earned time off."

Tier's gaze lifted to the Darkness as he rested his hands on his hips. "Is that all you have?" His eyes settled back on Erus. "You're a fool. The Darkness cannot be contained. It has no master. And not for the Grand Master's lack of trying."

"It is fickle," Erus dismissed. "However, I know its weak spot."

Tier gazed intensely into Erus' eyes, seeking until he found. "How suitable, a baby crying on its own latches onto another baby left abandoned. Your tantrums tire me."

"You always were my preferred. Whenever you wish to switch jobs I will only be so happy. But wait"—Erus burst in a fit of laughs—"I'm now the one on top. Enjoy the bottom of the barrel, brother. Maybe I'll ask again in a couple thousand years."

The Lord General Tier cast his gaze down to the beings of Light and scowled, narrowing his eyes back to Erus. "Do not force me to side with them brother."

"You appall me."

"End this now, Erus."

Erus considered it for half a moment with a cruel smile. "No."

"Very well," Tier said, slipping back through his portal and collapsing it to nothing.

The brief visit and sudden departure stung Erus for a moment before he remembered the role of a ruler was meant to be taken alone. He wouldn't be with anyone, not even his brothers, at the top.

But after another thought, he preferred it that way. Everyone beneath him.

A portal opened down below, far from the ring of light, but a friendly distance from the cemetery. Erus witnessed as Tier emerged first, followed closely by his force of shadows. Not like Erus'. There was uniformity uncharacteristic of shadows from the Pit. Shadows from Tier's forces were always scattered, placed in one area of the planet then suddenly whisked across the world. Erus' own army was always together. Always with souls. However for the most part, they only ever encountered other demons. It was forbidden for demons to be seen. Only tempt. The crevices on Erus' face deepened as he witnessed demon and angel fight against his shadows. And the angels never confused which shadow to attack. The slim chance of accidental attacks never came. While he refused to worry, even now, he watched solemnly.

The three armies fought one another and with one another for a time before Erus felt a tingle up his arms and down his spine. The only time he ever felt that tingle was with two others: the Grand Master, the rare times he visited Erus in his fortress; and with Paxiphen.

No, Erus assured himself. No matter what may come, he need not fear.

Far ahead of him into the distance, where the Darkness breached the horizon line, another portal opened. It flickered with static as larger shadows spilled out from the curving edges. When Erus caught sight of his eldest brother, who immediately sought the source of his trouble, he froze.

Out of habit, he assured himself. While the Lord General Paxiphen was a great space away, Erus could hear his brother incriminating rebukes.

"You called me down here," Paxiphen called, pointing a finger at Erus. "This isn't where I belong you—" Paxiphen began cursing from a roster of abuses. Erus clouded his voice, then watched as another army joined the battle.

How the tables have turned, Erus snickered sardonically. *Armies meant to fight one another now fight me. Damn them all. I am the embodiment of power.*

The culmination of armies stacked on one another until those on the ground began to lose sight of the Darkness cloud high above. Layers of ash and embers stacked over the soil. The blasts from rifles and pistols had paused as the people crowded together to watch the end times. The demons were too preoccupied to notice them and avenue after avenue, from the gardens to the roofs of unstable houses, the people of Shore watched an indescribable battle.

The forces of the Light weren't replenishing fast enough, and when the armies under the commands of the Lord Generals Tier and Paxiphen depleted, they were whisked away too far to return forthwith. However, his children, his beautiful Saplings and slaves of the Darkness only continued to grow. Only broaden and breed until there were three to every one of the enemy.

He smiled. Victory.

At last.

The moment was more glorious than he ever imagined it could be. All it should be. It shouldn't be this filling. He had been empty for so long, he had forgotten what it was like to be filled with such elation, such purpose, such fulfillment. Arms rose in victory, transformed to shape ink wings of a vulture.

A tear slid down his brightened face and fell. Down hundreds and thousands of feet to the ocean below where it joined the countless drops of water. What if every drop of the ocean was a tear from every human that had lived? One drop for every human.

Oh no, had he now joined their ranks? Was he now one of the filth?

The drop had dissipated among the water droplets before a baby's wail erupted from the Darkness. A violence jerked within him, then another, one dragging his center down. The hold he had on the Darkness weakened. All that filled him moments ago had begun to seep out. Drain him swiftly and tirelessly.

No. He half pleaded, half withheld.

Erus fell, thrashing into the air, desperately seeking a proffered hand.

There was none, which is why in the wide gap of free air between him and the ground, he wept.

40

Stepping backwards, through the synapses of memories and journeys over horizon bound to horizon bound, through jeers, a chorus of ridicule and despondency, beyond avarice and ease with the strength and fortitude of conviction woven into the fabric of a soul before nurture and nature and genesis, where empty eyes howl groaning weeps crowd a wandering Question before the rusted archway of eternity, guardless, vulnerable, a crown without a head. Time is here. Time was now. Existence's measure broken from its frame to foil and explode until a burden is a burden is a burden, doom's Sisyphean joke, where strangers and soulmates wear the same mask. Nothing is familiar. Nothing is alive. There is what is. A Never-End. The crippling darkness.

Pain.

Pain

Pain

41

Thirteen nights to the hour since the end of the world. That's what it had been. What other explanation was there for creatures of light and creatures of darkness to exist in reality? There were plenty of apocalyptic dooms in religions. Who ever thought they would hit that prophecy out of the park?

Aiden pressed his fingers lightly against the eyepiece and dipped his head slightly, looking at the lights once so bright, now dim. He wanted to know what had happened to the stars. They used to burn. After the end of the world, something had made them lose their luminosity. He needed an explanation. At least for the stars. If not for something else.

There had been no word of Jamie for thirteen days. Unlike most others, her body was never accounted for. All he knew was that she was last seen in the cathedral. One of the priests had tried to lead her out, but she refused and slipped his grasp, disappearing into the smoke before the walls caved into the hall. He was blocked from pursing her. There was so much smoke and with the unstable structure, the clergy had no choice but to evacuate immediately.

He didn't blame them. He understood. That day was the epitome of chaos. People weren't people. They'd become frenzied. He often wondered how and why he handled that day so well. He wondered if he was odd. If he was inhuman for his calm at seeing corpses in the street and some missing limbs or eyes or tongues.

The night sky suddenly blurred as he felt his nose burn, and a tear appeared on the glass. He gripped the eyepiece tightly as he rested his forehead against it, baring his teeth as he kept imminent tears back.

Watching the world end, he was calm. Watching as people disregarded others, he was calm. However now, reflecting on yet another family member, the closest he had bonded with now taken from him too, he couldn't contain himself. He was overrun by grief. He couldn't reach acceptance because her body was never found.

To fight his grief, he forced himself to wonder why it was so important that her body be at the funeral the next day. She was dead. Had she been alive, she would have returned by now. Unquestionably. There was no real reason why her body needed to be there. He and his mother would put her spirit to rest, with no less love and no less memory.

All the same, he needed a body. He needed some form of his sister to say goodbye to.

He straightened his back and wiped away the tears, looking back into the eyepiece. It still had the teardrop stained on it. He lifted the corner of his shirt and wiped it clean, looking through it again.

The night sky was clearer than ever, perfect weather to stargaze. The celestials were still dim. He needed an answer as to why. He wouldn't get one for his sister, so he needed one for the stars.

A slow-moving crescent entered the boundary of the focusing screen. Aiden stared for several moments before leaning back to see it in the sky. It was too far for the naked eye, so he used the eyepiece again.

A meteoroid, because if it had passed the Earth's atmosphere it would have burned, trailing a tail behind. However, it was too slow and too small. What other name could he give? How was he able to see it at this distance? It shone brighter than the stars in the background, and despite its existence, he marveled and monitored its sluggish—though intrepid—movement. After recording four time measures, he noted that the meteoroid took two minutes to reach the boundary of the circumference from one end to the other.

And it was subtle, since he stared at the light for over fifteen minutes straight, but it was definitely *growing*.

Coming closer.

Little by little he adjusted the angle of the telescope, more frequently over time, until nearly twenty minutes later, the white meteoroid began to pulsate and stretch. It had reached the Earth's atmosphere, though still moved slowly. No meteor he'd heard of lasted this long.

He looked up with his eyes again and spotted it. It stretched longer and the head of the meteor was as big as his thumb. It moved faster, suddenly weaving until it shifted from a slowly moving light in the horizon to a racing shooting star, catapulted across the flat night plane like a ball of fire; not unlike the ones he witnessed thirteen nights ago.

The tail behind the meteor stretched as wide from his pinky to his thumb. Not moments later, were he to have blinked, he would have missed another faint streak across the sky, trailing the glorious celestial. Wishing he could chase down the cosmic debris, he kept an eye out for any more stragglers. After being met with none for a long while, he bent down to the eyepiece again, trying to fill in a little more stargazing time before he went to bed and faced the hardest day of his life.

42

Rain. Like afternoon showers during the summer.

Waves beating against rocks. Like the ones on the rock pier near the southern curb of the beach.

Plus she was sweating.

Definitely Florida.

Jamie opened her eyes. Heavenly cushions below. Walls of beige. A fan clicked lightly against the rhythm of the palm leaf blades. The cherry-beamed vaulted ceiling matched the corresponding armoire and chairs. Filling in empty wall space were simply-sketched frames of local palm trees.

Last night was the hardest she'd slept in months. The best part was waking up, not remembering if she'd dreamt anything. Nothing good and nothing bad. When she sat up, her head wasn't heavy anymore.

A pulsing burn itched up her leg. When she flipped the blanket cover, there was a smeared handprint mark over her calf. Tenderly running her hand over it, the sting began to recede.

The French doors opened to the ocean not a far walk from the bedroom. Undeniably certain before, the view made her second guess herself. The water was clearer than Florida waters and the beach was cleaner.

This wasn't Shore.

There was a man on the beach, ambling along the sands with his face forward, not concentrating on anything. While she didn't want to bother a man in his reverie, she wasn't sure where she was or how she got there. Stepping from red Mexican tiles onto the scorching white sand, Jamie caught up to the stroller, smiling as the man turned to look at her.

He wasn't a stranger . . . He was the man who helped her in the cemetery. The man she'd met at the space launch.

"You."

His kind eyes were as she remembered. A feeling in her gut said that while she'd just woken up, a long time had passed since she'd last seen him. He looked the same, dark skin with dark hair and dark eyes. No, his eyes weren't dark before; they shone more white than light.

"Refreshed?"

Jamie nodded, using a hair band to hold back loose strands of hair from her face.

"You survived," she said incredulously. "I thought when you stayed behind you'd never make it out alive."

The disbelief mixed with concern humored him, stirring a smile to his lips. "What's more is the fact you survived. You were very deep, at the bottom of the tunnel."

Jamie knew if the cemetery and the tunnel to the church had been real, so had the tunnel below the church. However, that part of her memory, it seemed more up to grabs. Optional, more than true.

"How did I get out?"

The stranger squinted as the sun peeked out from a hefty Cumulus cloud, drifting his gaze toward the water. Jamie stepped beside him and looked over the ocean, mesmerized by the water at the shore, shifting slowly from light to dark as the shallow waters descended further and further. She hadn't seen water so clear since she'd visited Icacos Island near the northwestern shores of Puerto Rico.

"We're not in Florida. Where are we?" Jamie turned to him, her hands on her hips. "Who are you? What's your name?"

The stranger smiled kindly, turning to her. "Gerus."

Jamie proffered a hand. "Thank you for helping me Gerus."

He took it. "I haven't met more than ten people like you." When he noticed that she wanted him to elaborate, he obliged. "It's easy to do something when it's in the service of a friend, or part of your faith, but when you act against forces that contest with your beliefs, that's another type of selflessness. Not verily seen."

Jamie withdrew her hand. "I did what anyone would've done. Anyone at all."

"Anyone would have run home. Run back to their family. And from my understanding, you love your family. More than everyone, you love your brother."

She hadn't though. She was so caught up on doing what the gargoyles had asked she hadn't remembered her brother and mother

until she was in the cemetery. It was already too late for her to turn
back by then. Selflessness he called it. She knew it as negligence.

"Even traitors believe in something. Money or power. But you
thought there was nothing for you beyond what they asked. In fact,
absolutely nothing at all."

Jamie bit the inside of her bottom lip, sinking down to sit on
the sand, the high afternoon sun quickly blanketing her with warmth. It
wasn't that she disregarded a potential demise, only that it never
occurred to her. She hadn't spoken to the gargoyles in months, how
could she have expected what they were to ask of her? They hadn't even
known it would come to that since she was the one who brought news
of the chisel. If she hadn't told them, they would have never told her to
go down the tunnel. Never asked her to use it, *hoping* it could be an
effective weapon. Her hand strayed over the burn mark on her leg.

The coastal winds thrust striking showers of sand on them as
Gerus leaned down to sit beside her, folding his arms around his legs.

"Where are we?" she asked again. Gerus tilted his face to her,
however she continued. "I've seen Hell—even been there a couple
times. I've seen Heaven. Is this Purgatory?" The corner of Gerus' lips
lifted as Jamie exhaled, stretching her arms up to the sun and examining
them. "It won't take me long to get dark. Is there night in Purgatory?"

"You're very much on Earth. We're on one of the Canary
Islands."

"Refresh my memory. Ask Noel usually my geography's fine
but those islands are . . ."

"Off the western coast of Africa."

Jamie dismissed it with a nod, before really looking around
her. Back toward the way she came, there were no tall buildings, and
following the beach both ways, there were no people and no trash bins
or benches. She could be on any beach, whether the Atlantic, the
Pacific, or the Indian.

"How the hell did I get to west Africa!" Jamie turned to him.
Gerus pursed his lips, scratching his nose.

"Jamie, can you tell me what you remember before you slept?"

"Will you tell me what happened after?" Gerus nodded and
Jamie crossed her legs, leaning back. The scorch mark stole her
attention from the paradise. "Most of it I can't remember. I went down
the tunnel, found a fork, reached the bottom. Found the cave. I
destroyed the gate. At least I think I did."

She paused and Gerus didn't speak until he noticed her
struggling to remember past that, pressing her palms to her temples.
"You did destroy it. You didn't know—neither any of us. The Gate was
linked to Erus. His creation from his failure. We call it the Turn. He

sacrificed some of his power building the Gate. He used it to bring all of his forces here. When you destroyed it, it destroyed him."

Jamie was still pressing her temples. "I can't—I can't remember."

She destroyed the gate then it became black. Almost as soon as she brought the gate down everything in her world became nothing at all. Except. No that wasn't right. Her eyes were drawn back to the handprint. After everything became black, there was a pocket of something. A sizzling sound. An intense burn. It continued to escape her grasp whenever she reached for the memory.

"In the cave," Gerus continued for her. "You did what you had to. However, you never made it out. The tunnel, the cave you were in, collapsed."

Jamie looked up. "If it collapsed, how am I here?"

"The only way I can explain it is frankly. In this world, Jamie, you did die." He expected her to refute that but she said nothing. She wanted to hear it all before she decided. "And like any mortal who dies, you go to your next life. One decided by your beliefs. And for someone who did not accept any Paradise, regardless of your virtues, you went . . ." Jamie swallowed the name of the place as Gerus wiped his hands of the sand. The sand merely moved over another patch of his skin.

"It wasn't because of you. If you do not accept an afterlife, you cannot go there. I do know of that." Gerus pointed at her leg. "While the gate was being destroyed, Erus reached out a final time. He caught you. Brought you." Gerus pressed his lips together and exhaled. "The demon who distracted Erus in the cemetery, who gave us the distraction to escape, his name was Rephastion, otherwise known as the Gatekeeper. With Erus on Earth and with the Gatekeeper on Earth, whoever came to *that place*," he said delicately, "came to wander the lands lost and adrift. There is a certain order that happens. With the chain of command away, you were as misguided had you been dropped in a vacuum, with no light and no boundaries. Upon Erus' return he was whisked away. Believe it or not, there was chaos in the Pit. I do not know where he was taken, only that it was beyond the horizon.

"In the cemetery I kept the demons at bay for only so long before they found the tunnel and went after you. I'd been struck down, though I came to Rephastion's side when I saw he'd been bound. I told him where you were going." Gerus read the question in her eyes and tilted his head away. "Rephastion is another type of demon. Another type of creature. I'd say very unlike most, just like me. Demons are rather easy to understand. They are much like animals. Very primal. The intellect and love they possessed was abandoned after they abandoned our true home. Evolved, Rephastion had grown curious and needed answers to why I'd been banished from the Pit, why I was on

Earth, what trouble I'd been causing down here that would perturb one of the Lord Generals. All by me, a Sapling—"

"A Sapling?"

"A lesser class demon, according to the Lord Generals. I was no one important. Not different from multitudes of others. And yet, I still existed. A demon beyond the Pit.

"My history is long. I cannot tell you even a piece of it. Only that I'd been cast from the Pit, had found Earth, and made it my home. I'd evolved past my siblings. I became another species of my own. Independent, though still reliant on a love, a passion. I wandered Earth, and found my freedom and fascination to be lonely. I discovered a company of people in the mountains, praying. I joined them and they brought me in. While I watched generation after generation move on to the next life, and era after era evolve from one monumental achievement to another, I knew, that one day, mankind might evolve like me. I knew they would transcend the Earth and transcend after life." Gerus smiled brightly now, looking at Jamie with a gleam in his eyes. Only, the gleam didn't react to the sun. His eyes truly glowed white.

"I visited the Pit occasionally. Never for long, as I had been banished and was reluctant to learn what would happen if I'd been discovered. One time, I learned that Erus was planning for a battle. One that would tear the Earth apart. My Earth. I documented what I'd seen into my journal. One you found, Jamie." Gerus leaned up and pulled out the journal from a shadow behind him. She didn't understand what she'd just seen but was more marveled by the sight of the journal. The one that predicted the chaos. Seeing it in his hands, in anyone's but her own, felt unwonted. After watching him slowly flip mindlessly through the pages, the pressing feeling dissipated and the image of him holding his most precious treasure made her feel she was the intruder.

"I left my journal for someone to find and there were many. Some bringing it to the church unopened; others reading it and then returning it, thinking it nothing more than fiction or derangement; on one occasion a woman read it then tossed it. It hurt me to a degree but thankfully it never happened again. All however, never took it home, tried to understand where it'd come from; what king of being could write in such a way. Only you."

"It was my uncle," Jamie said softly. "If he hadn't shown me the gargoyles that first night I would have returned the journal and never thought of it again."

Gerus studied her silently before continuing. "I had always had a theory, that no matter what it is or who, no one is ever truly alone. In space and time maybe, but not in species. Not for all of time. I believed that one day, someone would go beyond what they were born into, evolve, and become a greater being than they were before."

"I've evolved?" Jamie smiled, twisting to look down her back, then when finding nothing sought Gerus' eyes again. "Thought I'd have wings."

"Maybe not yet," Gerus said, smiling as he looked forward. "Think back on your history. What does man evolve from?"

Jamie followed his eyes and then briefly looked back to him. He lifted his eyebrows like she could believe him or doubt him, but she merely accepted the dare and stood up, walking through the shallow waters and going just deep enough for her to sink completely under. She opened her eyes and saw the undulating waves, the sloping shore, and small groups of fish soaring past. On a count of two, she opened her mouth and inhaled, preparing to choke on water, pausing when she breathed normally. She ran her fingers over her neck and felt nothing but smooth skin, then looked up her arms for some form of gills, finding none. She returned to Gerus on the shore.

"What the hell! I mean, what the hell!"

Jamie grabbed her neck again, looking back toward the water as Gerus humored her with his eyes. "When you've already died, you can't die again. Soon, I'll show you how to use light and shadows to your advantage." He smirked. "And other tricks I've learned on my own."

"But I'm still a person. We don't have gills." Jamie registered what he said earlier. "This is what you said about evolving right? Are the gills somewhere else then?" Jamie patted her head and around her chest, still feeling nothing.

"While you were in the Pit, Jamie, you were alone for a while—All-time, not Earth time—until some allies found you and brought me to you, not far from the Gate; the one Rephastion guards. You did make it easy to find you, under the circumstances. I made a deal. Because you helped stop Erus, despite being brought there, for you to be free from the toil and mayhem of the Pit. To spend your eternity here on Earth."

"Who did you deal with?"

"The Lord Generals Tier and Paxiphen. Them—and someone else—though I only spoke to them."

"And they agreed? Just like that?"

"I made a good case for you. I've studied several practices of rhetoric over millennia."

Jamie sat down beside him again and the sun and breezes dried her off before she found what to ask next. "I'll be here with you? For the rest of time?"

Gerus studied her face for a moment, unsure she asked because it was for the rest of time or if it was in fear of being stuck with him. "If you wish not to see me, I will not find you. Only knowing you exist is enough."

Jamie brushed one hand against the other arm and shook her head. "It isn't that. Only, well, I've never known anyone older than ninety. Now you're telling me not only will I live past it, but I'll watch everyone else . . . *not*. My family . . ."

"You may not know them the rest of your life, but you can know others for the rest of theirs. And the beauty of this world is that there are many more people to meet and love. One thing I've learned after thousands of years is that humans can still surprise you."

"But, they won't be my family. I'll watch them all die." Jamie swept her hand through her hair to pull back the locks that snuck out of the ponytail. "I'm not good with death. I can't watch my family, *my* family, die. I'll never die, but it'll feel like I am. Over and over again."

A cloud blocked the sun. Gerus was silent at first. "Forgive me, I have never had a human heart and have never empathized with loss. A beginning yes, but my kind have never known a true end."

Jamie looked over to him. "But you have learned of human love. After all you've been through."

He nodded and smiled in appreciation. Jamie looked around them again. "So how did I get here?"

Her companion wiped sweat and sand from his neck. "When they agreed to banish you from the Pit, they cast you away. Your soul was flung among the stars and you sailed like a comet. It took you nearly two weeks to find Earth, and when you did, you landed not far from here. Fortunately, you found land."

The corners of her lips went up. "I was a comet? Did anyone see me? Was I on the news?"

"Not quite," Gerus said lightly. "Although, I believe someone close to you did."

Jamie took a handful of seconds to think of one such person. "Aiden." She swallowed hard. "So my family knows I'm dead."

He confirmed with a solemn nod. "It's been nearly two weeks. However, Jamie, your home is very different. It won't look like the Shore you remember."

Jamie ignored the warning. "Did they have a funeral for me?"

He stayed quiet a moment. "It's today."

"Why so late?"

"The town is *very* different. There are buildings and roads, however, many have lost what they've worked for. Most homes were wrecked and cars were crushed. But," he lightened his mood, "the beauty of humans has shone. Much like in Hurricane Irma last year or in the Pulse tragedy two years ago, many people, traveling from miles away—complete strangers—have come to bring the town out of its ruin. There are many reconstruction efforts to build communities again. Not just in Shore but in many cities around the world. Shore suffered the most destruction because Erus was here, but he slipped small forces across the Earth as soon as he arrived. Many cities on each continent."

"Where?"

"New York. Chongqing. Cairo. Bogotá. Tokyo. New Dehli. Sydney. Lagos. Kinshasa. Moscow. São Paulo. Istanbul. Every dense city in Europe, North America, the Indian Ocean. Any you can think of. Anywhere the damage would've been most destructive. The most devastating attack on the world."

Jamie shook her head. How could the world recover?

"It took a while to account for all dead and missing, so many delayed funerals. Some start today."

Jamie didn't ask the death count or how many were injured. At least it didn't get worse. It could have been so much worse. The gargoyles could have said nothing about the Gate and the opportunity to stopping him would have been lost.

"Is there anyone I know who didn't make it? Is there anyone, Gerus?"

A shadow of sadness crossed his face as he kept his jaw tight. "It is only right for you to see for yourself." He stood. Jamie followed him back to the beach house. "Would you like to shower first before we go?"

"Shower? Wait, you said the funeral was today. Even if we got on a plane, we wouldn't make it back in time. What's the commute for a plane crossing the Atlantic? Era told me it took her nine hours to get to France."

Gerus spoke over his shoulder. "We won't be needing a plane."

Underneath the patio awning, Gerus uttered undiscernible words before waving his hand through the air, stirring about a flat plane of shadow reaching from above his head to the ground. He looked back to her and held his hand up, though not to the portal, but the mirror nearby. When Jamie turned to it, she didn't recognize herself. Her eyes, they weren't the brown she'd known. But like Gerus' eyes. A radiant white. She turned back to Gerus, who now held his hand out toward the portal.

"For us, there are more convenient ways to travel."

* * * * * * * * * * * * * *

Living her entire life by the beach, she couldn't feel comfort in the white beach of the Canary Island. Living the past six months in darkness, she couldn't recognize the darkness she had once known when she stepped through demon's portal---exhilarated as she was stepping back on Floridian soil. An overwhelming weight of dispirit cloaked her as she stood in the desolated town. She struggled to believe that this was still her planet. Her home. All she knew.

Gerus led her down roads in repair, construction crews filling in sinkholes and homebuilders renovating weakly structured homes. Trees that were once abundant now were a rare find, let alone a tree still reaching skyward. While there was no way to look without landing on ruin, there were faces with cheer on them. A group of kids playing with a family dog and strangers reaching out to those who looked lost. At some houses, she noticed how even the kids were hard-working, helping to repaint walls and Caulk minor cracks. She didn't want to go by her house and so didn't ask. Suspecting, Gerus never mentioned it.

Walking down the cemetery lane, the same cemetery where her father was buried, she felt a case of deja vu. The weather was poor for a funeral.

Below overcast skies, Jamie looked over the gravestones to those gathered around the casket. The distance and their backs made it difficult for her to recognize anyone. When Jamie reached a skyward tree, she rested a hand on its bark, leaning around it, narrowing her eyes to better guess who was mourning her.

"They can't see us," Gerus said.

Jamie looked up at him. "Why not?"

"Another trick you'll learn. As a Shadow, even in bright sunlight, you can avoid being seen if you wish."

"Can we go closer?"

Gerus lifted a hand for her to do as she liked, but she didn't move. Despite the fact no harm could come to her now, she was afraid. She didn't want to see her mother's face.

Without realizing, one trick she learned on her own was that she could hear from a great distance. The conductor of the funeral, a priest, spoke loud enough for everyone gathered to hear. From the tree, she heard him as if she were another among the crowd.

When he finished, the crowd shuffled as another stepped to the head of the casket.

Her mother.

Jamie unconsciously walked closer, though stopped at the first gravestone she reached.

"Thank you for coming." Jamie had never heard her mother sound so defeated. Her feet brought her forward again. "Today will be the third time I've buried another part of my soul. All were in unnatural forms. The first was twenty-one years ago. He was small and unhealthy and didn't grow to be as strong as he should have become. His time was too short. Burying a baby who hadn't even lived for a week steals a lifetime from a mother I can't even put into words." She paused, inhaling deeply. "The second was three years ago. His body was broken, but my husband lived a good life. I know he regretted nothing." She took a moment. "Again, another part of me broken, but not defeated." Rosario fought to compose her face as the paper in her hand crumbled together, clutching onto the last of her strength of will; her hands trembling as she felt herself losing the fight. "But burying"—she gasped and inhaled deeply, letting out a soft cry in the exhale of air—"a coffin with no daughter to bury has been the hardest of them all." A trembling hand came to her cheek and she didn't hold back the sob.

By now, Jamie had reached the group. As Shadow, she slipped in between the shoulders of people as she stepped in the open space near the front. Not to look at the coffin. Not at the faces around her but at her mother, who she always believed never loved her the right way. Who she believed gave her a secondary love. Jamie focused on her mother's tears and wished now more than ever to tell her she loved her. She would be with her. Let her know she could cry until she couldn't cry anymore, whether that took ten minutes or ten lifetimes.

Aiden brought his arm around his mother. From behind Victor rested the hand not holding Riley's hand, onto her shoulder, squeezing it lightly. The crowd of mourners around the pit waited patiently for Rosario. When she collected herself, she took one of Aiden's hands and held onto it for support.

"I didn't love you the right amount," said her mother. "Not what you deserved. Not enough for you not to question it. But I think deep down you didn't believe that. You knew you were a part of my soul; that I couldn't love less than with all of me. *Te quiero, mi corazón. Te queiro. Para siempre.*"

Abuela came forward to stand on Rosario's other side as Victor stepped back, his head bowed. Rosario wrapped her arm around Aiden's back and rubbed it, encouraging him to say something. His face was red and Jamie assumed he wouldn't, but he stepped forward, and tentatively lifted a hand to the coffin. He brought his lips together and pulled them into his mouth as he knelt, his head hanging down. If they weren't standing nearby, they wouldn't have heard him. But Jamie could.

"I saw a meteor last night. It means something that I saw one last night, because I've never seen one before. A shooting star or a meteor or a comet or anything. Because they're bright, beautiful, and never last for too long. They demand to be appreciated because they don't last for long. You demanded that from me." A small smile spread over her face, but when she really looked at her brother, she understood that the reason why he hung his head down was because he couldn't look up. He'd been crying as he sassed her. Even here.

She bent down and rested her hand on his back, surprised that it landed there and not pass through him. However, he didn't feel anything. She looked up at her hand and examined how the skin could look so real but not embody anything. And that was what she was. No physical body. Only a shadow of a soul. On the Earth—only able to watch people grieve over a body that was deep below them in between all the pressures of the Earth's crust. She always knew she would get crushed by a dominating force, she just always assumed that force would be under the control of a human; distracted, and behind the steering wheel of a car.

Now all she wanted was to console her mother, comfort her brother. She brushed the back of his hair, wishing that if she spoke, he would hear.

"I wanted to protect you from all the bad in the world and I should've done a better job. A brother protects his sister. I'm sorry I couldn't this time." He lifted his face up, eyes red, tear stains trailed down his face. He patted the coffin. "I'll find you one day. Be ready. I'll miss you until then. I love you."

He stood up and stepped back beside his mother. Rosario wrapped both arms around him and leaned over to kiss the top of his head, rubbing his shoulder as if comforting him would lessen her grief.

Jamie stood up and looked at her family. The last of her blood. From brother, to mother, to Abuela. She loved them more than anything. She'd protect them from ever hurting again. She wouldn't be in their lives anymore but she would do that for them. Them, and any other person who loved this much.

Jamie looked forward and saw Minjae, dressed in a dress shirt and pants; his hands were tightly clasped in front of him. He was looking at the coffin and she couldn't know, but she *knew* what he was thinking. She loved him too. He was the closest to her outside of blood. He knew her just as well as her family, as well as Banafsha. Jamie found her too. She was behind Aiden, beside Victor, wearing a dark dress with a hijab Jamie had never seen her wear before. Jamie knew Banafsha wouldn't give her final regards here. She didn't need to though. Jamie knew what she wanted to say.

The casket was lowered and people dropped flowers into it. The gravedigger began filling the dirt back in as slowly, the mourners began to leave. Most people from school, others she'd shared classes with since elementary school, and others like Emily and Ms. Ava. Then Vienna. Then her coworkers, Era and Noel. Minjae's family said their goodbyes; even Daehyun flew from California to come. She hadn't known them very long, but Jamie watched as Penelope and her grandmother said their final respects; and their thank yous. They were the only ones outside of St. Luke's who knew what Jamie had done; why her body was never found. Several of the last to leave were the priests, Edgar and Elias, even Cadogan who she'd met only occasionally on her way to the gargoyles. But not her uncle. If he had lived, he would have been there.

Jamie inhaled deeply.

The last to remain were Victor, Riley, Banafsha, Minjae, Abuela, Aiden, and her mother. They stayed until the grave was dug; until it was a small mound over the grass blades.

Victor took Riley's hand and led her away. They would meet back at Rosario's house for dinner. Abuela took Banafsha's hand and both motherly parents to Jamie followed down the lane of graves back to the car.

It was now her three. Her favorite three. She wanted to hug them each one final time. What she wanted didn't matter though, so she settled for saying a goodbye of her own. Minjae came to Aiden and hugged him. Hugging Rosario, she kissed his cheek and patted his arm, thanking him. He inhaled deeply, giving the gravestone one final farewell before walking away.

Rosario and Aiden had spent enough time in the last three years before a grave, telling it the things they wished they could tell the person. Jamie didn't want them to do that for her. They needed to say their final wishes, then leave. Remember her, and move on. As the person whose memory was meant to be remembered instead of meaning to do the remembering, she could say for certain she wanted them to move on; embrace their life.

Eventually, mother and son followed the others.

Gerus stepped beside Jamie, crossing his hands in front of him as he breathed quietly. If Jamie hadn't looked, she wouldn't have known he was there.

"Thank you for bringing me back in time. Film strips . . . written words . . . spoken words—it wouldn't have been enough."

"You woke on your own. I guess instead, you should be thanking luck."

Jamie nodded. "What will I do now? What can I do?"

Kindness smiled.

"Learn to see the world."

"You need to learn?"

"There's so much out there. On Earth, out there . . . I think you'll find the years fly by."

And she would be able to see everything. Be a part of every major era in history. In the sidelines. And once learning Gerus' tricks, in the big moments.

It seemed, the future wasn't going to be as daunting anymore; but bright and promising, as it should have been all along.

43

All one could see when looking into the blue Florida sky was a stretching gray pillar. A guiding flame at its top, it kept rising into the atmosphere. Eventually one wouldn't be able to see it. The skies were clear and weather perfect for the Space Shuttle Intrepid. It reached the outer atmosphere, disappearing behind the smoke it cast behind it.

Jamie had a perfect seat for the launch. Over fifty miles north of Cape Canaveral, the third St. Luke's Cathedral stood colossal over the flat lands of Florida as it had done once before. The reconstruction project began within a year since its fall. Very little remained in the aftermath, but many sponsors around the world were eager to revive the country's largest cathedral back to its former glory. The church as a whole was more or less reconstructed to what it had been before, although this time, the original architect's wishes were honored. The installation of six large gargoyles now guarded from each of the outer faces of the bell towers. Not the same ones, certainly not, but every time Jamie looked upon their ram-like horns, their skyward wings, their unique celestial faces, she felt in the company of friends.

A seventh gargoyle was installed years after the others. It appeared in the night. Without whisper. Without fuss. His wings wrapped around his body but were large and protective. He was bent on one knee but his hands were reverential. His head was cast down but his eyes were open. A statue the height of two stories looked like a bug atop the eastern chapel. He was named the Silent Guardian, as some nights he was said to have disappeared, believed to be flying amongst the Heavens, protecting those of the Earth before the coming morn.

One of the anonymous patrons to the cathedral's reconstruction was Gerus. It was amazing how much money could accumulate when one saved it all. He could have funded the high-priced project all on his own but discovered early on that many had donated in their own way, from spare change to several hundred thousand. Jamie had several jobs in her travels and contributed her own small portion as well, simply under the name J. Diez. While her mother and brother would never know it was her, every time she passed by the roster of patrons near the narthex, she couldn't help but smile.

Gerus also helped Jamie in writing a will. Not necessarily written before her death, but by her hand. Under stealth and manipulation, Gerus made certain that the money in Jamie's bank account would go to Aiden when he reached legal age. Jamie would be damned if that money only ended up in the bank, and not in the promising hands of the future. Jamie had no doubt what her brother could accomplish and put her money where her faith was.

The light from the shuttle had disappeared for several minutes but she continued to watch the smoke from the exhaust slowly dissipate. Jamie was lying on her back on the southern parapet of the southern bell tower, one leg kicking back and forth over its edge. She'd lied on the summits of countless skyscrapers and the palm-inducing edges of cliffs, here on the cathedral, she felt . . . home.

Nothing made her prouder than knowing her little brother was on the Intrepid. At thirty-one, he was one of the youngest astronauts in American history. After the Battle, he'd never lost his passion and desire to travel into space. He'd studied, more ardently and tenaciously than before. While focused on his studies, he'd met a nice girl at UTSI, whom he later married. They'd been married for three years and were expecting their first baby in the spring of next year. Jamie liked to imagine the boy or girl having his brown eyes but her auburn hair, or maybe her green eyes but his dark wavy hair. No matter, they'd be tall like him. And kind and scholarly. They'd pursue a career in the arts, the complete opposite of their empirical father, or become an environmentalist. While she never missed not having children of her own, the possibilities of what they could have become passed through her thoughts when she thought on him. She prayed Aiden and Sasha would have more children.

And Jamie would have been an aunt. If she had aged with time, she would have been thirty-six.

Jamie wondered if he thought of her; wondered if he thought he was closer to her now in space than he'd been back on Earth.

She pursed her lips. They wouldn't know, but she would still be a part of the child's life. A part of every descendant's life. Growing up didn't mean anything unless she had someone to spend it with.

Though there was Gerus, though she could depend on him, she still wanted to be connected to her ties here on Earth that showed that she had once been human. Now having learned all of Gerus' tricks, it became easy to forget—ironically easy considering she was always around them—that she used to be one of them. Her soul was bright, but being without a body still made her forgetful.

"That's considered dangerous," said a voice.

Jamie smiled and sat up, looking over to Gerus as he approached.

"Heights have never frightened me before."

"It's nice knowing you'll always be here around this time."

Jamie nodded, bending one leg and hooking her hand around her knee. "It's convenient Aiden was launching off today. I arrived a couple days earlier." She had looked up to the pillar of smoke, but returned her focus back to him. "Where have you been?"

The question was never "how are you." As a culmination of beings, they were always the same. It was always: where have you been? Where are you going? What will you do next?

"Salar de Uyuni."

"I think you've been there five times since I've met you."

"And will many times again." Gerus chuckled. "Anywhere new for you?"

Gerus told her of the Battle, that the angels of the Heavens were as diverse and vast as the species of the Earth. And that while Earth was unique, it was not alone. There were other planets in other galaxies in other Times. They could travel together. Discover the wonders of the universe. One day, she had promised, after her mother and brother were no longer on Earth. Until then, there was plenty on this planet to appreciate.

"I was checking on Minjae in Pennsylvania when I learned Banafsha passed. I've been in Pakistan." Jamie passed her hand down her hairline and smiled in memory. "I know it's changed since she was little. I wish she could see it today." The place of her birth.

Jamie knew nothing would replace devotion to her Sunshine State. Whenever a storm passed in Europe, she waited for the clashing thunder and the flashing lightning. For the sunlight to peek behind the dark clouds when by the Indian Ocean. No place on Earth fulfilled her definition for thunderstorms than when she was in Florida.

"Have you been following anyone else?" While Gerus didn't know them, he'd adopted Jamie's loved ones as his own, and kept up-to-date with them as he knew she did.

Jamie nodded. "All of them. Everyone who was at my funeral."

When Jamie looked at him next, a question came to the tip of her tongue. A question which had lingered for years. And Gerus waited for her to ask. It was a simple question and it wasn't like she couldn't find out for herself. She had learned Gerus' trick of slipping into Hell long ago. What stopped her was it wasn't right.

After a silent stare-off, she smiled. "How long will you stay?"

"Until your father's anniversary."

There was a gleam in his white eyes. Yes, he certainly knew what she was thinking, and was willing and ready to answer when she asked.

Another day, she thought. She kept her mask as she twisted her neck to look back to the pillar in the sky, vanishing.

"Good, I could use the company." Jamie jumped up and led them toward the roof door. "Have you seen the new gallery? Inspired by a theatre south of Tallahassee from the late '30s—which is rather odd for a Gothic-inspired cathedral don't you think? You don't mind taking the stairs, do you?" Jamie opened the door for him and followed him through it. "Reminds you what we humans did once upon a time."

Jamie had found the brother she never came to know and he had become the brother she lost. He filled in the gaps of everyone out of her life. A father and brother and uncle and friend.

They would move on and discover another life after the one on Earth. Where beauty and light were more miraculous than songs could praise, and hell even further damning than the scriptures forewarned. All those she knew, and all those she didn't. All who had come before her, and all that would come after her time. They would meet. One way, one end or the other.

People had always debated whether there was a Heaven or Hell. Paradise or Inferno. Jamie often walked among them, wondering why they never feared to consider what if they faced another unknown.

ACKNOWLEDGMENTS

Eboné, *Trium* would be nothing without your initial feedback and constant support throughout its lifetime. May gargoyles fly by your inspiration.

Jonuel, my first reader. I write for people I'll never meet and for times I will no longer be here for. If it wasn't for your interest to read *Trium* and enthusiasm to read more of my work, I think I would have continued to keep my books hidden away on my computer.

Valerie, I follow your artistic footprints into the unknown and beyond. You've shown me the arts lead us to our full potential as human beings, but not without struggle to procure our dreams. May we continue to struggle over our mountains and create art and appreciate nature and explore this universe. Together. There's no one I'd rather enjoy the view with on the mountaintop. Forever your, Nike Eternal.

Abuela, who loved every draft I wrote. For the laughter. For the *embustes*. For keeping my writing dreams always possible and always obtainable.

Lastly and above all, Mom, who gave me freedom, who gave me opportunity, who introduced me to books and movies and music and language and the beauty of the unfamiliar. I'm a traveler, I'm a dreamer, I'm a goofball. I'm a writer. All because of you. May these words evolve into the full measure of their meaning: Thank you.

ABOUT THE AUTHOR

Nicole likes to spend her free time practicing photography, appreciating the art of film, and discovering new composers. She lives in Florida.
Trium is her first novel.

www.nicoledeleonauthor.com

@deleonwrites